Praise for

POPE JOAN

"It is so gratifying to read about those rare heroes whose strength of vision enables them to ignore the almost overpowering messages of their own historical periods. . . . Pope Joan has all the elements one wants: love, sex, violence, duplicity and long-buried secrets. Cross has written an engaging book." —*Los Angeles Times Book Review*

"A fascinating and moving account of a woman's determination to learn, despite the opposition of family and society. Highly recommended." —*Library Journal* (starred review)

"Cross makes an excellent, entertaining case that in the Dark Ages, a woman sat on the papal throne. . . . A colorful, richly imagined novel." —*Publishers Weekly*

"Pope Joan reveals the harsh realities of the Dark Ages. Violence is rife in the government, church and home; logic and reason are shunned as "dangerous ideas" and women are considered useful only as men's servants and child bearers. The novel explores the extraordinary life of an independent, intelligent and courageous woman who overcomes oppression and ascends to the highest level of religious power. . . . Cross' masterful use of anticipation, as well as the sweeping historical landscape of the story, keep *Pope Joan* intriguing. . . . An exciting journey through history as it's being made."
—*San Francisco Chronicle*

"Eloquently written and spellbinding in its account of this legendary figure." —*Arizona Republic*

POPE JOAN

A NOVEL

 DONNA WOOLFOLK CROSS

B\D\W\Y
Broadway Books
New York

Copyright © 1996, 2009 by Donna Woolfolk Cross

Published in the United States by Broadway Books, an imprint of the Crown Publishing Group, a division of Penguin Random House LLC, New York.
crownpublishing.com

Broadway Books and its logo, B \ D \ W \ Y, are trademarks of Penguin Random House LLC.

Originally published in hardcover in the United States by Crown Publishers, an imprint of the Crown Publishing Group, a division of Random House, Inc., New York, in 1996, and subsequently published in paperback in the United States by Three Rivers Press, an imprint of the Crown Publishing Group, a division of Penguin Random House LLC, New York, in 2009.

Library of Congress Cataloging-in-Publication Data
Cross, Donna Woolfolk.
    Pope Joan / Donna Cross.—1st Three Rivers Press ed.
    Originally published: New York : Crown, © 1996.
    1. Joan (Legendary Pope)—Fiction. 2. Popes—Legends—
Fiction. I. Title.
PS3553.R572P66   2009
813'.6—dc22   2008051919

ISBN 978-0-307-45236-8
EBOOK ISBN 978-0-307-45319-8

Printed in India

17

For my father,

William Woolfolk,

and there are no words

to add

⊱| Prologue |⊰

IT WAS the twenty-eighth day of Wintarmanoth in the year of our Lord 814, the harshest winter in living memory.

Hrotrud, the village midwife of Ingelheim, struggled through the snow toward the canon's *grubenhaus*. A gust of wind swept through the trees and drove icy fingers into her body, searching the holes and patches of her thin woolen garments. The forest path was deeply drifted; with each step, she sank almost to her knees. Snow caked her eyebrows and eyelashes; she kept wiping her face to see. Her hands and feet ached with cold, despite the layers of linen rags she had wrapped around them.

A blur of black appeared on the path ahead. It was a dead crow. Even those hardy scavengers were dying this winter, starved because their beaks could not tear the flesh of the frozen carrion. Hrotrud shivered and quickened her pace.

Gudrun, the canon's woman, had gone into labor a month sooner than expected. *A fine time for the child to come,* Hrotrud thought bitterly. *Five children delivered in the last month alone, and not one of them lasted more than a week.*

A blast of wind-driven snow blinded Hrotrud, and for a moment she lost sight of the poorly marked path. She felt a swell of panic. More than one villager had died that way, wandering in circles only a short distance from their homes. She forced herself to stand still as the snow swirled around her, surrounding her in a featureless landscape of white. When the wind let up, she could just make out the outline of the path. Again she began to move forward. She no longer felt pain in her hands and feet; they had gone completely numb. She knew what that could mean, but she could not afford to dwell on it; it was important to remain calm.

I must think of something besides the cold.

She pictured the home in which she had been raised, a *casa* with a prosperous manse of some six hectares. It was warm and snug, with walls of solid timber, far nicer than their neighbors' homes, made of simple wooden lathes daubed with mud. A great fire had blazed in the central hearth, the smoke spiraling up to an opening in the roof. Hrotrud's father had worn an expensive vest of otter skins over his fine linen *bliaud,* and her mother had had silken ribbons for her long, black hair. Hrotrud herself had had two large-sleeved tunics, and a warm mantle of the finest wool. She remembered how soft and smooth the expensive material had felt against her skin.

It had all ended so quickly. Two summers of drought and a killing frost ruined the harvest. Everywhere people were starving; in Thuringia there were rumors of cannibalism. Through the judicious sale of the family possessions, Hrotrud's father had kept them from hunger for a while. Hrotrud had cried when they took away her woolen mantle. It had seemed to her then that nothing worse could happen. She was eight years old; she did not yet comprehend the horror and cruelty of the world.

She pushed her way through another large drift of snow, fighting off a growing light-headedness. It had been several days since she had had anything to eat. *Ah, well. If all goes well, I will feast tonight. Perhaps, if the canon is well pleased, there will even be some bacon to take home.* The idea gave her renewed energy.

Hrotrud emerged into the clearing. She could see the blurred outlines of the grubenhaus just ahead. The snow was deeper here, beyond the screen of trees, but she drove ahead, plowing through with her strong thighs and arms, confident now that safety was near.

Arriving at the door, she knocked once, then immediately let herself in; it was too cold to worry about social courtesies. Inside, she stood blinking in darkness. The single window of the grubenhaus had been boarded up for winter; the only light came from the hearth fire and a few smoky tallows scattered about the room. After a moment, her eyes began to adjust, and she saw two young boys seated close together near the hearth fire.

"Has the child come?" Hrotrud asked.

"Not yet," answered the older boy.

Hrotrud muttered a short prayer of thanks to St. Cosmas, patron saint of midwives. She had been cheated of her pay that way more than once, turned away without a *denar* for the trouble she had taken to come.

At the hearth fire, she peeled the frozen rags from her hands and feet, crying out in alarm when she saw their sickly blue-white color. *Holy Mother, do not let the frost take them.* The village would have little use for a crippled midwife. Elias the shoemaker had lost his livelihood that way. After he was caught in a storm on his way back from Mainz, the tips of his fingers had blackened and dropped off in a week. Now, gaunt and ragged, he squatted by the church doors, begging his living off the charity of others.

Shaking her head grimly, Hrotrud pinched and rubbed her numbed fingers and toes as the two boys watched in silence. The sight of them reassured her. *It will be an easy birth,* she told herself, trying to keep her mind off poor Elias. *After all, I delivered Gudrun of these two easily enough.* The older boy must be almost six winters now, a sturdy child with a look of alert intelligence. The younger, his round-cheeked, three-year-old brother, rocked back and forth, sucking his thumb morosely. Both were darkavised, like their father; neither had inherited their Saxon mother's extraordinary white-gold hair.

Hrotrud remembered how the village men had stared at Gudrun's hair when the canon had brought her back from one of his missionary trips to Saxony. It had caused quite a stir at first, the canon's taking a woman. Some said it was against the law, that the Emperor had issued an edict forbidding men of the Church to take wives. But others said it could not be so, for it was plain that without a wife a man was subject to all kinds of temptation and wickedness. Look at the monks of Stablo, they said, who shame the Church with their fornications and drunken revelry. And certainly it was true that the canon was a sober and hardworking man.

The room was warm. The large hearth was piled high with thick logs of birch and oak; smoke rose in great billows to the hole in the thatched roof. It was a snug dwelling. The wooden timbers that formed the walls were heavy and thick, and the gaps between them were tightly packed with straw and clay to keep out the cold. The single window had been boarded over with sturdy planks of oak, an extra measure of protection against the *nordostroni,* the frigid northeast winds of winter. The house was large enough to be divided into three separate compartments, one containing the sleeping quarters of the canon and his wife, one for the animals that sheltered there in harsh weather—Hrotrud heard the soft scuffle and scrape of their hooves to her left—and this one, the central room, where the family worked and ate and the children slept. Other than the stone castle of the Emperor, still unfinished and therefore rarely inhabited, no one in Ingelheim had a finer home.

Hrotrud's limbs began to prickle and throb with renewed sensation. She examined her fingers; they were rough and dry, but the bluish cast had receded, supplanted by a returning glow of healthy reddish pink. She sighed with relief, resolving to make an offering to St. Cosmas in thanksgiving. For a few more minutes, Hrotrud lingered by the fire, enjoying its warmth; then, with a nod and an encouraging pat for the boys, she hurried around the partition to where the laboring woman was waiting.

Gudrun lay on a bed of peat topped with fresh straw. The canon, a dark-haired man with thick, beetling eyebrows that gave him a perpetually stern expression, sat apart. He nodded at Hrotrud, then returned his attention to the large wood-bound book on his lap. Hrotrud had seen the book on previous visits to the cottage, but the sight of it still filled her with awe. It was a copy of the Holy Bible, and it was the only book she had ever seen. Like the other villagers, Hrotrud could neither read nor write. She knew, however, that the book was a treasure, worth more in gold *solidi* than the entire village earned in a year. The canon had brought it with him from his native England, where books were not so rare as in Frankland.

Hrotrud saw immediately that Gudrun was in a bad way. Her breathing was shallow, her pulse dangerously rapid, her whole body puffed and swollen. The midwife recognized the signs. There was no time to waste. She reached into her sack and took out a quantity of dove's dung that she had carefully collected in the fall. Returning to the hearth, she threw the dung on the fire, watching with satisfaction as the dark smoke began to rise, clearing the air of evil spirits.

She would have to ease the pain so Gudrun could relax and bring the child forth. For that, she would use henbane. She took a bundle of the small, yellow, purple-veined flowers, placed them in a clay mortar, and skillfully ground them into powder, wrinkling her nose at the acrid odor that was released. Then she infused the powder into a cup of strong red wine and brought it to Gudrun to drink.

"What is that you mean to give her?" the canon asked abruptly.

Hrotrud started; she had almost forgotten he was there. "She is weakened from the labor. This will relieve her pain and help the child issue forth."

The canon frowned. He took the henbane from Hrotrud's hands, strode around the partition, and threw it into the fire, where it hissed briefly and then vanished. "Woman, you blaspheme."

Hrotrud was aghast. It had taken her weeks of painstaking search to gather that small amount of the precious medicine. She turned toward the canon, ready to vent her anger, but stopped when she saw the flinty look in his eyes.

"It is written"—he thumped the book with his hand for emphasis—"'In sorrow shalt thou bring forth children.' Such medicine is unholy!"

Hrotrud was indignant. There was nothing unchristian about *her* medicine. Didn't she recite nine paternosters each time she pulled one of the plants from the earth? The canon certainly never complained when she gave him henbane to ease the pain of *his* frequent toothaches. But she would not argue with him. He was an influential man. One word from him about "unholy" practices, and Hrotrud would be ruined.

Gudrun moaned in the throes of another pain. *Very well,* Hrotrud thought. If the canon would not allow the henbane, she would have to try another approach. She went to her sack and withdrew a long piece of cloth, cut to the True Length of Christ. Moving with brisk efficiency, she wound it tightly around Gudrun's abdomen. Gudrun groaned when Hrotrud shifted her. Movement was painful for her, but that could not be helped. Hrotrud took from her sack a small parcel, carefully wrapped in a scrap of silken fabric for protection. Inside was one of her treasures—the anklebone of a rabbit killed on Christmas Day. She had begged it off one of the Emperor's hunting party the previous winter. With utmost care, Hrotrud shaved off three thin slices and placed them in Gudrun's mouth.

"Chew these slowly," she instructed Gudrun, who nodded weakly. Hrotrud settled back to wait. From the corner of her eye, she studied the canon, who frowned in concentration on his book till his brows almost met over the bridge of his nose.

Gudrun moaned again and twisted in pain, but the canon did not look up. *He's a cold one,* Hrotrud reflected. *Still, he must have some fire in his loins, or he wouldn't have taken her to wife.*

How long had it been since the canon brought the Saxon woman home, ten—or was it eleven?—winters ago. Gudrun had not been young, by Frankish standards, perhaps twenty-three or twenty-four years old, but she was very beautiful, with the long white-gold hair and blue eyes of the *aliengenae*. She had lost her entire family in the massacre at Verden. Thousands of Saxons had died that day rather than accept the truth of Our Lord Jesus Christ. *Mad barbarians,* Hrotrud thought. *It wouldn't have happened to me.* She would have sworn to whatever they asked of her, would do it now for that matter, should the barbarians ever sweep through Frankland again, swear to whatever strange and terrible gods they wished. It changed nothing. Who was to know what went on in a person's heart? A wise woman kept her own counsel.

The fire sparked and flickered; it was burning low. Hrotrud crossed to the pile of wood stacked in the corner, chose two good-sized logs of birch, and put them on the hearth. She watched as they settled, hissing, into the fire, the flames licking upwards around them. Then she turned to check on Gudrun.

It was a full half hour since Gudrun had taken the shavings of rabbit bone, but there was no change in her condition. Even that strong medicine had failed to take effect. The pains remained erratic and ineffectual, and Gudrun was weakening.

Hrotrud sighed wearily. Clearly, she would have to resort to stronger measures.

THE canon proved to be a problem when Hrotrud told him she would need help with the birthing.

"Send for the village women," he said peremptorily.

"Ah, sir, that is impossible. Who is there to send?" Hrotrud raised her palms expressively. "I cannot go, for your wife needs me here. Your elder boy cannot go, for though he seems a likely lad, he could get lost in weather such as this. I almost did myself."

The canon glared at her from under his dark brows. "Very well," he said, "I will go." As he rose from his chair, Hrotrud shook her head impatiently.

"It would do no good. By the time you returned, it would be too late. It is *your* help I need, and quickly, if you wish your wife and babe to live."

"*My* help? Are you mad, midwife? That"—he motioned distastefully toward the bed—"is women's business, and unclean. I will have nothing to do with it."

"Then your wife will die."

"That is in God's hands, not mine."

Hrotrud shrugged. "It is all one to me. But you will not find it easy, raising two children without a mother."

The canon stared at Hrotrud. "Why should I believe you? She's given birth before with no trouble. I have fortified her with my prayers. You cannot know that she will die."

This was too much. Canon or not, Hrotrud would not tolerate his questioning her skill as a midwife. "It is *you* who know nothing," she said sharply. "You have not even looked at her. Go see her now; then tell me that she is not dying."

The canon went to the bed and looked down at his wife. Her damp hair was pasted to her skin, which had turned yellowish white, her dark-rimmed eyes were hollow and sunken into her head; but for the long, unsteady exhalation of breath, she might have been already dead.

"Well?" prodded Hrotrud.

The canon wheeled to face her. "God's blood, woman! Why didn't you bring the women with you?"

"As you said yourself, sir, your wife's given birth before without a speck of trouble. There was no reason to expect any this time. Besides, who would have come in weather such as this?"

The canon stalked to the hearth and paced back and forth agitatedly. At last he halted. "What do you want me to do?"

Hrotrud smiled broadly. "Oh, little enough, sir, little enough." She led him back to the bed. "For a start, help get her up."

Standing on either side of Gudrun, they grabbed her under the arms and heaved. Her body was heavy, but together they managed to lift her to her feet, where she swayed against her husband. The canon was stronger than Hrotrud had thought. That was good, for she would need all his strength for what came next.

"We must force the babe down into position. When I give the command, lift her as high as you can. And shake hard."

The canon nodded, his mouth set grimly. Gudrun hung like a dead weight between them, her head fallen forward on her chest.

"Lift!" shouted Hrotrud. They hoisted Gudrun by the arms and began to shake her up and down. Gudrun screamed and fought to free herself. Pain and fear gave her surprising strength; the two of them were hard put to restrain her. *If only he had let me give her the henbane,* Hrotrud thought. *She would be half-sensible by now.*

Quickly they lowered her, but she continued to struggle and cry out. Hrotrud gave a second command, and again they hoisted, shook, then lowered Gudrun to the bed, where she lay half-fainting, murmuring in her barbarous native tongue. *Good,* Hrotrud thought. *If I move quickly, it will all be over before she regains her senses.*

Hrotrud reached into the birth passage, probing for the opening to the womb. It was rigid and swollen from the long hours of ineffectual labor. Using her right index fingernail, which she kept long for just this purpose, Hrotrud tore at the resistant tissue. Gudrun groaned, then went completely limp. Warm blood poured over Hrotrud's hand, down her arms, and onto the bed. At last she felt the opening give way. With an exultant cry, Hrotrud reached in and took hold of the baby's head, exerting a gentle downward pressure.

"Take her by the shoulders and pull against me," she instructed the canon, whose face had gone quite pale. Nevertheless he obeyed; Hrotrud felt the pressure increase as the canon added his strength to hers. After a few minutes, the baby started to move down into the birth passage. She kept pulling steadily, careful not to injure the soft bones of the child's head and neck. At last the crown of the babe's head appeared, covered with a mass of fine, wet hair. Hrotrud eased the head out gently, then turned the body to permit the right shoulder, then the left, to emerge. One last, firm tug and the small body slid wetly into Hrotrud's waiting arms.

"A girl," Hrotrud announced. "A strong one too, by the look of her," she added, noting with approval the infant's lusty cry and healthy pink color.

She turned to meet the canon's disapproving stare.

"A girl," he said. "So it was all for nothing."

"Do not say so, sir." Hrotrud was suddenly fearful that the canon's disappointment might mean less for her to eat. "The child is healthy and strong. God grant that she live to do credit to your name."

The canon shook his head. "She is a punishment from God. A punishment for my sins—and hers." He motioned toward Gudrun, who lay motionless. "Will she live?"

"Yes." Hrotrud hoped that she sounded convincing. She could

not afford to let the canon think he might be doubly disappointed. She still hoped to taste meat that night. And there was, after all, a reasonable chance that Gudrun *would* survive. True, the birthing had been violent. After such an ordeal, many a woman came down with fever and the wasting disease. But Gudrun was strong; Hrotrud would treat her wound with a salve of mugwort mixed in fox's grease. "Yes, God willing, she will live," she repeated firmly. She did not feel it necessary to add that she would probably bear no more children.

"That's something, then," the canon said. He moved to the bed and stood looking down at Gudrun. Gently he touched the white-gold hair, darkened now with sweat. For a moment, Hrotrud thought he was going to kiss Gudrun. Then his expression changed; he looked stern, even angry.

"*Per mulierem culpa successit*," he said. "Sin came through a woman." He dropped the lock of hair and stepped back.

Hrotrud shook her head. *Something from the Holy Book, no doubt.* The canon was a strange one, all right, but that was none of her affair, God be thanked. She hurried to finish cleaning the blood and birth fluids off Gudrun so she could start back home while there was still daylight.

Gudrun opened her eyes and saw the canon standing over her. The beginnings of a smile froze on her lips as she saw the expression in his eyes.

"Husband?" she said doubtfully.

"A girl," the canon said coldly, not troubling to hide his displeasure.

Gudrun nodded, understanding, then turned her face to the wall. The canon turned to go, stopping briefly to glance at the infant already safely ensconced in her pallet of straw.

"Joan. She will be called Joan," he announced, and abruptly left the room.

1

THUNDER sounded, very near, and the child woke. She moved in the bed, seeking the warmth and comfort of her older brothers' sleeping forms. Then she remembered. Her brothers were gone.

It was raining, a hard spring downpour that filled the night air with the sweet-sour smell of newly plowed earth. Rain thudded on the roof of the canon's grubenhaus, but the thickly woven thatching kept the room dry, except for one or two small places in the corners where water first pooled and then trickled in slow, fat drops to the beaten earth floor.

The wind rose, and a nearby oak began to tap an uneven rhythm on the cottage walls. The shadow of its branches spilled into the room. The child watched, transfixed, as the monstrous dark fingers wriggled at the edges of the bed. They reached out for her, beckoning, and she shrank back.

Mama, she thought. She opened her mouth to call out, then stopped. If she made a sound, the menacing hand would pounce. She lay frozen, unable to will herself to move. Then she set her small chin resolutely. It had to be done, so she would do it. Moving with exquisite slowness, never taking her eyes off the enemy, she eased herself off the bed. Her feet felt the cool surface of the earthen floor; the familiar sensation was reassuring. Scarcely daring to breathe, she backed toward the partition behind which her mother lay sleeping. Lightning flashed; the fingers moved and lengthened, following her. She swallowed a scream, her throat tightening with the effort. She forced herself to move slowly, not to break into a run.

She was almost there. Suddenly, a salvo of thunder crashed overhead. At the same moment something touched her from behind. She yelped, then turned and fled around the partition, stumbling over the chair she had backed into.

This part of the house was dark and still, save for her mother's rhythmic breathing. From the sound, the child could tell she was deeply asleep; the noise had not wakened her. She went quickly to the bed, lifted the woolen blanket, and slid under it. Her mother lay on her side, lips slightly parted; her warm breath caressed the child's cheek. She snuggled close, feeling the softness of her mother's body through her thin linen shift.

Gudrun yawned and shifted position, roused by the movement. Her eyes opened, and she regarded the child sleepily. Then, waking fully, she reached out and put her arms around her daughter.

"Joan," she chastised gently, her lips against the child's soft hair. "Little one, you should be asleep."

Speaking quickly, her voice high and strained from fear, Joan told her mother about the monster hand.

Gudrun listened, petting and stroking her daughter and murmuring reassurances. Gently she ran her fingers over the child's face, half-seen in the darkness. She was not pretty, Gudrun reflected ruefully. She looked too much like *him*, with his thick English neck and wide jaw. Her small body was already stocky and heavyset, not long and graceful like Gudrun's people's. But the child's eyes were good, large and expressive and rich hued, green with dark gray smoke rings at the center. Gudrun lifted a strand of Joan's baby hair and caressed it, enjoying the way it shone, white-gold, even in the darkness. *My hair.* Not the coarse black hair of her husband or his cruel, dark people. *My child.* She wrapped the strand around her forefinger and smiled. *This one, at least, is mine.*

Soothed by her mother's attentions, Joan relaxed. In playful imitation, she began to tug at Gudrun's long braid, loosening it till her hair lay tumbled about her head. Joan marveled at it, spilling over the dark woolen coverlet like rich cream. She had never seen her mother's hair unbound. At the canon's insistence, Gudrun wore it always neatly braided, hidden under a rough linen cap. A woman's hair, her husband said, is the net wherein Satan catches a man's soul. And Gudrun's hair was extraordinarily beautiful, long and soft and pure white-gold, without a trace of gray, though she was now an old woman of thirty-seven winters.

"Why did Matthew and John go away?" Joan asked suddenly. Her mother had explained this to her several times, but Joan wanted to hear it again.

"You know why. Your father took them with him on his missionary journey."

"Why couldn't I go too?"

Gudrun sighed patiently. The child was always so full of questions. "Matthew and John are boys; one day they will be priests like your father. You are a girl, and therefore such matters do not concern you." Seeing that Joan was not content with that, she added, "Besides, you are much too young."

Joan was indignant. "I was four in Wintarmanoth!"

Gudrun's eyes lit with amusement as she looked at the pudgy baby face. "Ah, yes, I forgot, you are a big girl now, aren't you? Four years old! That does sound very grown-up."

Joan lay quietly while her mother stroked her hair. Then she asked, "What are heathens?" Her father and brothers had spoken a good deal about heathens before they left. Joan did not understand what heathens were, exactly, though she gathered it was something very bad.

Gudrun stiffened. The word had conjuring powers. It had been on the lips of the invading soldiers as they pillaged her home and slaughtered her family and friends. The dark, cruel soldiers of the Frankish Emperor Karolus. "Magnus," people called him now that he was dead. "Karolus Magnus." Charles the Great. Would they name him so, Gudrun wondered, if they had seen his army tear Saxon babes from their mothers' arms, swinging them round before they dashed their heads against the reddened stones? Gudrun withdrew her hand from Joan's hair and rolled onto her back.

"That is a question you must ask your father," she said.

Joan did not understand what she had done wrong, but she heard the strange hardness in her mother's voice and knew that she would be sent back to her own bed if she didn't think of some way to repair the damage. Quickly she said, "Tell me again about the Old Ones."

"I cannot. Your father disapproves of the telling of such tales." The words were half statement, half question.

Joan knew what to do. Placing both hands solemnly over her heart, she recited the Oath exactly as her mother had taught it to her, promising eternal secrecy on the sacred name of Thor the Thunderer.

Gudrun laughed and drew Joan close again. "Very well, little quail. I will tell you the story, since you know so well how to ask."

Her voice was warm again, wistful and melodic as she began to tell of Woden and Thor and Freya and the other gods who had peopled her Saxon childhood before the armies of Karolus brought the Word of Christ with blood and fire. She spoke liltingly of Asgard, the radiant home of the gods, a place of golden and silver palaces, which could only be reached by crossing Bifrost, the mysterious bridge of the rainbow. Guarding the bridge was Heimdall the Watchman, who never slept, whose ears were so keen he could even hear the grass grow. In Valhalla, the most beautiful palace of all, lived Woden, the father-god, on whose shoulders sat the two ravens Hugin, Thought, and Munin, Memory. On his throne, while the other gods feasted, Woden contemplated what Thought and Memory told him.

Joan nodded happily. This was her favorite part of the story. "Tell about the Well of Wisdom," she begged.

"Although he was already very wise," explained her mother, "Woden always sought greater wisdom. One day he went to the Well of Wisdom, guarded by Mimir the Wise, and asked for a draft from it. 'What price will you pay?' asked Mimir. Woden replied that Mimir could ask what he wished. 'Wisdom must always be bought with pain,' replied Mimir. 'If you wish a drink of this water, you must pay for it with one of your eyes.'"

Eyes bright with excitement, Joan exclaimed, "And Woden did it, Mama, didn't he? He did it!"

Her mother nodded. "Though it was a hard choice, Woden consented to lose the eye. He drank the water. Afterward, he passed on to mankind the wisdom he had gained."

Joan looked up at her mother, her eyes wide and serious. "Would *you* have done it, Mama—to be wise, to know about all things?"

"Only gods make such choices," she replied. Then, seeing the child's persistent look of question, Gudrun confessed, "No. I would have been too afraid."

"So would I," Joan said thoughtfully. "But I would *want* to do it. I would want to know what the well could tell me."

Gudrun smiled down at the intent little face. "Perhaps you would not like what you would learn there. There is a saying among our people. 'A wise man's heart is seldom glad.'"

Joan nodded, though she did not really understand. "Now tell about the Tree," she said, snuggling close to her mother again.

Gudrun began to describe Irminsul, the wondrous universe tree. It had stood in the holiest of the Saxon groves at the source of the Lippe River. Her people had worshiped at it until it was cut down by the armies of Karolus.

"It was very beautiful," her mother said, "and so tall that no one could see the top. It—"

She stopped. Suddenly aware of another presence, Joan looked up. Her father was standing in the doorway.

Her mother sat up in bed. "Husband," she said. "I did not look for your return for another fortnight."

The canon did not respond. He took a wax taper from the table near the door and crossed to the hearth fire, where he plunged it into the glowing embers until it flared.

Gudrun said nervously, "The child was frightened by the thunder. I thought to comfort her with a harmless story."

"Harmless!" The canon's voice shook with the effort to control his rage. "You call such blasphemy harmless?" He covered the distance to the bed in two long strides, set down the taper, and pulled the blanket off, exposing them. Joan lay with her arms around her mother, half-hidden under a curtain of white-gold hair.

For a moment the canon stood stupefied with disbelief, looking at Gudrun's unbound hair. Then his fury overtook him. "How dare you! When I have expressly forbidden it!" Taking hold of Gudrun, he started to drag her from the bed. "Heathen witch!"

Joan clung to her mother. The canon's face darkened. "Child, be-gone!" he bellowed. Joan hesitated, torn between fear and the desire somehow to protect her mother.

Gudrun pushed her urgently. "Yes, go. *Go quickly.*"

Releasing her hold, Joan dropped to the floor and ran. At the door, she turned and saw her father grab her mother roughly by the hair, wrenching her head back, forcing her to her knees. Joan started back into the room. Terror stopped her short as she saw her father withdraw his long, bone-handled hunting knife from his corded belt.

"*Forsachistu diabolae?*" he asked Gudrun in Saxon, his voice scarcely more than a whisper. When she did not respond, he placed the point of the knife against her throat. "Say the words," he growled menacingly. "*Say them!*"

"*Ec forsacho allum diaboles,*" Gudrun responded tearfully, her eyes blazing defiance, "*wuercum ende wuordum, thunaer ende woden ende saxnotes ende allum . . .*"

Rooted with fear, Joan watched her father pull up a heavy tress of her mother's hair and draw the knife across it. There was a ripping sound as the silken strands parted; a long band of white gold floated to the floor.

Clapping her hand over her mouth to stifle a sob, Joan turned and ran.

In the darkness, she bumped into a shape that reached out for her. She squealed in fear as it grabbed her. The monster hand! She had forgotten about it! She struggled, pummeling at it with her tiny fists, resisting with all her strength, but it was huge, and held her fast.

"Joan! Joan, it's all right. It's me!"

The words penetrated her fear. It was her ten-year-old brother Matthew, who had returned with her father.

"We've come back. Joan, stop struggling! It's all right. It's *me*." Joan reached up, felt the smooth surface of the pectoral cross that Matthew always wore, then slumped against him in relief.

Together they sat in the dark, listening to the soft, splitting sounds of the knife ripping through their mother's hair. Once they heard Mama cry out in pain. Matthew cursed aloud. An answering sob came from the bed where Joan's seven-year-old brother, John, was hiding under the covers.

At last the ripping sounds stopped. After a brief pause the canon's voice began to rumble in prayer. Joan felt Matthew relax; it was over. She threw her arms around his neck and wept. He held her and rocked her gently.

After a time, she looked up at him. "Father called Mama a heathen."

"Yes."

"She isn't," Joan said hesitantly, "is she?"

"She *was*." Seeing her look of horrified disbelief, he added, "A long time ago. Not anymore. But those were heathen stories she was telling you."

Joan stopped crying; this was interesting information.

"You know the first of the Commandments, don't you?"

Joan nodded and recited dutifully, "Thou shalt have no other gods before me."

"Yes. That means that the gods Mama was telling you about are false; it is sinful to speak of them."

"Is that why Father—"

"Yes," Matthew broke in. "Mama had to be punished for the good of her soul. She was disobedient to her husband, and that also is against the law of God."

"Why?"

"Because it says so in the Holy Book." He began to recite, " 'For the husband is the head of the wife; therefore, let the wives submit themselves unto their husbands in everything.' "

"Why?"

"Why?" Matthew was taken aback. No one had ever asked him that before. "Well, I guess because . . . because women are by nature inferior to men. Men are bigger, stronger, and smarter."

"But—" Joan started to respond, but Matthew cut her off.

"Enough questions, little sister. You should be in bed. Come now." He carried her to the bed and placed her beside John, who was already sleeping.

Matthew had been kind to her; to return the favor, Joan closed her eyes and burrowed under the covers as if to sleep.

But she was far too troubled for sleep. She lay in the dark, peering at John as he slept, his mouth hanging slackly open.

He can't recite from the Psalter and he's seven years old. Joan was only four, but she already knew the first ten psalms by heart.

John wasn't smart. But he was a boy. Yet how could Matthew be wrong? He knew everything; he was going to be a priest, like their father.

She lay awake in the dark, turning the problem over in her mind.

Toward dawn she slept, restlessly, troubled by dreams of mighty wars between jealous and angry gods. The angel Gabriel himself came from Heaven with a flaming sword to do battle with Thor and Freya. The battle was terrible and fierce, but in the end the false gods were driven back, and Gabriel stood triumphant before the gates of paradise. His sword had disappeared; in his hand gleamed a short, bone-handled knife.

2

THE wooden stylus moved swiftly, forming letters and words in the soft yellow wax of the tablet. Joan stood attentively near Matthew's shoulder as he copied out the day's lessons. From time to time he stopped to wave a candle flame over the tablet to keep the wax from hardening too quickly.

She loved to watch Matthew work. His pointed bone stylus pushed the shapeless wax into lines that held for her a mysterious beauty. She longed to understand what each mark meant and followed every movement of the stylus intently, as if to discover the key to the meaning in the shape of the lines.

Matthew put the stylus down and leaned back in the chair, rubbing his eyes. Sensing an opportunity, Joan reached over to the tablet and pointed to a word.

"What does that say?"

"Jerome. That is the name of one of the great Fathers of the Church."

"Jerome," she repeated slowly. "The sound is like my name."

"Some of the letters are the same," Matthew agreed, smiling.

"Show me."

"I'd better not. Father wouldn't like it if he found out."

"He won't," Joan pleaded. "Please, Matthew. I want to know. Please show me?"

Matthew hesitated. "I suppose there is no harm in teaching you to write your own name. It may be useful one day when you are married and have a household of your own to manage."

Placing his hand over her small one, he helped her trace the letters of her name: J-O-H-A-N-N-A, with a long, looped *a* at the end.

"Good. Now try it yourself."

Joan gripped the stylus hard, forcing her fingers into the odd, constricted position, willing them to form the letters she pictured in her mind. Once, she cried aloud in frustration when she could not make the stylus go where she wished.

Matthew soothed her. "Slowly, little sister, slowly. You are only six. Writing does not come easy at that age. That is when I started also, and I remember. Take your time; it will come to you in the end."

THE next day, she rose early and went outside. In the loose earth surrounding the livestock pen, she traced the letters over and over again until she was sure she had them right. Then she proudly called Matthew over to witness her handiwork.

"Why, that's very good, little sister. Really very good." He caught himself with a start and muttered guiltily, "But it will not do for Father to find out about this." He scuffed at the dirt with his feet, erasing the marks she had made.

"No, Matthew, no!" Joan tried to pull him away. Disturbed by the noise, the pigs started a chorus of grunting.

Matthew bent to embrace her. "It's all right, Joan. Don't be unhappy."

"B-but you said my letters were good!"

"They *are* good." Matthew was surprised by how good they were; better than John could do, and he was three years older. Indeed, if Joan weren't a girl, Matthew would have said that she would make a fine scribe one day. But it was better not to put wild ideas in the child's head. "I could not leave the letters for Father to see; that is why I erased them."

"Will you teach me more letters, Matthew? Will you?"

"I have already showed you more than I should have."

She said with grave seriousness, "Father won't find out. I won't ever tell him, I promise. And I will erase the letters very carefully when I am done." Her deep-set gray-green eyes held his intently, willing him to agree.

Matthew shook his head in rueful amusement. She was certainly persistent, this little sister of his. Affectionately he chucked her under the chin. "Very well," he agreed. "But, remember, we must keep it our secret."

AFTER that, it became a kind of game between them. Whenever the chance presented itself, not nearly as often as Joan would have liked, Matthew would show her how to trace letters in the earth. She was an eager student; though wary of the consequences, Matthew found it impossible to resist her enthusiasm. He, too, loved learning; her eagerness spoke directly to his heart.

Nevertheless, even he was shocked when she came to him one day carrying the huge, wood-bound Bible that belonged to their father.

"What are you doing?" he cried. "Put that back; you should never have touched it!"

"Teach me to read."

"What?" Her audacity was astonishing. "Now, really, little sister, that's asking too much."

"Why?"

"Well . . . for one thing, reading is a lot more difficult than merely learning the abecedarium. I doubt you could even learn to do it."

"Why not? You did."

He smiled indulgently. "Yes. But I am a man." This was not quite true, as he had not yet attained thirteen winters. In a little over a year, when he turned fourteen, he would truly be a man. But it pleased him to claim the privilege now, and besides, his little sister didn't know the difference.

"I *can* do it. I know I can."

Matthew sighed. This was not going to be easy. "It's not only that, Joan. It is dangerous, and unnatural, for a girl to read and write."

"Saint Catherine did. The bishop said so in his sermon, remember? He said she was loved for her wisdom and learning."

"That's different. She was a saint. You are just a . . . girl."

She was silent then. Matthew was pleased at having won the debate so handily; he knew how determined his little sister could be. He reached for the Bible.

She started to give it to him, then pulled it back. "Why is Catherine a saint?" she asked.

Matthew paused, his hand still extended. "She was a holy martyr who died for the Faith. The bishop said so in his sermon, remember?" He could not resist parroting her.

"Why was she martyred?"

Matthew sighed. "She defied the Emperor Maxentius and fifty of his wisest men by proving, through logical debate, the falseness of paganism. For this she was punished. Now come, little sister, give me the book."

"How old was she when she did this?"

What odd questions the child asked! "I don't want to discuss it any further," Matthew said, exasperated. "Just give me the book!"

She backed away, keeping tight hold of it. "She was old when she went to Alexandria to debate the Emperor's wise men, wasn't she?"

Matthew wondered if he should wrest the book from her. No, better not. The fragile binding might come loose. Then they would both be in more trouble than he cared to think about. Better to keep talking, answering her questions, silly and childish as they were, until she tired of the game.

"Thirty-three, the bishop said, the same age as Christ Jesus at His crucifixion."

"And when St. Catherine defied the Emperor, she was already admired for her learning, like the bishop said?"

"Obviously." Matthew was condescending. "How else could she have bested the wisest men in all the land in such a debate?"

"Then"—Joan's small face was alight with triumph—"she must have learned to read *before* she was a saint. When she was just a girl. Like me!"

For a moment Matthew was speechless, torn between irritation and surprise. Then he laughed aloud. "You little imp!" he said. "So that's where you were headed! Well, you have a gift for disputation, that's for certain!"

She handed him the book then, smiling expectantly.

Matthew took it from her, shaking his head. What a strange creature she was, so inquisitive, so determined, so sure of herself. She was not at all like John or any other young child he had ever met. The eyes of a wise old woman shone forth from her little girl's face. No wonder the other girls in the village would have nothing to do with her.

"Very well, little sister," he said at last. "Today, you begin to learn to read." He saw the gleeful anticipation in her eyes and hastened to caution her. "You must not expect much. It is far more difficult than you think."

Joan threw her arms around her brother's neck. "I love you, Matthew."

Matthew extricated himself from her grasp, opened the book, and said gruffly, "We will begin here."

Joan bent over the book, picking up the pungent smell of parchment and wood as Matthew pointed out the passage, "The Gospel of
John, chapter one, verse one. *In principio erat verbum et verbum erat
apud Deum et verbum erat Deus*": "In the beginning was the Word
and the Word was with God and the Word was God."

THE summer and fall that followed were mild and fruitful; the harvest was the best the village had had in years. But in Heilagmanoth,
snow fell, and the wind drove in from the north in icy blasts. The
window of the grubenhaus was boarded up against the cold, snow
drifted high against its walls, and the family stayed indoors most of
the day. It was more difficult for Joan and Matthew to find time for
lessons. On good days the canon still went on his ministry, taking
John with him—for Matthew he left to his all-important studies.
When Gudrun went into the forest to gather wood, Joan would hurry
to the desk where Matthew bent over his work and open the Bible to
the place where they had left off the previous lesson. In this way Joan
continued to make rapid progress, so that before Lent she had mastered almost all of the Book of John.

One day, Matthew withdrew something from his scrip and held it
out to her with a smile. "For you, little sister." It was a wooden
medallion attached to a loop of rope. Matthew ringed the loop
around Joan's head; the medallion swung down onto her chest.

"What is it?" Joan asked curiously.

"Something for you to wear."

"Oh," she said, and then, realizing that something more was
needed, "Thank you."

Matthew laughed, seeing her puzzlement. "Look at the front of
the medallion."

Joan did as he told her. Carved into the wooden surface was the
likeness of a woman. It was crudely done, for Matthew was no
woodworker, but the woman's eyes were well made, even striking,
looking straight ahead with an expression of intelligence.

"Now," Matthew directed her, "look at the back."

Joan turned it over. In bold letters ringing the edge of the medallion, she read the words "Saint Catherine of Alexandria."

With a cry, Joan clasped the medallion to her heart. She knew
what this gift signified. It was Matthew's way of acknowledging her

abilities and the faith he had in her. Tears welled in her eyes. "Thank you," she said again, and this time he knew she meant it.

He smiled at her. She noticed dark circles around his eyes; he looked tired and drawn.

"Are you feeling well?" she asked with concern.

"Of course!" he said, just a shade too heartily. "Let's begin the lesson, shall we?"

But he was restless and distracted. Uncharacteristically, he failed to catch her up when she made a careless error.

"Is there anything wrong?" Joan asked.

"No, no. I am a little tired, that is all."

"Shall we stop, then? I don't mind. We can go on tomorrow."

"No, I am sorry. My mind wandered, that's all. Let's see, where were we? Ah yes. Read the last passage again, and this time be careful of the verb: *videat, not videt.*"

THE next day Matthew woke complaining of a headache and a sore throat. Gudrun brought him a hot posset of borage and honey.

"You must stay in bed for the rest of the day," she said. "Old Mistress Wigbod's boy has the spring flux; it may be that you are coming down with it."

Matthew laughed and said it was nothing of the kind. He worked several hours at his studies, then insisted on going outside to help John prune the vines.

The next morning he had a fever, and difficulty swallowing. Even the canon could see that he looked really ill.

"You are excused from your studies today," he told Matthew. This was an unheard-of dispensation.

They sent to the monastery of Lorsch for help, and in two days' time the infirmarian came and examined Matthew, shaking his head gravely and muttering under his breath. For the first time Joan realized that her brother's condition might be serious. The idea was terrifying. The monk bled Matthew profusely and exhausted his entire repertoire of prayer and holy talismans, but by the Feast of St. Severinus, Matthew's condition was critical. He lay in a feverish stupor, shaken by fits of coughing so violent that Joan covered her ears to try to shut them out.

Throughout the day and into the night the family kept vigil. Joan knelt beside her mother on the beaten earth floor. She was frightened by the alteration in Matthew's appearance. The skin on his face was stretched taut, distorting his familiar features into a horrible mask. Beneath his feverish flush was an ominous undertone of gray.

Above them, in the dark, the canon's voice droned into the night, reciting prayers for his son's deliverance. *"Domine Sancte, Pater omnipotens, aeterne Deus, qui fragilitatem conditionis nostrae infusa virtutis tuae dignatione confirmas . . ."* Joan nodded drowsily.

"No!"

Joan wakened suddenly to her mother's wailing cry.

"He is gone! Matthew, my son!"

Joan looked at the bed. Nothing appeared to have changed. Matthew lay motionless as before. Then she noticed his skin had lost its feverish flush; he was entirely gray, the color of stone.

She took his hand. It was flaccid, heavy, though not so hot as before. She held it tightly, pressing it to her cheek. *Please don't be dead, Matthew.* Dead meant that he would never again sleep beside her and John in the big bed; she would never again see him hunched over the pine table, brow furrowed in concentration as he labored at his studies, never again sit beside him while his finger moved across the pages of the Bible, pointing out words for her to read. *Please don't be dead.*

AFTER a while, they sent her away so her mother and the village women could wash Matthew's body and prepare it for burial. When they were done, Joan was allowed to approach to pay her final respects. But for the unnatural grayness of his skin, he looked to be merely sleeping. If she touched him, she imagined, he would wake, his eyes would open and gaze upon her again with teasing affection. She kissed his cheek, as her mother instructed her. It was cold and oddly unresistant, like the skin of the dead rabbit Joan had fetched from the cooling shed only last week. She drew back quickly.

Matthew was gone.

There would be no more lessons now.

SHE stood alongside the livestock pen, staring at the patches of black earth beginning to show under the melting snow, the earth in which she had traced her first letters.

"Matthew," she whispered. She sank to her knees. The wet snow penetrated her woolen cloak, soaking through to the skin. She felt

very cold, but she could not go back in. There was something she had
to do. With her forefinger, she traced the familiar letters from the
Book of John in the wet snow.

Ubi sum ego vos non potestis venire. "Where I am you cannot
come."

"WE WILL all do penance," the canon announced after the burial,
"to atone for the sins that have visited God's wrath upon our family."
He made Joan and John kneel in silent prayer on the hard wooden
board that served as the family altar. They stayed there all that day
with nothing to eat or drink until at last, with the coming of night,
they were released and permitted to sleep in the bed, big and empty
now without Matthew. John whimpered with hunger. In the middle
of the night, Gudrun woke them, her finger pressed warningly to her
lips. The canon was asleep. Quickly, she handed them several pieces
of bread and a wooden cup filled with warm goat's milk—all the food
she dared smuggle from the larder without arousing her husband's
suspicions. John gobbled down his bread and was still hungry; Joan
shared her portion with him. As soon as they were done, Gudrun
took away the wooden cup and left, pulling the woolen covers up
under their chins. The children nestled together for comfort and were
quickly asleep.

With the first light, the canon woke them, and without breaking
fast, sent them to the altar to resume their penance. The morning came
and went, and the dinner hour, and still they remained on their knees.

The rays of the late afternoon sun slanted onto the altar, spilling
through the slit in the grubenhaus window. Joan sighed and shifted
position on the makeshift altar. Her knees were sore, and her stomach growled. She struggled to concentrate on the words of her prayer,
"*Pater Noster qui es in caelis, sanctificetur nomen tuum, adveniat
regnum tuum . . .*"

It was no use. The discomforts of her present situation kept in-
truding. She was tired and hungry, and she missed Matthew. She
wondered why she did not cry. There was a sensation of pressure in
her throat and chest, but the tears would not come.

She stared at the small wooden crucifix that hung on the wall before the altar. The canon had brought it with him from his native
England when he had arrived to carry out his missionary work
among the heathen Saxons. Fashioned by a Northumbrian artist, the

Christ figure had more power and precision than most Frankish work. His body stretched on the cross, all elongated limbs and emaciated ribs, the lower half twisted to emphasize His mortal agony. His head was fallen back, so that the Adam's apple bulged—a strangely disconcerting reminder of His human maleness. The wood was deeply etched to reveal the tracks of blood from His many wounds.

The figure, for all its power, was grotesque. Joan knew she should be filled with love and awe at Christ's sacrifice, but instead she felt revulsion. Compared with the beautiful, strong gods of her mother, this figure seemed ugly, broken, and defeated.

Beside her, John started to whimper. Joan reached out and took his hand. John took punishment hard. She was stronger than he was, and she knew it. Though he was ten years old, and she only seven, she found it entirely natural that she should nurture and protect him, rather than the other way around.

Tears started to form in his eyes. "It's not fair," he said.

"Don't cry." Joan was worried that the noise might bring Mama—or worse yet, Father. "Soon the penance will be over."

"That's not it!" he responded with wounded dignity.

"What's the matter, then?"

"You wouldn't understand."

"Tell me."

"Father will want me to take over Matthew's studies. I know he will. And I can't do it; I can't."

"Perhaps you can," said Joan, though she understood why her brother was worried. Father accused him of laziness and beat him when he did not progress in his studies, but it was not John's fault. He tried to do well, but he was slow; he always had been.

"No," John insisted. "I'm not like Matthew. Did you know that Father planned to take him to Aachen, to petition for his acceptance in the Schola Palatina?"

"Truly?" Joan was astonished. The Palace School! She had no idea that her father's ambitions for Matthew had reached so high.

"And I can't even read Donatus yet. Father says that Matthew had mastered Donatus when he was only nine, and I am almost ten. What will I do, Joan? What will I do?"

"Well . . ." Joan tried to think of something comforting to quiet him, but the strain of the last two days had driven John into a state past all caring.

"He will beat me. I know he will beat me." Now John started to wail in earnest. *"I don't want to be beaten!"*

Gudrun appeared in the doorway. Nervously casting a glance into the room behind her, she hurried over to John. "Stop it. Do you want your father to hear you? Stop it, I tell you!"

John rocked clumsily off the altar, threw his head back, and bawled. Oblivious to his mother's words, he continued to wail, tears streaming down red-blotched cheeks.

Gudrun gripped John's shoulders and shook him. His head flopped wildly, back to front; his eyes were closed, his mouth hanging open. Joan heard the sharp click of teeth as his mouth snapped shut. Startled, John opened his eyes and saw his mother.

Gudrun hugged him to her. "You will not cry anymore. For your sister's sake, and mine, you must not cry. All will be well, John. But now you will be quiet." She rocked him, soothing and remonstrating at the same time.

Joan watched thoughtfully. She recognized the truth in what her brother said. John was not smart. He could not follow in Matthew's footsteps. But— Her face flushed with excitement as a thought struck with the force of revelation.

"What is it, Joan?" Gudrun had seen the odd expression on her daughter's face. "Are you unwell?" She was concerned, for the demons that carried the flux were known to linger in a house.

"No, Mama. But I have an idea, a wonderful idea!"

Gudrun groaned inwardly. The child was full of ideas that only got her into trouble.

"Yes?"

"Father wanted Matthew to go to the Schola Palatina."

"I know."

"And now he will want John to go in Matthew's place. That is why John is crying, Mama. He knows he cannot do it, and he's afraid that Father will be angry."

"Well?" Gudrun was puzzled.

"*I* can do it, Mama. I can take over Matthew's studies."

For a moment Gudrun was too shocked to respond. *Her* daughter, her baby, the child she loved best—the only one with whom she had shared the language and the secrets of her people—*she* to study the sacred books of the Christian conquerors? That Joan would even consider such a thing was deeply wounding.

"What nonsense!" Gudrun said.

"I can work hard," Joan persisted. "I like to study and learn about things. I can do it, and then John won't have to. He isn't good at it." There was a muffled sob from John, whose head was still buried in his mother's chest.

"You are a girl; such things are not for you," Gudrun said dismissively. "Besides, your father would never approve."

"But, Mama, that was before. Things have changed. Don't you see? Now Father may feel differently."

"I forbid you to speak of this to your father. You must be lightheaded from lack of food and rest, like your brother. Otherwise you would never speak so wildly."

"But, Mama, if I could only show him—"

"No more, I say!" Gudrun's tone left no room for further discussion.

Joan fell silent. Reaching inside her tunic, she clasped the medallion of St. Catherine that Matthew had carved for her. *I can read Latin, and John cannot,* she thought stubbornly. *Why should it matter that I am a girl?*

She went to the Bible on the little wooden desk. She lifted it, felt its weight, the familiar grooves of the gilt-edged tracings on the cover. The smell of wood and parchment, so strongly associated with Matthew, made her think of their work together, of all he had taught her, all she still wanted to learn. *Perhaps if I show Father what I have learned . . . perhaps then he will see I can do it.* Once again, she felt a rise of excitement. *But there could be trouble. Father might be very angry.* Her father's anger frightened her; she had been struck by him often enough to know and fear the force of his rage.

She stood uncertainly, fingering the smooth surface of the Bible's wooden binding. On an impulse, she opened it; the pages fell open to the Gospel of St. John, the text Matthew had used when he first taught her to read. *It is a sign,* she thought.

Her mother was sitting with her back to Joan, cradling John, whose sobs had subsided into forlorn hiccuping. *Now is my chance.* Joan held the book open and carried it into the next room.

Her father was hunched in a chair, head bowed, hands covering his face. He did not stir as Joan approached. She halted, suddenly afraid. The idea was impossible, ridiculous; Father would never approve. She was about to retreat when he took his hands from his face and looked up. She stood before him with the open book in her hands.

Her voice was nervously unsteady as she began to read, *"In principio erat verbum et verbum erat apud Deum et verbum erat Deus . . ."*

There was no interruption; she kept on, gaining confidence as she read. "All things were made by Him; and without Him was not any thing made that was made. In Him was life; and the life was the light of men. And the light shone in the darkness, and the darkness comprehended it not." The beauty and power of the words filled her, leading her onward, giving her strength.

She came to the end, flushed with success, knowing she had read well. She looked up and saw her father staring at her.

"I can read. Matthew taught me. We kept it a secret so no one would know." The words spilled out in a breathless jumble. "I can make you proud, Father, I know I can. Let me take over Matthew's studies and I—"

"You!" Her father's voice rumbled with anger. "It was you!" He pointed at her accusingly. "You are the one! You brought God's wrath down upon us. Unnatural child! Changeling! *You murdered your brother!"*

Joan gasped. The canon came toward her with arm raised. Joan dropped the book and tried to run, but he caught her and spun her round, bringing his fist down on her cheek with a force that sent her reeling. She landed against the far wall, striking her head.

Her father stood over her. Joan braced herself for another blow. None came. Moments passed, and then he began to make hoarse, guttural noises in his throat. She realized he was crying. She had never seen her father cry.

"Joan!" Gudrun hurried into the room. "What have you done, child?" She knelt beside Joan, taking note of the swelling bruise under her right eye. Keeping her body between her husband and Joan, she whispered, "What did I tell you? Foolish girl, look what you've done!" In a louder voice, she said, "Go to your brother. He needs you." She helped Joan up and propelled her quickly toward the other room.

The canon watched Joan darkly as she went to the door.

"Forget the girl, Husband," Gudrun said to distract him. "She's of no importance. Do not despair; remember, you have yet another son."

≽ 3 ≼

IT WAS Aranmanoth, the wheat-blade month, in the autumn of her ninth year, when Joan first met Aesculapius. He had stopped at the canon's grubenhaus on his way to Mainz, where he was to be teaching master at the cathedral *schola*.

"Be welcome, sir, be welcome!" Joan's father greeted Aesculapius delightedly. "We rejoice in your safe arrival. I trust the journey was not too arduous?" He bowed his guest solicitously through the door. "Come refresh yourself. Gudrun! Bring wine! You do my humble home great honor, sir, with your presence." From her father's behavior, Joan understood that Aesculapius was a scholar of some standing and importance.

He was Greek, dressed in the Byzantine manner. His fine white linen chlamys was clasped with a simple metal brooch and covered with a long blue cloak, bordered with silver thread. He wore his hair short, like a peasant, and kept it smoothly oiled back from his face. Unlike her father, who shaved in the manner of the Frankish clergy, Aesculapius had a long, full beard—white, like his hair.

When her father called her over to be presented, she suffered a fit of shyness and stood awkwardly before the stranger, her eyes fixed on the intricate braid work of his sandals. At last the canon intervened and sent her off to help her mother prepare the evening meal.

When they sat down at the table, the canon said, "It is our custom to read from the Holy Book before we partake of food. Would you do us the honor of reading this night?"

"Very well," said Aesculapius, smiling. Carefully he opened the wooden binding and turned the fragile parchment pages. "The text is Ecclesiastes. *Omnia tempus habent, et momentum suum cuique negotio sub caelo...*"

Joan had never heard Latin spoken so beautifully. His pronunciation was unusual: the words were not all run together, Gallic style; each was round and distinct, like drops of clear rainwater. "For everything there is a season, and a time to every purpose under

Heaven. A time to be born, and a time to die; a time to plant, and a time to pluck up that which is planted . . ." Joan had heard her father read the same passage many times before, but in Aesculapius's reading, she heard a beauty she had not previously imagined.

When he was finished, Aesculapius closed the book. "An excellent volume," he said appreciatively to the canon. "Written in a fair hand. You must have brought it with you from England; I have heard that the art still flourishes there. It is rare these days to find a manuscript so free from grammatical barbarisms."

The canon flushed with pleasure. "There were many such in the library at Lindisfarne. This one was entrusted to me by the bishop when he ordained me for the mission in Saxony."

The meal was splendid, the most lavish the family had ever prepared for a guest. There was a haunch of roast salted pork, cooked till the skin crackled, boiled barley-corn and beetroot, pungent cheese, and loaves of crusty bread freshly baked under the embers. The canon brought out some Frankish ale, spicy, dark, and thick as country soup. Afterward, they ate fried almonds and sweet roasted apples.

"Delicious," Aesculapius pronounced at the end of the meal. "It has been a long while since I have dined so well. Not since I left Byzantium have I tasted pork so sweet."

Gudrun was pleased. "It is because we keep our own pigs, and fatten them before the slaughter. The meat of the black forest pigs is tough and unappetizing."

"Tell us about Constantinople!" John said eagerly. "Is it true the streets are paved with precious stones, and the fountains spew liquid gold?"

Aesculapius laughed. "No. But it is a marvelous place to behold." Joan and John listened gape-mouthed as Aesculapius described Constantinople, perched on a towering promontory, with buildings of marble domed in gold and silver rising several stories high, overlooking the harbor of the Golden Horn, in which ships from all over the world lay at anchor. It was the city of Aesculapius's birth and youth. He had been forced to flee when his family had become embroiled in a religious dispute with the basileus, something to do with the breaking of icons. Joan did not understand this, though her father did, nodding with grave disapproval as Aesculapius described his family's persecution.

Here the discussion turned to theological matters, and Joan and her brother were trundled off to the part of the house where their parents slept; as an honored guest, Aesculapius was to have the big bed near the hearth all to himself.

"Please, can't I stay and listen?" Joan pleaded with her mother.

"No. It is well past time for you to be asleep. Besides, our guest is done with telling stories. This schoolroom talk will not interest you."

"But—"

"No more, child. Off to bed with you. I will need your help in the morning; your father wishes us to prepare another feast for his visitor tomorrow. Any more such guests," Gudrun grumbled, "and we will be ruined." She tucked the children into the straw pallet, kissed them, and left.

John was quickly asleep, but Joan lay awake, trying to hear what the voices were saying on the other side of the thick wooden partition. Finally, overcome with curiosity, she got out of bed and crept over to the partition, where she knelt, peering out from the darkness to where her father and Aesculapius sat talking by the hearth fire. It was chilly; the warmth of the fire did not reach this far, and Joan was wearing only a light linen shift. She shivered but did not consider returning to the bed; she *had* to hear what Aesculapius was saying.

The talk had turned to the cathedral schola. Aesculapius asked the canon, "Do you know anything of the library there?"

"Oh yes," said the canon, obviously pleased to have been asked. "I have spent many hours in it. It houses an excellent collection, upwards of five and seventy codices." Aesculapius nodded politely, though he did not appear impressed. Joan could not imagine so many books all in one place.

The canon said, "There are copies of Isidore's *De scriptoribus ecclesiasticus* and Salvianus's *De gubernatione Dei*. Also the complete *Commentarii* of Jerome, with wondrously skilled illustrations. And there is a particularly fine manuscript of the *Hexaëmeron* by your countryman St. Basil."

"Are there any manuscripts of Plato?"

"Plato?" The canon was shocked. "Certainly not; his writing is no fit study for a Christian."

"Ah? You do not approve of the study of logic, then?"

"It has its place in the trivium," the canon replied uneasily, "with the use of proper texts such as those of Augustine and Boethius. But faith is grounded in the authority of Scripture, not the evidence of logic; out of foolish curiosity men do sometimes shake their faith."

"I see your point." Aesculapius's words were spoken more out of courtesy than agreement. "Perhaps, however, you can answer me this: How does it happen that man can reason?"

"Reason is the spark of the divine essence in man. 'So God created man in His own image; In the image of God created He him.' "

"You have a good command of Scripture. So you would agree, then, that reason is God-given?"

"Most assuredly."

Joan crept closer, moving out from behind the shadow of the partition; she did not want to miss what Aesculapius said next.

"Then why fear to expose faith to reason? If God gave it to us, how then should it lead us from Him?"

The canon shifted in his seat. Joan had never seen him look so uncomfortable. He was a missionary, trained to lecture and to preach, unaccustomed to the give-and-take of logical debate. He opened his mouth to reply, then closed it.

"Indeed," Aesculapius went on, "is it not *lack* of faith that leads men to fear the scrutiny of reason? If the destination is doubtful, then the path must be fraught with fear. A robust faith need not fear, for if God exists, then reason cannot help but lead us to Him. '*Cogito, ergo Deus est,*' argues St. Augustine, '*I think, therefore God is.*'"

Joan was following the argument so intently that she forgot herself and exclaimed aloud in appreciative understanding. Her father looked sharply toward the partition. She darted back into the shadows and waited, scarcely breathing. Then she heard the hum of voices again. *Benedicite,* she thought, *they did not see me.* She crept softly back to the pallet, where John lay snoring.

Long after the voices ceased, Joan lay awake in the dark. She felt incredibly lighthearted and free, as if an oppressive weight had been lifted from her. It was *not* her fault that Matthew had died. Her desire to learn had not killed him, despite what her father said. Tonight, listening to Aesculapius, she had discovered that her love of knowing was not unnatural or sinful but the direct consequence of a God-given ability to reason. *I think, therefore God is.* In her heart, she felt the truth of it.

Aesculapius's words had turned a light on in her soul. *Perhaps to-*

morrow I can speak to him, she thought. *Perhaps I will have a chance to show him I can read.*

The prospect was so pleasing that she could not let go of it. She did not fall asleep until dawn.

EARLY the next morning, her mother sent Joan into the woods to gather beechnuts and acorns as fodder for the pigs. Anxious to return to the house and Aesculapius, Joan hurried to complete the chore. But the ground of the autumn forest was thick with fallen leaves, and the nuts were hard to find; she could not go back until the wicker basket was full.

By the time she returned, Aesculapius was readying to leave.

"Ah, but I had hoped you would do us the honor of dining with us again," said the canon. "I was interested in your ideas on the mystery of the Triune Oneness and would like to discuss the subject further."

"You are kind, but I must be in Mainz this evening. The bishop expects me, and I am eager to take up my new duties."

"Of course, of course." After a pause the canon added, "But you do remember our conversation about the boy. Will you stay to observe his lesson?"

"It is the least I can do for so generous a host," Aesculapius said with studied politeness.

Joan took up her sewing and stationed herself in a chair a short distance apart, trying to be as inconspicuous as possible, so her father would not send her away.

She need not have worried. The canon's attention was focused entirely on John. Hoping to impress Aesculapius with the extent of his son's learning, he began the lesson by questioning John on the rules of grammar following Donatus. This was a mistake, for grammar was John's weakest subject. Predictably, he performed dismally, confusing the ablative with the dative case, botching his verbs, and in the end showing himself utterly unable to parse a sentence correctly. Aesculapius listened solemnly, the line of a frown creasing his forehead.

Red-faced with embarrassment, the canon retreated to safer ground. He began with the great Alcuin's catechism of riddles, in which John had been thoroughly drilled. John made it through the first part of the catechism well enough:

"What is a year?"

"A cart with four wheels."

"What horses pull it?"

"The sun and the moon."

"How many palaces has it?"

"Twelve."

Pleased with this small success, the canon moved on to more difficult parts of the catechism. Joan feared what was coming, for she saw that John was now in a state of near panic.

"What is life?"

"The joy of the blessed, the sorrow of the sad, and . . . and . . ." John broke off.

Aesculapius shifted in his chair. Joan closed her eyes, concentrating on the words, willing John to utter them.

"Yes?" prodded the canon. "And what?"

John's face lit with inspiration. "And a search for death!"

The canon nodded curtly. "And what is death?"

Stricken, John stared at his father like a netted deer who sees at last the approach of the huntsman.

"What is death?" repeated the canon.

It was no use. The near miss on the last question and his father's mounting displeasure destroyed the last of John's composure. He could no longer remember anything. His face crumpled; Joan saw that he was going to cry. Her father glared at him. Aesculapius looked on with pitying eyes.

She could stand it no longer. Her brother's distress, her father's anger, the intolerable humiliation before the eyes of Aesculapius overwhelmed her. Before she knew what she was doing, she burst out: "An inevitable happening, an uncertain pilgrimage, the tears of the living, the thief of man."

Her words struck the others like a thunderbolt. All three looked up at once, their faces registering a range of emotions. On John's there was chagrin, on her father's outrage, on Aesculapius's astonishment. The canon found his voice first.

"What insolence is this?" he demanded. Then, remembering Aesculapius, he said, "Were it not for the presence of our guest, you would be given a proper thrashing right now. As it is, your punishment will have to wait. Be gone from my sight."

Joan rose from her chair, fighting for control until she reached the door of the grubenhaus and pulled it shut behind her. Then she ran, as fast and hard as she could, all the way to the bracken at the edge of the forest, where she threw herself down on the ground.

She thought she would burst with pain. To have been disgraced before the eyes of the one person she had most wanted to impress! *It isn't fair. John didn't know the answer, and I did. Why shouldn't I give it?*

For a long time she sat watching the lengthening shadows of the trees. A robin fluttered to the ground nearby and began to peck in the bracken, hunting for worms. It found one and, puffing out its chest, strutted in a little circle, displaying its prize. *Like me*, she thought with wry recognition. *All puffed with pride over what I've done.* She knew pridefulness was a sin—she had been chastised for it often enough—yet she could not help the way she felt. *I am smarter than John. Why should he be able to study and learn and not me?*

The robin flew off. Joan watched it become a distant flutter of color among the trees. She fingered the medal of St. Catherine that hung around her neck and thought of Matthew. He would have sat with her, talked with her, explained things so she could understand. She missed him so much.

You murdered your brother, Father had said. A sick feeling rose in her throat as she remembered. Still her spirit rebelled. She *was* prideful, wanting more than God intended for a woman. But why would God punish Matthew for her sin? It didn't make sense.

What was it in her that would not let go of her impossible dreams? Everyone told her that her desire to learn was unnatural. Yet she thirsted for knowledge, yearned to explore the larger world of ideas and opportunities that was open to people of learning. The other girls in the village had no such interest. They were content to sit through mass without understanding a single word. They accepted what they were told and did not look further. They dreamed of a good husband, by which they meant a man who would treat them kindly and not beat them, and a workable piece of soil; they had no desire ever to go beyond the safe, familiar world of the village. They were as inexplicable to Joan as she was to them.

Why am I different? she wondered. *What is wrong with me?*

Footsteps sounded beside her, and a hand touched her shoulder. It was John.

He said sulkily, "Father sent me. He wants to see you."

Joan took his hand. "I'm sorry."

"You shouldn't have done it. You're only a girl."

This was hard to take, but she owed him an apology for shaming him before their guest.

"I was wrong. Forgive me."

He tried to maintain his pose of wounded virtue but could not. "All right, I forgive you," he relented. "At least Father isn't angry at *me* anymore. Now—well, come and see for yourself."

He pulled her up from the damp ground and helped her dust off the clinging pieces of bracken. Holding hands, they walked back toward the cottage.

At the door, John ushered Joan in ahead of him. "Go on," he said. "It's you they want to see."

They? Joan wondered what he meant, but she could not ask, for she was already facing her father and Aesculapius, who waited before the hearth fire.

She approached and stood submissively before them. Her father had a peculiar look on his face, as if he had swallowed something sour. He grunted and motioned her toward Aesculapius, who beckoned to her. Taking her hands in his, Aesculapius fixed her with a penetrating gaze. "You know Latin?" he said.

"Yes, sir."

"How do you come by this knowledge?"

"I listened, sir, whenever my brother had his lessons." She could imagine her father's reaction to this information. She dropped her eyes. "I know that I should not have done so."

Aesculapius asked, "What other knowledge have you gained?"

"I can read, sir, and write a little. My brother Matthew taught me when I was small." From the corner of her eye Joan saw her father's start of anger.

"Show me." Aesculapius opened the Bible, searched for a passage, then held the book out to her, marking the place with his finger. It was the parable of the mustard seed from the Gospel of St. Luke. She began to read, stumbling at first over some of the Latin words—it had been a while since she had read from the book: *"Quomodo assimilabimus regnum Dei aut in qua parabola ponemus illud?"*—"Unto what is the kingdom of God like? And whereunto shall I resemble it?" She continued without hesitation until the end: "Then he said, It is like a grain of mustard seed which a man took, and cast into his garden, and it grew, and waxed a great tree, and the fowls of the air lodged in the branches of it."

She stopped reading. In the silence that followed she could hear the soft rustle of the autumn breeze passing through the thatching on the roof.

Aesculapius said quietly, "And do you understand the meaning of what you have read?"

"I think so."

"Explain it to me."

"It means that faith is like a mustard seed. You plant it in your heart, just like a seed is planted in a garden. If you cultivate the seed, it will grow into a beautiful tree. If you cultivate your faith, you will gain the Kingdom of Heaven."

Aesculapius tugged at his beard. He gave no indication of whether he approved of what she had said. Had she given the wrong interpretation?

"Or—" She had another idea.

Aesculapius's eyebrows went up. "Yes?"

"It could mean that *the Church* is like a seed. The Church started small, growing in darkness, cared for only by Christ and the Twelve Apostles, but it grew into a huge tree, a tree that shades the whole world."

"And the birds who nest in its branches?" Aesculapius asked.

She thought quickly. "They are the faithful, who find salvation in the Church, just as birds find protection in the branches of the tree."

Aesculapius's expression was unreadable. Again he tugged solemnly at his beard. Joan decided to give it one more try.

"Also . . ." She reasoned it out slowly as she spoke. "The mustard seed *could* represent Christ. Christ was like a seed when he was buried in the earth, and like a tree when he was resurrected and rose toward Heaven."

Aesculapius turned to the canon. "You heard?"

The canon's face twitched. "She is only a girl. I am sure she did not mean to presume . . ."

"The seed as faith, as the Church, as Christ," said Aesculapius. "*Allegoria, moralis, anagoge.* A classic threefold scriptural exegesis. Rather simply expressed, of course, but still, as complete an interpretation as that of the great Gregory himself. And that without any formal education! Astonishing! The child demonstrates an extraordinary intelligence. I will undertake to tutor her."

Joan was dazed. Was she dreaming? She was afraid to let herself believe this was actually happening.

"Not, of course, at the schola," Aesculapius continued, "for that would not be permitted. I will arrange to come here once a week. And I will provide books for her to study in between."

The canon was displeased. This was not the outcome he had envisioned. "That's all very well," he said testily. "But what about the boy?"

"Ah, the boy? I'm afraid he shows no promise as a scholar. With further training, he might qualify as a country priest. The law requires only that they read and write, and know the correct form of the sacraments. But I should look no further than that. The schola is not for him."

"I can scarcely credit my ears! You will undertake to teach the girl, but not the boy?"

Aesculapius shrugged. "One has talent; the other has not. There can be no other consideration."

"A woman as scholar!" The canon was indignant. "She to study the sacred texts while her brother is ignored? I will not permit it. Either you teach both or neither."

Joan held her breath. Surely she could not have come this close only to have it taken away. She started to recite a prayer under her breath, then stopped. Perhaps God would not approve. She reached under her tunic and gripped the medallion of St. Catherine. *She* would understand. *Please*, she prayed silently. *Help me to have this. I will make a fine offering to you. Only please let me have this.*

Aesculapius looked impatient. "I have told you the boy has no aptitude for study. To tutor him would be a waste of time."

"Then it is settled," said the canon angrily. Joan watched, disbelieving, as he rose from his chair.

"A moment," said Aesculapius. "I see you are fixed in your intention."

"I am."

"Very well. The girl shows every sign of a prodigious intellect. She could accomplish much with the proper education. I cannot let such an opportunity pass. Since you insist, I will tutor them both."

Joan let her breath out in a rush. "Thank you," she said, as much to St. Catherine as to Aesculapius. It was all she could do to keep her voice steady. "I will work to be deserving."

Aesculapius looked at her, his eyes filled with a penetrating intelligence. *Like a fire from within,* Joan thought. A fire that would light the weeks and months ahead.

"Indeed you will," he said. Underneath the thick, white beard there was the trace of a smile. "Oh yes, indeed you will."

⊁ 4 ⊰

Rome

THE vaulted marble interior of the Lateran Palace was deliciously cool after the blistering heat of the Roman streets. As the huge wooden doors of the papal residence swung shut behind him, Anastasius stood blinking, momentarily blinded in the darkness of the Patriarchium. Instinctively, he reached for his father's hand, then drew back, remembering.

"Stand tall, and do not cling to your father," his mother had said that morning as she fussed over his attire. "You are twelve now; time enough to learn to play the part of a man." She tugged firmly on his jeweled belt, pulling it into place. "And look squarely at those who address you. The family name is second to none; you must not appear to be deferential."

Now, recalling her words, Anastasius drew his shoulders back and lifted his head high. He was small for his age, a continuing source of grief for him, but he tried always to hold himself so as to appear as tall as possible. His eyes began to adjust to the dim light, and he looked around curiously. It was his first visit to the Lateran, the majestic residence of the Pope, and the seat of all power in Rome, and Anastasius was impressed. The interior was enormous, a vast structure containing the archives of the Church and the Treasure Chamber, as well as dozens of oratories, triclinia, and chapels, among them the celebrated private chapel of the Popes, the Sanctum Sanctorum. Before Anastasius, on the wall of the Great Hall, hung a huge *tabula mundi,* an annotated wall map depicting the world as a flat disk surrounded by oceans. The three continents—Asia, Africa, and Europe—were separated by the great rivers Tanais and Nile as well as the Mediterranean. At the very center of the world was the holy city of Jerusalem, bounded on the east by the terrestrial paradise. Anastasius studied the map, his attention riveted to the large open spaces, mysterious and frightening, at the outmost edges, where the world fell off into darkness.

A man approached, wearing the white silk dalmatic of the members of the papal household. "I give you greeting and the blessing of our Most Holy Father, Pope Paschal," he said.

"May he live long, that we may continue to prosper from his benevolent guidance," replied Anastasius's father.

The required formalities over, both men relaxed.

"Well, Arsenius, how is it with you?" said the man. "You are here to see Theodorus, I suppose?"

Anastasius's father nodded. "Yes. To arrange the appointment of my nephew Cosmas as *arcarius*." Lowering his voice, he added, "The payment was made weeks ago. I cannot think what has delayed the announcement so long."

"Theodorus has been quite busy of late. There was that nasty dispute, you know, over the possession of the monastery at Farfa. The Holy Father was much displeased with the imperial court's decision." Bending close, he added in a conspiratorial whisper, "And even more displeased with Theo for championing the Emperor's cause. Be prepared: there may be little that Theo can do for you just now."

"The thought had occurred to me." Anastasius's father shrugged. "Nevertheless, Theo is still *primicerius,* and the payment has been made."

"We shall see."

The conversation halted abruptly as a second man, also clad in the white dalmatic, came toward them. Anastasius, standing close by his father's side, sensed the slight stiffening of his back. "May the blessings of the Holy Father be conferred upon you, Sarpatus," said his father.

"And on you, my dear Arsenius, and on you," the man replied. His mouth had an odd twist. "Ah, Lucian," he said, turning to the first man. "You were so intent on your conversation with Arsenius just now. Have you some interesting news? I should love to hear it." He yawned elaborately. "Life is so tedious here since the Emperor left."

"No, Sarpatus, of course not. If I had any news, I should tell you," Lucian replied nervously. To Anastasius's father he said, "Well, Arsenius, I must go now. I have duties to attend to." He bowed, turned on his heel, and quickly walked away.

Sarpatus shook his head. "Lucian has been edgy of late. I wonder why." He looked pointedly at Anastasius's father. "Well, well, no matter. I see that you have company today."

"Yes. May I present my son Anastasius? He is to take the exam to become a *lector* soon." Anastasius's father added with emphasis, "His uncle Theo is especially fond of him; that is why I brought him along with me to our meeting."

Anastasius bowed. "May you prosper in His Name," he said formally, as he had been taught.

The man smiled, amusement twisting the corners of his lips even more.

"My! The boy's Latin is excellent; I congratulate you, Arsenius. He will prove to be an asset to you—unless, of course, he shares his uncle's deplorable lack of judgment." He continued, precluding any reply, "Yes, yes, a fine boy. How old is he?" The question was addressed to Anastasius's father.

Anastasius replied, "I turned twelve just after Advent."

"Indeed! You look younger." He patted Anastasius's head.

A dislike for the stranger rose inside Anastasius. Drawing himself up as tall as possible, he said, "And I think that my uncle's judgment cannot be so very bad, or else how did he come to be primicerius?"

His father squeezed Anastasius's arm in warning, but his eyes were mild and there was a hint of a smile on his lips. The stranger stared at Anastasius, something—surprise? anger?—registering in his eyes. Anastasius met his gaze levelly. After a long moment the man broke the gaze and returned his attention to Anastasius's father.

"Such family loyalty! How touching! Well, well, let us hope that the boy's thinking proves to be as correct as his Latin."

A loud noise drew their attention to the far side of the hall as the heavy doors were opened.

"Ah! Here comes the primicerius now. I shall intrude upon you no longer." Sarpatus bowed elaborately and withdrew.

A hush fell over the assembly as Theodorus entered, accompanied by his son-in-law Leo, recently elevated to the position of nomenclator. He stopped just inside the doors to converse briefly with a few of the clerics and nobles standing nearby. In his ruby silk dalmatic and golden cingulum, Theodorus was by far the most elegantly attired of the group; he loved fine materials and favored a certain ostentation in his dress, a characteristic that Anastasius admired.

Finishing with the formal greetings, Theodorus scanned the hall. Catching sight of Anastasius and his father, he smiled and started across the floor toward them. As he drew closer, he winked at Anastasius, and his right hand moved toward the fold in his dalmatic. Anastasius grinned, for he knew what that meant. Theodorus, who had a love for children, always carried some special treats to hand out. *What will it be today?* Anastasius wondered, his mouth watering in anticipation. *A plump fig, a honeyed filbert, a creamy lump of sweetened almond paste?*

Anastasius's attention was focused so intently on the fold in Theodorus's dalmatic that at first he did not see the other men. They came up quickly—three of them—from behind; one clapped a hand over Theodorus's mouth, drawing him backward. Anastasius thought it was some kind of prank. Smiling, he looked at his father for explanation; his heart leapt when he saw the fear in his father's eyes. He turned back and saw Theodorus struggling to break loose. Theodorus was a big man, but the contest was hopelessly unequal. The men surrounded him, pinning his arms, dragging him down. The front of Theodorus's ruby dalmatic was torn, the fine silk hanging in jagged ribbons, exposing patches of white skin. One of the attackers entwined his fingers in Theodorus's thick black hair and wrenched his head back. Anastasius saw a glint of steel. There was a scream, and then Theodorus's face seemed to explode in a fountain of red. Anastasius flinched as a fine spray hit his face. He reached up, then stared numbly at his hand. It was blood. Across the room someone shouted; Anastasius saw Leo, Theodorus's son-in-law, disappear beneath a swarm of attackers.

The men released Theodorus, and he fell forward onto his knees. Then he raised his head, and Anastasius screamed in terror. The face was dreadful. Blood poured from the black and empty holes where Theodorus's eyes had been, streaming from his chin onto his shoulders and chest.

Anastasius buried his face in his father's side. He felt his father's large hands on his shoulders and heard his voice, strong and unwavering. "No," his father said. "You cannot hide, my son." The hands impelled him, pushing him away, turning him back toward the grisly scene before him.

"Watch," the voice commanded, "and learn. This is the price exacted for lack of subtlety and art. Theodorus pays now for wearing his loyalty to the Emperor so openly."

Anastasius stood like a post while the attackers carried Theodorus and Leo to the center of the hall. Several times they stumbled and almost fell on the tile floor, slippery with blood. Theodorus was shouting something, but the words were unintelligible. With his mouth open and moving, his face was even more frightful.

The men forced Theodorus and Leo to their knees and pulled their heads forward. One man raised a long sword over Leo's neck and with one quick stroke, decapitated him. But Theodorus's neck was thick, and he continued to struggle; it took three or four sword strokes to cleave his head from his body.

Anastasius saw, for the first time, that the attackers wore the scarlet cross of the papal militia. "Father!" he blurted. "It's the guards! The guards of the militia!"

"Yes." He drew Anastasius close.

Anastasius fought against the rise of hysteria. "But why? Why, Father? Why would they do it?"

"They were ordered to."

"Ordered to?" said Anastasius. He tried to make sense of it. "Who would give such an order?"

"Who? Ah, my son, *think*." His father's face was ashen, but his voice was steady as he replied, "You must learn to think so you will never suffer such a fate. Consider now: Who has the power? Who is capable of giving such an order?"

Anastasius stood speechless, overwhelmed by the enormity of the idea that had begun to break upon him.

"Yes." His father's hands were gentle now on Anastasius's shoulders. "Who else," he said, "but the Pope?"

5

"NO, NO, *no.*" Aesculapius's voice was edged with impatience. "You must make your letters much smaller. See how your sister pens her lesson?" He tapped Joan's paper. "You must learn a greater respect for your parchment, my boy—there's a whole sheep gone to make just one folio. If the monks of Andernach sprawled their words across the page in that manner, the herds of Austrasia would be wiped out in a month!"

John cast a resentful glance at Joan. "It's too hard; I can't do it."

Aesculapius sighed. "Very well; return to practicing on your tablet. When you have achieved a better control, we will try the parchment again." He asked Joan, "Have you finished the *De inventione?*"

"Yes, sir," Joan replied.

"Name the six evidentiary questions used to determine the circumstances of human acts."

Joan was ready. "*Quis, quid, quomodo, ubi, quando, cur?*"— "Who, what, how, where, when, why?"

"Good. Now identify the rhetorical *constitutiones.*"

"Cicero specifies four different *constitutiones:* dispute about fact, dispute about definition, dispute about the nature of the act, and—"

There was a thud as Gudrun kicked the door open and entered, stooping from the weight of the heavy wooden water buckets she carried, one in each clenched hand. Joan rose to help her, but Aesculapius put a hand on her shoulder, returning her to her seat.

"And?"

Joan hesitated, her eyes still on her mother.

"Child, continue." Aesculapius's tone indicated that he would tolerate no disobedience.

Joan hastened to reply. "Dispute about jurisdiction or procedure."

Aesculapius nodded, satisfied. "Provide an illustration of the third *status*. Write it out on your parchment, and make sure it will be worth the keeping."

Gudrun bustled about, blowing up the fire, bringing the pot to

45

boil, laying the table in preparation for the afternoon meal. Once or twice she looked over her shoulder resentfully.

Joan felt a stab of guilt but forced her attention back to her work. This time was precious—Aesculapius came only once a week—and her studies mattered more than anything else.

But it was hard, working under the weight of her mother's displeasure. Aesculapius obviously noticed it too, though he attributed it to the fact that the lessons took Joan away from household chores. Joan knew the real cause. Her studies were a betrayal, a violation of the private world she shared with her mother, a world of Saxon gods and Saxon secrets. By learning Latin and studying Christian texts, Joan aligned herself with the things her mother most detested—with the Christian God who had destroyed Gudrun's homeland and, more to the point, with the canon, her husband.

The truth was that Joan worked mostly with pre-Christian, classical texts. Aesculapius revered the "pagan" texts of Cicero, Seneca, Lucan, and Ovid, regarded as anathema by most scholars of the day. He was teaching Joan to read Greek using the ancient texts of Menander and Homer, whose poetry the canon regarded as nothing less than pagan blasphemy. Taught by Aesculapius to appreciate clarity and style, Joan never considered the question of whether Homer's poetry was acceptable in terms of Christian doctrine; God was in it, because it was beautiful.

She would have liked to explain this to her mother but knew it would make no difference. Homer or Bede, Cicero or St. Augustine—to Gudrun it was all one: it was not Saxon; nothing else mattered.

Joan's concentration had wandered; she blundered and made an ugly blotch on her parchment. She looked up to see Aesculapius regarding her with penetrating dark eyes.

"Never mind, child." His voice was unexpectedly gentle; usually he was harsh with careless errors. "It is no matter. Begin again here."

THE townspeople of Ingelheim were gathered round the village pond, chattering animatedly. A witch was to be tried today, an event sure to inspire horror, pity, and delight—welcome respite from the daily drudgery of their lives.

"*Benedictus.*" The canon began the blessing of the water.

Hrotrud tried to run, but two men seized her and dragged her back to where the canon stood, his dark brows meeting in frowning disapproval. Hrotrud cursed and struggled as her captors wrested her clawed hands behind her and tied them together with strips of linen cloth, causing her to cry out in pain.

"*Maleficia*," someone muttered, close to where Joan and Aesculapius were standing among the crowd of witnesses. "St. Barnabas, preserve us from the evil eye."

Aesculapius said nothing but shook his head sadly.

He had arrived at Ingelheim that morning for the weekly lesson, but the canon had refused to let the children receive instruction, insisting they first attend the trial of Hrotrud, formerly the village midwife.

"For you will learn more about the ways of God from observing this holy trial than you will from any heathen writing," the canon had said, looking pointedly at Aesculapius.

Joan did not like delaying her lesson, but she was curious about the trial. She wondered what it would be like; she had never seen anyone tried for witchcraft. She was sorry that it was Hrotrud, however. Joan liked Hrotrud, who was an honest woman and no hypocrite. She had always spoken fairly to Joan, treating her kindly and not ridiculing her as so many of the villagers did. Gudrun had told Joan how Hrotrud had assisted at her birthing—a grueling ordeal, according to her mother, who credited Hrotrud with saving her life and Joan's that day. As Joan stared at the crowd of villagers, the thought came to her that Hrotrud had doubtless helped to birth almost everyone gathered there—those, at least, who had reached six winters or more. One would never know it from the way they gawked at her now. She had become an annoyance to them, a goad to their Christian charity, for ever since the wasting pain had crooked her hands, destroying her usefulness as a midwife, she had lived off the alms of her neighbors—that, and what little she could earn from selling medicinal herbs and philters of her own devising.

Her skill in this last had proved to be her undoing, for her ability to work cures for sleeplessness and pains of the tooth, stomach, and head appeared to the simple villagers to be nothing less than sorcery.

Finishing with the blessing of the water, the canon turned to Hrotrud. "Woman! You know the crime of which you are accused. Will you now freely confess your sins in order to ensure the salvation of your immortal soul?"

Hrotrud regarded him consideringly from the corners of her eyes. "If I confess, you will let me go free?"

The canon shook his head. "It is expressly forbidden in the Holy Book: 'You shall not permit a sorceress to live.' " He added, for authority, "Exodus, chapter twenty-two, verse eighteen. But you will die a consecrated death, and a swift one, and through it gain the immeasurable rewards of Heaven."

"No!" Hrotrud retorted defiantly. "I am a Christian woman, and no witch, and anyone who says otherwise is a foul liar!"

"Sorceress! You will suffer the fires of Hell for all eternity! Can you deny the evidence of your own eyes?" From behind his back the canon pulled a soiled linen belt, mutilated by a series of crude knots. He thrust it accusingly at Hrotrud, who started and stepped back.

"See how she shrinks from it?" someone whispered close to Joan. "She is guilty, sure, and should be burned!"

Anyone would be startled by so sudden a move, Joan thought. *Surely that is no proof of guilt.*

The canon held the belt up for the crowd to observe. "This belongs to Ebo, the miller. It went missing a fortnight ago. Immediately thereafter he took to his bed, afflicted with a terrible pain in the bowels."

The faces in the crowd looked solemn. They did not especially like Ebo, who was widely suspected of cheating with his weights. "What is the boldest thing in the world?" began a riddle that they loved to repeat. "Ebo's shirt, for it clasps a thief by the throat every day!" Nevertheless, the illness of their miller was of grave concern to the entire community. Without him, none of their grain could be turned into flour, for by law no villager could mill his own harvest.

"Two days ago"—the canon's voice was dark with accusation— "this belt was discovered in the woods near Hrotrud's cottage."

There was an awed murmur from the crowd, punctuated by scattered cries: "Witch!" "Sorceress!" "Burn her!"

The canon said to Hrotrud, "You stole the belt and made the knots in it to aid your evil incantations, which have brought Ebo to the very brink of death."

"Never!" Hrotrud shouted indignantly, struggling against the bonds that held her. "I did no such thing! I've never seen that belt before! I never—"

Impatiently, the canon signaled to the men, who hoisted Hrotrud like a sack of oats, swung her back and forth several times, then released her at the height of the last swing. Hrotrud cried out in fear and anger as she sailed through the air and dropped with a splash directly into the center of the pond.

Joan and Aesculapius were jostled as people strained forward, trying to see. If Hrotrud rose to the surface of the pond and floated, that meant the priest-blessed waters had rejected her; she would be revealed as a sorceress and a witch and burned at the stake. If she sank, her innocence was proved and she was saved.

In tense silence, all eyes remained fixed on the surface of the pond. Ripples circled slowly outward from the spot where Hrotrud had entered the water; otherwise the surface was still.

The canon grunted and signaled the men, who immediately dashed into the water and dived down to search for Hrotrud.

"She is innocent of the charges against her," the canon pronounced. "God be praised."

Was it only Joan's imagination, or did he look disappointed?

The men kept diving and surfacing with no result. At last one of them broke the surface holding Hrotrud. She lay limp in his arms, her face swollen and discolored. He carried her to the edge of the pond and put her down. She did not stir. He bent over her, listening for a heartbeat.

After a moment he sat up. "She is dead," he announced.

A murmur went up from the crowd.

"Most unfortunate," the canon said. "But she died innocent of the crime of which she was accused. God knows His own; He will give recompense and rest to her soul."

The villagers dispersed, some making their way over to where Hrotrud's body lay, examining it curiously, some breaking into little groups that murmured and chattered in low tones.

Joan and Aesculapius walked back to the grubenhaus in silence. Joan was deeply disturbed by Hrotrud's death. She was ashamed of the excitement she had felt beforehand about witnessing the trial. But then she had not expected Hrotrud to die. Surely Hrotrud was not a witch; therefore Joan had believed God would prove her innocence.

And He had.

But then why did He let her die?

✣

SHE didn't speak about it until later, after she had resumed her lesson back at the grubenhaus. She lowered her stylus in the middle of writing and asked suddenly, "Why would God do it?"

"Perhaps He didn't," Aesculapius responded, taking her meaning at once.

Joan stared at him. "Are you saying that such a thing could have happened in spite of His will?"

"Perhaps not. But the fault may lie in the nature of the trial rather than in the nature of God's will."

Joan considered that. "My father would say that this is how witches have been tried for hundreds of years."

"True enough."

"But that doesn't necessarily make it right." Joan looked at Aesculapius. "What would be a better way?"

"That," he said, "is for you to tell me."

Joan sighed. Aesculapius was so different from her father, or even Matthew. He refused to tell her things, insisting instead that she reason her own way to the answer. Joan tugged gently on the tip of her nose as she often did when thinking out a problem.

Of course. She had been blind not to see it at once. Cicero and the *De inventione*—until now, it had been merely an abstraction, a rhetorical ornament, an exercise for the mind.

"The evidentiary questions," Joan said. "Why couldn't they be brought to apply in this case?"

"Explain," Aesculapius said.

"*Quid:* there is the fact of the knotted belt—that is indisputable. But surely there is an argument about what it means. *Quis:* Who put the knots in the belt and placed it in the woods? *Quomodo:* How was it taken from Ebo? *Quando, Ubi:* When and where was it taken? Did anyone actually see Hrotrud with it? *Cur:* Why should Hrotrud wish harm to Ebo?" Joan spoke rapidly, excited by the possibilities of the idea. "Witnesses could be brought forward and questioned. And Hrotrud and Ebo too—they could be questioned. Their answers might have determined Hrotrud's innocence. And"—Joan concluded ruefully—"she would not have had to die to prove it!"

They were on dangerous ground, and they knew it. They sat together in silence. Joan was overwhelmed by the enormity of the concept that had burst upon her: the application of logic to divine revelation, the possibility of an earthly justice in which the assumptions of faith were governed by rational inquiry, and belief was supported by the powers of reason.

Aesculapius said, "It would probably be wise not to mention this conversation to your father."

THE Feast of St. Bertin was just past, the days were growing shorter, and so, of necessity, were the children's lessons. The sun was low in the sky when Aesculapius finally stood up.

"That, children, is enough for today."

"May I go now?" John asked. Aesculapius waved in dismissal, and John bounded from his seat and hurried outdoors.

Joan smiled ruefully at Aesculapius. John's obvious dislike for their studies embarrassed her. Aesculapius was frequently impatient, even sharp, with John. But her brother was a slow and unwilling student. "I can't do it!" he would wail the moment he met some new difficulty. There were times when Joan would have liked to shake him and shout, "Try! Try! How do you know you can't do it unless you try!"

Afterward, Joan reproached herself for such thoughts. John could not help being slow. Without John there would have been no lessons at all these past two years—and life without lessons had become unthinkable.

As soon as John had gone, Aesculapius said seriously, "I have something to tell you. I have been informed that my services are no longer needed at the schola. Another scholar, a Frankishman, has applied to be teaching master, and the bishop finds him more suitable for the position than I."

Joan was bewildered. "How can this be? Who is the man? He cannot possibly know as much as you!"

Aesculapius smiled. "That statement shows loyalty, if not wisdom. I have met the man; he is an excellent scholar, whose interests are better suited to the teachings of the schola than mine." Seeing that Joan did not take his meaning, he added, "There is a place for the kind of knowledge you and I have pursued together, Joan, and it is not within the walls of a cathedral. Remember what I tell you, and be careful: some ideas are dangerous."

"I understand," Joan said, though she didn't, completely. "But—what will you do now? How will you live?"

"I have a friend in Athens, a countryman who has achieved success as a merchant. He wants me to tutor his children."

"You are leaving?" Joan was unable to believe what he was telling her.

"He is prosperous; his offer is generous. I have little choice but to accept."

"You mean to go to Athens?" It was so far away. "When will you go?"

"In a month. I would have gone by now save for the pleasure I have taken in our work together."

"But—" Joan's mind raced, trying to think of something, anything to prevent this awful thing from happening. "You could live here, with us. You could be our tutor, John's and mine, and we could have lessons every day!"

"That is impossible, my dear. Your father has barely enough to sustain your family through the winter as it is. There is no room at your hearth or at your table for a stranger. Besides, I must go where I can continue my own work. The cathedral library will no longer be permitted me."

"Don't go." Grief rose within her like a palpable substance, forming a hard knot at the base of her throat. "Please don't go."

"My dear girl, I must. Though truly I wish it were not so." He stroked Joan's white-gold hair fondly. "I have learned much from teaching you; I do not look to have so apt a pupil again. You have a rare intelligence; it is God-given, and you must not deny it"—he glanced meaningfully at her—"whatever the cost."

Joan was afraid to speak lest her voice betray her emotions.

Aesculapius took her hand in his. "You must not worry. You will be able to continue your studies. I will make arrangements. I do not know exactly where, as yet, or how, but I will. Yours is too promising an intellect to lie fallow. We will find the seeds with which to sow it, I promise." He grasped her hand tightly. "Trust me in this."

After he had gone, Joan did not move from her little desk. She sat alone in the gathering darkness until her mother returned, carrying logs for the hearth.

"Ah, so you are finished?" said Gudrun. "Good! Now come help me build the fire."

☩

AESCULAPIUS came to see her the day he left, dressed in his long blue traveling cloak. In his hands he carried a package wrapped in cloth.

"For you." He placed the package in her hands.

Joan unwrapped the strips of linen, then gasped as she saw what they had concealed. It was a book, bound in the Eastern fashion with leather-covered wooden boards.

"It is my own," said Aesculapius. "I made it myself, some years ago. It is an edition of Homer—the original Greek in the front half of the book, and a Latin translation in the back. It will help you keep your knowledge of the language fresh until the time you can begin your studies again."

Joan was speechless. A book of her own! Such a privilege was enjoyed only by monks and scholars of the highest rank. She opened it, looking at line after line of Aesculapius's neat uncial letters, filling the pages with words of inexpressible beauty. Aesculapius watched her, his eyes filled with tender sadness.

"Do not forget, Joan. Do not ever forget."

He opened his arms to her. She went to him, and for the first time they embraced. For a long while they clung to each other, Aesculapius's tall, broad form cradling Joan's small one. When at last they parted, his blue cloak was wet with Joan's tears.

She did not watch as he rode away. She stayed inside where he had left her, holding on to the book, grasping it so tightly that her hands ached.

JOAN knew her father would not permit her to keep the book. He had never approved of her studies, and now, with Aesculapius gone, there was no one to stop him from enforcing his will. So she hid the book, rewrapping it carefully in its cloth and burying it under the thick straw on her side of the bed.

She was on fire to read it, to see the words, to hear again in her mind the joyous beauty of the poetry. But it was too dangerous; someone was usually in or near the cottage, and she feared discovery. Her only opportunity was at night. After everyone was asleep, she could read without risk of sudden interruption. But she needed some light—a candle, or at least some oil. The family got only two dozen candles a year—the canon was loath to take them from the sanctuary—and these were carefully conserved; she could not use one unnoticed. But the church storehouse had a huge stockpile of wax—the coloni of Ingelheim were required to supply the sanctuary with a hundred pounds a year. If she could get hold of some, she could fashion her own candle.

It wasn't easy, but in the end she managed to pilfer enough wax to make a small candle, using a piece of linen cord for a wick. It was a makeshift job—the flame was scarcely more than a flicker—but it was enough to provide light for study.

The first night she was cautious. She waited until long after her parents had retired to their bed behind the partition and she could hear the canon's snoring before daring to move. Finally she slid out of bed, silent and watchful as a fawn, careful not to disturb John, who lay beside her. He slept soundly, his head burrowed beneath the covers. Gently Joan removed the book from its hiding place in the straw and carried it to the small pine desk in the far corner of the room. She took her candle to the hearth and lit it in the glowing embers.

Returning to the desk, she held the candle close to the book. The light was faint and unsteady, but with an effort she could make out the lines of dark black ink. The neat letters danced in the flickering light, beckoning, inviting. Briefly Joan paused, savoring the moment. Then she turned the page and began.

THE warm days and cool nights of Windumemanoth, the wine harvest month, passed swiftly. The harsh nordostroni winds arrived earlier than usual, blowing in from the northeast in strong, bone-chilling gusts. Once again the window of the grubenhaus was boarded up, but the frigid winds penetrated every crevice; to keep warm, they had to leave the hearth fire burning all day long, filling the place with sooty smoke.

Every night after her family slept, Joan rose and studied for hours in the darkness. She exhausted her candle and was forced to wait impatiently till she had pilfered some more wax from the church storehouse. When at last she was able to resume work, she drove herself relentlessly. She finished the book and then returned to the beginning, this time studying the complicated verb forms and copying them painstakingly onto her tablet until she knew them by heart. Her eyes were red and her head ached from the strain of working in the bad light, but it never occurred to her to stop. She was happy.

The Feast of St. Columban came and went, and there was still no word, no news of any arrangements for formal tutoring. Nevertheless, Joan kept faith with Aesculapius's promise. As long as she had his book, there was no cause for despair. She was continuing to learn, to make progress. Surely, surely something would happen soon. A tutor would arrive in the village, asking for her by name, or she would be summoned by the bishop and told of her acceptance into a schola.

Joan started work a little earlier each night. Sometimes she did not even wait till she heard her father's snoring. When she spilled some hot wax on the desk, she did not even notice.

One night she was working out a particularly difficult and interesting problem of syntax. Impatient to get started, she settled in at the desk not long after her parents had retired. She had been working only a few minutes when she heard a muffled sound from behind the partition.

She snuffed the candle flame and sat like a stone in the darkness, listening, feeling the leap of her pulse in her throat.

Several moments passed. There was no further sound. It must have been her imagination. Relief washed through her like a warm current. Still, she let a long time pass before she rose from the desk, went to the hearth to relight the wick, and returned with the glowing taper. The spark flared brightly, creating a little circle of light around the desk. At the edge of the circle, where the light met the shadows, was a pair of feet.

Her father's feet.

The canon stepped out of the darkness. Instinctively, Joan moved to hide the book from him, but it was too late.

His face, lit from below by the unsteady flame, was ghastly, terrifying.

"What wickedness is this?"

Joan's voice was a whisper. "A book."

"A book!" He stared at it as if he could scarcely believe the evidence of his eyes. "How do you come by this? What are you doing with it?"

"Reading it. It—it's mine, it was given to me by Aesculapius. It's mine."

The force of her father's blow caught her by surprise, knocking her off the stool. She lay on the ground in a heap, the earthen floor cool against her cheek.

"Yours! Insolent child! *I* am master in this house!"

Joan raised herself on one elbow and watched helplessly as her father bent over the book, squinting to make out the words in the uncertain light. After a few moments he jerked upright, making the sign of the cross in the air above the desk. "Christ Jesus, protect us." Without taking his gaze from the book, he beckoned to Joan. "Come here."

Joan got up from the floor. She was dizzy, and there was a painful ringing in one ear. Slowly she walked over to her father.

"This is not the language of Holy Mother Church." He pointed to the open page before him. "What is the meaning of these marks? Answer me truly, child, as you value your immortal soul!"

"It is poetry, Father." Despite her fear, Joan felt a swell of pride in the knowledge. She did not dare add that the poetry was by Homer, whom her father regarded as a godless heathen. The canon knew no Greek. If he did not look at the Latin translation in the back, perhaps he would not realize what she had done.

Her father placed both hands on Joan's head, his broad peasant's fingers encircling her head just above the brow. "*Exorcizo te, immundissime spiritus, omnis incursio adversarii, omne phantasma . . .*" His hands tightened, squeezing so hard that Joan cried out in fear and pain.

Gudrun appeared in the doorway. "By all that's holy, Husband, what is the matter? Be careful with the child!"

"Silence!" the canon barked. "The child is possessed! Her demon must be exorcised." The pressure of his hands increased until Joan thought her eyes would burst.

Gudrun seized his arm. "Stop! She is just a child! Husband, stop! Would you kill her in your madness?"

The excruciating pressure ceased abruptly as the canon released his grip. He wheeled and with a single blow propelled Gudrun to the other side of the room. "Begone!" he roared. "This is no time for woman's weakness! I found the girl practicing magic in the night! With a witch's book! She is possessed!"

"No, Father, no!" Joan shrieked. "It is not witchcraft! It is poetry! Poetry written in Greek, that is all! I swear it!" He reached for her, but she ducked under his arm and circled behind him. He turned and advanced on her, eyes dark with menace.

He was going to kill her.

"Father! Turn to the back! The back of the book! It is written in Latin! You will see it! It is in Latin!"

The canon hesitated. Hurriedly Gudrun brought him the book. He did not look at it. He stared at Joan, considering.

"Please, Father. Only look at the back of the book. You can read it for yourself. It is not witchcraft!"

He took the book from Gudrun. She ran to get the candle and held it close to the page so he could see. He bent to examine the book, his thick, dark brows knitted in concentration.

Joan could not stop talking. "I was studying. I read by night so no one would know. I knew you would not approve." She would say anything, confess anything to make him believe. "It is Homer. The book of the *Iliad*. Homer's poem. It is not witchcraft, Father." She started to sob. "Not witchcraft."

The canon paid no attention. He read intently, his eyes close to the page, his mouth silently forming the words. After a moment he looked up.

"God be praised. It is not witchcraft. But it is the work of a godless heathen, and therefore an offense against the Lord." He turned to Gudrun. "Build up the fire. This abomination must be destroyed."

Joan gasped. Burn the book! Aesculapius's beautiful book, which he had given to her in trust!

"Father, the book is valuable! It is worth money; we could fetch a good price for it or"—her mind raced—"you could present it to the bishop as a gift for the cathedral library."

"Wicked child, you are so far sunk in sin it is a wonder you have not drowned in it. This is no fit gift for the bishop, nor for any Godfearing soul."

Gudrun went to the corner where the wood was stored and selected a few small logs. Joan watched numbly. She had to find some way to keep this from happening. If only the pain in her head would stop, she could think.

Gudrun stoked the embers, preparing the hearth for the fresh wood.

"Hold a moment." Abruptly, the canon addressed Gudrun. "Leave the fire be." He fingered the pages of the book appraisingly. "It is true that the parchment is valuable and might be put to good use." He placed the book on the desk and vanished into the next room.

What did it mean? Joan looked at her mother, who shrugged in bewilderment. Directly to her left, John sat upright in the bed. Awakened by the noise, he stared at Joan with large, round eyes.

The canon returned, carrying something long and shiny. It was his bone-handled hunting knife. As always, the sight of it filled Joan with a strong and bewildering sense of dread. The dim play of forgotten memory teased the edges of her awareness. Then it was gone, before she could remember what it was.

Her father sat at the desk. Turning the knife at an oblique angle so the sharp edge lay flat against the page, he scraped at the vellum. One of the letters on the page disappeared. He gave a little grunt of satisfaction.

"It works. I saw it done, once, at the monastery of Corbie. It leaves the pages clean so they can be used again. Now"—he motioned peremptorily to Joan—"you do it."

This, then, was to be her punishment. Her hand would be the one to destroy the book, to obliterate the forbidden knowledge and with it all her hopes.

Her father's eyes glittered with malevolent expectation.

Woodenly, she took the knife and sat at the desk. For a long moment she stared at the page. Then, holding the knife as she had seen her father do it, she moved the blade slowly over the surface of the page.

Nothing happened.

"It doesn't work." She looked up hopefully.

"Like this." The canon placed his hand over hers, applying pressure with a small lateral movement of the blade. Another letter disappeared. "Try again."

She thought of Aesculapius, of his long hours of labor making this book, of the faith he had shown in her when he entrusted it to her. The page blurred as tears rose to her eyes.

"Please. Don't make me. Please, Father."

"Daughter, you have offended God with your disobedience. In penance, you will work day and night until these pages are wholly cleansed of their ungodly contents. You will take nothing but bread and water until the task is complete. I will pray for God to have mercy upon you for your grievous sin." He pointed to the book. "Begin."

Joan placed the knife on the page and scraped as her father had shown her. One of the letters flaked, paled, and then disappeared. She moved the knife; another letter was obliterated. Then another. And another. Soon an entire word was gone, leaving only the rough, abraded surface of the parchment.

She moved the knife to begin on the next word. Ἀλήθεια. Aletheia. *Truth.* Joan stopped, her hand poised over the word.

"Continue." Her father's voice was stern, commanding.

Truth. The round lines of the uncial letters stood out boldly against the pale parchment.

A fierce denial rose within her. All the fear and misery of the night gave way before one overwhelming conviction: *This must not be!*

She put down the knife. Slowly she looked up to meet her father's eyes. What she saw there made her draw her breath in sharply.

"Take up the knife." The menace in his voice was unmistakable.

Joan tried to speak, but her throat constricted and no words came. She shook her head no.

"Daughter of Eve, I will teach you to fear the tortures of Hell. Bring me the switch."

Joan went to the corner and retrieved the long, black stick which her father used on such occasions.

"Prepare yourself," the canon said.

She knelt on the floor in front of the hearth. Slowly, for her hands were shaking, she unclasped her gray woolen mantle and pulled off her linen tunic, exposing the bare flesh of her back.

"Begin the paternoster." Her father's voice was a low rumble behind her.

"Our Father, who art in Heaven—"

The first lash struck cleanly between the shoulders, parting the flesh, sending a piercing shaft of pain up her neck into her skull.

"Hallowed be thy Name—"

The second lash was harder. Joan bit her arm to keep from crying out. She had been beaten before, but never like this, never with such relentless, implacable force.

"Thy Kingdom come—"

The third lash bit deep into her torn flesh, drawing blood. The warm wetness trickled down her sides.

"Thy will be done—" The shock of the fourth lash jolted Joan's head upwards. She saw her brother watching intently from the bed. There was an odd expression on his face. Was it fear? Curiosity? Pity?

"On earth as it is—" The lash descended again. In the flash of a second before pain forced her eyes shut, Joan recognized the look on her brother's face. It was exultation.

"In Heaven. Give us this day—" The lash struck heavily. How many was it? Joan's senses reeled. She had never had to endure more than five.

Lash. Distantly, she heard someone screaming.

"Our daily bread. And forgive us . . . forgive—" Her mouth moved, but she could not form the words.

Lash.

With what power of thought was left her, Joan suddenly understood. This time it would not end. This time her father would not stop. This time he would continue until she was dead.

Lash.

The ringing in her ears built to a deafening crescendo. Then there was nothing but silence, and merciful darkness.

⇥ 6 ⇤

FOR days the village buzzed with the news of Joan's beating. The canon had lashed his daughter to within an inch of her life, it was said, and would have killed her had his wife's screams not attracted the attention of some villagers. It had taken three strong men to drag him away from the child.

But it wasn't the savagery of the beating that caused people to talk. Such things were common enough. Hadn't the blacksmith knocked his wife down and kicked her in the face until all her bones were broken, because he was tired of her nagging? The poor creature was disfigured for life, but there was nothing to do about it. A man was master in his own home, no one questioned that. The only law governing his absolute right to dispense punishment as he saw fit was one that limited the size of the club he could use. The canon had not used a club, in any case.

What was really interesting to the villagers was the fact that the canon had so far lost control of himself. Such violent emotion was unexpected, unseemly, in a man of God—so naturally everyone delighted in talking about it. Not since he had taken the Saxon woman to his bed had they had so much to gossip about. In little groups they whispered together, breaking off abruptly when the canon passed by.

Joan knew nothing of this. For an entire day after the beating, the canon forbade anyone to go near her. All that night and the following day Joan lay on the floor of the cottage unconscious. Dirt from the beaten earth floor clung to her lacerated flesh. By the time Gudrun was permitted to tend her, the wounds had corrupted and a dangerous fever set in.

Gudrun nursed her solicitously. She cleaned Joan's wounds with fresh water and bathed them with strong wine. Then, working with utmost gentleness to avoid further damage to the raw flesh, she applied a cooling paste of mulberry leaves.

It's all the fault of the Greek, Gudrun thought bitterly, as she made a hot posset and fed it to Joan, lifting her head and trickling the liquid into her mouth a few drops at a time. *Giving the child a book, filling her head with worthless ideas.* She was a girl, and therefore not meant for book study. The child was meant to be with her, to share the hidden secrets and the language of her people, to be the comfort and balm of her old age. *Evil the hour the Greek entered this house. May the wrath of all the gods descend upon him.*

Nevertheless, Gudrun's pride had been sparked by the child's display of bravery. Joan had defied her father with the fierce, heroic strength of her Saxon ancestors. Once Gudrun too had been strong and brave. But the long years of humiliation and exile in an alien land had gradually drained the will to fight out of her. *At least,* she thought proudly, *my blood runs true. The courage of my people runs strong within my daughter.*

She stopped to stroke Joan's throat, helping her swallow the healing broth. *Get well, little quail,* she thought. *Get well, and return to me.*

THE fever broke early in the morning of the ninth day. Joan woke to find Gudrun bending over her.

"Mama?" Her voice sounded hoarse and unfamiliar in her ears.

Her mother smiled. "So you have returned to me at last, little quail. For a time I feared I had lost you."

Joan tried to raise herself but fell back heavily onto the straw. Pain pierced her, bringing back memory.

"The book?"

Gudrun's face tightened. "Your father has scraped the pages clean, and set your brother to copying some new nonsense onto it."

So it was gone.

Joan felt inexpressibly weary. She was sick; she wanted to sleep.

Gudrun held out a wooden bowl filled with steaming liquid. "Now you must eat to regain your strength. See, I have made you some broth."

"No." Joan shook her head weakly. "I don't want any." She did not want to get her strength back. She wanted to die. What was left to live for? She would never break free from the narrow confines of life in Ingelheim. Life had closed her in; there was no further hope of escape.

"Take a little now," Gudrun prodded, "and while you eat, I will sing you one of the old songs."

Joan turned her head away.

"Leave such things to the foolishness of priests. We have our own

secrets, don't we, little quail? We will share them again, as we used to."
Gudrun stroked Joan's forehead gently. "But first you must get well.
Sip some broth. It is a Saxon recipe, with strong healing properties."

She held the wooden spoon to Joan's lips. Joan was too weak to
resist; she allowed her mother to trickle a little broth into her mouth.
It was good, warm and rich and comforting. Despite herself, she
began to feel a little better.

"My little quail, my sweetheart, my darling." Gudrun's voice caressed Joan softly, seductively. She dipped the wooden ladle in the
steaming broth and held it out to Joan, who sipped some more.

Her mother's voice rose and fell in the sweet, lilting strains of the
familiar Saxon melody. Lulled by the sound and her mother's ca-
resses, Joan drifted slowly into sleep.

WITH the fever past, Joan's strong young body mended quickly. In a
fortnight, she was on her feet again. Her wounds closed cleanly,
though it was plain she would bear the marks for the rest of her life.
Gudrun lamented over the scars, long, dark stripes that turned Joan's
back into an ugly patchwork, but Joan did not care. She did not care
about anything very much. Hope was gone. She existed, that was all.

She spent all her time with her mother, rising at daybreak to help
her feed the pigs and chickens, collect eggs, gather wood for the
hearth fire, and haul heavy bucketfuls of water from the creek. Later
they worked side by side preparing the day's meal.

One day they were making bread together, their fingers working
to shape the heavy dough—for yeast and other leavenings were rarely
used in this part of Frankland—when Joan asked suddenly, "Why did
you marry him?"

The question took Gudrun aback. After a moment she said, "You
cannot imagine what it was like for us when the armies of Karolus
came."

"I know what they did to your people, Mama. What I can't
understand is why, after that, you came away with the enemy—
with *him*?"

Gudrun did not reply.

I've offended her, Joan thought. *She will not tell me now.*

"By winter," Gudrun began slowly, "we were starving, for the
Christian soldiers had burned our crops along with our homes." She
looked past Joan, as if picturing something distant. "We ate anything

we could find—grass, thistles, even the seeds contained in the dung of animals. We were not far from death when your father and the other missionaries arrived. They were different from the others; they carried no swords or weapons, and they dealt with us like people, not brute beasts. They gave us food in return for our promise to listen to them preach the word of the Christian God."

"They traded food for faith?" Joan asked. "A sorry way to win people's souls."

"I was young and impressionable, sick unto death of hunger and misery and fear. Their Christian God must be greater than ours, I thought, or else how had they succeeded in defeating us? Your father took a special interest in me. He had great hopes for me, he said, for though I was heathen born, he was sure I had the capacity to understand the True Faith. From the way he looked at me, I knew he desired me. When he asked me to come away with him, I consented. It was a chance at life, when all around was death." Her voice dropped to a whisper. "It was not long before I realized how great a mistake I'd made."

Her eyes were red rimmed, brimming with barely suppressed tears. Joan put an arm around her. "Don't cry, Mama."

"You must learn from my mistake," Gudrun said fiercely, "so you do not repeat it. To marry is to surrender everything—not only your body but your pride, your independence, even your life. Do you understand? *Do you?*" She gripped Joan's arm, fixing her with an urgent look. "Heed my words, daughter, if you ever mean to be happy: *Never give yourself to a man.*"

The scarred flesh on Joan's back quivered with the remembered pain of her father's lash. "No, Mama," she promised solemnly, "I never will."

IN OSTARMANOTH, when warm spring breezes caressed the earth and the animals were set out to pasture, the monotony was broken by the arrival of a stranger. It was a Thursday—Thor's Day, Gudrun still called it when the canon was not around to hear—and the rumble of that god's thunder was sounding in the distance as Joan and Gudrun worked together in the family garden. Joan was pulling up nettles and destroying molehills, while Gudrun followed after her, tracing the furrows and crushing the clods with a thick oaken plank. As she worked, Gudrun sang and told tales of the Old Ones. When Joan answered in Saxon, Gudrun laughed with pleasure. Joan had just finished a row when she looked up and saw John hurrying across the field toward them. She tapped her mother's arm in warning; Gudrun saw her son, and the Saxon words died on her lips.

"Quick!" John was breathless from running. "Father wants you at the house now. Hurry!" He pulled Gudrun by the arm.

"Gently, John," Gudrun reprimanded. "You're hurting me. What has happened? Is anything wrong?"

"I don't know." John kept tugging on his mother's arm. "He said something about a visitor. I don't know who. But hurry. He said he'd box my ears if I didn't bring you right away."

The canon was waiting for them at the grubenhaus door. "It took you long enough," he said.

Gudrun stared at him coolly. A tiny spark of anger ignited in the canon's eyes; he drew himself up importantly. "An emissary is coming. From the Bishop of Dorstadt." He paused for effect. "Go and prepare a suitable meal. I will meet him at the cathedral and lead him here." He dismissed her with a wave of the hand. "Be quick, woman! He will arrive soon." He left, slamming the door behind him.

Gudrun's face was rigidly expressionless. "Start with the pottage," she said to Joan. "I'll go collect some eggs."

Joan poured water from the oaken bucket into the large iron pot the family used for cooking and set the pot over the hearth fire. From a woolen sack, almost empty now after the long winter, she took handfuls of dried barley and threw them into the pot. She noticed, with surprise, that her hands shook with excitement. It had been so long since she had felt anything.

But an emissary from Dorstadt! Could it have anything to do with her? After all this time, had Aesculapius finally managed to find a way for her to resume her studies?

She cut off a slab of salt pork and added it to the pot. No, it was impossible. It was almost a year since Aesculapius had left. If he had been able to arrange anything, she would have heard long ago. It was dangerous to hope. Hope had nearly destroyed her once; she would not be so foolish again.

Nevertheless, she could not still her excitement when the door opened one hour later. Her father entered, followed by a dark-haired man. He was not at all what she had imagined. He had the blunt, unintelligent features of a *colonus,* and he carried himself more like a soldier than a scholar. His tunic, bearing the insignia of the bishop, was rumpled and dusty from travel.

"You will do us the honor of supping with us?" Joan's father indicated the pot boiling on the hearth.

"Thank you, but I cannot." He spoke in Theodisk, the common tongue, not Latin, another surprise. "I left the rest of the escort at a *cella* outside Mainz—the forest path is too slow and narrow for ten men and horse—and came ahead alone. I must rejoin them tonight; in the morning we begin the return journey to Dorstadt." He withdrew a parchment scroll from his scrip and handed it to the canon. "From his Eminence the Lord Bishop of Dorstadt."

Carefully the canon broke the seal; the stiff parchment crackled as it was unrolled. Joan watched her father closely as he squinted to make out the writing. He read all the way to the bottom, then began again, as if searching for something he had missed. Finally he looked up, his lips tight with anger.

"What is the meaning of this? I was told your message had to do with me!"

"So it does." The man smiled. "Insofar as you are the child's father."

"The bishop has nothing to say about my work?"

The man shrugged. "All I know, Father, is that I am to escort the child to the schola in Dorstadt, as the letter says."

Joan cried out in a sudden rush of emotion. Gudrun hurried over and placed an arm protectively around her.

The canon hesitated, eyeing the stranger. Abruptly, he came to a decision. "Very well. It's true that it is a fine opportunity for the child, though it will be hard enough for me without his help." He turned to John. "Gather your belongings, and be quick. Tomorrow you ride for Dorstadt, to begin studies at the cathedral in accordance with the bishop's express command."

Joan gasped. *John* was being called to study at the schola? How could this be?

The stranger shook his head. "With all respect, Holy Father, I believe it's a girl child I'm supposed to bring back with me. A girl by the name of Johanna."

Joan stepped out of her mother's encircling arm. "I am Johanna."

The bishop's man turned to her. The canon stepped quickly between them.

"Nonsense. It's my son Johannes the bishop wants. Johannes, Johanna. *Lapsus calami.* A slip of the pen. A simple mistake on the part of the bishop's amanuensis, that is all. It happens often enough, even among the best of scribes."

The stranger looked doubtful. "I don't know . . ."

"Use your head, man. What would the bishop want with a girl?"

"It did strike me as odd," the man agreed.

Joan started to protest, but Gudrun drew her back and placed a warning finger over her lips.

The canon continued. "My son, on the other hand, has been studying the Scriptures since he was a babe. Recite from the Book of Revelation for our honored guest, Johannes."

John paled and began to stammer. *"Acopa . . . Apocalypsis Jesu Christi quo . . . quam dedit illi Deus palam fa . . . facere servis—"*

The stranger impatiently signaled a stop to the unsteady flow of words. "There is no time. We must leave immediately if we are to reach the cella before dark." He looked uncertainly from John to Joan. Then he turned to Gudrun.

"Who is this woman?"

The canon cleared his throat. "A Saxon heathen whose soul I am laboring to bring to Christ."

The bishop's man took note of Gudrun's blue eyes and slim form and the white-gold hair peeking out from under her white linen cap. He smiled, a broad, knowing, gap-toothed grin, then addressed himself directly to her.

"You are the children's mother?"

Gudrun nodded wordlessly. The canon flushed.

"What do you say, then? Is it the boy the bishop wants, or the girl?"

"Disrespectful dog!" The canon was furious. "You dare to question the word of a sworn servant of God!"

"Calm yourself, Holy Father." The man emphasized the word *holy* ever so slightly. "Let me remind you of the duty you owe to the authority I represent."

The canon glared at the bishop's man, his face purpling.

Again the man asked Gudrun, "Is it the boy? Or the girl?"

Joan felt Gudrun's arms tighten around her, drawing her close. There was a long pause. Then she heard her mother's voice behind her, musical and sweet, filled with the broad Saxon vowels that still marked her, unmistakably, as a foreigner. "The boy is the one you want," Gudrun said. "Take him."

"Mama!" Shocked at this unexpected betrayal, Joan could only utter the single, startled cry.

The bishop's messenger nodded, satisfied. "Then it is settled." He turned toward the door. "I must see to my horse. Have the boy ready as quickly as possible."

"No!" Joan tried to stop him, but Gudrun held her tight, whispering in Saxon, "Trust me, little quail. It is for the best, I promise you."

"No!" Joan struggled to free herself. It was a lie. This was Aesculapius's doing. Joan was certain of it. He had not forgotten her; he had found a way at last for her to continue what they had begun together. John wasn't the one being called to study at the schola. It was all wrong.

"No!" She twisted sharply, broke loose, and made straight for the door. The canon reached for her, but she evaded him. Then she was outside, running swiftly toward the retreating messenger. Behind her, in the cottage, she heard her father shouting, then her mother's voice, tense, tearful, raised in reply.

She caught up with the man just as he reached his horse. She tugged at his tunic, and he looked at her. From the corner of her eye, Joan saw her father advancing toward them.

There wasn't much time. Her message had to be convincing, unmistakable.

"*Magna est veritas et praevalebit,*" she said. It was a passage from Esdras, obscure enough to be recognized only to those well versed in the writings of the Holy Fathers. "The truth is great, and it will prevail." He was the bishop's man, a man of the Church, he would know it. And the fact that she knew it, that she spoke Latin, would prove that *she* was the scholar the bishop sought.

"*Lapsus calami non est,*" she continued in Latin. "There is no error in the writing. I am Johanna; I am the one you want."

The man looked at her, his eyes kind. "Eh? What's this, bright eyes? What a mighty stream of words!" He chucked her under the chin. "Sorry, child. I speak none of your Saxon tongue. Though having seen your mother, I begin to wish I did." He reached into a pouch tied to his saddle and withdrew a honeyed date. "Here, have a sweet."

Joan stared at the date. The man hadn't understood a word. A scion of the Church, the bishop's emissary, and he had no Latin. How was it possible?

Her father's footsteps sounded close behind her. His arm gripped her painfully around the waist; then she was lifted off the ground and carried back toward the house.

"No!" she screamed. Her father's large hand covered her nose and mouth, pressing so hard she could not breathe. She kicked and struggled. Inside the cottage he released her, and she fell to the floor, gulping air. He raised his fist over her.

"No!" Suddenly Gudrun was between them. "You will not touch her." There was a tone in her voice that Joan had never heard before. "Or I will tell the truth."

The canon stared in disbelief. John appeared in the doorway, carrying a linen sack stuffed with his belongings.

Gudrun nodded toward him. "Our son needs your blessing for the journey."

For a long time the canon held her gaze. Then, very slowly, he turned to face his son.

"Kneel, Johannes."

John knelt. The canon placed his hand on his bowed head. "O God, Who didst call Abraham to leave his home and didst protect him in all his wanderings, unto Thee we commit this boy."

A thin stream of late afternoon sun filtered through the window, illuminating John's dark hair with a rich light.

"Watch over him and provide all things needful for his soul and body . . ." The canon's voice assumed a singsong rhythm as he prayed.

Keeping his head bowed, John looked up and met his sister's gaze, his eyes wide and frightened, eloquent with appeal. *He doesn't want to go,* Joan realized suddenly. Of course! Why had she not seen it before? She had not given a thought to John's feelings. *He is afraid. He cannot keep up with the demands of a schola, and he knows it.*

If only I could go with him.

A plan began to formulate in her mind.

". . . and when life's pilgrimage is over," the canon finished, "may he arrive safely at the heavenly country, through Christ Jesus our Lord. Amen."

The blessing over, John rose to his feet. Stolid, unresisting, like a sheep before the sacrifice, he endured his mother's embraces and his father's last-minute admonitions. But when Joan approached and put her arms around him, he clutched her and began to sob.

"Don't be afraid," she murmured reassuringly.

"Enough," the canon said. He placed an arm around his son's shoulder, shepherding him toward the door. "Keep the girl inside," he commanded Gudrun, and then they were gone. The door swung shut with a hollow thud.

Joan ran to the window and peered out. She saw John mount behind the bishop's emissary, his plain woolen tunic contrasting with the rich red of the stranger's robes. The canon stood nearby, his dark, squat figure outlined against the budding green of the landscape. With a last shout of farewell, they rode off.

Joan turned from the window. Gudrun stood in the middle of the room, watching her.

"Little quail . . . ," Gudrun began hesitantly.

Joan walked past her as if she did not exist. She took up her pile of mending and sat by the hearth. She needed to think, to prepare. There wasn't much time, and everything had to be worked out very carefully.

It would be difficult, probably even dangerous. The thought frightened her, but it made no difference. With a certainty at once wonderful and terrifying, Joan knew what she must do.

IT'S *not fair,* John thought. He rode sullenly behind the bishop's man, scowling at the insignia on the red tunic. *I don't want to go.* He hated his father for making him. He reached inside his tunic, searching for the object he had secretly placed there before he left. His fingers touched the smooth handle of the knife—his father's bone-handled knife, one of his treasures.

A small, vengeful smile touched John's lips. His father would be furious when he discovered it missing. No matter. By then John would be miles away from Ingelheim, and there was nothing his father could do about it. It was a small triumph, but he clung to it in the misery of his situation.

Why didn't he send Joan? John asked himself angrily. Black resentment simmered inside him. *It's all her fault,* he thought. Because of Joan, he had already endured over two years of lessons from Aesculapius, that tedious and evil-tempered old man. Now he was being sent away to the schola at Dorstadt in *her* place. Oh, it was Joan the bishop wanted, John was sure of it. It had to be Joan. *She* was the smart one, *she* knew Latin and Greek, *she* could read Augustine when he still hadn't mastered all the psalms.

He might have forgiven her that, and more besides. She was, after all, his sister. But there was one thing that John could not forgive: Joan was Mama's pet. He had overheard them often enough, laughing and whispering together in Saxon, then breaking off abruptly when he joined them. They thought he didn't hear them, but he did. Mama never spoke the Old Tongue with him. *Why?* John asked himself bitterly for the thousandth time. *Does she think I'd tell Father? I wouldn't—not for anything, no matter what he did, not even if he beat me.*

It isn't fair, he thought again. *Why should she prefer Joan to me? I'm her son, which everybody knows is better than a useless daughter.* Joan was a sorry excuse for a girl. She couldn't sew or spin or weave half as well as other girls her age. Then there was her interest in book learning, which everyone knew to be unnatural. Even Mama saw there was something wrong there. The other children in the village constantly mocked Joan. It was embarrassing, having her as a sister; John would gladly disclaim her, if he could.

Immediately after he had the thought, he felt a twinge of conscience. Joan had always been good to him, had stood up for him when Father was angry, even done his work for him when he couldn't understand. He was grateful for her help—she had saved him from many a beating—but at the same time, he resented it. It was humiliating. After all, he was her older brother. *He* was the one who should look after her, not the other way around.

Now, because of her, he was riding behind this strange man toward a place he did not know and a life he did not want. He pictured his life at the schola, trapped inside some dreary room all day, surrounded by piles of boring, awful books.

Why couldn't Father understand that he didn't want to go? *I'm not Matthew; I'll never be good at book studies.* Nor did he mean to be a scholar or a cleric. He knew what he wanted: to be a warrior, a warrior in the Emperor's army, battling to subdue the heathen hordes. He had gotten the idea from Ulfert, the saddler, who had gone with Count Hugo on the old Emperor's campaign against the Saxons. What wonderful tales the old man told, sitting in his workshop, his tools temporarily forgotten by his side, his eyes lit with the memory of that great victory! "Like the thrushes that fly over the autumn vineyards, pecking at the grapes"—John remembered every word exactly as old Ulfert had spoken them—"we flew over the land, a holy canticle on our lips, ferreting out the heathens hiding in the woods and marshes and concealed in the ditches, men and women and children alike. There was not one of us whose bucklers and swords were not red with blood that day. By sunset, there was no soul left alive who had not renounced their godless ways and sworn eternal allegiance on their knees to the True Faith." Then old Ulfert had brought out his sword, which he had wrested, still warm, from the dead hand of one of the heathens. Its handle shone with glassy gems; its shaft was a gleaming yellow. Unlike Frankish swords, which were fashioned of iron, it was made from gold—an inferior material, Ulfert explained, lacking the solidity and bite of Frankish weapons, but beautiful nonetheless. John's heart had swelled at the sight of it. Old Ulfert had held it out to him, and John had grasped it, feeling its balance, its weight. His hand fit the gemmed handle as if it were made for it. He swung the sword over his head; it sliced the air with a thrumming sound that kept rhythm with the singing in his blood. He had known then he was born to be a warrior.

There were rumors, even now, of a new campaign in the spring. Perhaps Count Hugo would answer the Emperor's call again. If so, John planned to go with him, no matter what Father said. He would be fourteen soon, a man's age—many had gone to war at that age, even younger. He would run off, if necessary, but he would go.

Of course, that would be difficult now that he was to be imprisoned in the schola at Dorstadt. Would word of the new conscript even travel so far? he wondered. And if it did, would he be able to get away?

The thought was upsetting, and he put it out of his mind. Instead, he called up his favorite daydream. He was in the front ranks of the battle, the silver banners of the count gleaming before him, drawing him forward. They were driving the scattered and defeated heathens before them. They flew from him, desperate and frightened, the women's long, white-gold hair waving in the wind. He ran them down, wielding his long sword with great skill, slashing and killing, offering no mercy, until finally they submitted to him, repenting their blindness and showing themselves willing to accept the Light.

The corners of John's mouth lifted in a drowsy smile as the steady beat of the horse's hooves signaled their progress through the darkening forest.

✝

THERE was a whirring sound, followed by a heavy thud.

"Unnhh." The bishop's man jolted backward. His shoulder rammed into John, jarring him from sleep.

"Hey!" John protested, but already the man was falling, the weight of his pendulous body dragging John irresistibly from the saddle.

They dropped to the ground together. John landed on top of the bishop's man, who lay unmoving where he fell. As John put his hand out to raise himself, his fingers closed around something long and round and smooth.

It was the shaft of an arrow, yellow feathers at the end. The tip was buried deep in the middle of the man's chest.

John rose to his feet, all his senses alert. From the thick trees on the other side of the path, a man emerged, dressed in tattered clothes. In his hands he carried a bow, and on his back a quiverful of yellow-feathered arrows.

Does he mean to kill me too?

The man came toward him. John looked around, seeking a path of escape. The trees grew dense in this part of the woods; if he ran, he might be able to elude the attacker.

The man was almost upon him, close enough for John to read the menace in his eyes.

John tried to run, but it was too late. The man grabbed him by the arm. John struggled, but the man, taller than he by a head and powerfully built, held him fast, lifting him slightly so that his toes barely touched the ground.

John remembered the knife. With his free hand, he reached inside his tunic; frantically his fingers sought the bone handle, found it, gripped it. He pulled the knife out and plunged it home in one swift motion. With an exhilarating rush, John felt it sink deep into the man's flesh, striking bone before John withdrew it with a wicked twist. The man swore and grabbed his wounded shoulder, letting go of John.

John ran into the woods. Sharp branches tore at his clothes and scratched his skin, but he kept running. Despite the moonlight, it was dark under the canopy of trees. Looking behind him to see if he was being pursued, John bumped into a beech with low-hanging branches. He leapt for the bottommost branch, caught it, and started to scramble up quickly, his lithe young body snaking expertly through the branches, stopping only when the limbs became too small and pliant to support his weight. Then he waited.

There was no sound except the soft rustle of leaves. Twice a night owl called, its cry echoing eerily in the stillness. Then John heard footsteps crashing through the forest. He gripped the knife, holding his breath, grateful for his plain brown cloak, which merged so well with the blackness of the night.

The footsteps came closer and closer. John could hear the man's ragged, uneven breathing.

The footsteps stopped directly beneath him.

JOAN stepped out of the silent darkness of the grubenhaus into the moonlit night. Shapes of familiar objects loomed eerily, transformed by shadows. She shivered, recalling stories of *Waldleuten,* evil sprites and trolls that haunted the night. Gathering her cloak of rough gray hemp around her, she moved into the shadows, searching the changed landscape for the entrance to the path through the forest. The light was good—it lacked only two days till full moon—and in a moment she was able to make out the old oak, split by lightning, that marked the spot. She ran quickly across the field toward it.

At the edge of the woods she paused. It was dark in there, the moon filtered by the trees into pale threads of light. She looked back at the grubenhaus. Washed by moonlight, surrounded by the fields and animal pens, it was solid, warm, familiar. She thought of her comfortable bed, the coverings probably still warm from the heat of her body. She thought of Mama, to whom she had not even said good-bye. She took a step toward home, then stopped. All that mattered, all she wanted, lay in the other direction.

She entered the woods. The trees closed over her head. The path was strewn with rocks and underbrush, but she moved ahead swiftly. It was fifteen miles to the cella, and she had to be there before dawn.

She concentrated on keeping a steady pace. It was hard going; in the darkness it was easy to stray toward the edge of the path, where branches tore at her clothes and hair. The path became more and more uneven. Several times she tripped on rocks or broken roots; once she fell, bruising her hands and knees.

After several hours, the sky began to show light above the roof of trees. It was nearing dawn. Joan was exhausted, but she quickened her pace, half-walking, half-running down the path. She had to make it before they left. She had to.

Her left foot caught on something. She tried to regain her balance, but she was moving too quickly and she fell, breaking her fall clumsily with her arms.

She lay still, the breath knocked out of her. Her right arm hurt where a sharp twig had scraped it, but otherwise she did not seem to be injured. She pushed herself into a sitting position.

On the ground beside her, a man lay with his back to her. Sleeping? No. He would have wakened when she stumbled over him. She touched his shoulder; he rolled onto his back. The dead eyes of the bishop's emissary glared up at her, lips frozen in a gap-toothed grimace. His rich tunic was ripped and bloody. The middle finger of his left hand was missing.

Joan leapt to her feet. "John!" she shouted. She scanned the woods and the ground nearby, afraid of what she might find.

"Here." A patch of pale skin showed faintly in the darkness.

"John!" She ran to him, and they embraced, holding on to each other tightly.

"Why are you here?" John asked. "Is Father with you?"

"No. I'll explain later. Are you hurt? What happened?"

"We were attacked. A brigand, I think, after the emissary's gold ring. I was riding behind when the arrow struck him."

Joan said nothing, but hugged him closer.

He pulled out of her arms. "But I defended myself. I did!" His eyes glittered with a strange excitement. "When he came for me, I struck him with this!" He held up the canon's bone-handled hunting knife. "Got him in the shoulder, I think. Anyway, it stopped him long enough for me to get away!"

Joan stared at the blade, discolored with blood. "Father's knife."

John's expression turned sullen. "Yes. I took it. Why not? He made me go—I didn't want to."

"All right," Joan said briskly. "Put it away. We must hurry if we are to make it to the cella before dawn."

"The cella? But I don't have to go to Dorstadt now. After

what happened"—he thrust his head in the direction of the murdered emissary—"I can go home."

"No, John. *Think.* Now that Father knows the bishop's intentions, he will not permit you to stay at home. He'll find some way to get you to the schola, even if he has to take you himself. Besides"— Joan pointed to the knife—"by the time we get back, he will have discovered that you took this."

John looked startled. Obviously he had not thought of that.

"It will be all right. I'll be there with you, I'll help you." She took his hand. "Come."

Hand in hand, under the steadily brightening sky, the two children made their way to the cella, where the rest of the bishop's men were waiting.

≽| 7 |≼

THEY arrived at the cella while the sun was still low in the sky, but the bishop's men were already awake, impatiently awaiting their companion's return. When Joan and John told them what had transpired, the men became suspicious. They took John's bone-handled knife and examined it carefully. Joan breathed a prayer of thanks that she had thought to clean it thoroughly in the forest stream, washing off all trace of blood. The men rode back to find their companion's body, taking Joan and John with them; the discovery of the yellow-feathered arrow confirmed the children's story. But what should they do with the body? It was out of the question to carry it all the way to Dorstadt, a fortnight's journey, not with the spring sun making the days so warm. In the end they buried their companion in the forest, marking the spot with a rough wooden cross. Joan said a prayer over the grave, which impressed the men, for, like their companion, they knew no Latin. Expecting to escort a girl child, the men did not, at first, want to take John.

"There's no mount for him," their leader said, "nor food neither."

"We can ride tandem," Joan offered. "And share a ration."

The man shook his head. "The bishop sent for *you*. There's no point bringing your brother."

"My father made a compact with your companion," Joan lied. "I was permitted to go only on condition that John accompany me. If he doesn't, my father will call me home again—and you'll be put to the trouble of escorting me back."

The man frowned; having just endured the discomforts of a long journey, he did not relish the prospect of another.

Joan pressed her advantage. "If that happens, I'll tell the bishop that I tried my best to explain the situation, and you wouldn't listen. Will he be pleased to learn that the entire misunderstanding was your fault?"

The man was stunned. He had never heard a girl speak so boldly.

Now he understood why the bishop wanted to see her; she was a curiosity, that was for certain.

"Very well," he agreed grudgingly. "The boy can come."

IT WAS an exhausting journey to Dorstadt, for the men of the escort were eager to get home and rode long and hard every day. The rigors of the journey did not trouble Joan; she was fascinated by the ever-changing landscape and the new world which every day opened before her. At last she was free, free from Ingelheim and the confines of her existence there. She rode through squalid little villages and bustling towns with equal delight, full of curiosity and wonder. John, however, quickly grew irritable from lack of sufficient food and rest. Joan tried to soothe him, but his ill humor was only inflamed by his sister's good-natured solicitude.

They reached the bishop's palace at noontide of the tenth day. The palace steward took one disapproving look at the two children, in their stained and rumpled peasants' garments, and gave orders for baths and clean clothing before he would permit them to be admitted to the bishop's presence.

For Joan, accustomed to hurried washings in the stream that ran behind the grubenhaus, the bath was an extraordinary experience. The bishop's palace had indoor baths, with heated water, a luxury she had never even heard of. She remained in the warm water for almost an hour while serving women scrubbed her till her skin glowed pink and almost raw. Her back, however, they cleansed with utmost gentleness, clucking their tongues sympathetically over the jagged scars. They washed her hair and twisted the long, white-gold mass into shining plaits that framed her face. Then they brought her a new tunic of green linen. The texture was so soft, the weaving so fine, Joan found it hard to believe it had been made by human hands. When she was dressed, the women brought her a looking glass set in gold. Joan lifted it and saw the face of a stranger. She had never viewed her own features, except in occasional distorted fragments reflected by the muddy water of the village pond. Joan was astonished by the clarity of the image in the mirror. She held the mirror up, scrutinizing herself critically.

She was not pretty, but she knew that. She did not have the high, pale forehead, delicate chin, and frail, slope-shouldered form so favored by minstrels and lovers. She had a ruddy, healthy, boyish look. Her brow was too low, her chin too firm, her shoulders too straight for beauty. But her hair—Mama's hair—was lovely, and her eyes were good—deep-set gray-green orbs, fringed with thick lashes. She shrugged and put the glass down. The bishop had not sent for her to discover if she was pretty.

John was brought in, equally resplendent in tunic and mantle of blue linen. The two children were taken to the palace steward.

"Better," the steward said, examining them appraisingly. "Much better. Very well, then, follow me."

They walked down a long corridor whose walls were covered with enormous tapestries intricately worked with gold and silver thread. Joan's pulse leapt nervously in her throat. She was going to meet the bishop.

Will I be able to answer his questions? Will he accept me in the schola? All at once she felt inadequate and unsure. She tried to remember a single thing she had studied, but her mind went blank. When she thought of Aesculapius, of the faith he had shown in her by arranging this interview, her stomach clenched.

They stopped before a huge pair of double-sided oaken doors. From inside came a din of voices and a clattering of plates. The palace steward nodded at the house knave positioned at the entrance, and the man swung the heavy doors open.

Joan and John walked into the room, then stopped, gaping. Some two hundred people were gathered in the hall, seated at long tables piled high with food. Platters filled with every variety of roasted meat—capons, geese, moorhens, and several haunches of stag—crowded together on the tables within easy reach of the diners, who pulled off chunks of flesh with their fingers and stuffed it in their mouths, wiping their hands on their sleeves. In the center of the largest table, half devoured but still recognizable, rested the enormous head of a roasted boar, larded with sauce. There were pottages and pasties, peeled walnuts, figs, dates, white and vermilion sweetmeats, and many other dishes which Joan could not identify. She had never seen so much food in one place in her life.

"A song! A song!" Pewter cups banged on the wooden tables, rhythmic, insistent. "Come, Widukind, a song!" A tall, fair-skinned young man was prodded to his feet and rose, laughing.

"*Ik gihorta dat seggen dat sih urhettun aenon muo tin, hiltibraht enti hadubrant . . .*"

Joan was surprised. The young man sang in Theodisk, the common tongue—the canon would have called it the pagan tongue.

"This I have heard told, that warriors met singly, Hildebrand and Hadubrand between two armies . . ."

The men stood and joined in, holding their cups high. ". . . they let glide spears of ashwood, sharp showers; they stepped together and cleft the battle boards until their shields of limewood shattered hacked by the weapons . . ."

An odd song for a bishop's table. Joan glanced sidelong at John, but he was listening raptly, eyes alight with excitement.

With an exultant shout, the men finished the song. There was a loud scraping of wood as they sat, pulling the long planked benches up to the tables.

Another man rose with a taunting smile. "I heard of something rising in a corner . . ." He paused expectantly.

"A riddle!" someone cried, and the crowd bellowed its approval. "One of Haido's riddles! Yes! Yes! Let's have it."

The man called Haido waited till the noise abated. "I heard of something rising in a room," he repeated, "swelling and lifting its cover. The bold-hearted bride grabbed at that boneless wonder with her hands . . ."

A knowing chuckle began to build among the guests.

". . . she covered that swelling thing with a swirl of cloth." Haido's smiling eyes raked the room challengingly. "What is it?"

"Look between your legs," someone shouted, "and you'll find the answer right enough!" This was followed by more laughter and a barrage of obscene gestures. Joan watched in astonishment. *This* was a bishop's residence?

"Wrong!" Haido retorted merrily. "You are all wrong!"

"The answer, then! The answer!" People shouted and banged their cups on the tables.

Haido paused a moment for dramatic effect.

"Dough!" he announced triumphantly, and sat down as a wave of shouting laughter shook the room.

When the noise subsided, the steward said, "Come with me," and led the two children to the far end of the hall, where the high table rested on its dais. The bishop sat in the center, still chuckling, dressed in magnificent yellow silk stained with drops of grease and wine. A soft down pillow cushioned his place on the bench. He did not look at all as Joan had imagined him. He was a big man, thick necked; the muscularity of his chest and shoulders showed through his thin silken tunic. His large belly and florid face were those of a man who enjoyed his food and wine. As they approached, he leaned over and held a crimson sweetmeat to the lips of a buxom woman seated beside him. She bit it, then whispered something in his ear, and they both laughed.

The palace steward cleared his throat. "My lord, the men have returned from Ingelheim with the child."

The bishop stared at the steward opaquely. "Child? Eh? What child?"

"The one you sent for, my lord. A candidate for the schola, I believe. Recommended to you by the Gr—"

"Yes, yes." The bishop waved impatiently. "I remember now." His arm rested lightly around the woman's shoulders. He looked at Joan and John. "Well, Widukind, am I seeing double?"

"No, Lord. The canon sent his son as well. The two of them arrived at the cella together and would not be separated."

"Well." The bishop's face shone with amusement. "What do you think of that? I ask for one and get two. Would the Emperor were so generous with his favors as this country prelate!"

The table roared with laughter. There were several shouts of "Hear, hear!" and "Amen!"

The bishop reached over and ripped a leg off a roast hen. He said to Joan, "Are you the scholar you have been made out to be?"

Joan hesitated, unsure of what to say. "I have studied hard, Eminence."

"Pah! Studying!" The bishop snorted. He took a bite of chicken. "The schola is filled with dunderheads who study but know nothing. What do you *know*, child?"

"I can read and write, Eminence."

"In Theodisk or in Latin?"

"In Theodisk, in Latin, and in Greek."

"Greek! Now that is something. Even Odo has no Greek, have you, Odo?" He grinned at a thin-faced man a few seats away.

Odo spread his mouth in a humorless smile. "It is a pagan tongue, Sire, a tongue of idolaters and heretics."

"Quite correct, quite correct." The bishop's tone was taunting. "Odo is always correct, aren't you, Odo?"

The cleric sniffed. "You know well, Eminence, that I do not approve of this latest whim of yours. It is dangerous, and ungodly, to allow a woman into the schola."

From the back of the hall a voice called out, "She's no woman yet, from the looks of her." Another tide of laughter swept the hall, accompanied by lewd remarks.

A burning warmth crept from Joan's throat up to her cheeks. How could these people behave so in the presence of the bishop?

"It is also pointless," the man called Odo continued when the noise died down. "Women are, by nature, quite incapable of reasoning." His eyes flicked over Joan dismissively, then returned to the bishop. "Their natural humors, which are cold and moist, are unpropitious for cerebral activity. They cannot comprehend the higher spiritual and moral concepts."

Joan stared at the man.

"I have heard that opinion expressed," the bishop said. He smiled at Odo with the look of a man who was enjoying himself immensely. "But how then do you explain the girl's scholarly attainments—her knowledge of Greek, for example, which even *you*, Odo"—he lingered over the words—"have not mastered?"

"She has boasted of her abilities, but we have seen no proof of them." Odo sniffed. "You are credulous, Sire. The Greek may have been less than honest in reporting her accomplishments?"

This was too much. First this hateful man insulted her, and now he dared to attack Aesculapius! Joan's lips started to form an angry reply when she caught the sympathetic gaze of a red-haired knight seated beside the bishop.

No. He signaled her silently. She hesitated, struck by the message in his compelling indigo eyes. He turned to the bishop and whispered something. The bishop nodded and addressed the thin-faced cleric. "Very well, Odo, examine her."

"My lord?"

"Examine her. See if she is fit for study at the schola."

"Here, my lord? It hardly seems appro—"

"Here, Odo. Why not? We will all profit from the example."

Odo frowned. He turned to Joan. His narrow face aimed at her like an ax.

"*Quicunque vult.* What does it mean?"

Joan was surprised. So easy a question? Perhaps it was a trick. Perhaps he was trying to put her off her guard. Cautiously she responded, "It is the doctrine asserting that the three Persons of the Trinity are cosubstantial. That Christ was fully divine just as He was fully human."

"The authority for this doctrine?"

"The first council of Nicaea."

"*Confessio Fidei.* What is it?"

"It is the false and pernicious doctrine"—Joan knew what to say, having been cautioned by Aesculapius on this point—"which asserts that Christ was first a human being and only secondarily divine. Divine, that is, only through his adoption by the Father." She studied Odo's face, but it was unreadable. "*Filius non proprius, sed adoptivus,*" she added for good measure.

"Explain the false nature of this heresy."

"If Christ is God's Son by grace and not by nature, then He must be subordinate to the Father. This is a false heresy and an abomination," Joan recited dutifully from memory, "because the Holy Spirit proceeds not only from the Father but also from the Son; there is only one Son, and He is not an adopted son. *'In utraque natura proprium eum et non adoptivum filium dei confitemur.'*"

The people at the tables snapped their fingers in applause. "*Litteratissima!*" someone shouted across the room.

"Amusing little oddity, isn't she?" a woman's voice muttered close behind Joan, just a shade too loudly.

"Well, Odo," the bishop said expansively. "What do you say? Was the Greek right about Joan, or not?"

Odo looked like a man who has tasted vinegar. "It appears the child has some knowledge of orthodox theology. Nevertheless, this in itself does not prove anything." He spoke condescendingly, as if to a difficult child. "There is, in some women, a highly developed imitative ability which allows them to memorize and repeat the words of men, and so give the appearance of thought. But this imitative skill is not to be confused with true reason, which is essentially male. For, as is well known"—Odo's voice assumed an authoritative ring, for now he was on familiar ground—"women are innately inferior to men."

"Why?" The word was out of Joan's mouth before she was even aware of having spoken.

Odo smiled, his thin lips drawing back unpleasantly. He had the look of the fox when it knows it has the rabbit cornered. "Your ignorance, child, is revealed in that question. For St. Paul himself has asserted this truth, that women are beneath men in conception, in place, and in will."

"In conception, in place, and in will?" Joan repeated.

"Yes." Odo spoke slowly and distinctly, as if addressing a half-wit. "In conception, because Adam was created first, and Eve afterward; in place, because Eve was created to serve Adam as companion and mate; in will, because Eve could not resist the Devil's temptation and ate of the apple."

Among the tables, heads nodded in agreement. The bishop's expression was grave. Beside him, the red-haired knight gave no outward sign of his thoughts.

Odo smirked. Joan felt an intense dislike for this man. For a moment she stood silently, tugging on her nose.

"Why," she said at last, "is woman inferior in conception? For though she was created second, she was made from Adam's side, while Adam was made from common clay."

There were several appreciative chuckles from the back of the hall.

"In place"—the words tumbled out as Joan's thoughts raced ahead and she reasoned her way through—"woman should be preferred to man, because Eve was created inside Paradise, but Adam was created outside."

There was another hum from the audience. The smile on Odo's face wavered.

Joan continued, too interested in the line of her argument to consider what she was doing. "As for will, woman should be considered *superior* to man"—this was bold, but there was no going back now—"for Eve ate of the apple for love of knowledge and learning, but Adam ate of it merely because she asked him."

There was shocked silence in the room. Odo's pale lips pressed together angrily. The bishop was staring at Joan as if he could not quite believe what he had just heard.

She had gone too far.

Some ideas are dangerous.

Aesculapius had warned her, but she had become so involved in the debate she forgot his advice. That man, that Odo, had been so sure of himself, so bent on humiliating her before the bishop. She had ruined her chance for the schola and she knew it, but she would not give the hateful little man the satisfaction of seeing her dismay. She stood before the high table with chin lifted, eyes blazing.

The silence stretched on interminably. All eyes were on the bishop, whose assessing gaze remained fixed on Joan. Then, slowly, very slowly, a long, low rumble of mirth escaped his lips.

The bishop was laughing.

Beside him, the buxom woman giggled nervously. Then the room erupted with noise. People cheered and pounded on the tables and laughed, laughed so hard the tears coursed down their faces and they had to wipe them off with their sleeves. Joan looked at the red-haired knight. He was grinning broadly. She met his eyes, and he winked at her.

"Come now, Odo," said the bishop, when at last he could draw breath, "you must admit it. The girl has outwitted you!"

Odo gave the bishop a poisonous look. "What of the boy, Eminence? Do you wish to have him examined as well?"

"No, no. We'll take him too, since the girl is so attached to him. We'll take them both! To be sure, the girl's education has been a bit"—he sought the right word—"unorthodox. But she is entirely refreshing. Just what the schola needs! Odo, you have acquired some new students. Take good care with them!"

Joan stared at the bishop in shock. What did he mean? Could Odo be the master of the schola? The one who would teach her?

What had she done?

Odo looked down his narrow nose at the bishop. "You have, of course, made arrangements for the child's accommodation? She cannot board in the boys' quarters."

"Ah . . . accommodations." The bishop hesitated. "Let us see . . ."

"My lord." The red-haired knight interrupted. "The child could stay with me. My wife and I have two daughters, who would make her welcome. She would be a good companion for my Gisla."

Joan looked at him. He was a man in the prime of life, some twenty-five years of age, strong, well favored, with high cheekbones and a fine, full beard. His thick hair, really an extraordinary color of red, was parted in the middle and curled thickly to his shoulders. His startling blue eyes were intelligent and kind.

"Excellent, Gerold." The bishop thumped him warmly on the back. "It is all settled. The girl will stay with you."

A servant came by with a tray heaped with sweetmeats. John's eyes widened at the sight of the honeyed treats, oozing with butter.

The bishop smiled. "Children, you must be hungry after your long trip. Come sit by me." He moved closer to the woman beside him, clearing a space between him and the red-haired knight.

Joan and John went around the table and sat. The bishop himself served them sweetmeats. John ate greedily, taking huge bites of the gooey treats, the sticky syrup mustaching his mouth.

The bishop returned his attention to the woman seated beside him. They drank from the same cup, laughing, and he stroked her hair, disarranging her coif. Joan fixed her eyes on the plate of sweetmeats. She nibbled at one of them but could not finish it; the honeyed sweetness was sickening. She yearned to be away from this place, away from the noise, the unfamiliar people, and the puzzling behavior of the bishop.

The red-haired knight named Gerold spoke to her. "You have had a long day. Would you like to leave?"

Joan nodded. Seeing them rise, John stuffed in one last mouthful of candy and got up.

"No, son." Gerold placed a hand on John's shoulder. "You stay here."

John said plaintively, "I want to go with her."

"Your place is here, with the other boys. When the meal is finished, the steward will show you to your quarters."

John paled, but he mastered himself and said nothing.

"That is an interesting piece." Gerold pointed to the bone-handled knife strapped to John's waist. "May I see it?"

John pulled it from his belt and handed it to Gerold. He turned it over, admiring the working on the handle. The blade glinted, reflecting the flickering torches around the room. Joan remembered how it had glowed in the candlelight of the grubenhaus, before it bit into the parchment of Aesculapius's book, erasing, destroying.

"Very fine. Roger has a sword whose handle has similar working. Roger." Gerold called to a youth at a table nearby. "Come show this young man your sword."

Roger held out a long iron sword with an elaborate handle.

John regarded it reverently. "May I touch it?"

"You can hold it if you like."

"You'll be given a sword of your own," Gerold said. "And a bow. A lance too, if you've the strength for it. Tell him, Roger."

"Yes. We have lessons every day in fighting and weaponry."

John's eyes registered surprise and delight.

"See the little nick here on the side of the blade? That's where I struck a blow against the heavy sword of the master of weapons himself!"

"Really?" John was fascinated.

Gerold said to Joan, "Shall we go? I think your brother will not mind our leaving now."

At the doorway, Joan turned to look back at John. With the sword across his lap, he was talking animatedly to Roger. She felt an odd reluctance to part from him. They had often been more rivals than friends, but John was her link to home, to a world familiar and comprehensible. Without him, she was alone.

Gerold had gone ahead and was striding down the corridor. He was very tall, and his long legs carried him quickly; Joan had to take little running steps to catch up.

For several minutes they did not speak. Then Gerold said abruptly, "You did well, back there with Odo."

"I do not think he likes me."

"No. He wouldn't. Odo guards his dignity closely, as a man guards his coins when there are hardly any left."

Joan smiled up at Gerold, liking him.

On an impulse, she decided to trust him.

"Was that the bishop's . . . wife?" She stumbled over the word, embarrassed. All her life she had been aware of the shameful impropriety of her parents' marriage. It was a child's awareness, never spoken or even fully acknowledged, but deeply felt. Once, observing Joan's sensitivity on the subject, Aesculapius had told her that such marriages were not uncommon among the lower clergy. But for a bishop . . .

"Wife? Oh, you mean Theda." Gerold laughed. "No, my lord bishop is not the marrying kind. Theda is one of his paramours."

Paramours! The bishop kept paramours!

"You are shocked. You needn't be. Fulgentius—my lord bishop— is not a man of pious disposition. He inherited the title from his uncle, who was bishop before him. He never took priest's orders and makes no pretense of holiness, as you will have noted. But you will find him a good enough man for all that. He admires learning, though he is not lettered himself. It was he who established the schola here."

Gerold had spoken to her plainly, not as a child but as someone who could be expected to understand. Joan liked that. But his words were troubling. Could it be right for a bishop, a prince of the Church, to live like this? To keep . . . paramours? Everything was so different from what she had expected.

They arrived at the outside doors to the palace. Pages dressed in red silk swung the huge oaken panels open; the brightness of the torchlit hall spilled into the darkness.

"Come," said Gerold. "You will feel better after a night's sleep." He strode quickly in the direction of the stables.

Uncertain, Joan followed him into the cool night.

"THERE it is!" Gerold pointed off to the left, and Joan followed the direction of his arm. In the distance she could just make out dark shapes of buildings outlined against the moonlit sky. "There's Villaris, my home—and yours now as well, Joan."

Even in the darkness, Villaris was magnificent. Situated commandingly on the slopes of a hill, it appeared enormous to Joan's wondering eyes. It consisted of four tall, heavy-timbered buildings connected through a series of courtyards and splendid wooden porticoes. Gerold and Joan rode through the sturdy oak palisades guarding the main entrance and past several outbuildings: a kitchen, a bakery, a stable, a granary, and two barns. They dismounted in a small forecourt, and Gerold handed his mount over to the waiting hands of the stable master. Resin torches placed at regular intervals lit their way down a long, windowless corridor upon whose thick oak walls rows of gleaming weapons were displayed: long swords, lances, spears, crossbows, and scramasaxes, the short, heavy, single-edged blades favored by the fierce Frankish infantrymen. They emerged into a large second courtyard ringed by covered porticoes and passed through into the great hall itself, a vast, echoing space hung with richly decorated tapestries.

In the center of the room stood the most beautiful woman Joan had ever seen, apart from her own mother. But whereas Gudrun was tall and fair, this woman was small and slight, with ebony hair and large, proud, dark eyes. Coolly those eyes raked Joan, inspecting her with an expression that clearly found her wanting.

"What is this?" she asked abruptly as they drew near.

Ignoring her rudeness, Gerold replied, "Joan, this is my wife, Richild, the lady of this manor. Richild, may I present Joan of Ingelheim, who has today arrived to begin study at the schola."

Joan made an awkward attempt at a curtsy, which Richild regarded with contempt before returning her attention to Gerold. "The schola? Is this some kind of jest?"

"Fulgentius has admitted her, and she is to reside here at Villaris for the duration of her studies."

"Here?"

"She can share a bed with Gisla, who could use a sensible companion for a change."

Richild's graceful black eyebrows arched haughtily. "She looks like a colona."

Joan flushed with the insult.

"Richild, you forget yourself," Gerold admonished sharply. "Joan is a guest in this house."

Richild sniffed. "Well"—she fingered Joan's new green linen tunic—"at least she appears to be clean." She signaled imperiously to one of the servants. "Show her to the *dortoir*." Without another word she swept from the room.

LATER, lying on the soft straw mattress in the upstairs dortoir beside a snoring Gisla (who had not awakened even when Joan crawled in beside her), Joan wondered about her brother. Beside whom was John sleeping now—if, that is, he was able to sleep? She certainly could not; her mind was aswirl with troubling thoughts and emotions. She longed for the familiar surroundings of home, longed especially for her mother. She wanted to be held and caressed and called "little quail" again. She should not have run off the way she did—in silence and in anger, without a word of farewell. Gudrun had betrayed her with the bishop's emissary, it was true, but Joan knew that she had done it from an excess of love, because she could not bear to see her daughter leave. Now Joan might never see her mother again. She had leapt at the chance for escape without considering the consequences. For she could never return home, that was certain. Her father would kill her for her disobedience. Her place was here now, in this strange and friendless country, and here, for good or ill, she must remain.

Mama, she thought as she stared into the forbidding darkness of the unfamiliar room, and a single tear slid silently down her cheek.

⨝ 8 ⨞

THE classroom, a small, stone-walled chamber adjacent to the cathedral library, remained cool and moist even on this warm fall afternoon. Joan loved its coolness and the rich smell of parchment that permeated the air, an enticement to explore the vast holding of books that lay just next door.

An enormous painting covered the wall at the front of the room. It was a picture of a woman dressed in the long, flowing robes of the Greeks. In her left hand she held a pair of shears; in her right, a whip. The woman represented Knowledge; her shears were to prune away error and false dogma, her whip was to reprimand lazy students. The brows of Knowledge were sharply drawn together, and the corners of her mouth curved down, creating a stern expression. The dark eyes glared from the painted wall, seeming to focus on the observer, their look hard and commanding. Odo had commissioned the work shortly after assuming the position of teaching master at the schola.

"*Bos mugit, equus hinnit, asinus rudit, elephans barrit . . .*"

On the left side of the room, the less advanced students chanted monotonously, practicing simple verb forms.

"Cows moo, horses neigh, donkeys bray, elephants roar . . ."

Odo motioned rhythmically with his right hand, setting the pace of the chant. Meanwhile, his eyes swept the room with practiced skill, monitoring the work of his other students.

Ludovic and Ebbo huddled together over one of the psalms. They were supposed to be memorizing it, but the tilt of their heads toward each other indicated that they had ceased to concentrate on their work. Without letting his other hand miss a beat of the chanting rhythm, Odo smacked both boys sharply on the backs of their heads with a long wooden rod. They yelped and bent over their tablets again, models of industriousness.

Nearby, John was working on a chapter of Donatus. He was clearly having great difficulty. He read slowly, painstakingly forming each vowel and consonant with his lips, stopping frequently to scratch his head in puzzlement over some unfamiliar word pattern.

Sitting apart from the others—for they would have nothing to do with her—Joan was intent on the task to which Odo had set her, preparing a gloss of a life of St. Antony. She worked quickly, her stylus traveling across the parchment with confidence and precision. She did not look up, nor did her attention waver for an instant. Her concentration was absolute.

Odo said shortly, "That is enough for today. This group"—he gestured toward the novices—"is dismissed. The rest of you will remain at your seats until I have checked your work."

The novices rose excitedly from their desks, exiting the room as quickly as decorum permitted. The other students put down their styluses and watched Odo expectantly, eager to be released to the pleasures of the warm afternoon.

Joan remained studiously bent over her work.

Odo frowned. The girl's zeal had admittedly surprised him. His hand itched to use the rod on her, but so far she had given him no occasion. She actually seemed to want to learn.

Odo walked to her desk and stood over her pointedly. She stopped working then, her expression registering surprise and even—was it possible?—disappointment.

"Did you call on me, sir? Pardon me; I was concentrating on my work and did not hear you," Joan said politely.

She acts her part well, Odo thought. *But I am not deceived.* Oh, she pretended respect and submission whenever he addressed her, but he read the truth in her eyes. In her soul, she mocked and challenged him. That Odo would not tolerate.

He bent to examine her work, shuffling the pieces of parchment in silence.

"The hand," he said, "is not sufficiently fair. See here—and here"—he stabbed at the parchment with one long, white finger—"you do not round your letters sufficiently. Child, what explanation can you offer for such sloppy work?"

Sloppy work! Joan was indignant. She had just glossed ten pages of text—far more than any of the other students could have done in twice the time. Her explanations were accurate and complete—even Odo did not try to deny that. She had seen his eyes flicker as they scanned the passage with her elegant handling of the subjunctive.

"Well?" Odo prodded her. He wanted her to defy him, to answer him boldly. *Arrogant and unnatural creature.* He knew she sought to violate the God-given order of the universe by usurping men's rightful authority over her. *Go ahead,* he willed her. *Speak your mind.* If she did, he would have her where he wanted her.

Joan fought to keep her emotions under control. She knew what Odo was trying to do. But no matter how hard he provoked her, she would not oblige him. She would not provide him with a reason to dismiss her from the schola. Keeping her voice flat, she replied dryly, "I have no excuse, sir."

"Very well," Odo said. "As punishment for your indolence, you will copy out the passage from First Timothy, chapter two, verses eleven and twelve, twenty-five times in a *good* hand before you leave."

Dark resentment boiled inside Joan. Nasty, narrow-minded man! If only she could tell him what she thought of him!

"Yes, sir." She kept her eyes lowered, so he could not read her thoughts.

Odo was disappointed. Still, the girl could not keep this up forever. Sooner or later—the thought made him smile—she would give herself away. When she did, he would be waiting.

He left her and went to check on his other students.

Joan sighed and picked up her stylus. First Timothy, chapter two, verses eleven and twelve. She knew it well enough; it was not the first time Odo had levied this punishment. It was a quotation from St. Paul: "I do not permit a woman to be a teacher, nor must a woman domineer over a man; she should be quiet and listen with due submission."

SHE was halfway through the writing when she first sensed something wrong. She looked up. Odo was gone. The boys were standing in a knot by the door, talking. That was odd. Usually they rushed from the room as soon as lessons were over. She watched them warily. John stood on the outer fringe of the little group, listening. She caught his eye, and he smiled and waved.

She smiled in return, then went back to her writing. But a tiny prickle of alarm raised the hairs on her neck. Were the boys planning something? They frequently teased and tormented her—Odo did nothing to stop them—and though she had steeled herself to their abuse, she still dreaded it.

Hurriedly she finished the last few lines and rose to leave. The boys were standing by the door. She knew they were waiting for her. She lifted her chin determinedly. Whatever they had in store for her, she would walk past quickly and have done with it.

Her cloak hung on a wooden peg near the door. Making an elaborate gesture of ignoring the boys, she retrieved it, fastened it carefully round her neck, and pulled up the hood.

Something heavy and wet pooled on the top of her head. Immediately she tugged at the hood, but it would not come off. The sticky wetness oozed downward. She reached up and touched it; her fingers came away coated with a thick, mucousy substance. *Gum arabic.* A common material in schoolrooms and *scriptoria,* it was used, with vinegar and charcoal, to make ink. She wiped her hand on her cloak, but the gum arabic clung stickily. Frantically, she pulled at the hood again and yelped as her hair was yanked painfully by the roots.

Her cry elicited a shout of laughter from the boys. She walked quickly toward the door. The group parted as she drew near, forming a line on either side.

"*Lusus naturae!*" they taunted her. "Freak of nature!"

Halfway down the line she saw John. He was laughing and shouting insults along with the others. She met his eyes; he flushed and looked away.

She kept walking. Too late she saw the flash of blue cloth near the floor. She tripped and fell clumsily, landing heavily on her side.

John, she thought. *He tripped me.*

She got to her feet, wincing as a sharp pain shot down her side. The disgusting slime oozed from under the hood onto her face. She wiped at it, trying to keep it out of her eyes, but it was no use. It slid glutinously over her eyebrows onto her lids, gumming her eyelashes, making it impossible to see clearly.

Laughing, the boys crowded in, shoving her back and forth, trying to make her fall again. She heard John's voice among the others, calling out insults. Through the thick film that covered her eyes, the room spun dizzyingly in alternating patterns of light and color. She could no longer make out the door.

She felt a sudden sting of tears.

Oh no, she thought. That was what they wanted—to make her weep and plead for mercy, to show some weakness, so they could mock her as a coward of a girl.

They shall not have that. I will not give them that.

She held herself straight, willing herself not to cry. This display of self-control only inflamed them, and they began to hit harder. The biggest of the boys struck her forcefully on the neck. The blow staggered her, and she fought to keep her feet.

A man's voice shouted in the distance. Had Odo come at last to put an end to this?

"What is happening here?"

This time she recognized the voice. Gerold. There was a tone in his voice she had never heard before. The boys backed away from her so suddenly she almost fell again.

Gerold's arm was around her shoulder, steadying her. She leaned into him gratefully.

"Well, Bernhar." Gerold addressed the biggest boy, the one who had hit her on the neck. "Wasn't it just last week I watched you at weapons practice, trying so desperately to keep out of range of Eric's sword that you could not manage a single strike? Yet I see that you have no difficulty fighting when your opponent is a defenseless girl."

Bernhar stammered an explanation, but Gerold cut him off.

"You may tell that to His Lordship the bishop. He will send for you when he learns of this. Which he will, this very day."

The silence around them was absolute. Gerold lifted Joan in his arms. She felt with some surprise the rippling power of his arms and back. He was so tall and lean, she had not realized he was so strong. She tilted her head away so the disgusting slime that covered her would not mar his tunic.

Halfway to his mount, Gerold turned. "One thing more. From what I have witnessed, she is braver than any of you. Yes, and smarter too, for all that she is a girl."

Joan felt the start of tears in her eyes. No one had ever spoken for her like that save Aesculapius.

Gerold was—different.

The bud of a rose grows in darkness. It knows nothing of the sun, yet it pushes at the darkness that confines it until at last the walls give way and the rose bursts forth, spreading its petals into the light.

I love him.

The thought was as startling as it was sudden. What could it mean? She could not be in love with Gerold. He was a nobleman, a great lord, and she was a canon's daughter. He was a mature man of twenty-eight winters, and Joan knew he thought of her as a child, though in fact she was almost thirteen and would soon be a woman grown.

Besides, he had a wife.

Joan's mind was a whirl of confusing emotions.

Gerold lifted her onto his horse and mounted behind. The boys stood huddled before the door, not daring to speak. Joan leaned back into Gerold's arms, feeling his strength, drawing upon it.

"Now," Gerold said, spurring the horse into a canter, "I will take you home."

≽| 9 |≼

COUNT Gerold, *grafio vir illuster* of this far northeastern march of the imperial realm, flicked his new chestnut into a gallop as he neared the motte on which his manor stood. The horse responded smartly, anticipating a warm stable and a pile of fresh hay. Beside him, the horse carrying Osdag, Gerold's venery servant, also lengthened its stride, though the weight of the slaughtered stag tied across its back caused it to lag.

It had been a good day's hunt. On a whim, for usually a hunting sortie consisted of six or more men, Gerold had gone out with only Osdag and two of the brachet hounds as companions. Luck had been with them; almost immediately they found deer's spoor, which Osdag scooped up in his hunting horn and scrutinized with a trained eye. "A hart," he announced, "and a big one." They tracked him for the better part of an hour until they sighted him in a small clearing. Gerold lifted his ivory oliphant to his lips and blew a series of soft, one-pitch notes, and the brachet hounds leapt eagerly to the chase. It had not been easy bringing the beast to bay with only two men and two dogs, but they had cornered it at last, and Gerold had dispatched it with one quick thrust of his lance. It was, as Osdag had predicted, a fine, large beast; with winter coming on, it would make a welcome addition to the Villaris larder.

Some distance away, Gerold spied Joan sitting cross-legged on the grass. He sent Osdag ahead to the stables and rode toward her. He had grown surprisingly attached to the girl over the past year. She was a strange one, there was no denying it—too much alone, too solemn for her years, but with a good heart and a keen intelligence that Gerold found very appealing.

Drawing near to where Joan sat still as one of the reliefs on the cathedral door, Gerold dismounted and led the chestnut forward. Joan was so deep in concentration that he got within ten yards of her before she saw him. Then she rose to her feet, blushing. Gerold was amused. She was incapable of disguise—a trait Gerold found quite charming, as it was so different from . . . what he was used to. There was no mistaking her childlike infatuation with him.

"You were deep in thought," he said.

"Yes." She rose and came over to admire the chestnut. "Did he handle well?"

"Perfectly. He's a fine mount."

"Oh yes." She stroked the chestnut's shining mane. She had an excellent appreciation of horses, perhaps because she had grown up without them. From what Gerold had been able to make out, her family had lived as poorly as any coloni, though her father was a canon of the Church.

The horse nuzzled her ear, and she laughed delightedly. An attractive girl, Gerold thought, though she would never be a beauty. Her large, intelligent eyes were set deep, her strong jaw and wide, straight shoulders gave her a boyish appearance, heightened now by the short white-gold hair that curled around her face, reaching barely to the tops of her ears. After that episode at the schola, they had been obliged to cut her hair down to the scalp; there had been no other way to remove the gum arabic smeared through every strand.

"What were you thinking about?"

"Oh. Just something that happened at the schola today."

"Tell me."

She looked at him. "Is it true that the cubs of the white wolf are born dead?"

"What?" Gerold was accustomed to her odd questions, but this one was stranger than usual.

"John and the other boys were talking. There's going to be a hunt for the white wolf, the one in the forest of Annapes."

Gerold nodded. "I know the one. A bitch, and a savage one—it hunts alone, apart from any pack, and knows no fear. Just last winter it attacked a band of travelers and carried off a small child before anyone could lift hand to bow to stop it. They say it now has a belly full of kits—I suppose they mean to kill it before it gives birth?"

"Yes. John and the others are excited, for Ebbo said his father promised to take him along on the hunt."

"So?"

"Odo was adamant against it. He would personally see the hunt called off, he said, for the white wolf is a holy beast, a living manifestation of Christ's resurrection."

Gerold's eyebrows lifted skeptically.

Joan continued. " 'Its cubs are born dead,' Odo said, 'and then in three days' time their sire licks them into life. It is a miracle so rare and so holy that none has ever witnessed it.' "

"What did you say to that?" Gerold asked. He knew her well enough by now to know that she would have had something to say.

"I asked how this was known to be true, if it had never been witnessed."

Gerold laughed out loud. "I'll wager our schoolmaster did not appreciate the question!"

"No. It was irreverent, he said. And also illogical, for the moment of the Resurrection was also never witnessed, yet no one doubts *its* truth."

Gerold laid a hand on Joan's shoulder. "Never mind, child."

There was a pause, as if she were debating whether to say anything further. Suddenly she looked up at him, her young face intent and deeply earnest. "How *can* we be sure of the truth of the Resurrection? If no one ever witnessed it?"

He was so startled that he jerked on the reins, and the chestnut started. Gerold placed a hand on the russet flank, gentling him.

Like most of his peers in this northern part of the Empire, landed magnates who had reached their manhood under the reign of old Emperor Karolus, who held to the old ways, Gerold was a Christian in the loosest sense. He attended mass, gave alms, and was careful to keep the feasts and outward observances. He followed those teachings of church doctrine that did not interfere with the execution of his manorial rights and duties, and ignored the rest.

But Gerold understood the way of the world, and he recognized danger when he saw it.

"You did not ask that of Odo!"

"Why not?"

"God's teeth!" This could mean trouble. Gerold had no liking for Odo, a little man of narrow ideas and even narrower spirit. But this was exactly the kind of weapon Odo needed to embarrass Fulgentius and force Joan from the schola. Or—it did not bear thinking of— even worse.

"What did he say?"

"He did not answer. He was very angry, and he . . . reprimanded me." She flushed.

Gerold let out his breath in a soft whistle. "Well, what did you expect? You are old enough now to know that there are some questions one does not ask."

"Why?" The large, gray-green eyes, so much deeper and wiser than other children's, fixed on him intently. *Pagan eyes,* Gerold thought, *eyes that would never look down before man or God.* It troubled him to think what must have gone into the making of those eyes.

"Why?" she asked again, insistent.

"One simply doesn't, that's all." He was irritated by her prodding. Sometimes the girl's intelligence, which so far outpaced her physical growth, was unsettling.

Something—hurt, or was it anger?—flared briefly in her eyes and then was masked. "I should return to the house. The tapestry for the hall is nearing completion, and your lady may need help with the finishing." Chin lifted, she turned to go.

Gerold was amused. So much wounded dignity in one so young! The thought of Richild, his wife, requiring Joan's help with the tapestry was absurd. She had frequently complained to him about Joan's clumsiness with the needle; Gerold himself had witnessed the girl's frustrated efforts to force her awkward fingers to obey, and seen the sorry results of her labors.

His irritation dissipated, he said, "Don't be offended. If you wish to get on in the world, you must have more patience with your betters."

She peered at him sideways, assessing his words, then threw her head back and laughed. The sound was delightful, full throated and musical, wholly infectious. Gerold was charmed. The girl could be stubborn and quick to anger, but she had a warm heart and a ready wit.

He cupped her chin. "I did not mean to be harsh," he said. "It's just that you surprise me sometimes. You are so wise about some things, and so stupid about others."

She started to speak, but he held a finger to her lips. "I don't know the answer to your question. But I know the question itself is dangerous. There are many who would say such a thought is heresy. Do you understand what that means, Joan?"

She nodded gravely. "It is an offense against God."

"Yes. It is that, and more than that. It could mean the forfeit of your hopes, Joan, of your future. Of—your very life."

There. He had said it. The gray-green eyes regarded him unwaveringly. There was no going back now. He would have to tell her all of it.

"Four winters ago a group of travelers was stoned to death, not far from here, in the fields bordering the cathedral. Two men, a woman, and a boy, not much older than you are now."

He was a seasoned soldier, a veteran of the Emperor's campaigns against the barbarian Obodrites, yet his flesh crawled, remembering. Death, even horrible death, held no surprises for him. But he had recoiled from this killing. The men were unarmed, and the other two . . . The dying had taken a long time, the woman and the boy suffering the longest, since the men had tried to shield them with their bodies.

"Stoned?" Joan's eyes were wide. "But why?"

"They were Armenians, members of the sect known as Paulicians. They were on their way to Aachen, and they were unfortunate enough to pass through just after a hailstorm struck the vineyards. In less than an hour, the entire crop was lost. In such times, people seek a reason for their troubles. When they looked around, there they were—strangers, and of a suspect set of mind. *Tempestarii*, they were called, who had used enchantments to unchain the violent storm. Fulgentius tried to defend them, but they were questioned and their ideas found to be heretical. Ideas, Joan"—he fixed her with a level gaze—"not so very different from the question you asked Odo today."

She fell silent, staring off into the distance. Gerold said nothing, giving her time.

"Aesculapius once said something like that to me," she said at last. "Some ideas are dangerous."

"He was a wise man."

"Yes." Her eyes softened with remembrance. "I will be more careful."

"Good."

"Now," she said, "tell me. How *do* we know that the story of the Resurrection is true?"

Gerold laughed helplessly. "You"—he rumpled the cropped white-gold hair—"are incorrigible." Seeing that she still waited for an answer, he added, "Very well. I'll tell you what I think."

Her eyes lit with eager interest. He laughed again.

"But not now. Pistis needs tending. Come find me before vespers and we will talk."

Joan's admiration shone undisguised in her eyes. Gerold stroked her cheek. She was hardly more than a child, but there was no denying that she moved him. Well, his own marital bed was cold enough,

God knew, for him to enjoy the warmth of such innocent affection without too great a burden of conscience.

The chestnut nuzzled Joan. She said, "I have an apple. May I give it to him?"

Gerold nodded. "Pistis deserves a reward. He did well today; he'll make a first-rate hunter one day, or I'm much mistaken."

She reached into her scrip, withdrew a small greenish red apple, and held it out to the chestnut, who lipped it gently, then took the whole fruit into his mouth. As she withdrew her hand, Gerold saw a flash of red. She realized he had seen and tried to hide the hand, but he caught it and held it up to the light. A deep furrow of torn flesh and drying blood scored the tender inside of the palm, cut clear across.

"Odo?" Gerold said quietly.

"Yes." She winced as he gently fingered the edges of the wound. Odo had obviously used the rod more than once, and with considerable force; the wound was deep and needed immediate tending to prevent corruption from setting in.

"We must see to this right away. Return to the house; I will meet you there." It was an effort to keep his voice steady. He was surprised at the intensity of his emotion. Odo had undeniably been within his rights to discipline her. Indeed, it was probably for the best that he had struck her, for, having vented his anger in this way, he was less likely to carry the matter further. Nevertheless, the sight of the wound roused in Gerold a strong, unreasoning fury. He would have liked to throttle Odo.

"It is not so bad as it looks." Joan was watching him closely with those wise, deep eyes.

Gerold checked the wound again. It was deep, centered right in the most sensitive part of the hand. Any other child would have wept and cried out with pain. She had not said a word, even when questioned.

Yet just a few weeks ago, when they had to cut her hair to get the gum arabic out, she had screamed and fought like a Saracen. Later, when Gerold asked why she had resisted so, she could offer no clearer explanation than that the sound of the knife ripping through her hair had frightened her.

A strange girl, no doubt of it. Perhaps that was why he found her so intriguing.

"Father!" Dhuoda, Gerold's younger daughter, burst into view, running down the hill of the motte toward where Joan and he stood among the trees. They waited till she drew up to them, flushed and panting from her run. "Father!" Dhuoda raised her arms expectantly, and Gerold grabbed her and swung her up and around while she squealed exuberantly. When he thought she had had enough, he set her down.

Flushed and excited, Dhuoda tugged on his arm. "Oh, Father, come see! Lupa has given birth to five pups. May I have one for my own, Father? Can it sleep on my bed?"

Gerold laughed. "We'll have to see. But first"—he held her firmly, for she had already turned to race back to the house ahead of him— "first take Joan back to the house; her hand is injured and needs looking after."

"Her hand? Show me," she demanded of Joan, who held out her hand with a rueful smile. "Ooooooh." Dhuoda's eyes widened in horrified fascination as she examined it. "How did it happen?"

"She can tell you on the way back," Gerold interrupted impatiently. He did not like the look of that wound; the sooner it was seen to, the better. "Hurry now, and do as I told you."

"Yes, Father." Dhuoda said to Joan sympathetically, "Does it hurt *very* much?"

"Not enough to keep me from reaching the gate first!" Joan replied, and broke into a run.

Dhuoda squealed with delight and took off after her. The two girls ran up the hill of the motte together, laughing.

Gerold watched, smiling, but his eyes were troubled.

WINTER came, marked indelibly in Joan's mind by her passage into womanhood. She was thirteen and should have expected it, but still it took her by surprise—the sudden appearance of a dark brown stain on her linen tunic and the tightening pain in her abdomen. She knew immediately what it was—she had heard her mother and the women in Gerold's household talk about it often enough, and seen them washing out their rags each month. Joan spoke to a maidservant, who ran to bring her a tall pile of clean rags, winking knowingly as she handed them over.

Joan hated it. Not just the pain and the bother, but the very idea of what was happening. She felt betrayed by her own body, which appeared to be rearranging itself almost daily into new and unfamiliar contours. When the boys at the schola began to take mocking notice of her budding breasts, she bound them tightly with strips of cloth. It was painful, but the effect was worth it. Her gender had been a source of misery and frustration for as long as she could remember, and she meant to fight this emerging evidence of her femininity as long as possible.

WINTARMANOTH brought an iron frost that gripped the land like an oppressive fist. The cold was enough to make one's teeth ache. Wolves and other forest predators prowled nearer the town than ever before; few villagers ventured abroad without a pressing reason.

Gerold urged Joan not to go to the schola, but she would not be dissuaded. Every morning, excepting the Sabbath, she donned her thick wool cloak and belted it tightly around her waist to keep out the wind; then, hunching her body against the cold, she walked the two miles to the cathedral. When the high, frigid winds of Hornung came, driving the cold across the roads in bitter gusts, Gerold had a horse saddled every day and rode Joan to and from the schola himself.

Though Joan saw her brother every day at the schola, John never spoke to her now. He was still dismally slow at his studies, but his skill in the use of sword and lance had won the respect of the other boys, and he visibly flourished in their companionship. He had no wish to jeopardize his newfound sense of belonging by acknowledging a sister who was an embarrassment. He turned away whenever she approached.

The girls of the town kept their distance as well. They regarded Joan with suspicion, excluding her from their games and gossip. She was a freak of nature—male in intellect, female in body, she fit in nowhere; it was as if she belonged to a third, amorphous sex.

She was alone. Except, of course, for Gerold. But Gerold was enough. Joan was happy just to be near him, to talk and laugh and speak of things she could discuss with no one else in the world.

One cold day after she and Gerold had returned from the schola, he beckoned to her. "Come," he said, "I have something to show you."

He led her through the winding hall of the manor to the solar and the small cabinet in which he kept his papers. From it he withdrew a long, rectangular object and handed it to her.

A book! Somewhat old and frayed at the edges, but intact. In fine gold letters on the wooden cover was written the title: *De rerum natura.*

De rerum natura. The great work of Lucretius! Aesculapius had frequently spoken of its importance. There was only one copy extant, it was said, and that one kept close and carefully in the great library of Lorsch. Yet here was Gerold offering it to her as casually as if it were a choice piece of meat.

"But how . . . ?" She lifted wondering eyes to his.

"What is written may be copied," he answered with a conspiratorial smile. "For a price. A considerable price, in this case. The abbot bargained hard, saying he was short of scribes. And, indeed, it has taken more than ten months to complete the work. But here it is. And not one denarius more than it's worth."

Joan's eyes glowed as she fingered the cover of the book. In all her months at the schola, she had never been allowed to work with texts such as this. Odo absolutely forbade her to read the great classical works in the cathedral library, restricting her to the study of sacred texts, which were, he said, the only ones suitable for her weak and impressionable female mind. Proudly she had not let him see how deeply this grieved her. *Go ahead, bar your library,* she thought defiantly. *You cannot put bars on my mind.* Nevertheless, it had been infuriating, knowing what treasures of knowledge were locked away from her. Gerold had seen that; he always seemed to know what she was thinking and feeling. How could she help but love him?

"Go on," Gerold said. "And when you have done, come to me and we will talk over what you have read. You will be most interested in what he has to say."

Joan's eyes opened wide in astonishment. "Then you—"

"Yes. I have read it. Does that surprise you?"

"Yes. I mean no—but—" Joan's cheeks pinkened as she stumbled for a reply. She had not known he could read Latin. It was rare for nobles and men of property to read and write at all. It was the job of the manor steward, a man of letters, to keep accounts and carry out any necessary correspondence. Naturally Joan had assumed . . .

Gerold laughed, plainly enjoying her embarrassment. "It's all right. You could not have known. I was some years studying at the Schola Palatina when old Emperor Karolus was alive."

"The Schola Palatina!" The name was legend. The school founded by the Emperor had turned out some of the finest minds of the day. The great Alcuin himself had been the master teacher.

"Yes. My father sent me, intending me for a scholar. The work was interesting, and I enjoyed it well enough, but I was young and hadn't the temperament to make a steady diet of it. When the Emperor called for men to campaign with him against the Obodrites, I went, though I was only thirteen. I was gone some years, perhaps would be there still, but then my eldest brother died, and I was called home to assume inheritance of this estate."

Joan regarded him wonderingly. He was a scholar, a man of letters! How could she not have known! She should have guessed from the way he had spoken with her about her studies.

"Off with you." Gerold shooed her away amiably. "I know you cannot wait. There's an hour yet before supper. But listen carefully for the bell."

Joan ran upstairs to the dortoir she shared with Dhuoda and Gisla. She went to her bed and opened the book. She read slowly, savoring the words, stopping occasionally to make note of a particularly elegant phrase or argument. When the light in the room faded with the dusk, she lit a candle and kept working.

She read on and on, completely forgetting the time and would have missed supper entirely had not Gerold, in the end, sent a servant to fetch her.

THE weeks passed quickly, charged with the excitement of Joan and Gerold's work together. Waking each morning, Joan wondered impatiently how she would ever make it until after vespers, when, supper over and the necessary devotions past, she and Gerold could resume their study of Lucretius.

De rerum natura was a revelation—a wonder of a book, rich in knowledge and wisdom. In order to discover truth, Lucretius said, one had only to observe the natural world. It was an idea which made good sense in Lucretius's time but which was extraordinary, even revolutionary in anno domini 827. Nevertheless, it was a philosophy that appealed strongly to Joan's and Gerold's practical turn of mind.

It was, in fact, entirely because of Lucretius that Gerold trapped the white wolf.

Joan returned from the schola one day to find Villaris in an uproar. The household dogs were barking themselves hoarse; the horses ran wildly round the perimeter of their corral; the entire bailey was echoing with a deafening series of terrifying growls.

In the middle of the forecourt, Joan found the object of all the excitement. A large white wolf fought and twisted and hurled itself furiously against the sides of an oblong cage. The bars of the cage, constructed of sturdy oakwood three inches thick, cracked and groaned under the fury of the beast's assault. Gerold and his men ringed the area warily, bows and spears at the ready, lest the creature should succeed in breaking loose. Gerold gestured to Joan to stay back. As she watched the she-wolf's strange pink eyes, glittering with hatred, Joan found herself willing the bars to hold firm.

After a time the wolf tired and stood panting, legs planted stolidly and head lowered, glowering. Gerold lowered his spear and came over to Joan.

"Now we put Odo's theory to the test!"

For a fortnight the two of them kept vigil, determined, if at all possible, to observe the very moment of birth. Nothing happened. The wolf sulked in her cage and showed no sign of an impending delivery. They had almost begun to doubt whether the beast was pregnant when she abruptly went into labor.

It happened during Joan's turn at the watch. The wolf alternately paced and shifted restlessly on the floor, as if unable to get comfortable. Finally she grunted and began to heave. Joan ran to get Gerold and found him in the solar with Richild. Bursting in upon them like a whirlwind, Joan dispensed with the normal courtesies. "Come quickly! It's started!"

Gerold rose immediately. Richild frowned and looked as if she would speak, but there was no time to waste. Joan spun around and ran back along the covered portico that led to the main courtyard. Gerold, who had stopped to fetch a lantern, followed close behind. Neither one of them witnessed the look on Richild's face as she watched them go.

By the time they reached the bailey, the wolf was straining hard. Joan and Gerold watched as the tip of one small paw began to emerge, followed by another, and then by a tiny, perfect head. Finally, with a last heave from the bitch, a small, dark body slid wetly onto the straw lining the bottom of the cage and lay still.

Joan and Gerold strained to see into the darkness of the cage. The newborn pup lay inert, completely covered by the birth sac, so they could hardly make out head from tail. His dam licked the sac off and ate it.

Gerold raised the lantern high against the bars of the cage to give more light. The newborn did not appear to be breathing.

The mother began to strain with the effort of a second delivery. Moments passed, and still the newborn cub did not move or give any sign of life.

Joan looked at Gerold with dismay. Was it so? Would it lie lifeless, waiting for its father to lick it into life? Had Odo been right, after all?

If so, then they had killed it, for they had taken it far from the father who would have given it life.

Once again the mother grunted; a second small body slid out, landing partly on top of the first. The impact jolted the firstborn, which twitched and let out a soft squeal of protest.

"Look!" The two of them prodded each other and pointed in exultant unison. They laughed, well pleased with the results of their experiment.

The two pups bumped their way over to their mother's side to nurse, even before she finished the throes of a third delivery.

Together, Gerold and Joan watched the beginning of this new family. Their hands reached out for each other in the dark, meeting and clasping in mutual understanding.

Joan had never felt so close to anyone in her life.

"WE MISSED you at vespers." Richild glared at them reprovingly from the portico. "It is the Eve of St. Norbert, have you forgotten? It sets a poor example when the lord of the manor absents himself from the holy devotions."

"I had something else to attend to," Gerold replied coolly.

Richild started to respond, but Joan interrupted excitedly.

"We watched the white wolf give birth to her pups! They are not born dead, despite what people say," she announced jubilantly. "Lucretius was right!"

Richild stared at her as if she were mad.

"All things in nature are explainable," Joan continued. "Don't you see? The pups were born alive, with no reliance on the supernatural, just like Lucretius said!"

"What godless speech is this? Child, are you feverish?"

Gerold stepped quickly between them. "Go to bed, Joan," he said over his shoulder. "It is late." He took Richild by the arm and firmly steered her into the house.

Joan remained where she was, listening to Richild's voice echo shrilly through the calm evening air.

"This is what comes of educating the girl beyond her capacity to learn. Gerold, you must cease to encourage her in these unnatural pursuits!"

Joan slowly made her way back to her sleeping chamber.

THEY killed the white wolf after she weaned her pups. She was dangerous, having already attacked and carried off one small child, and such a man-killer could not be set free. Her last-born did not survive; it was a sickly thing that lived only a few days. But the other two grew into robust and active pups, whose playful antics delighted Joan and Gerold. One had a coat of brown and gray mottled fur, typical of the forest wolves in this part of Frankland; Gerold made a gift of him to Fulgentius, who derived a wicked pleasure in pointedly displaying him to Odo. The other pup, the firstborn, had his mother's snow white coat and singular, opalescent eyes; this one they kept. "Luke," Joan and Gerold called him, in Lucretius's honor, and their affection for the frisky, energetic pup strengthened the developing bond between them.

10

THERE was to be a fair in St.-Denis! The news was astonishing—there had not been a fair or a market in the entire kingdom for more years than most people could count. But some of the old ones—like Burchard, the tanner—remembered a time when there had actually been two or three fairs a year in Frankland. So they said, though it was hard to credit the truth of it. Of course, those were in the days when Emperor Karolus of blessed memory was in his prime, and the roads and bridges still well maintained, no thieves or charlatans plying the ways, nor yet—God defend it!—the swift, savage terror of the Norsemen swooping down without warning upon the land. Now travel was too hazardous to make fairs profitable; merchants did not dare to transport precious goods over the unsafe roads, and people did not wish to chance their lives on the journey.

Nevertheless, there was to be a fair. And it would be a wonder, if even half of what the herald who brought the news said was true. There would be merchants from Byzantium bringing exotic spices, silks, and brocades; Venetian traders with cloaks of peacock feathers and embossed leather; Frisian slave dealers with their human cargo of Slavs and Saxons; Lombards with bags of salt piled high inside ships whose bright orange sails bore the signs of the zodiac; and all manner of amusements: rope dancers and acrobats, storytellers, jongleurs, performing dogs and bears.

St.-Denis was not close by—in fact, it was some one hundred fifty miles from Dorstadt, a fortnight's journey, over crumbling roads and fast-rushing rivers. But no one was daunted by that. Everyone who could get hold of a horse or mule or even a pony was going.

Gerold's entourage, as befitted that of a count, was large. Fifteen of Gerold's *fideles,* well armed, would ride with them, as well as several servants to attend the family. Joan was to go, and as a special courtesy—Joan was sure it was Gerold's idea—John was invited as well. Richild's preparations had been exacting; she had taken pains to ensure they would want for nothing in comfort and safety for the journey. For days now, wagons had been pulled into the castle bailey and loaded with goods.

The morning of the departure, Villaris was astir with activity. Grooms scurried about, feeding and loading the packhorses; the pantler and his scullions sweated over the great oven, whose tall chimney belched huge puffs of smoke; the blacksmith worked furiously at his forge, finishing the last of a supply of horseshoes, nails, and wagon fittings. Sounds blended and rose in noisy confusion: maidservants shouted to one another above the deeper calls and whistles of the grooms, cows mooed and stamped as they were hastily milked, one overladen donkey brayed loudly in protest against its load. The bustling activity stirred up dust from the dry earth; it rose into the air and hung in a shimmering mist, lit by the brilliant spring sunshine.

Joan lingered in the courtyard, watching the last-minute preparations, enjoying the excitement. Luke pranced around her, ears pricked and opalescent eyes alight with expectation. He was going on the journey too, for, as Gerold had declared, the six-month-old pup had become so attached to Joan there was no separating them. Joan laughed and petted Luke, his white fur soft under her hand; he licked her cheek and sat back with his mouth stretched wide, as if he were laughing too.

"If you've nothing better to do than stand about gaping, give the pantler a hand." Richild gave Joan a push toward the kitchen, where the pantler waved flour-coated hands in a frenzy of activity. He had been up all night, baking rolls and pies for the journey.

By midmorning, the household was packed. The chaplain offered a brief prayer for the safe deliverance of the travelers, and the procession of wagons and horses moved out slowly onto the road. Joan rode in the first cart, behind Gerold and his men, along with Richild, Gisla, and Dhuoda, and the three villein girls who served as the ladies' personal attendants. The women jounced against the hard wooden seats as the cartwheels bumped over the pitted, uneven road. Luke trotted alongside, keeping a watchful eye on Joan. Joan looked ahead and saw John riding with the men, seated comfortably astride a fine roan mare.

I sit a horse as well as he, Joan thought. Gerold had spent many hours teaching her to ride, and she was now an accomplished horsewoman.

As if suddenly aware of her scrutiny, John turned around and gave her a knowing smile, at once intimate and malicious. Then he kicked his horse into a canter and rode up next to Gerold. They spoke; Gerold threw back his head and laughed.

Jealousy rose sharply within her. What could John have to say to Gerold that would amuse him so? They had nothing in common. Gerold was a learned man, a scholar. John knew nothing of such matters. Yet now he rode beside Gerold, talked with him, laughed with him, while she lurched along behind in this miserable dogcart.

Because she was a girl. Not for the first time she cursed the stroke of fate that had made her so.

"It is impolite to stare, Joan." Richild's dark eyes regarded Joan disdainfully.

Joan tore her eyes away from Gerold. "I'm sorry, my lady."

"Keep your hands folded on your lap," Richild remonstrated, "and your eyes turned down, as befits a modest woman."

Joan obediently followed her bidding.

"Proper deportment," Richild continued, "is a higher virtue in a lady than an ability to read—something you would know if you had been gently raised." She stared at Joan coolly for a few moments before returning her attention to her embroidery.

Joan watched her now out of the corner of her eye. She was certainly beautiful, in the pale, ascetic, slope-shouldered fashion of the day. Her creamy skin rose to an extremely high forehead, crowned by lustrous coils of thick black hair. Her eyes, fringed by long, dark lashes, were so deep a brown they appeared almost black. Joan felt a sharp pang of envy. Richild was everything that she was not.

"Come now, you must help us decide." Gisla, the elder daughter, beamed at Joan. "Which of my gowns should I wear for the wedding feast?" She giggled excitedly.

Gisla was fourteen, only a few weeks older than Joan, and already betrothed to Count Hugo, a Neustrian nobleman. Gerold and Richild were pleased, as the union was an advantageous match. The wedding was some six months away.

"Oh, Gisla, you have so many lovely things." And it was true. Joan had been astonished at the size of Gisla's wardrobe—enough to wear a different tunic every day for a fortnight if she chose. In Ingelheim, a girl had but one tunic, of strong woolen cloth if she was lucky, and she kept it carefully, for it would have to last many years. "I am sure Count Hugo will think you beautiful in any of them."

Gisla giggled again. A good-hearted but somewhat simple girl, she erupted into nervous laughter every time her affianced's name was mentioned.

"No, no," she said breathlessly. "You cannot wriggle out of it so easily. Listen. Mother thinks I should wear the blue, but I say the yellow. Come now, give me a proper answer."

Joan sighed. She liked Gisla, for all her giddiness and silly ways. They had shared a bed from the very first night, when Gerold had brought Joan home from the bishop's palace, weary and frightened. Gisla had welcomed Joan, been kind to her, and Joan would always be grateful. Still, there was no denying that conversation with Gisla could be trying, for her interests were entirely confined to clothes, food, and men. For the last few weeks, she had talked incessantly about the wedding, and it was beginning to try everyone's patience.

Joan smiled, making an effort to be obliging. "I think you should wear the blue. It matches your eyes."

"The blue? Really?" Gisla's brow furrowed. "But the yellow has the lovely lace trim on the front."

"Well, the yellow then."

"Still, the blue *does* match my eyes. Perhaps it would be better. What do you think?"

"*I* think that if I hear any more about that stupid wedding feast I shall scream," said Dhuoda. She was nine years old and resentful of all the attention her older sister had been getting over the past few weeks. "Who cares what color tunic you wear anyway!"

"Dhuoda, that remark is unbecoming a lady." Richild looked up from her embroidery to chastise her younger daughter.

"I'm sorry," Dhuoda said to Gisla contritely. But as soon as her mother looked away she stuck out her tongue at Gisla, who smiled back at her good-humoredly.

Richild said, "As for you, Joan, it is not for you to offer an opinion; Gisla will wear whatever *I* think best."

Joan flushed at the reprimand but said nothing.

"Count Hugo is such a handsome man." Bertha, one of the serving wenches, spoke up. A red-cheeked girl of no more than sixteen winters, she was new to household service, having been brought in a month ago to replace a girl dead of typhoid. "He looks so fine on his charger, with his ermine cloak and gloves."

Gisla giggled delightedly. Encouraged, Bertha continued. "And, mistress, from the way he looks at you, it cannot matter what tunic you wear. Come the wedding night, he'll have it off you quick enough!"

She laughed boisterously, pleased with her joke. Gisla tittered. The others in the wagon sat quietly, watching Richild.

Richild put down her embroidery, her eyes dark with anger. "What did you say?" she asked, in a tone ominously quiet.

"Uh—nothing, my lady," Bertha said.

"Oh, Mother, I am sure she did not mean—" Gisla tried ineffectually to intervene.

"Coarseness and filth! I will not suffer it in my presence!"

"I'm sorry, my lady," Bertha said, chastened. But she still smiled a little, not believing Richild could be truly angry.

Richild motioned Bertha to the open back of the cart. "Out."

"But, my lady!" Bertha wailed, at last comprehending the enormity of her error. "I did not mean—"

"Out!" Richild was adamant. "In penance for your impudence, you will walk the rest of the way."

It was a punishing journey to St.-Denis. Bertha looked ruefully at her feet, covered with rough, hemp-soled buskins. Joan felt sorry for her. Her remark had been heedless and ill advised, but the girl was young and new to service, and obviously had not meant to give offense.

"You will recite the paternoster aloud while you walk."

"Yes, my lady," Bertha said resignedly. She clambered out of the cart, took up a position alongside, and after a minute slowly began to recite, *"Pater Noster qui es in caelis . . ."* She spoke in an odd singsong style that emphasized all the wrong words. Joan was sure she had no idea what she was saying.

Richild returned to her embroidery. Her black hair shone in the sunlight as she bent her head over her stitching. Her lips were tight, her eyes hard with anger as she drove the needle through the thick cloth.

She is an unhappy woman, Joan thought. This was difficult to understand, for was she not married to Gerold? Yet theirs had been an arranged marriage, and although many such matches turned out to be happy ones, this one obviously had not. They slept in separate beds, and, if the servants' gossip was correct, had not known each other as man and wife for many years.

"Would you care to ride?" Gerold smiled down at her from astride his chestnut stallion. In his right hand he held the reins of Boda, a lively bay mare he knew Joan especially favored.

Joan blushed, embarrassed by what she had just been thinking. She had been so lost in thought that she had not seen Gerold ride back to retrieve Boda from the group of spare mounts and lead her toward the wagon.

"Ride with the men?" Richild frowned. "I won't permit it! It would not be proper!"

"Nonsense!" Gerold replied. "It does no harm, and the girl wants to ride, don't you, Joan?"

"I . . . I . . . ," she said awkwardly, caught in the middle and reluctant to further offend Richild.

Gerold raised an eyebrow. "Of course, if you'd rather remain in the wagon . . ."

"No!" Joan said quickly. "Please, I'd love to ride Boda." She stood in the cart and reached out her arms. Gerold laughed and caught her about the waist, swinging her high onto the saddle before him. Then, keeping the horses close, he hoisted her sideways onto Boda's back.

She settled into the saddle. In the wagon Gisla and Dhuoda looked on with surprise, Richild with glaring disapproval. Gerold appeared not to notice. Joan prodded Boda into a canter and rode quickly toward the front of the line. The smooth, rhythmic strides of the horse were a joy compared with the stiff jerking of the wagon. Luke ran alongside, tail held high, his laughing mouth registering a delight almost as great as Joan's.

She pulled up next to John, who could not conceal his dismay. Joan laughed, her spirits soaring. The road to St.-Denis would not be so long after all.

THEY crossed the tributary of the Rhine with no difficulty; the bridge there was sturdy and wide, one of those built in the days of Emperor Karolus and still maintained by the lord of that county. But the Meuse, at whose banks they arrived on the eighth day, presented a problem, for the bridge there had fallen into disrepair. The planks were rotten, and there were holes where one or two had dropped out completely, making passage impossible. Someone had improvised a rough bridge by tying a string of wooden boats together in a line; a person could cross by stepping through each of the boats in turn. But the boat bridge would not serve for so many people, horses, and wagons laden with goods. Gerold and two of his men ranged south along the riverbank, looking for a place to ford. An hour later they returned to report a likely spot two miles down where the river widened into shallows.

The party set off again, the wagons lurching wildly over the dense undergrowth along the riverbank. The women clutched the sides of their cart with both hands to keep from being thrown out. Bertha still walked alongside, her lips moving in unending recitation. The hemp on her buskins was worn through to the skin, and she had begun to limp; her toes were swollen, her soles cut and bleeding. Nevertheless, Joan noticed that she occasionally stole sidewards glances at Richild and her daughters and seemed to derive some small satisfaction from watching them pitch about in the wagon.

At last they reached the fording place. Gerold and several of the other mounted men rode down into the river first, to test the depth and levelness of the bottom. The water quickly swirled round them; it reached the bottom of their kirtles in midstream before it began to recede where the riverbed sloped upward to the opposite bank.

Gerold rode back, motioning the others forward. Without hesitation, Joan headed into the river, followed closely by Luke, who plunged in and swam with sure, confident movements. After a moment's hesitation, John and the others came after them.

The cold waters of the Meuse circled Joan. She gasped as the chill penetrated her clothes and reached her skin. Behind her the wagons slowly bumped down into the river, drawn forward by the mules. Bertha labored to keep up, pushing her way through the chilly water, which rose nearly to her shoulders.

Looking back, Joan saw that Bertha was in trouble. She rode toward her. The mare could carry both of them across with no trouble. She was no more than five feet away when the girl vanished, slipping beneath the surface of the water as quickly as if pulled by the feet. Joan halted, unsure what to do; then she urged her mount toward the widening rings of water marking the spot where Bertha had gone under.

"Stay back!" Gerold's hand grabbed the bridle, halting the mare. He broke a long branch off an overhanging birch, dismounted, and walked slowly back toward the bank, probing the riverbed. An arm's length away from the place where Bertha had disappeared, he stumbled and almost fell as the branch sank deep into the water.

"A hole!" He ripped off his mantle and dove in.

Suddenly everything was confusion. Men rode back and forth through the water, shouting instructions and beating the water with sticks.

Gerold was down there. They could be trampling him, hurting him, why couldn't they see that?

"Stop!" Joan screamed, but they paid no attention. She rode to Egbert, chief of Gerold's retainers, and grabbed him fiercely by the arm. "Stop!" she said.

Startled, Egbert was about to shrug her off, but she stared him down. "Tell them to stop; they are making it worse." He drew up, signaling the others. They reined in, ringing the water hole, and waited in tense concentration.

A minute passed. Behind them the first wagon gained the far bank and bumped safely onto land. Joan did not notice. Her eyes were fixed on the spot where Gerold had dived under.

Fear moistened her palms, made her hands slip on the reins. The bay mare, sensing trouble, whinnied and shifted. Luke threw back his head and howled.

Deus Misereatur, she prayed. *Dear God, take pity. Demand what sacrifice You will, only let him rise from this.*

Two minutes.

It was too long. He needed to come up for air.

She swung down out of the saddle into the cold water. She could not swim, but she did not stop to think of that. She began splashing wildly toward the hole. Luke leapt back and forth in front of her, trying to block her advance, but she shoved past him. Only one thought occupied all her mind—reach Gerold, pull him out, save him.

She was half a yard from the water hole when there was a splash and a plume of water. Gerold broke the surface in one leap and stood gasping, his red hair smeared across his face.

"Gerold!" Joan's exultant shout sounded clear above the cheers of the men. Gerold turned to her and nodded. Then he took a deep breath, ready to dive again.

"Look!" The mule driver in the first wagon pointed downriver.

A round blue object rose and fell gently against the far bank. Bertha's robe was blue.

They remounted and rode downriver. In the water, caught in branches and debris that had accumulated along the bank, Bertha was floating on her back, limbs thrown wide as if discarded, her lifeless features fixed into a terrible expression of helplessness and fear.

"Take her up." Gerold spoke brusquely to his men. "We will bear her to the church in Prüm for a decent burial."

Joan began to tremble violently, unable to pull her eyes away from Bertha. In death, she looked so much like Matthew had—the pale gray skin, the half-closed eyes, the slackened mouth.

Suddenly Gerold's arms were around her, turning her head away, pressing it to his shoulder. She closed her eyes and clung to him. The men dismounted and splashed into the water; she heard the soft, wet rustle of the river reeds as they released the weight of Bertha's body.

"You were coming after me back there, weren't you?" Gerold whispered, his mouth close to her ear. He spoke wonderingly, as if the realization had just struck him.

"Yes." She nodded, never taking her head from his shoulder.

"Can you swim?"

"No," she admitted, and felt Gerold's arms tighten around her as they stood together by the river's edge.

Behind them, the men slowly carried Bertha's body toward the wagons. The chaplain walked alongside, his head bowed as he recited the prayer for the dead. Richild was not praying with him. Her head was high, and she was staring at Joan and Gerold.

Joan stepped out of the circle of Gerold's arms.

"What is it?" His look was warm with affection and concern.

Richild was still watching them.

"N-nothing."

He followed the direction of her gaze. "Ah." Gently he lifted a stray lock of white-gold hair from her face. "Shall we rejoin the others then?"

Side by side they walked to the wagons. Then Gerold left to consult with the chaplain about the disposition of the body.

Richild said, "Joan, you will ride in the wagon for the rest of the journey. You will be far safer here with us."

It was useless to protest. Joan climbed into the wagon.

The men gently laid Bertha in one of the rear wagons, moving sacks aside to make room. A household servant, an older woman, cried out and threw herself onto Bertha's body.

The woman began the traditional keening wail for the dead.

Everyone waited in a respectful, embarrassed silence. After a decent interval, the chaplain approached and spoke softly to the woman. She raised her head; her eyes, wild with grief and pain, fixed on Richild.

"You!" she screamed. "It was you, lady! You killed her! She was a good girl, my Bertha, she would have served you well! Her death is on your head, lady. On your head!"

Two of Richild's retainers grabbed the woman roughly and hurried her away, still screaming imprecations.

The chaplain approached Richild, wringing his hands in nervous apology. "She is Bertha's mother. Grief has driven the poor woman quite out of her senses. Of course the child's death was an accident. A tragic accident."

"No accident, Wala," Richild said sternly. "It was God's will."

Wala blanched. "Of course, of course." As Richild's chaplain, a private "house priest," Wala held a position little better than that of a common colonus; if he displeased her, she could have him whipped— or worse yet, cast out to starve. "God's will. God's will, lady, most assuredly."

"Go and speak to the woman, for the extremity of her grief has surely placed her soul in mortal danger."

"Ah, lady!" He fluttered long, white hands skyward. "Such heavenly forbearance! Such *caritas*!"

She dismissed him impatiently, and he hurried away, looking like a man who has been cut loose from the gallows just before the trap opens.

Gerold gave the command to start up, and the procession moved out, bumping along the riverbank back toward the road to St.-Denis. Behind them, in the rearmost wagon, the mother's screams gradually subsided into a steady, heart-wrenching sobbing. Dhuoda's eyes were moist with tears; even Gisla's unflagging high spirits were quenched. But Richild appeared entirely unshaken. Joan studied her appraisingly. Could anyone be that skillful at hiding her emotions, or was she really as cold as she appeared? Did the girl's death not weigh upon her conscience at all?

Richild looked at her. Joan turned her eyes away so she could not read her thoughts.

God's will?

No, my lady.

Your command.

THE first day of the fair was in full swing. People streamed through the huge iron gate that led to the open field fronting the Abbey of St.-Denis—peasants in ragged *bandelettes* and shirts of rude linen; noblemen and *fideles* in silk tunics crossed with golden baldrics, their wives elegantly bedecked in fur-trimmed mantles and jeweled head-dresses; Lombards and Aquitanians in their exotic bouffant pantaloons and boots. Never had Joan seen so odd or so large a conglomeration of humanity.

On the field, the stalls of the merchants crowded closely together, their various goods displayed in a gaudy, incoherent riot of color and form. There were robes and mantles of purple silk, scarlet phoenix skins, peacock's feathers, stamped leather jerkins, rare delicacies such as almonds and raisins, and all manner of scents and spices, pearls, gems, silver and gold. Still more merchandise poured through the gates, heaped high on wagons or carried in unwieldy piles upon the backs of the poorer vendors, bent almost double under the weight. More than one of these would not sleep that night from the pain of muscles strained past endurance, but in this way they avoided the ex-pensive tolls, the *rotaticum* and *saumaticum,* charged against goods carried in on wheeled vehicles and beasts of burden.

Inside the gate, Gerold said to Joan and John, "Hold out your hands." Into each of their outstretched palms, he placed a silver denarius. "Spend it wisely."

Joan stared at the shiny coin. She had seen denarii only once or twice before, and those at a distance, for in Ingelheim trade was ac-complished by barter; even her father's income, the *decima* tithed from the peasants of his parish, had been offered in goods and foodstuffs.

A whole denarius! It seemed a fortune beyond measure.

They wandered down the narrow, crowded passageways between the stalls. All around vendors hawked their merchandise, customers bargained hotly over prices, and performers of every kind—dancers, jugglers, acrobats, bear and monkey trainers—plied their trades. The din of innumerable deals, jests, and arguments surrounded them on every side, conducted in a hundred dialects and tongues.

It was easy to get lost in the jostling crowds. Joan took John's hand—to her surprise, he did not protest—and kept close to Gerold's side. Luke stayed right behind them, inseparable, as always, from Joan. Their small group was soon parted from Richild and the others, who had walked more slowly. Halfway down the first row of stalls, they stopped and waited for the others to catch up. Off to their left, a woman stood screaming at a pair of merchants pulling at either end of a piece of linen cloth laid out beside a long wooden ruler measuring exactly one ell.

"Stop!" the woman shouted. "You dunderheads! You are stretching it!" And indeed, it appeared as if the men would rip the cloth in half to make the most of its measure.

There was a loud burst of shouting and laughter from a crowd circling a small open enclosure a short distance ahead.

"Come on." John pulled on Joan's arm. She hesitated, not wanting to leave Gerold, but he saw what John wanted and good-naturedly shooed them in that direction.

Another great shout rose from the crowd as they drew close. Joan saw a man fall to his knees in the center of the enclosure, clutching his shoulder as if it were hurt. Quickly he got back up to his feet, and now Joan could see that in his other hand he held a thick, sturdy birch bough. Another man stood in the ring, similarly armed. The two of them circled each other, swinging the heavy sticks with ferocious abandon. There was an odd, high-pitched squeal as a blood-spattered pig ran frantically between the two men, its stubby legs pumping like matched butter churns. The two men swung at the pig, but their aim was wild; the one who had just fallen shrieked as he took a solid hit on his nether parts. The crowd roared with laughter.

John laughed along with the others, his eyes lit with interest. He tugged on the sleeve of a short, pockmarked peasant who stood beside them. "What's going on?" he asked excitedly.

The man grinned down at him, the holes in his face widening as the skin creased. "Why, they're after the pig, lad, d'ye see? Him as kills it, takes it home for his table."

Odd, Joan thought, as she watched the two men compete for the prize. They swung their sticks forcefully, but their blows were random and undirected, falling on thin air or on each other more often than on the hapless pig. There was something strange about the appearance of the man facing her. She looked more closely and saw a milky whiteness where his pupils should have been. Now the other man turned to face her; his eyes looked normal enough, but they stared out fixedly into space, vacant and unfocused.

The men were blind.

Another blow found its mark, and the milky-eyed man staggered sideways, clutching his head. John jumped up, clapping his hands and shouting with laughter along with the rest of the crowd. His eyes glittered with a strange excitement.

Joan turned away.

"Psst! Young mistress!" a voice called out to her. Across the way, a vendor was gesturing at her. She left John cheering on the bizarre combat and went to the man's stall, fronted by a long table displaying an assortment of religious relics. There were wooden crosses and medallions of every kind and description, as well as holy relics of several locally popular saints: a strand of hair from St. Willibrord, a fingernail of St. Romaric, two teeth of St. Waldetrudis, and a scrap of cloth from the robe of the virgin martyr St. Genovefa.

The man pulled a vial from his leather scrip.

"Know what this holds?" His voice was so low she could barely hear him over the surrounding din. She shook her head.

"Several drops of the milk"—his voice dropped still further—"of the Holy Virgin Mother."

Joan was stunned. So great a treasure! Here? Surely it should be enshrined in some great monastery or cathedral.

"One denarius," the man said.

One denarius! She fingered the silver coin in her pocket. The man held the vial out to her, and she took it, its surface cool in her hand. She had a brief vision of the look on Odo's face when she returned with such a prize for the cathedral.

The man smiled, holding out his hand, fingers waggling to coax the coin from her.

Joan hesitated. Why would this man sell so great a treasure for such a sum? It was worth a fortune to some great abbey or cathedral in need of a holy relic for pilgrims to venerate.

She lifted the cap off the vial and peered inside. Halfway down the length of the tube, the pale surface of the milk shimmered smooth and blue-white in the sunlight. Joan reached down and touched it with the tip of her little finger. Then she looked up, her keen eyes scanning the area around the stall. She laughed, lifted the vial to her lips, and drank.

The man gasped. "Are you woodly?" His face was contorted with anger.

"Delicious," Joan said, recapping the vial and handing it back to him. "My compliments to your goat."

"Why, you . . . you . . . ," the man sputtered, unable to find the words to express his rage and frustration. For a moment it seemed as if he might come round the table after her. There was a low growl; Luke, who until then had been sitting quietly, moved in front of Joan, a deep line furrowing the length of his muzzle, lifted at the sides to reveal a row of menacing white teeth.

"What is that?" The vendor stared at Luke's glittering eyes.

"That," a voice said behind Joan, "is a wolf."

It was Gerold. He had come up quietly during her interchange with the vendor. He stood loosely, his arms at his sides, his body relaxed, but his eyes were hard with warning. The vendor turned away, mumbling something under his breath. Gerold put his arm around Joan's shoulders and led her away, calling to Luke, who growled at the vendor one more time, then ran to join them.

Gerold didn't speak. They walked together in silence, Joan quickening her pace to keep up with his long strides.

He is angry, she thought, her high spirits quenched as suddenly as a smothered hearth fire.

What was worse, she knew he was right. She had acted recklessly with the merchant. Hadn't she promised to be more careful? Why did she always have to question and challenge things? Why couldn't she learn it: *Some ideas are dangerous.*

Maybe I am woodly.

She heard a low rumble of sound; Gerold was laughing.

"The look on the man's face when you lifted the vial and drank! I shall never forget it!" He pulled her close in a warm hug. "Ah, Joan, you are my pearl! But tell me, how did you know that it wasn't the Virgin's milk?"

Joan grinned, relieved. "I was mistrustful from the first, for if the thing were truly holy, why would it fetch so small a price? And why did the vendor keep his goat tethered behind the stall, where it couldn't be seen? If it was received in barter, surely there was no need to hide it."

"True. But to actually *drink* the stuff"—there was another burst of laughter from Gerold—"surely you must have known something else."

"Yes. When I uncapped the vial, the milk was uncurdled and perfectly fresh, as if produced this morning, though the Virgin's milk would be over eight hundred years old."

"Ah"—Gerold smiled, his eyebrows arched, testing her—"but perhaps its great holiness kept it pure and uncorrupted."

"True," Joan admitted. "But when I touched the milk, it was still warm! So holy a thing might perhaps remain uncorrupted, but why should it be warm?"

"A pretty observation," Gerold said appreciatively. "Lucretius himself could have done no better!"

Joan beamed. How she loved to please him!

They had walked almost to the end of the long row of stalls, where the huge wooden cross of St.-Denis marked the boundary of the fair, protecting the holy tranquillity of the abbey brothers. This was where the parchment merchants had set up their stalls.

"Look!" Gerold spied them first, and they hurried over to inspect the merchandise, which was of very high quality. The vellum, in particular, was extraordinary: the flesh side of the skin was perfectly even, the color whiter than Joan had ever seen; the other side was, as usual, somewhat yellower, but the pittings where the calf's hair had been rooted were so tiny and shallow as to be almost invisible.

"What a pleasure it must be to write on such sheets!" Joan exclaimed, fingering them gently.

Gerold immediately called one of the merchants over. "Four sheets," he ordered, and Joan gasped, overwhelmed at his extravagance. Four sheets! It was enough for an entire codex!

While Gerold paid for his purchase, Joan's attention wandered to a few sheets of ragged-looking parchment scattered untidily toward the rear of the stall. The edges of the sheets were torn, and there was writing on them, very faint and obliterated in places by ugly brown stains. She bent close to read the writing better, then flushed with excitement.

Seeing her interest, the merchant hurried over.

"So young, and already a fine eye for a bargain," he said unctuously. "The sheets are old, as you see, but still good for their purpose. Look!"

Before she could speak, he took a long, flat tool and scraped it quickly across the page, effacing several letters.

"Stop!" Joan spoke sharply, remembering a different piece of parchment and a different knife. "Stop!"

The merchant looked at her curiously. "You needn't worry, lass, it's only pagan writing." He pointed proudly to the page. "See? Nice and clean and ready to write on!" He lifted the tool to demonstrate the trick again, but Joan grabbed his hand.

"I'll give you a denarius for them," she said tersely.

The man feigned being insulted. "They're worth three denarii, at least."

Joan took the coin from her scrip and held it out to him. "One," she repeated. "It's all I have."

The merchant hesitated, searching her face assessingly. "Very well," he said testily. "Take them."

Joan thrust the coin at him and gathered up the precious parchment before he could change his mind. She ran to Gerold.

"Look!" she said excitedly.

Gerold stared at the pages. "I don't recognize the letters."

"It's written in Greek," Joan explained. "And it's very old. An engineering text, I think. See the diagrams?" She pointed to one of the pages, and Gerold studied the drawing.

"Some kind of hydraulic device." His interest was kindled. "Fascinating. Can you provide a translation of the text?"

"I can."

"Then I might be able to rig it up."

They smiled at each other, conspirators in a fine new scheme.

"Father!" Gisla's voice pierced the noise of the crowd. Gerold turned, searching for her. He was taller by a head than anyone around him; in the sun his thick, red hair gleamed like colored gold. Joan's heart jumped unevenly in her chest as she watched him. *You are my pearl,* he had said. She grasped the papers tightly as she watched him, holding on to the moment.

"Father! Joan!" Gisla finally appeared, pushing her way through the crowd, followed by one of the household servants, his arms laden with goods. "I've been looking everywhere!" she remonstrated good-naturedly. "What have you got there?" Joan started to explain, but Gisla waved her aside. "Oh, just more of your silly old books. Look what *I* found," she enthused. She dangled a length of multicolored cloth. "For my wedding dress! Isn't it *perfect*?"

The cloth shimmered as Gisla displayed it. Examining it more closely, Joan saw that it was woven through with slender, perfect threads of gold and silver.

"It's astonishing," she said sincerely.

Gisla giggled. "I know!" Without waiting for a reply, she grabbed Joan's arm and started toward a stall some distance ahead. "Oh, look," she said, "a slave auction! Let's go see!"

"No." Joan hung back. She had seen the slave traders passing through Ingelheim, their human cargo bound together with heavy ropes. Many of them were Saxons, like her mother.

"No," she said again, and would not budge.

"Aren't you a goose!" Gisla tweaked Joan playfully. "They're only heathens. They don't have feelings, at least not like us."

"I wonder what's in here?" Joan said, anxious to distract her. She led Gisla toward a tiny stall at the end of the row. It was dark and sealed, every panel closed. Luke circled it, sniffing curiously at the walls.

"How strange," Gisla said.

In the bright afternoon sun, with business in full swing all around, the quiet, darkened stall *was* an oddity. Her curiosity piqued, Joan tapped gently on the closed shutter.

"Come in," a cracked voice spoke from within. Gisla jumped at the sound but did not back away. The two girls circled to the side of the stall and pushed cautiously on the planked timber door, which creaked and groaned as it opened inward, spilling slanting rays of light into the gloom.

They stepped inside. A strange smell pervaded the stall, cloying and sweet, like fermented honey. In the center of the enclosure, a tiny figure sat cross-legged—an old woman, dressed simply in a loose, dark robe. She appeared unbelievably ancient, perhaps seventy winters or more; her hair was gone, save for some fine white strands at her crown, and her head shook constantly as if she were afflicted with the ague. But her eyes shone alertly in the darkness, focusing on Joan and Gisla with shrewd assessment.

"Pretty little doves," she croaked. "So pretty and so young. What do you want of Old Balthild?"

"We just wanted to—to—" Joan faltered as she searched uneasily for an explanation. The old woman's gaze was unsettling.

"To find out what is for sale here," Gisla finished boldly.

"What's for sale? What's for sale?" The old woman cackled. "Something that you want but will never own."

"What?" Gisla asked.

"Something that is already yours though you have it not." The old woman grinned at them toothlessly. "Something beyond price and yet it can be bought."

"What *is* it?" Gisla said sharply, impatient with the old woman's riddles.

"The future." The old woman's eyes glittered in the dimness. "Your future, my little dove. All that will be and is not yet."

"Oh, you're a fortune-teller!" Gisla clapped her hands together, pleased to have deciphered the puzzle. "How much?"

"One *solidus*."

One solidus! It was the price of a good milking cow, or a pair of fine rams!

"Too dear." Gisla was in her element now, confident and assured, a shrewd customer looking to strike a bargain.

"One *obole*," she offered.

"Five denarii," the old woman countered.

"Two. One for each of us." Gisla withdrew the coins from her scrip and held them out on her palm for the woman to see.

The old woman hesitated, then took the coins, motioning the girls to the floor beside her. They sat; the woman clasped Joan's strong young hands in her shaking grasp and fixed her odd, disquieting gaze upon her. For a long time, she said nothing; then she began to speak.

"Changeling child, you are what you will not be; what you will become is other than you are."

This made little sense, unless it meant simply that she would soon be a woman grown. But then why had the old woman called her a "changeling"?

Balthild continued, "You aspire to that which is forbidden." Joan started with surprise, and the old woman tightened her clasp. "Yes, changeling, I see your secret heart. You will not be disappointed. Greatness will be yours, beyond your dreams, and grief, beyond your imaginings."

Balthild dropped Joan's hands and turned toward Gisla, who winked at Joan with an expression that said, *Wasn't that* fun?

The old woman took Gisla's hands, her bent, gnarled fingers curling around Gisla's smooth, pink ones.

"You will marry soon, and richly," she said.

"Yes!" Gisla giggled. "But, old woman, I did not pay you to tell me what I already know. Will the union be a happy one?"

"No more than most, but no less either," Balthild said. Gisla raised her eyes to the ceiling in mock despair.

"A wife you shall be, though never a mother," Balthild crooned, swaying with the rhythm of the words, her voice singsong, melodic.

Gisla's smile vanished. "Shall I be barren, then?"

"The future lies before you all dark and empty." Balthild's voice rose in a keening wail. "Pain shall be yours, and confusion, and fear."

Gisla sat transfixed, like a stoat held fast by the stare of a snake.

"Enough!" Joan pried Gisla's hands from the old woman's grasp. "Come with me," she said. Gisla obeyed, compliant as a babe.

Outside the stall, Gisla began to cry.

"Don't be silly," Joan soothed. "The old woman's mad, pay no attention to her. There is no truth in such fortune-telling."

Gisla would not be comforted. She cried and cried; finally, Joan led her to the sweetmeat stalls, where they bought honeyed figs and gorged themselves until Gisla felt somewhat better.

THAT night, when they told Gerold what had happened, he was furious.

"What now, sorcery? Joan and Gisla, you will take me to this stall tomorrow. I have some words to say to this old woman who frightens young girls. In the meantime, Gisla, you must not give heed to such nonsense. Why did you even seek such false counsel?" To Joan he said reproachfully, "I would have thought that *you*, at least, would have known better."

Joan accepted the chastisement. Still, there was a part of her that wanted to believe in Balthild's powers. Hadn't the old woman said that she would realize her secret desire? If she was right, then Joan *would* achieve greatness, despite the fact that she was a girl, despite what everyone else believed possible.

But if Balthild was right about Joan's future, then she was also right about Gisla's.

When they returned to the stall with Gerold the next day, it was empty. No one could tell them where the old woman had gone.

IN WINNEMANOTH, Gisla was married to Count Hugo. There had been some difficulty finding a date suitable for the immediate consummation of the marriage. The Church forbade all marital relations on Sundays, Wednesdays, and Fridays, as well as for forty days before Easter, eight days after Pentecost, and five days before the taking of communion, or on the eve of any great feast or rogation day. In all, on some two hundred and twenty days of the year sexual intercourse was prohibited; when these, as well as Gisla's monthly bleeding time, were taken into account, there were not many dates left to choose from. But at last they settled on the twenty-fourth of the month, a date that pleased everyone save Gisla, who was impatient for the festivities to begin.

At last the great day arrived. The entire household rose before prime to fuss over Gisla. First she was helped into her long-sleeved, yellow linen undertunic. Over this was placed the resplendent new tunic fashioned from the shimmering silver and gold fabric purchased at the St.-Denis fair. It draped from her shoulders to the floor in graceful folds that were echoed in the wide sleeves opening out at her elbows. Around her hips was fastened a heavy kirtle set with good-luck stones—agate to guard against fever, chalk to defend against the evil eye, bloodstone for fertility, jasper for safe delivery in childbirth. Finally a delicate, finely worked silken veil was fastened on her head. It billowed to the ground, covering her shoulders and completely hiding her auburn hair. Standing there in her wedding dress, hardly able to move or even sit for fear of crumpling it, she looked, Joan thought, like an exotic game bird, stuffed and trussed and ready for carving.

Not I, Joan vowed. She did not mean to wed, although in seven months she would be fifteen, a more than marriageable age. In three more years, she would be an old maid. It was incredible to her that girls her age were so eager for marriage, for it immediately plunged a woman into a state of serflike bondage. A husband had absolute control of his wife's goods and property, her children, even her life. Having endured her father's tyranny, Joan meant never to give any man such power over her again.

Gisla, simple creature that she was, went to her bridegroom with eager enthusiasm, all blushes and nervous giggles. Count Hugo, magnificent in a tunic and mantle edged with ermine, waited for her at the sacred portal to the cathedral. She took his proffered hand and stood proudly while Wido, the steward of Villaris, publicly recited all the lands, servants, animals, and goods that Gisla brought as dowry. Then the wedding party entered the cathedral, where Fulgentius waited before the altar to perform the solemn wedding mass.

"*Quod Deus conjunxit homo non separet.*" The Latin words issued haltingly from Fulgentius's tongue. He had been a soldier before inheriting the bishopric late in life; having begun book study tardily, the proper forms of Latin were forever beyond him.

"*In nomine Patria et Filia . . .*" Joan winced as Fulgentius mangled the blessing, confusing his declensions so that instead of "In the name of the Father and the Son and the Holy Spirit" it came out "In the name of the Country and the Daughter."

Finishing with this part of the mass, Fulgentius turned, with obvious relief, to Theodisk.

"May this woman be amiable as Rachel, faithful as Sarah, fertile as Leah." He rested his hand kindly on Gisla's head. "May she bring forth many sons to bring honor to her husband's house."

Joan saw Gisla's shoulders shake and knew she was repressing a giggle.

"Let her copy the behavior of a dog who always has his heart and his eye upon his master; even if his master whip him and throw stones at him, the dog follows, wagging his tail." This seemed hard to Joan, but Fulgentius was regarding Gisla with a benign, even affectionate expression and obviously did not mean to offend. "Wherefore for a better and stronger reason," he continued, "a woman should have a perfect and indestructible love for her husband."

He turned to Count Hugo. "May this man be brave as David, wise as Solomon, strong as Samson. May his lands increase even as his fortune. May he be a just lord to this lady, never administering to her more than reasonable punishments. May he live to see his sons do honor to his name."

They began the exchange of vows. Count Hugo gave his promise first, then placed a ring of Byzantine turquoise on Gisla's fourth finger, which contained the vein leading to the heart.

It was Gisla's turn. Joan listened to Gisla recite her marriage vows. Her voice was high and merry, her mind untroubled by doubt, her future seemingly assured.

What, Joan wondered, *does* my *future hold?*

She could not continue at the schola forever—at most, she had another three years. She let herself daydream, picturing herself as teaching master at one of the great cathedral scholas, Rheims, perhaps, or even the Schola Palatina, her days spent exploring the wisdom of the ages with minds as eager and inquisitive as her own. The daydream was, as always, intensely pleasing.

But—the thought struck like a loosed shaft—*that would mean leaving Villaris. Leaving Gerold.*

She knew she would have to leave Villaris one day. But over the past few months, she had put that thought away, content to live in the present, in the joy of being with Gerold every day.

She let her gaze rest upon him. His profile was strong and well chiseled, his form tall and straight; his red hair curled thickly to his shoulders.

The handsomest man I have ever seen, she thought, not for the first time.

As if he had read her mind, he turned toward her. Their eyes met. Something in his expression—a momentary softening, a tenderness— thrilled her. In an instant the look had vanished, before she was even sure of it, but its warmth lingered.

I am wrong to worry, she thought. *Nothing needs to be decided yet.*

Three years was a long time.

A lot could happen in three years.

RETURNING from the schola the following week, Joan found Gerold waiting for her on the portico.

"Come with me." His tone indicated that he had a surprise in store. He motioned to her and started toward the foregate. Passing through the gated palisade, they followed the road for several miles, then abruptly turned aside into the woods, emerging a short time later into a small clearing, in the midst of which was a sunken hut. No longer inhabited, it had fallen into disrepair. But it must once have been a snug freeman's dwelling, for the wattle-and-daub walls still appeared tight, and the door was made of sturdy oak. It reminded Joan of her own home in Ingelheim, though this grubenhaus was far smaller and its thatched roof was holed with rot.

They stopped before it. "Wait here," Gerold commanded. Joan

watched curiously as he circled the structure once, then returned and stood beside her, facing the door.

"Behold," Gerold said with feigned solemnity. Raising his hands above his head, he clapped loudly three times.

Nothing happened. Joan looked questioningly at Gerold, who stared at the hut expectantly. Evidently something was supposed to happen. But what?

With a loud groan, the heavy oak door began to swing open— slowly at first, then more quickly, exposing the vacant darkness within. Joan peered into the hut. No one was there. The door had moved on its own.

Astounded, Joan gaped at the door. A dozen questions thronged her brain, but only one found its way out. "How?"

Gerold raised his eyes to Heaven in mock piety. "A holy miracle."

Joan snorted.

He laughed. "Sorcery, then." He eyed her challengingly, enjoying the game.

Joan took up the challenge. She marched to the door and examined it. "Can you close it?" she asked.

Gerold raised his hands again. He clapped three times. After a pause, the door groaned and began to swing inward on its hinges. Joan followed as it moved, studying it. The heavy wooden panels were smooth and tightly jointed—no sign of anything unusual there. There was nothing unusual about the plain wooden handle, either. She examined the hinges. They were ordinary iron hinges. It was infuriating. She could not fathom what was making the door move.

The door was fast closed once more. It was a mystery.

"Well?" Gerold's indigo eyes were lit with amusement.

Joan hesitated, unwilling to forfeit the game.

Just as she was about to admit defeat, she heard something, a slender thread of sound coming from somewhere above her. At first she could not place it; the noise was familiar yet strangely out of place.

Then she recognized it. Water. The sound of trickling water.

She said excitedly, "The hydraulic device! The one in the manuscript from the St.-Denis fair! You built it!"

Gerold laughed. "Adapted it, rather. For it was designed to pump water, not to open and close doors!"

"How does it work?"

Gerold showed her the mechanism, located just under the decaying roof of the hut a full ten feet from the door, which was why she had not seen it. He demonstrated the complicated system of levers, pulleys, and counterweights, connected to two slender iron rods attached to the inside of the door so that they were barely visible. By stepping on a rope when he had circled the hut, Gerold had activated the device.

"Amazing!" she said when he finished explaining. "Do it again." Now that she understood how the device worked, she wanted to observe it in action.

"I can't. Not without fetching more water."

"Then let's fetch it," she said. "Where are the buckets?"

Gerold laughed. "You are incorrigible!" He pulled her close in an affectionate hug. His chest was hard and firm, his arms strong around her. Joan felt as if her insides were melting.

Abruptly, he let her go. "Come on, then," he said gruffly. "The buckets are over here."

They carried the empty buckets to the stream a quarter of a mile away, filled them, carried them back, poured them into the receptacle, then returned to fetch more. Three times they made the trip, and by the third they were feeling somewhat giddy. The sun was warm, the air full of spring promise, and their spirits high from the excitement of their project and the joy of each other's company.

"Gerold, look!" Joan called, standing knee-deep in the cool water of the stream. When he turned to her, she playfully slung the water from her bucket at him, wetting the front of his tunic.

"You imp!" he roared.

He filled his bucket and doused her in turn. So they continued, splashing each other in a flurry of sparkling spray, until Joan was hit by a stream of water from Gerold's bucket just as she was bending over to fill her own. Caught off balance, she slipped and fell heavily into the stream. The cool water closed over her head, and for a brief moment she panicked, unable to find her footing on the shifting pebbles of the riverbed.

Then Gerold's arms were around her, pulling her up, setting her on her feet.

"I've got you, Joan, I've got you." His voice, close to her ear, was warm and reassuring. Joan felt her whole body thrum to its cadence. She clung to him. Their wet clothes stuck to each other, molding their bodies together in unambiguous intimacy.

"I love you," she said simply. "I love you."

"Oh, my dearest, my perfect girl," Gerold murmured thickly, and then his mouth was on hers, and she was kissing him back, their passion fueled by the sudden release of emotions long held in check.

The very air seemed to hum in Joan's ears. *Gerold,* it sang. *Gerold.*

Neither of them guessed that from behind the little copse of trees on the crest of the hill, someone was watching.

ODO had been on his way to Héristal to pay a visit to his uncle, one of the holy brothers of that abbey, when his mule had chanced to stray from the path in pursuit of a particularly succulent-looking patch of clover. He cursed the mule, pulling on its bridle and whipping it with a willow rod, but it was stubborn and would not be dissuaded. He had no choice but to leave the road and follow the stupid beast. Then he looked up, toward the stream, and saw.

A learned woman is never chaste. St. Paul's words, or were they Jerome's? No matter. Odo had always believed it to be true, and now he had the proof with his own eyes!

Odo patted the mule's flank. *You shall have an extra portion of feed tonight,* he thought. Then he reconsidered. Feed was expensive, and besides, the beast had only served as God's instrument.

Odo hurried back to the road. His errand would have to wait. First he must get to Villaris.

A short time later, the towers of Villaris loomed ahead. In his excitement, he had walked more quickly than usual. He passed through the gated palisade and was greeted by a guardsman.

Odo waved aside the greeting. "Take me to Lady Richild," he commanded. "I must speak with her at once."

GEROLD removed Joan's arms from his neck and stepped back. "Come," he said, his voice heavy with emotion, "we must go back."

Woolly-headed with love, Joan moved to embrace him again.

"No," Gerold said firmly. "I must take you home now, while I have the will to do so."

Joan stared at him dazedly. "You don't . . . want me?" She lowered her head before he could answer.

Gerold cupped her chin gently, forcing her eyes to meet his. "I want you more than I have ever wanted any woman."

"Then why . . . ?"

"God's teeth, Joan! I am a man, with a man's desires. Do not tempt me beyond my limits!" Gerold sounded almost angry. Seeing the start of tears to her eyes, he gentled his tone. "What would you have me do, my love? Make you my mistress? Ah, Joan, I would take you right here on this sward if I thought it would make you happy. But it would spell your ruin, can't you see that?"

Gerold's indigo eyes held hers commandingly. He was so handsome that it took her breath away. All she wanted was for him to take her in his arms again.

He stroked her white-gold hair. She began to speak, but her voice broke. She breathed deeply, trying to steady her emotions, sick with shame and frustration.

"Come." Gerold took Joan's hand, folding it into his tenderly. She did not protest as he led her back to the road. Wordlessly, hand in hand, they walked the long, comfortless miles toward Villaris.

≽⊣ 11 ⊢≼

"L ADY Richild, Countess of Villaris," the herald announced as Richild swept regally into the bishop's reception hall.

"Eminence." She made a graceful reverence.

"Lady, you are welcome," Fulgentius said. "What news from your lord? God grant he has not met with misfortune on his journey?"

"No, no." She was pleased to find him so transparent. Of course he must wonder at the purpose of her visit! He must have thought—Gerold had been gone five days now, time enough to have met with some disaster on the dangerous roads.

"We have had no word of any difficulties, Eminence, nor do we expect any. Gerold took twenty men with him, well armed and well provisioned; he will not take any chances on the road, as he is on the Emperor's business."

"We heard as much. He is gone as *missus*—to Westphalia, is it?"

"Yes. To settle a dispute about *wergeld*. There are some minor matters of property to be settled as well. He will be away a fortnight or more." *Time enough,* she thought, *just time enough.*

They spoke briefly of local affairs—the shortage of grain at the mill, the repair of the cathedral roof, the success of the spring calving. Richild was careful to observe the necessary courtesies, but nothing more. *I am the scion of better stock than his.* Just as well to remind him of that before coming to the matter of her visit. Obviously he suspected nothing. So much the better; surprise would be her ally in this day's work.

Finally, she judged the time was right. "I have come to ask your help with a domestic matter."

He looked gratified. "Dear lady, I am only too happy to help. What is the nature of your difficulty?"

"It is the girl Joan. She is no longer a child; she"—Richild chose her words delicately—"has now reached womanhood. It is no longer seemly for her to remain under our roof."

"I see," Fulgentius said, though it was apparent he did not. "Well, I should think we could find some other lodg—"

"I have arranged an advantageous match," Richild interrupted. "With the son of Bodo, the farrier. He is a fine young man, well favored, and will be farrier himself when his father dies—there are no other sons."

"This comes as a surprise. Has the girl expressed any inclination for marriage?"

"Surely that is not for her to decide. It is a far better marriage than she has any right to expect. Her family is poor as coloni, and her odd ways have given her something of a . . . reputation."

"Perhaps," the bishop replied amiably. "But she seems devoted to her studies. And she could not, of course, continue at the schola if she married the farrier's boy."

"That is why I have come. As it was you who contracted to bring her to the schola, you would have to agree to her release."

"I see," he said again, though he still did not, quite. "And how does the count feel about the match?"

"He does not know of it. The opportunity only just offered itself."

"Well, then." Fulgentius looked relieved. "We will wait till his return. There's no need to rush the matter, surely."

Richild persisted. "The opportunity may not be open long. The boy is reluctant—seems he's taken a fancy to one of the town girls—but of course I have seen to it that this match will be far more beneficial for him. His father and I are agreed upon the dowry. The boy now says he will carry out his father's wishes—but he is young and of a changeable disposition. Best if the wedding take place immediately."

"Nevertheless . . ."

"I remind you, Eminence, that I am mistress of Villaris, and the girl has been placed in my care. I am fully capable of making this decision in my husband's absence. Indeed, I am better suited to make it. To speak frankly, Gerold's partiality for the girl clouds his judgment where she is concerned."

"I see," Fulgentius said, and this time he did, only too well.

Richild said quickly, "My concern is strictly monetary, you understand. Gerold has spent a small fortune obtaining books for the girl—a wasteful expense, since she has no possible future as a scholar. Someone must provide for her future; now I have done so. You must see that the match is a good one."

"Yes," Fulgentius admitted.

"Good. Then you agree to release her?"

"My apologies, dear lady, but my decision must attend upon the count's return. I assure you I will discuss the matter fully with him. And with the girl. For though the match is . . . advantageous, as you say, I am loath to commit her to it against her will. If the match proves agreeable to all, we will proceed with dispatch."

She started to speak, but he cut her off. "I know you believe the match will be compromised if it is not concluded immediately. But, forgive me, lady, I cannot agree. A fortnight, or even a month, will make little difference."

Again she tried to object, and again he silenced her. "I am quite decided. There is no point in further discussion."

Her cheeks burned with the insult. *High-handed fool! Who does he think he is to dictate to me? My family was living in royal palaces while his was still tilling fields!*

She eyed him levelly. "Very well, Eminence, if that is your decision, I must accept it." She began to pull on her riding gloves as if preparing to leave.

"By the way"—she kept her tone deliberately casual—"I have just had a letter from my cousin, Sigimund, Bishop of Troyes."

The bishop's face registered a gratifying respect. "A great man, a very great man."

"You know that he is to lead the synod which convenes in Aachen this summer?"

"So I had heard."

Now that she had ceased pressing him, his manner was once again relentlessly cheerful.

"Perhaps you have also heard what is to be the chief topic of discussion at this gathering?"

"I should be interested to learn," he responded politely. He obviously guessed nothing of where she was leading.

"Certain . . . irregularities"—she baited the trap carefully—"in the conduct of the episcopacy."

"Irregularities?"

He did not take her meaning. She would have to be plainer.

"My cousin plans to address the question of adherence to episcopal vows, especially"—she looked him directly in the eyes—"the vow of chastity."

The color drained from his face. "Indeed?"

"Apparently he means to make great issue of it at the synod. He's gathered a good deal of evidence about the Frankish bishoprics, which he finds most disturbing. But he is not so familiar with episcopacies in this part of the Empire and must therefore rely on local reports. In his letter he specifically requests me to share any information I may have about *your* episcopacy, Eminence." She used the title with open scorn and was gratified to see him flinch.

"I intended to reply before now," she went on smoothly. "But the details of the girl's betrothal kept me far too busy. Indeed, the plans for the wedding feast would make it impossible for me to respond at all. Of course, now that the wedding is to be delayed . . ." She let the end of the thought hang delicately.

He sat like a stone, silent, noncommittal. She was mildly surprised. He was going to be better at this than she had anticipated.

Only one thing gave him away. Deep inside his sleepy, heavy-lidded eyes, there was a tiny, unmistakable spark of fear.

Richild smiled.

JOAN sat on a rock, troubled and sad. Luke lay down in front of her and put his head in her lap, staring up at her with his opalescent eyes.

"You miss him too, don't you, boy?" she said, gently ruffling the young wolf's white fur.

She was alone now, except for Luke. Gerold had been gone for over a week. Joan missed him with an ache that surprised her with its physicality. She could put her hand over the exact spot in her chest where the pain was most acute; it felt as if her heart had been removed from her body, beaten, and replaced.

She knew why he had gone. After what passed between them at the riverbank, he *had* to go. They needed time apart, time to let heads clear and passions cool. She understood, yet her heart rebelled.

Why? she asked for the thousandth time. *Why must it be this way?* Richild did not love Gerold, nor he her.

She reasoned with herself, rehearsing the arguments why this must be so, why it might even be for the best, but in the end she always came back to one unalterable fact: she loved Gerold.

She shook her head, angry with herself. If Gerold was strong enough to do this for her sake, could she be less so? What could not be changed must somehow be endured. She fixed her mind on a new resolve: when Gerold returned, things would be different. She would be content just to be near him, to talk and laugh as they always had . . . before. They would be like teacher and student, priest and nun, brother and sister. She would erase from her mind the memory of his arms around her, of his lips on hers . . .

Wido, the steward, came up suddenly beside her. "My lady wants to speak with you."

Joan followed him through the gated palisade into the forecourt, Luke trotting by her side. When they reached the main courtyard, Wido pointed to Luke. "Not the wolf."

Richild disliked dogs and forbade them to come inside the house walls, as they did on other manses.

Joan told Luke to lie down and wait in the courtyard.

The guard led her through the covered portico into the great hall, teeming with servants preparing the afternoon meal. They pushed their way through to the solar, where Richild was waiting.

"You sent for me, lady?"

"Sit down." Joan started for a nearby chair, but Richild motioned imperiously toward a wooden stool set before a small writing table. Joan sat down.

"You will take a letter."

Like all the noblewomen in this part of the Empire, Richild could neither read nor write. Wala, the Villaris chaplain, was usually her scribe. Wido could also write a little and sometimes served Richild in this capacity.

Why, then, has she sent for me? Joan wondered.

Richild tapped her foot impatiently. With a practiced eye, Joan surveyed the quills on the desk and selected the sharpest. She took a leaf of fresh parchment, dipped the quill in the inkwell, and nodded at Richild.

"From Richild, Countess, doyenne of the estate of Villaris," Richild dictated.

Joan wrote quickly. The scratching of the quill grated in the stony silence of the room.

"To the canon of the village of Ingelheim, Greetings."

Joan looked up. "My father?"

"Continue," Richild commanded in a tone that indicated she

would tolerate no questions. "Your daughter, Joan, having attained almost fifteen years, and thus being of a marriageable age, will no longer be permitted to continue her studies at the schola."

Joan stopped writing altogether.

"As the girl's guardian, ever vigilant for her welfare," Richild continued, keeping up the pretense of dictation, "I have arranged an advantageous match with Iso, son of the farrier of this town, a prosperous man. The wedding will take place in two days. The terms of the arrangement are as follows—"

Joan jumped up, knocking over her stool. "Why are you doing this?"

"Because I choose to." A small, malicious smile lifted the corners of Richild's mouth. "And because I can."

She knows, Joan thought. *She knows about Gerold and me.* The blood rose into her neck and face so suddenly it felt as if her skin were on fire.

"Yes. Gerold told me everything about that pitiful little interlude by the riverbank." Richild laughed mirthlessly. She was enjoying this. "Did you really believe your clumsy kisses would please him? We laughed about them together that very night."

Joan was too shocked to respond.

"You are surprised. You shouldn't be. Did you think you were the only one? My dear, you are only the latest bead in Gerold's long necklace of conquests. You shouldn't have taken him so seriously."

How does she know what passed between us? Did Gerold tell her? Joan felt suddenly cold, as if caught in a chance wind.

"You do not know him," she said staunchly.

"I am his wife, you insolent child."

"You do not love him."

"No," she admitted. "But neither do I mean to be . . . discomforted by the worthless daughter of coloni!"

Joan tried to steady her thoughts. "You cannot do this without Bishop Fulgentius's approval. He brought me to the schola; you cannot remove me without his permission."

Richild held out a sheet of parchment, marked with Fulgentius's seal.

Joan read it quickly, then once again slowly, to be sure she had not made a mistake. There was no room for doubt; Fulgentius had terminated her studies at the schola. The document bore Odo's signature as well. Joan could imagine the pleasure it must have given him to pen it.

Richild's heart rejoiced as she watched Joan read. The arrogant little nobody was discovering just how insignificant she was. She said, "There is no point in further arguing. Sit down and finish taking the letter to your father."

Joan replied defiantly, "Gerold will not let you do this."

"Foolish child, it was his idea."

Joan thought quickly. "If this marriage were Gerold's idea, why did you wait until he left to arrange it?"

"Gerold is tenderhearted . . . to a fault. He lacks the heart to tell you. I have seen it happen before, with the others. He asked me to take care of the problem for him. And so I have."

"I don't believe you." Joan backed away, fighting back tears. "I don't believe you."

Richild sighed. "The matter is settled. Will you finish taking the letter, or shall I call Wala?"

Joan whirled and ran from the room. Before she reached the great hall, she heard the tinkle of Richild's bell, calling for her chaplain.

LUKE was waiting where she had left him. Joan flung herself to her knees beside him. His body pressed against hers affectionately, his large head resting on her shoulder. His warm, comforting presence helped calm Joan's seething emotions.

I mustn't panic. That's just what she wants me to do.

She had to think, to plan what to do. But her thoughts spun round unproductively, all leading to the same place.

Gerold.

Where is he?

If he were here, Richild could not do this. *Unless of course she was telling the truth, and the marriage* was *Gerold's idea.*

Joan banished the traitorous thought. Gerold loved her; he would not let her be married off against her will to a man she didn't even know.

He might still return in time to stop it. He might—

No. She could not let her future hang on so slim a reed of chance. Joan's mind, numbed by shock and fear, was yet clear enough to understand that.

Gerold is not due back for two more weeks. The wedding will take place in two days.

She had to save herself. She could not go through with this marriage.

Bishop Fulgentius. I must get to him, talk to him, persuade him that this wedding cannot take place.

Joan was sure Fulgentius had not signed that document with a happy heart. Through dozens of small kindnesses, he had made it plain that he liked Joan and took pleasure in her achievements at the schola—particularly since they were so effective a thorn in Odo's side.

Richild must have some hold over him to have gotten him to agree to this.

If Joan could speak to him, she might convince him to call off the wedding—or at least delay it until Gerold's return.

But perhaps he will not see me. However he had been won round to the marriage, he would be reluctant—even embarrassed—to meet with her now. If she requested an audience, she would probably be denied.

She fought down fear, forcing herself to think logically. *Fulgentius will lead the high mass on Sunday. He will ride in procession to the cathedral beforehand. I'll approach him then, throw myself at his feet if I have to. I don't care. He will stop and hear me; I will make him.*

She looked at Luke. "Will it work, Luke? Will it be enough to save me?"

He tilted his head inquisitively, as if trying to understand. It was a mannerism that always amused Gerold. Joan hugged the white wolf, burying her face in the thick fur ringing his neck.

THE notaries and other clerical officers came into view first, walking in stately procession toward the cathedral. Behind them, on horseback, rode the officials of the Church, the deacons and subdeacons, all splendidly attired. Odo rode among them, dressed in plain brown robes, his narrow face haughty and disapproving. As his gaze fell on Joan, standing with the group of beggars and petitioners awaiting the bishop, his thin lips parted in a malevolent smile.

At last the bishop appeared, robed in white silk, riding a magnificent steed caparisoned in crimson. Immediately behind rode the chief dignitaries of the episcopal palace: the treasurer, the controller of the wardrobe, and the almoner. The procession halted as ragged beggars pressed in eagerly all around, crying out for alms in the name of St. Stephen, patron saint of the indigent. Wearily the almoner distributed coins among them.

Joan moved quickly to where the bishop waited, his horse pawing the ground impatiently.

She fell to her knees. "Eminence, hear my plea—"

"I know this case," the bishop interrupted, not looking at her. "I have already rendered judgment. I will not hear this petitioner."

He spurred his horse, but Joan leapt up and grabbed the bridle, staying him. "This marriage will be my ruin." She spoke quickly and quietly, so no one else would hear. "If you can do nothing to stop it, will you at least delay it for a month?"

He made as if to ride on again, but Joan kept tight hold of the bridle. Two of the guards rushed over and would have pulled her away, but the bishop checked them with a wave of his hand.

"A fortnight?" Joan pleaded. "I entreat you, Eminence, give me a fortnight!" Mortifyingly, for she had resolved to be strong, she began to sob.

Fulgentius was a weak man, with many faults, but he was not hard-hearted. His eyes softened with sympathy as he reached down to pat Joan's white-gold hair.

"Child, I cannot help you. You must resign yourself to your fate, which is, after all, natural enough for a woman." He bent down and whispered, "I have inquired after the young man who is to be your husband. He's a comely lad; you will not find your lot difficult to bear."

He signaled the guards, who pried Joan's hands from the bridle and shoved her back into the crowd. A path opened for her. As she passed through, trying to hide her tears, she heard the villagers' whispered laughter.

In the rear of the crowd, she saw John. She went to him, but he backed off.

"Stay away!" He scowled. "I hate you!"

"Why? What have I done?"

"You know what you've done!"

"John, what is it? What's wrong?"

"I have to leave Dorstadt!" he cried. "Because of you!"

"I don't understand."

"Odo told me, 'You don't belong here.'" John mimicked the schoolmaster's nasal intonation. "'We only let you stay because of your sister.'"

Joan was shocked. She had been so involved in her own dilemma that she had not thought of the consequences for John. He was a poor student; they'd kept him on only because of his kinship to her.

"This marriage is not of my choosing, John."

"You've always spoiled things for me, and now you're doing it again!"

"Didn't you hear what I said to the bishop just now?"

"I don't care! It's all your fault. Everything's always been your fault!"

Joan was puzzled. "You hate book studies. Why do you care if they send you from the schola?"

"You don't understand." He looked behind her. "You never understand."

Joan turned and saw the boys of the schola huddled together. One of them pointed and whispered something to the others, followed by muffled laughter.

So they already know, Joan thought. *Of course. Odo would not spare John's feelings.* She regarded her brother with sympathy. It must have been difficult, almost unbearable, for him to be separated from his friends because of her. He had often joined with them against her, but Joan understood why. John never wanted anything more than to be accepted, to belong.

"You'll be all right, John," she said soothingly. "You're free to go home now."

"Free?" John laughed harshly. "Free as a monk!"

"What do you mean?"

"I'm to go to the monastery at Fulda! Father sent instructions to the bishop after we first arrived. If I failed at the schola, I was to be sent to join the Fulda brotherhood!"

So this was the source of John's anger. Once consigned to the brotherhood, he would not be able to leave. He would never be a soldier now, nor ride in the Emperor's army as he had dreamed.

"There may still be a way out," Joan said. "We can petition the bishop again. Perhaps if we both plead with him, he will—"

Her brother glared at her, his mouth working as he searched for words strong enough to express what he felt. "I . . . I wish you'd never been born!" He turned and ran.

Dispiritedly, she started back toward Villaris.

JOAN sat by the stream where she and Gerold had embraced only a few weeks ago. An eternity had passed since then. She looked at the sun; it lacked only an hour or two until sext. By this time tomorrow, she would be wed to the farrier's son.

Unless . . .

She studied the line of trees marking the edge of the woods. The forest surrounding Dorstadt was dense and broad; a person could hide in there for days, even weeks, without being discovered. It would be a fortnight or more before Gerold returned. Could she survive for that long?

The forest was dangerous; there were wild boars, and aurochs, and . . . wolves. She remembered the savage violence of Luke's dam as she fought against the bars of her cage, her sharp teeth glinting in the moonlight.

I'll take Luke with me, she thought. *He will protect me, and help me hunt for food as well.* The young wolf was already a skilled hunter of rabbits and other small game, which were plentiful this time of year.

John, she thought. *What about John?* She couldn't just run off without letting him know where she had gone.

He can come with me! Of course! It was the solution to both their problems. They would hide together in the woods and await Gerold's return. Gerold would set everything right—not only for her but for her brother.

She must get word to John. Tell him to meet her in the forest tonight, bringing his lance and bow and quiver.

It was a desperate plan. But she *was* desperate.

SHE found Dhuoda in the dortoir. Though she was only ten, she was a big girl, well developed for her age. Her resemblance to her sister Gisla was unmistakable. She greeted Joan excitedly. "I've just heard! Tomorrow is your wedding day!"

"Not if I can prevent it," Joan responded bluntly.

Dhuoda was surprised. Gisla had been so eager to wed. "Is he old, then?" Her face lit with childish horror. "Is he toothless? Does he have scrofula?"

"No." Joan had to smile. "He's young and comely, I am told."

"Then why—"

"There's no time to explain, Dhuoda," Joan said urgently. "I've come to ask a favor. Can you keep a secret?"

"Oh, yes!" Dhuoda leaned forward eagerly.

Joan pulled a piece of rolled parchment from her scrip. "This letter is for my brother, John. Take it to him at the schola. I would go myself, but I am expected in the solar to have a new tunic fit for the wedding. Will you do this for me?"

Dhuoda stared at the piece of parchment. Like her mother and sister, she could not read or write.

"What does it say?"

"I can't tell you, Dhuoda. But it's important, very important."

"A secret message!" Her face was aglow with excitement.

"It's only two miles to the schola. You can go and come in an hour if you hurry."

Dhuoda grabbed the parchment. "I'll be back before that!"

DHUODA hurried through the main courtyard, dodging to avoid the servants and craftsmen who always filled the place this time of day. Her senses were alive with an intimation of adventure. She felt the cool smoothness of the parchment in her hand and wished she knew what was written on it. Joan's ability to read and write filled her with awe.

This mysterious errand was a welcome change from the boredom of her daily routine at Villaris. Besides, she was glad to help Joan. Joan was always nice to her; she took time to explain all kinds of interesting things—not like Mama, who was so often short-tempered and angry.

She was almost to the palisade when she heard a shout.

"Dhuoda!"

Mama's voice. Dhuoda kept going as if she hadn't heard, but as she passed through the gate, the porter grabbed her and forced her to wait.

She turned to face her mother.

"Dhuoda! Where are you going?"

"Nowhere." Dhuoda thrust the parchment behind her. Richild caught the sudden movement, and her mouth set with suspicion.

"What is that?"

"N-nothing," Dhuoda stammered.

"Give it to me." Richild held out her hand imperiously.

Dhuoda hesitated. If she gave Mother the parchment, she would betray the secret Joan had entrusted her with. If she resisted . . .

Her mother glared at her, her dark eyes reflecting a building anger. Looking into those eyes, Dhuoda knew she had no choice.

FOR this last night before Joan's wedding, Richild had insisted that she sleep in the small warming room adjoining her own chamber—a privilege customarily reserved only for sick children or favored servants. It was a special honor accorded to the bride-to-be, Richild said, but Joan was sure that she simply wanted to keep her under close observation. No matter. Once Richild was asleep, Joan could slip out of this room just as easily as the dortoir.

Ermentrude, one of the serving girls, came into the little room, carrying a wooden cup filled with spiced red wine. "From the Lady Richild," she said simply. "To honor you on this night."

"I don't want it." Joan waved it away. She would not accept favors from the enemy.

"But the Lady Richild said to stay while you drink it and then take the cup away." Ermentrude was anxious to do things right, being only twelve and new to household service.

"Have it yourself, then," Joan said irritably. "Or empty it on the ground. Richild will never know."

Ermentrude brightened. The idea had not occurred to her. "Yes, mistress. Thank you, mistress." She turned to go.

"A moment." Joan called her back, reconsidering. The wine brimmed the cup, rich and thick, shimmering in the dim light. If she was going to survive for a fortnight in the forest, she would need all the sustenance she could get. She could not afford foolish gestures of pride. She took the cup and gulped the warm wine greedily. It mustached her lips, leaving a strange sour taste. She wiped her mouth with her sleeve, then handed the cup to Ermentrude, who hurriedly left.

Joan blew out the candle and lay on the bed in the dark, waiting. The feather mattress surrounded her with alien softness; she was accustomed to the thin straw on her bed upstairs in the dortoir. She wished Richild had let her sleep in her own bed, beside Dhuoda. She had not seen Dhuoda since handing her the message, having been

cloistered in Richild's chambers all afternoon while the serving
women fussed over her wedding dress and assembled the clothing
and personal items that would go with her as dowry.

Had Dhuoda given John the message? There was no way to be
sure. She would wait for John in the forest clearing; if he did not
come, she and Luke would go on alone.

In the adjoining room, she heard Richild's deep, slow breathing.
Joan waited another quarter of an hour, to be sure Richild was
asleep. Then she slipped silently from under the blankets.

She stepped through the door into Richild's chamber. Richild lay
still, her breathing regular and deep. Joan slipped along the wall and
out the door.

As soon as she had gone, Richild's eyes flew open.

JOAN moved soundlessly through the halls until at last she reached
the open air of the courtyard. She breathed deeply, feeling a bit giddy.

All was still. A single guard sat with his back to the wall near the
gate, his head on his chest, snoring. Her lengthened shadow spilled
across the moonlit earth, grotesquely huge. She moved her hand, and
a giant gesture mocked her.

Joan whistled softly to Luke. The guard stirred and shifted in his
sleep. Luke did not come. Keeping to the shadows, she started toward the corner where Luke usually slept; she would not risk waking
the guard by making any further sound.

Suddenly, the ground seemed to shift beneath her. She felt a rise of
nausea and dizzily held on to a post to steady herself. *Benedicite. I
can't be sick now.*

Fighting the giddiness, she made her way across the courtyard. In
the far corner she saw Luke. The young wolf lay on his side, his
opalescent eyes staring blindly into the night, his tongue lolling
limply out of his mouth. She bent to touch him and felt the coldness
of his body beneath the soft white fur. She gasped and drew back.
Her eyes fell on a half-eaten piece of meat on the ground. She stared
at it dazedly. A fly settled on the bloody wetness surrounding the
meat. It remained there, drinking, then flew upward, circling errati-
cally before it dropped abruptly to the ground. It did not move again.

There was a loud humming in Joan's ears. The air seemed to un-
dulate around her. She backed away, turning to run, but again the
ground lurched and shifted, then rose suddenly to meet her.

She did not feel the arms that lifted her roughly from where she lay and carried her back inside.

THE creaking of the wheels kept melancholy rhythm with the clopping of horses' hooves as the cart bumped along the road toward the cathedral, carrying Joan to her wedding mass.

She had been dragged awake this morning, too dazed to realize what had happened. She stood numbly while the servants fussed over her, putting on her wedding dress and fixing her hair.

But the effects of the drug were wearing off, and Joan began to remember. *It was the wine,* she thought. *Richild put something in the wine.* Joan thought of Luke, lying cold and alone in the night. A lump rose in her throat. He had died without comfort or companionship; Joan hoped he had not suffered long. It must have given Richild pleasure to poison his meat; she had always hated him, sensing the bond he represented between Gerold and Joan.

Richild was riding in the cart just ahead. She was magnificently dressed in a tunic of gleaming blue silk, her black hair coiled elegantly around her head and secured with a silver tiara set with emeralds. She was beautiful.

Why, Joan wondered dully, *didn't she just kill me too?*

Sitting in the cart drawing her ever closer to the cathedral, sick in body and heart, with Gerold far away and no way of escape, Joan wished that she had.

THE wheels clattered noisily onto the uneven cobblestones of the cathedral forecourt, and the horses were reined to a stop. Immediately, two of Richild's retainers appeared alongside. With elaborate obsequiousness, they helped Joan from the cart.

An enormous crowd was gathered outside the cathedral. It was the Feast of the First Martyrs, a solemn religious holiday, as well as Joan's wedding mass, and the entire town had turned out for the occasion.

In front of the crowd Joan caught sight of a tall, ruddy, big-boned boy standing awkwardly beside his parents. The farrier's son. She noted his sullen expression and the dejected set of his head. *He doesn't want me for a wife any more than I want him for a husband. Why should he?*

His father prodded him; he came toward Joan and held out his hand. She took it, and they stood side by side as Wido, Richild's steward, read the list of items composing Joan's dowry.

Joan looked toward the forest. She could not possibly run and hide there now. The crowd encircled them, and Richild's men stood close beside her, eyeing her warily.

In the crowd Joan saw Odo. Gathered around him were the boys of the schola, whispering together as usual. John was not among them. She searched the crowd and found him standing off to one side, ignored by his companions. They were both alone now, except for each other. Her eyes sought his, seeking and offering comfort. Surprisingly, he did not look away but returned her gaze, his face openly registering his pain.

They had been strangers for a long time, but in that moment they were two again, brother and sister, leagued in understanding. Joan kept her eyes fixed on him, reluctant to break the fragile bond.

The steward stopped reading. The crowd waited expectantly. The farrier's son led Joan into the cathedral. Richild and her household swept in behind them, followed by the townspeople.

Fulgentius was waiting by the altar. As Joan and the boy came toward him, he motioned them to sit. First the holy feast would be celebrated, then the wedding mass.

Omnipotens sempiterne Deus qui me peccatoris. As usual, Fulgentius was mangling the Latin service, but Joan hardly noticed. He signaled an acolyte to prepare for the offertory and began the oblation prayer. *Suscipe sanctum Trinitas* . . . Beside her, the farrier's son bent his head reverently. Joan tried to pray, too, bowing her head and mouthing the words, but there was no substance to the form; inside her there was only emptiness.

The mixing of the water with the wine began. *Deus qui humanae substantiae* . . .

The doors of the cathedral burst open with a loud crack. Fulgentius abandoned his struggles with the Latin mass and stared incredulously at the entrance. Joan craned her neck, trying to make out the source of this unprecedented intrusion. But the people behind her blocked her view.

Then she saw it. An enormous creature, manlike but taller by a head than any man, stood outlined in the blinding light of the doorway, its shadow spilling into the dim interior. Its face was curiously expressionless and shone with a metallic gleam, the eyes so deep in their dark sockets that Joan could not make them out.

Somewhere in the crowded assembly, a woman screamed.

Woden, Joan thought. She had long ago ceased to believe in her mother's gods, but here was Woden, exactly as her mother had described him, striding boldly up the aisle right toward her.

Has he come to save me? she thought wildly.

As he drew closer, she saw that the metallic face was a mask, part of an elaborate battle helmet. The creature was a man and no god. From the back of his head, where the helmet ended, long golden hair curled down to his shoulders.

"Norsemen!" someone shouted.

The intruder continued past without breaking stride. Reaching the altar, he raised a heavy, two-sided broadsword and brought it down with savage force on the bald tonsure of one of the assisting clerics. The man dropped, blood spurting from the deep cleft where his head had been.

Everything erupted into chaos. All around Joan people were screaming and shoving to get away. Joan was dragged along with the crowd, packed so tightly between struggling bodies that her feet lost contact with the floor. The wave of terrified villagers swept toward the doors, then abruptly halted.

The exit was blocked by another intruder, dressed for battle like the first, except that he carried an ax instead of a sword.

The crowd swayed uncertainly. Joan heard shouting outside, and then more of the Norsemen—a dozen at least—piled through the doors. They came in at a run, shouting hoarsely and swinging enormous iron axes over their heads.

The villagers fought and climbed over one another to get out of the way of the murderous blades. Joan was pushed hard from behind and fell to the ground. She felt feet on her sides and back, and she threw up her arms to protect her head. Someone stepped heavily on her right hand, and she cried out in pain. "Mama! Help me! Mama!"

Struggling to extricate herself from the crush of bodies, she crawled sideways until she reached an open area. She looked toward the altar and saw Fulgentius surrounded by Norsemen. He was striking at them with the huge wooden cross that had hung behind the altar. He must have pried it from the wall, and now he swung it around with fierce strength as his attackers darted back and forth, attempting to strike him with their swords but unable to get inside the circle of his defense. As she watched, Fulgentius dealt one Norseman a blow that sent him flying halfway across the room.

She crawled through the noise and the smoke—was there a fire?—searching for John. All around her were shrieks, war cries, and howls of pain and terror. The floor was littered with overturned chairs and sprawled bodies, wet with spilled blood.

"John!" she called. The smoke was thicker here; her eyes burned, and she could not see clearly. "John!" She hardly heard her own voice over the din.

A rush of air on the back of her neck warned her, and she reacted instinctively, hurling herself to the side. The Norseman's blade, aimed for her head, tore a gash in her cheek instead. The blow threw her to the floor, where she rolled in agony, clutching her wounded face.

The Norseman stood above her, his blue eyes murderous through the appalling mask. She crawled backwards, trying to get away, but she could not move fast enough.

The Norseman raised his sword for the death blow. Joan shielded her head with her arms, turning her face aside.

The blow did not come. She opened her eyes to see the sword drop from her attacker's hands. Blood trickled from the corners of his mouth as he sank slowly to the floor. Behind him stood John, grasping the reddened blade of Father's bone-handled knife.

His eyes glittered with a strange exhilaration. "I took him right through the heart! Did you see? He would have killed you!"

The horror of it flooded her. "They will kill us all!" She clutched at John. "We must get away, we must hide!"

He shrugged her off. "I got another one. He came at me with an ax, but I got inside and took him through the throat."

Joan looked round frantically for somewhere to hide. A few feet ahead was the reredos. It was wrought of wood, fronted with gilded panels depicting the life of St. Germanus. And it was hollow. There might just be enough room . . .

"Quickly," she shouted to John. "Follow me!" She grasped the sleeve of his tunic, pulling him down beside her on the floor. Motioning him to follow, she crawled to the side of the reredos. Yes! There was an interstice, just big enough to squeeze through.

It was dark inside. Only a thin stream of light trickled in from the seam in front where the panels were inexpertly joined.

She squatted in the far corner, tucking her legs under to leave room for John. He did not appear. She crawled back to the opening and peered out.

A few feet away she saw him, bending over the body of the Norseman he had killed. He was pulling at the man's clothes, trying to pry something loose.

"John!" she shouted. "In here! Hurry!"

He stared at her, a mad, glittering gaze, his hands still working under the Norseman's body. She didn't dare shout again for fear she would reveal the precious hiding place. After a moment he gave an exultant yell and stood, holding the Norseman's sword. She gestured for him to join her. He lifted the sword in mocking salute and ran off.

Shall I go after him? She edged toward the opening.

Someone—a child?—screamed nearby, a hideous shriek that hung in the air, then abruptly ceased. Fear overwhelmed her, and she drew back. Tremulously she put an eye to the seam between the panels and peered out, searching for John.

There was fighting directly in front of her peephole. She heard the clang of metal on metal, caught a brief glimpse of yellow cloth, the gleam of an uplifted sword. A body thumped down heavily. The fighting moved off to the side, and she was looking straight down the nave toward the cathedral entrance. The heavy doors stood ajar, propped open by a grotesque jumble of bodies.

The Norsemen were herding their victims away from the entrance toward the right side of the cathedral.

The way stood clear.

Now, she told herself. *Run for the doors.* But she could not bring herself to move; her limbs seemed to be locked.

A man appeared at the edge of her narrow field of vision. He looked so wild and disheveled that for a moment she did not recognize him as Odo. He was lurching toward the entrance, dragging his left leg. In his arms he clutched the huge Bible from the high altar.

He was almost to the doors when two Norsemen intercepted him. He faced his attackers, holding the Bible aloft as if warding off evil spirits. A heavy sword sliced through the book and took him directly in the chest. For a moment he stood, astonished, clutching the two halves of the book in his hands. Then he fell backwards and did not move again.

Joan shrank back into the darkness. The screams of the dying were all around her. Hunched in a ball, she buried her head in her arms. Her rapid heartbeat sounded in her ears.

THE screaming had stopped.

She heard the Norsemen calling out to one another in their guttural tongue. There was a loud noise of splintering wood. At first she did not understand what was happening; then she realized they were stripping the cathedral of its treasures. The men laughed and shouted. They were in high spirits.

It did not take them long to complete their plundering. Joan heard them grunting under the weight of their loot, their voices receding into the distance.

Rigid as a post, she sat in the dark and strained to hear. Everything was quiet. She inched toward the opening of the reredos until she reached the edge of the narrow crack of light.

The cathedral lay in ruins. Benches were overturned, hangings were torn off walls, statuary lay in pieces on the floor. There was no sign of the Norsemen.

Bodies lay everywhere, piled in careless heaps. A few feet away, at the bottom of the stairs leading to the altar, Fulgentius was sprawled beside the great wooden cross. It was splintered, the gilded crosspiece broken and wet with blood. Beside him lay the bodies of two Norsemen, their skulls crushed within their shattered helmets.

Cautiously, Joan crept forward until her head and shoulders were out of the reredos.

In the far corner of the room, something moved. Joan shrank back out of the light.

A pile of clothing twisted, then separated itself from the heap of bodies.

Someone was alive!

A young woman rose, her back toward Joan. She stood, shakily, and then began to stagger toward the door.

Her golden dress was ripped and bloodied, and her hair, torn loose from its cap, tumbled over her shoulders in auburn coils.

Gisla!

Joan called her name, and she turned, swaying unsteadily, toward the reredos.

There was a sudden burst of laughter outside the cathedral.

Gisla heard and wheeled to run, but it was too late. A group of Norsemen came through the door. They fell on Gisla with a jubilant shout, lifting her above their heads.

They carried her to an open space beside the altar and spread-eagled her, pinning her down by the wrists and ankles. She twisted violently to free herself. The tallest of the men dragged her tunic up over her face and dropped full length on her. Gisla screamed. The man dug his hands into her breasts. The others laughed and shouted encouragement as he raped her.

Joan gagged, clamping hand over mouth to mask the sound.

The Norseman stood up, and another one took his place. Gisla lay slack and unmoving. One of the men took hold of her hair and twisted it to make her jump.

A third man took her, and a fourth; then they left her alone while they retrieved several sacks piled near the door. There was a ringing of metal as they hoisted them; the sacks must have been filled with more of the cathedral's plundered treasure.

It was for these that they had returned.

Before they left, one of the men strode over to Gisla, pulled her up, still limp and unresisting, and slung her over his shoulder like a sack of grain.

They left by the far door.

Deep inside the reredos Joan heard only the eerie, echoing stillness of the cathedral.

LIGHT coming through the front seam of the reredos cast long shadows. There had been no sound for several hours. Joan stirred and crept cautiously through the narrow opening.

The high altar still stood, though stripped of its gold plating. Joan leaned against it, staring at the scene around her. Her wedding tunic was splattered with blood—her own? She could not tell. Her torn cheek throbbed with pain. Woodenly, she picked her way through the jumbled bodies, searching.

In a pile of corpses near the door, she came upon the farrier and his son, their arms sprawled as if each had tried to protect the other.

In death the boy looked shrunken and old. Only a few hours ago, he had stood beside her in the cathedral, tall and ruddy and full of youthful strength and vigor. *There will be no marriage now,* Joan thought. Yesterday that thought would have filled her with profound relief and joy; now she felt nothing but numbing emptiness. She left him lying beside his father and continued her search.

She found John in the corner, his hand still gripping the Norseman's sword. The back of his head had been smashed in with a heavy blow, but the violence of his death had left no mark on his face. His blue eyes were clear and open; his mouth was drawn back slightly in what appeared to be a smile.

He had died a soldier's death.

SHE ran, stumbling, toward the door and pushed it open. It swung away from her crookedly, the hinges broken by the Norsemen's axes. She rushed outside and stood gasping, breathing the fresh, sweet air in great gulps, ridding herself of the stench of death.

The landscape was bare. Smoke curled upward in lazy spirals from heaps of rubble that only this morning had been a lively clutter of homes and buildings surrounding the cathedral.

Dorstadt was in ruins.

Nothing stirred. No one was left. All the townspeople had been gathered in the cathedral for the mass.

She looked east. Above the trees obscuring her view, black smoke mushroomed skyward, darkening the sky.

Villaris.

They had burned it.

She sat down on the ground and put her face in her hands, cradling her wounded cheek.

Gerold.

She needed him to hold her, comfort her, make the world recognizable again. Scanning the horizon with narrowed eyes, she half-expected him to appear, riding toward her on Pistis, red hair streaming behind him like a banner.

I must wait for him. If he returns and does not find me, he will think I was carried off by the Norsemen, like poor Gisla.

But I can't stay here. Fearfully she surveyed the ruined landscape. There was no sign of the Norsemen. Had they gone? Or would they be back, looking for more plunder?

What if they find me? She had seen what mercy an unprotected female could expect from them.

Where could she hide? She started toward the trees that marked the edge of the forest circling the town, slowly at first, then at a run. Her breath came sobbingly; at every step, she expected hands to grab her from behind, spinning her around to face the hideous, metallic masks of the Norsemen. Reaching the safety of the trees, she threw herself on the ground.

After a long while, she forced herself to sit up. Night was coming on. The forest around her was dark and foreboding. She heard a rustle of leaves and flinched in fear.

The Norsemen might be nearby, camping in these woods.

She had to escape from Dorstadt and somehow get word to Gerold about where she had gone.

Mama. She longed for her mother, but she could not go home. Her father had not forgiven her. If she returned now, bringing news of the death of his only remaining son, he would have his revenge upon her, that was certain.

If only I were not a girl. If only . . .

For the rest of her life she would remember this moment and wonder what power of good or evil had directed her thoughts. But now there was no time to consider. It was a chance. There might never be another.

The red sun glittered on the horizon. She had to act quickly.

She found John lying as she had left him, sprawled in the dim interior of the cathedral. His body was limp and unresistant as she rolled him onto his side. The death rigor had not yet set in.

"Forgive me," she whispered as she unclasped John's mantle.

When she was done, she covered him with her own discarded cloak. Gently she closed his eyes and arranged him as decently as she could. She stood, shifting her arms, adjusting to the weight and feel of her new clothes. They were not so different from her own, except for the sleeves, close-fitted at the wrists. She fingered the bone-handled knife she had taken from John's belt.

Father's knife. It was old, the white bone handle darkened and chipped, but the blade was sharp.

She went to the altar. Loosening her cap, she placed a mass of her hair upon the altar. It curled thickly over the smooth stone surface, almost white in the dimming light.

She lifted the knife.

Slowly, deliberately, she began to cut.

AT TWILIGHT, the figure of a young man stepped from the door of the ruined cathedral, scanning the landscape with keen gray-green eyes. The moon was rising in a sky quickening with stars.

Beyond the rubble of buildings, the eastern road shimmered mackerel-silver in the gathering darkness.

The figure slipped furtively out of the shadow of the cathedral. No one was left alive to watch as Joan hurried down the road, toward the great monastery of Fulda.

⊱⊱ 12 ⊰⊰

THE hall was crowded and clamorous, jammed with people who had traveled from miles around the small Westphalian village to witness the proceedings of the *mallus*. They stood shoulder to shoulder, jostling, scuffling the clean rushes that had been scattered across the beaten earth floor, uncovering the ancient accumulation of beer, grease, spittle, and animal excrement that lay beneath. The rank odor rose into the hot, close air. But no one gave it much mind, such odors being common in Frankish dwellings. Besides, the focus of the crowd's attention lay elsewhere: on the red-haired Frisian count who had come as missus to render judgment and deliver justice in the Emperor's name.

Gerold turned to Frambert, one of the seven *scabini* assigned to assist him in his work. "How many more today?" The mallus had convened at first light; it was now midafternoon, and they had been hard at it for over eight hours. Behind the high table at which Gerold sat, his retainers drooped wearily over their swords. He had brought twenty of his best men, just in case. Ever since the death of the Emperor Karolus, the Empire had been sinking into disarray; the position of imperial *missi* had become increasingly precarious. They were sometimes met with bold-faced defiance from wealthy and powerful local lords, men who were unused to having their authority questioned. The law was nothing if it could not be enforced; that was why Gerold had brought so many men, though this had meant leaving Villaris with only a handful of defenders. But the manor's strong wooden palisades were sufficient guarantee against the depredations of the solitary thieves and brigands who had been the only threat to the peace and security of the surrounding countryside for many years.

Frambert checked the list of complainants, written on a strip of parchment eight inches wide, its segments stitched together end to end to form a roll some fifteen feet long.

"Three more today, my lord," Frambert said.

Gerold sighed wearily. He was tired and hungry; his patience for dealing with the endless stream of petty accusations, countercharges, and complaints was wearing thin. He wished he were back at Villaris, with Joan.

Joan. How he missed her—her husky voice, her rich, deep laughter, her fascinating gray-green eyes, which regarded him with such knowledge and love. But he must not think of her. That was why he had agreed to serve as missus after all—to put distance between them, give him time to regain control of the ungovernable intensity of emotion that had been building inside him.

"Call the next case, Frambert," Gerold commanded, putting a check on his errant thoughts.

Frambert lifted the roll of parchment and read aloud, straining to be heard over the buzzing crowd.

"Abo complains of his neighbor Hunald, that he has unlawfully and without just compensation taken his livestock from him."

Gerold nodded knowingly. The situation was all too common. In these illiterate times, rare was the property owner who could keep written account of his holdings; the absence of such records left his fields open to all kinds of thievery and false dealing.

Hunald, a big, florid-faced man, dressed ostentatiously in scarlet linen, stepped forward to deny the charge.

"The beasts are mine. Bring me the reliquary." He pointed to the box of holy relics on the high table. "Before God"—he posed dramatically, raising his arms toward Heaven—"I will swear to my innocence on these sacred bones."

"They are my cows, my lord, not Hunald's, as well he knows," responded Abo, a small man whose quiet demeanor and simple dress made him a study in contrast with Hunald. "Hunald can swear as he likes; it will not change the truth."

"What, Abo, do you question God's judgment?" Hunald remonstrated. His voice registered the correct note of pious indignation, but Gerold caught the undertone of triumph. "Mark it, my lord Count, this is blasphemy!"

"Have you any proof the beasts are yours?" Gerold asked Abo.

The question was highly irregular; there were no laws of witness or evidence in Frankland. Hunald glowered at Gerold. What was this strange Frisian count trying to do?

"Proof?" This was a new idea; Abo had to think for a moment.

"Well, Berta—that's my wife—can name every one, and so can my four children, for they have known them since they were babes. They can tell you which ones have a temper when milked, and which prefer clover to grass." Another thought struck him. "Bring me to them and let me call them; they will come to me readily, for they know the sound of my voice and the touch of my hand." A tiny flicker of hope ignited in Abo's eyes.

"Nonsense!" Hunald exploded. "Is this court supposed to accept the unthinking actions of dumb beasts before the sacred laws of Heaven? I demand just trial by compurgation. Bring the box of relics and let me swear!"

Gerold stroked his beard, considering. Hunald was the accused; he was within his rights to request the oath taking. God would not permit him to swear falsely with his hand on the holy relics, or so said the law.

The Emperor set great store by such trials, but Gerold had his doubts. There were certainly men who, caring more for the solid advantages of this world than for the vague and insubstantial terrors of the next, would not hesitate to lie. *If it came to that, I would do it myself,* Gerold thought, *if the stakes were high enough.* He would swear to a lie on a whole cartful of relics to protect the safety of anyone he loved.

Joan. Again her image rose irresistibly to his mind, and he forced it aside. There would be time enough for such thoughts when the day's work was done.

"My lord." Frambert spoke quietly into his ear. "I can vouch for Hunald. He is a fine man, a generous man, and this claim against him is falsely brought."

Below the level of the table, out of sight of the crowd, Frambert played with a magnificent ring, an amethyst set in silver, engraved with the figure of an eagle. He twirled it round his middle finger so Gerold could see how it gleamed in the light.

"Ah, yes, a most *generous* man." Frambert slipped the ring off his finger. "Hunald wished me to tell you that it is yours. A gesture of his appreciation for your support." A small, tentative smile played at the corners of his lips.

Gerold took the ring. It was a magnificent piece of work, the finest he had ever seen. He handled it, admiring its weight and the perfect workmanship of its artisan. "Thank you, Frambert," he said decisively. "This makes my judgment easier."

Frambert's smile widened into a broad, conspiratorial grin.

Gerold turned to Hunald. "You wish to submit yourself to the judgment of God."

"Yes, my lord." Hunald swelled with confidence, having witnessed the exchange between Gerold and Frambert. The servant with the box of relics stepped forward, but Gerold waved him back.

"We will seek God's judgment through the *judicium aquae ferventis.*"

Hunald and Abo looked blank; like everyone else in the room, they knew no Latin.

"*Kesselfang,*" Gerold translated.

"Kesselfang!" Hunald blanched; he had not thought of this. Ordeal by boiling water was a well-known form of trial, but it had not been employed in this part of the Empire for some years.

"Bring the caldron," Gerold commanded.

There was a moment of stunned silence. Then the room dissolved into a chaotic bustle of conversation and activity. Several of the scabini rushed outside to search the nearby houses for a pot with water already on the boil. Minutes later they returned, carrying a black iron caldron, deep as a man's arm from top to bottom, filled with steaming hot water. Placed on the hearth in the center of the room, the water soon foamed and bubbled.

Gerold nodded, satisfied. Given Hunald's talent for bribery, it might have been a smaller pot.

Hunald scowled. "My lord Count, I protest!" Fear had rendered him indifferent to appearances. "What about the ring?"

"My thought exactly, Hunald." Gerold held the ring up for all to see, then threw it into the caldron. "On the accused's suggestion, this ring shall be the servitor of God's judgment."

Hunald swallowed hard. The ring was small and slippery; it would be hellishly difficult to retrieve. But he could not refuse the trial without admitting his guilt and returning Abo's cows—and they were worth well over seventy solidi. He cursed the foreign count who was so inexplicably immune to the mutually beneficial exchange of favors that had characterized his dealings with other missi. Then he took a deep breath and plunged his arm into the pot.

His face creased with pain as the boiling water seared his skin. Frantically he groped round the bottom of the pot, searching for the ring. A howl of anguish broke from his lips as it slipped through his hand. His tortured fingers scuttled after it in pursuit and—praise God!—closed upon it. He withdrew his hand and held the ring aloft.

"Aaaaaaah." A fascinated moan passed through the crowd as they saw Hunald's arm. Blisters and boils were already starting to form over the angry red surface of his skin.

"Ten days," Gerold announced, "shall be the time of God's judgment."

There was a stir from the crowd, but it held no tone of protest. Everyone understood the law: if the wounds on Hunald's hand and arm healed within ten days, his innocence was proved, and the cattle were his. If not, he was guilty of theft, and the cattle would be returned to their rightful owner, Abo.

Privately Gerold doubted the wounds would heal in so short a time. This was what he had intended, for he had little doubt that Hunald was guilty of the crime. And if Hunald's wounds should happen to heal in the allotted time—well, the ordeal would make him think twice before stealing his neighbor's cattle again. It was rough justice, but it was all the law provided, and it was far better than none. *Lex dura, sed lex.* The imperial statutes were the sole pillars supporting the rule of law in these disordered times; strike them flat, and who knew what wild winds would blow across the land, casting down weak and powerful alike.

"Call the next case, Frambert."

"Aelfric accuses Fulrad of refusing to pay the lawful blood price."

The case seemed straightforward enough. Fulrad's son Tenbert, a boy of sixteen, had killed a young woman, one of Aelfric's coloni. The crime itself was not in dispute, only the amount of the blood price. The laws regarding wergeld were detailed and specific for every person in the Empire, depending on rank, property holdings, age, and sex.

"It was her own fault," said Tenbert, a tall, loose-jointed boy with mottled skin and a sullen expression. "She was only a colona; she should not have fought so hard against me."

"He raped her," Aelfric explained. "Came across her harvesting grapes in my vineyard and took a fancy to her. She was a pretty little thing of only twelve winters—still a child, really, and she didn't understand. She thought he meant to harm her. When she wouldn't submit willingly, he beat her senseless." There was a long murmur from the crowd; Aelfric paused, content to let it register. "She died the next day, bruised and swollen and calling out for her mother."

"You have no cause for complaint," Fulrad, Tenbert's father, broke in hotly. "Did I not pay the wergeld the next week—fifty gold solidi, a generous sum! And the girl only a common colona!"

"The girl is dead; she will not tend my vines again. And her mother, one of my best weavers, is gone woodly with grief and is of no use anymore. I demand the lawful wergeld—one hundred gold solidi."

"An outrage!" Fulrad spread his arms wide in appeal. "Your Eminence, with what I have given him, Aelfric can purchase twenty fine milk cows—which everyone knows are worth far more than a wretched girl, her mother, and the loom combined!"

Gerold frowned. This bartering over blood price was repellent. The girl had been about the same age as Gerold's daughter Dhuoda. The idea of this sullen, disagreeable youth forcing himself on her was grotesque. Such things happened all the time, of course—any colona who made it to the age of fourteen with her virtue intact was extraordinarily lucky, or ugly, or both. Gerold was not naive, he knew the way of the world, but he did not have to like it.

A huge leather-bound codex gold-stamped with the imperial seal rested on the table before him. In it were inscribed the ancient laws of the Empire, the *Lex Salica*, as well as the *Lex Karolina*, which included revisions and additions to the code of law issued by the Emperor Karolus. Gerold knew the law and had no need of the book. Nevertheless, he made solemn show of consulting it; its symbolic value would not be lost on the litigants, and the judgment he was about to render would require all of its authority.

"The Salic code is very clear on this point," he said at last. "One hundred solidi is the lawful wergeld for a colona."

Fulrad cursed aloud. Aelfric grinned.

"The girl was twelve years of age," Gerold continued, "and had therefore reached her childbearing years. By law her blood price must be tripled to three hundred gold solidi."

"What, is the court mad?" Fulrad shouted.

"The sum," Gerold continued equably, "is to be paid as follows: two hundred solidi to Aelfric, the girl's lawful lord, and one hundred to her family."

Now it was Aelfric's turn to be outraged. "One hundred solidi to her *family*?" he said incredulously. "To coloni? I am lord of the landholding; the girl's wergeld is mine by rights!"

"Are you trying to ruin me?" Fulrad interrupted, too absorbed in his own problem to take pleasure in his enemy's distress. "Three hundred solidi is almost the blood price of a warrior! Of a priest!" He moved aggressively toward the table where Gerold sat. "Even, perhaps"—the threat in his voice was unmistakable—"of a count?"

A short shriek of alarm came from the crowd as a dozen of Fulrad's retainers pushed their way to the front. They were armed with swords, and they looked like men who knew how to use them.

Gerold's men moved to counter them, their hands on their half-drawn swords. Gerold stayed them with a gesture of his hand.

"In the Emperor's name"—Gerold's voice rang out, steely as a knife blade—"judgment in this case has been rendered and received." His cool indigo eyes stared Fulrad down. "Call the next case, Frambert."

Frambert did not answer. He had slid out of his seat and was hiding under the table.

Several moments passed in tense silence, the restive, murmuring crowd utterly stilled.

Gerold sat back in his chair, giving every appearance of confidence and ease, but his right hand dangled carelessly above his sword, so close his fingertips brushed the cold steel.

Abruptly, with a muttered curse, Fulrad spun on his heel. Grabbing Tenbert roughly by the arm, he dragged him toward the door. Fulrad's men followed, the crowd giving way before them. As they passed through the door, Fulrad struck Tenbert a hard blow to the head. The boy's yelp of pain sounded through the hall, and the crowd exploded into raucous, tension-breaking laughter.

Gerold smiled grimly. If he knew anything about human nature, Tenbert was in for quite a beating. Perhaps it would teach him a lesson, perhaps not. Either way, it could no longer help the murdered girl. But her family would receive part of her wergeld. With it, they would be able to buy their freedom and build a better life for themselves, their remaining children, and their children's children.

Gerold signaled his men; they resheathed their swords and withdrew to their positions behind the judicial table.

Frambert crawled out from under the table and reoccupied his seat with an air of ruffled dignity. His face was pale, and his voice shook as he read off the last case. "Ermoin, the miller, and his wife complain of their daughter, that she has willfully and against their express command taken a slave to husband."

Again the crowd parted to let pass an elderly couple, gray haired, patrician, robed in fine cloth—testimony to Ermoin's success in his trade. Behind them came a youth, dressed in the worn and tattered tunic of a slave, and finally a young woman, who entered with head modestly bowed.

"My lord." Ermoin spoke without waiting to be addressed. "You see before you our daughter, Hildegarde, joy of our aging hearts, the sole surviving child of eight born to us. She has been tenderly reared, my lord—too tenderly, as we have learned to our grief. For she has repaid our loving kindness with willful disobedience and ingratitude."

"What redress do you seek from this court?" Gerold asked.

"Why, the choice, my lord," Ermoin said with surprise. "The spindle or the sword. She must choose, as the law requires."

Gerold looked grave. In his career as missus he had presided over one other such case; he did not relish witnessing another.

"The law, as you say, provides for such a circumstance. But it seems harsh, especially for one who has been raised so—tenderly. Is there no other way?"

Ermoin took his meaning. The man price could be paid, the boy bought out of slavery and made a freedman.

"No, my lord." He shook his head vehemently.

"Very well," Gerold said resignedly. There was no way to avoid it—the girl's parents knew the law and would insist on carrying out the ugly business to its conclusion.

"Bring a spindle," Gerold commanded. "And Hunric"—he gestured to one of his men—"lend me your sword." He would not use his own weapon; it had never yet bitten into undefended flesh, nor ever would while Gerold carried it.

Some moments of bustle and commotion ensued while a spindle was procured from a nearby house.

The girl looked up as it was carried in. Her father spoke sharply to her, and she quickly dropped her eyes. But in that brief moment, Gerold got a glimpse of her face. She was exquisite—huge carnelian eyes islanded in a sea of milky skin, a fine, delicate brow, sweetly curving lips. Gerold could understand her parents' fury: with such a face the girl might have captured the heart of a great lord, even a nobleman, and bettered her family's fortunes.

Gerold placed one hand on the spindle; with his other he raised the sword. "If Hildegarde chooses the sword," Gerold said loudly so all might hear, "then her husband, the slave Romuald, will immediately die by it. If she chooses the spindle, then she herself will become a slave."

It was a terrible choice. Once Gerold had witnessed a different girl, not so lovely but just as young, face the same alternatives. That one had chosen the sword and stood by while the man she loved was slain with it before her eyes. Yet what else could she have done? Who would willingly choose vile debasement, not only for herself but for her children, and all future generations of her line?

The girl stood silent and unmoving. She had not reacted with so much as a quiver when Gerold had explained the trial.

"Do you understand the significance of the choice you must make?" Gerold asked her gently.

"She does, my lord," said Ermoin, tightening his grip on his daughter's arm. "She knows exactly what to do."

Gerold could well imagine it. The girl's cooperation had doubtless been secured by means of dire threats and curses, perhaps even blows.

The guards flanking the young man took hold of his arms to prevent any struggle to escape. He eyed them scornfully. He had an interesting face—a low, common brow crowned with a thatch of coarse hair, but intelligent eyes, a well-formed jaw, and a fine, strong nose; he looked to have some of the old Roman blood.

He might be a slave, but he had courage. Gerold signaled the guards to stand off.

"Come, child," Gerold said to the girl. "It is time."

Her father whispered something in her ear. She nodded, and he loosed his grip on her arm and pushed her forward.

She raised her head and looked at the young man. The undisguised love that shone in her eyes took Gerold aback.

"No!" The girl's father tried to stop her, but it was too late. With her gaze fixed on her husband, she unhesitatingly approached the spindle, sat down, and started to spin.

RIDING home to Villaris the next day, Gerold thought about what had happened. The girl had sacrificed everything—her family, her fortune, even her freedom. The love he had seen in her face fired his imagination and moved him in ways he did not entirely understand. All he knew, with a conviction that swept everything else aside, was that he wanted it—that purity and intensity of emotion that made all else seem pale and meaningless. It was not too late for him; surely it was not too late. He was only thirty-one—no longer young, perhaps, but still in the prime of his years.

He had never loved his wife, Richild, nor had she ever made any pretense of loving him. She would not, he knew, sacrifice so much as a single jeweled hair comb for him. Theirs had been a carefully negotiated marriage of fortunes and families. This was quite as things should be, and until recently Gerold had looked for no more. When, following Dhuoda's birth, Richild had announced that she wanted no more children, he had acceded to her wishes with no sense of loss. He had had no difficulty finding willing partners to share pleasures away from the marital bed.

But now, because of Joan, all that was changed. He pictured her in his mind, her fine, white-gold hair circling her face, her wise, gray-green eyes belying her years. His longing for her, stronger even than desire, tugged at his heart. He had never known anyone like her. Her probing intelligence, her willingness to challenge and question ideas the rest of the world accepted as unshakable truths, filled him with awe. He could talk to her as he could talk to no one else. He could trust her with anything, even his life.

It would be easy enough to make her his mistress—their last encounter at the riverbank had left no doubt about that. Uncharacteristically, he had held back, wanting something more, though he had not, at the time, known what.

Now he knew.

I want her as my wife.

It would be difficult, and no doubt costly, to free himself from Richild, but that did not matter.

Joan will be my wife, if she will have me.

With this resolve came a sense of peace. Gerold breathed deeply, reveling in the rich, exciting smells of the spring forest, feeling happier and more alive than he had for years.

THEY were very near home. A low-lying cloud hung heavily in the air, obscuring Gerold's view of Villaris. Joan was there, waiting for him. Impatient, he urged Pistis into a canter.

An unpleasant scent filled the air, penetrating his senses.

Smoke.

The cloud over Villaris was smoke.

Then they were all riding recklessly through the forest at an open run, unmindful of the branches tearing at their hair and their clothes. They emerged into the clearing and reined in sharply, staring in bewilderment.

Villaris was gone.

Beneath the cloud of slowly spiraling smoke, a blackened pile of rubble and ash was all that remained of the home they had left only two weeks before.

"Joan!" Gerold shouted. "Dhuoda! Richild!" Had they escaped, or were they dead, buried beneath the smoldering heap of debris?

His men were on their knees in the middle of the heap, searching for anything recognizable—a scrap of clothing, a ring, a headpiece. Some of them wept openly as they tore at the rubble, fearful that any moment they would find what they were seeking.

Off to one side, under a pile of blackened beams, Gerold saw something that made his heart sink.

It was a foot. A human foot.

He ran over and began pulling off the beams, clawing at them with his hands till they bled, though he did not know it. Gradually, the body underneath was revealed. It was a man's body, so badly burned that the features were scarcely recognizable, but from the amulet around the neck Gerold knew that it was Andulf, one of the guards. In his right hand was a sword. Gerold bent to take it up, but the dead man's hand followed, refusing to loose its grip. The heat of the fire had melted the handle, fusing flesh and iron into one.

Andulf had died fighting. But whom? Or what? Gerold surveyed the landscape with a soldier's practiced eye. There was no sign of any encampment, no weapons or materials left behind to lend a clue to what had happened. The surrounding forest lay motionless in the bright spring afternoon.

"My lord!" His men had found the bodies of two more guards. Like Andulf, they had died fighting, their weapons still in their hands. The discovery fueled a renewed search, but it was fruitless. There was no sign of anyone else.

Where are they all? They had left over two score people behind in Villaris—they couldn't all have vanished, without even a trace of bone or blood.

Gerold's heart pounded with a wild hope. Joan was alive, she must be alive. Perhaps she was nearby, hiding in the forest with the others who were missing—or perhaps they had fled to the town!

He mounted Pistis in a single leap, calling to his men. They rode into town at a gallop, slowing only when they reached the vacant, deserted streets.

Quietly, Gerold and his men scattered, reconnoitering, into the long row of silent houses. Gerold took Worad and Amalwin and rode on to the cathedral. The heavy oaken doors hung crookedly open on broken hinges. Warily they dismounted and approached, swords in hand. Climbing the steps, Gerold stumbled on something slippery. A pool of darkening blood lay atop the well-worn wood, fed by a slow, steady trickle from the other side of the door.

Gerold stepped inside.

For one merciful moment, the darkness of the interior obscured his sight. Then his vision cleared.

Behind him, Amalwin began to retch. Gerold felt his own gorge rise, but he swallowed hard, mastering himself. He covered his mouth and nose with his sleeve and moved forward into the nave of the church. It was difficult to avoid stepping on the densely sprawled bodies. He heard Worad and Amalwin cursing, heard the sound of his own rapid, shallow breath. He continued as in a dream, picking his way among the ghastly human debris, searching.

Near the high altar, he came across the members of his household. There was Wala, the chaplain, and Wido, the steward. Irminon, the chambermaid, lay nearby, her lifeless arms still cradling her dead babe. There was a howl from Worad, her husband, as he spied them. He fell to his knees and clasped them, pressed his hands to their wounds, smearing himself with their blood.

Gerold turned away. His eyes fell upon a familiar gleam of emerald and silver. Richild's tiara. She lay on her back beside it, her black hair spread across her body like a shroud. He picked up the tiara and went to replace it in her hair. At his touch Richild's head twisted grotesquely, then slowly rolled away from her body.

Startled, Gerold stepped backwards. His foot struck another body, and he almost fell. He looked down. At his feet lay Dhuoda, her body twisted as if she had tried to dodge her attacker's blow. With a groan, Gerold dropped to his knees beside his daughter's body. Gently he touched her, stroking her fine, soft child's hair, rearranging her limbs so she rested more comfortably. He kissed her cheek and passed his hand over the vacant eyes, closing them. It was all wrong. She should have been the one to perform these final respects for him.

With leaden expectation, he rose and resumed his grisly search through the sprawled bodies. Joan must be there somewhere, among the others; he had to find her.

He traversed the room, staring into every one of the cold, dead faces, recognizing in each of them the familiar features of a townsman, neighbor, or friend. But he did not find Joan.

Could she have somehow, miraculously, escaped? Was it possible? Gerold scarcely dared hope. He started to search the room again.

"My lord! My lord!" Voices rose urgently outside the cathedral. Gerold reached the door as the rest of his men came riding up.

"Norsemen, my lord! Down by the river! Loading their ships—"

But Gerold was already out the door, running toward Pistis.

THEY rode hell-bent for the river, their horses' hooves drumming on the hard earth of the road. They gave no thought to surprise; reckless with grief, they were fixed only on revenge.

Rounding a corner, they saw a long, shallow-drafted ship with a high wooden prow carved in the shape of a dragon's head with gaping mouth and long, curving teeth. Most of the Norsemen were already aboard, but a score remained onshore guarding the ship while the last of the booty was loaded.

With a great wordless battle shout, Gerold spurred forward, leveling his spear. His men followed close behind. The unmounted Norsemen dived and stumbled to get out of the way; several fell screaming beneath the trampling hooves. Gerold raised his barbed javelin, taking aim at the nearest Norseman, a gold-helmeted giant with a yellow beard. The giant turned, lifted his shield, and the javelin landed in it, shuddering.

Suddenly the air was filled with arrows; the Norsemen were shooting at them. Pistis reared wildly, then lurched to the ground, a feathered shaft in his eye. Gerold jumped clear, landing awkwardly on his left leg. He drew his sword and ran limping toward the giant, who was struggling to cut the javelin free from his shield. Gerold placed his foot on the butt of the javelin as it trailed on the ground, pulling the Norseman's shield down and away. The giant looked at Gerold with surprise and lifted his ax, but it was too late; with a single stroke Gerold took him through the heart. Without waiting to see him fall, Gerold whirled and struck at another Norseman, cleaving him through the head. Bloody shreds of tissue spattered Gerold's face, and he wiped his eyes to see. He was in the thick of the fighting now. He raised his sword, striking all around him with reckless exhilaration, the tightly coiled emotions of the past hour sprung forth in a welcome delirium of killing and blood.

"They're leaving! They're leaving!" The shouts of his men sounded in Gerold's ears; he looked toward the shore and saw the dragon-headed ship pulling away, its red sail fluttering in the wind. The Norsemen were fleeing.

A riderless black-maned bay danced nervously a few feet away. Gerold leapt on his back. The horse panicked and reared, but Gerold stayed with him, hands firm on the bridle. The bay turned smartly and headed for the shore. With a shout to his men to follow, Gerold rode straight into the water. An unused spear dangled from the saddle. Gerold withdrew the spear and hurled it with a force that almost propelled him over the neck of the bay. The spear sliced the air, its iron tip shimmering in the sun, and dropped into the water just short of the grinning dragon's mouth.

There was a burst of jeering laughter from the ship. The Norsemen called out derisively in their rough tongue. Two of them hoisted a golden bundle for display, only it wasn't a bundle, it was a woman hanging limply between them, a woman with auburn hair.

"Gisla!" Gerold shouted in an agony of recognition. What was she doing here? She should be safe at home with her husband.

Dazedly Gisla lifted her head. "Father!" she screamed. "Fatherrrrrr!" Her cry resonated in the fiber of his being.

Gerold spurred the bay, but he whinnied and backed off, refusing to advance any farther into the deepening dark water. He jabbed him in the hindquarters with his sword to force him to obey, but it only panicked him; he bucked wildly, his hooves flailing. A less skilled rider would have been thrown, but Gerold held on determinedly, fighting to bend the bay to his will.

"My lord! My lord!" Gerold's men were all around him, grabbing the bridle, pulling him back.

"It's hopeless, my lord." Grifo, Gerold's lieutenant, spoke clearly in his ear. "There's nothing more we can do."

The red sails of the Viking ship had ceased fluttering; they curved smoothly as the ship glided rapidly away from shore. There was no way to pursue it, no boats anywhere, even had Gerold and his men known how to sail them; the craft of shipbuilding had long been forgotten in Frankland.

Numbly, Gerold allowed Grifo to lead the bay to shore. Gisla's cry still echoed in his ears. *Fatherrrrr!* She was lost, irretrievably lost. There had been reports of young girls taken during the Norsemen's increasingly frequent raids along the coast of the Empire, but Gerold had never thought, never imagined . . .

Joan! The thought struck him with the force of an arrow shaft, robbing him of breath. They had taken her too! Gerold's disordered thoughts spun round, seeking another possibility, but found none. The barbarians had abducted Joan and Gisla, stolen them away to unspeakable horrors, and there was nothing, nothing he could do to save them.

His eyes fell on one of the dead Norsemen. He leapt off the bay, grabbed the long-handled ax from the dead man's clenched hand, and began striking at the corpse. The limp body jumped with every blow. The golden helmet came off, revealing the beardless face of a young boy, but Gerold kept striking, raising the ax again and again. Blood spurted everywhere, drenching his clothes.

Two of his men moved to stop him, but Grifo held them back.

"No," he said quietly. "Let him be."

A few moments later Gerold released the ax and dropped to his knees, covering his face with his hands. Warm blood coated his fingers, sticking them together. Sobs rose explosively in his throat, and he no longer tried to resist. Brokenly and unashamedly he wept.

Colmar | June 24, 833

The Field of Lies

ANASTASIUS pulled aside the heavy curtains covering the opening of the Pope's tent and slipped inside.

Gregory, fourth of that name to occupy the Throne of St. Peter, was still at prayer, kneeling on the silken pillows placed before the exquisite carved ivory figure of Christ that occupied the place of honor in his tent. The figure had survived the perilous journey over ruined roads and bridges, through the high and treacherous passes of the Alps, without a scratch. It gleamed as brightly here, in a crude tent pitched on this alien Frankish land, as it had in the safety and comfort of Gregory's private chapel in the Lateran Palace.

"*Deus illuminatio mea, Deus optimus et maximus,*" Gregory prayed, his face alight with devotion.

Watching soundlessly from the entryway, Anastasius wondered, *Was I ever so simple in my faith?* Perhaps once, when he was very small. But his innocence had died the day his uncle Theodorus had been murdered in the Lateran Palace before his eyes. "Watch," his father had told him then, "and learn."

Anastasius had watched, and learned—learned how to conceal his true feelings behind the mask of manners, learned how to manipulate and deceive, even betray, if necessary. The rewards of that knowledge had been gratifying. At nineteen, Anastasius was already *vestiarius*—the youngest man ever to hold so high a position. Arsenius, his father, took great pride in him. Anastasius meant to make him prouder still.

"Christ Jesus, give me the wisdom I need this day," Gregory continued. "Show me the way to avert this unholy war and reconcile these rebellious sons to the Emperor their father."

Is it possible that he does not know, even yet, what he stands to lose this day? Anastasius could scarcely believe it. The Pope was such an innocent. Anastasius was only nineteen, less than half Gregory's age, and already he understood far more about the world.

He is ill suited to be Pope, Anastasius thought, not for the first time. Gregory was a pious soul, there was no denying that, but piety was an overrated virtue. The man had a nature better suited to the cloister than the papal court, whose subtle politics were forever beyond his reach. Whatever had Emperor Louis been thinking of when he had asked Gregory to make the long journey from Rome to the empire of the Franks to serve as mediator in this crisis?

Anastasius coughed discreetly, to attract Gregory's attention, but he was lost in prayer, gazing at the Christ figure with a look of exaltation.

"It is time, Holiness." Anastasius did not hesitate to interrupt the Pope's devotions. Gregory had been at prayer for over an hour, and the Emperor was waiting.

Startled, Gregory looked around, and seeing Anastasius, nodded, crossed himself, and stood, smoothing the bell-shaped purple *paenula* which he wore over the papal dalmatic.

"I see you have drawn strength from the Christ figure, Holiness," Anastasius said, helping Gregory put on the pallium. "I too have felt its power."

"Yes. It is magnificent, isn't it?"

"Indeed. Especially the beauty of the head, which is large in proportion to the body. It always reminds me of the first Epistle to the Corinthians: 'And the head of Christ is God.' A glorious expression of the idea that Christ combines in His person both natures, Godhood and manhood."

Gregory beamed appreciatively. "I don't think I have ever heard that thought so well expressed. You make a fine vestiarius, Anastasius; the eloquence of your faith is an inspiration."

Anastasius was pleased. Such papal praise might well translate into another promotion—to nomenclator, perhaps, or even primicerius? He was young, it was true, but such high honors were not beyond ambition. Indeed, they were but way stations on the path to the single overarching ambition of Anastasius's life: to be Pope himself one day.

"You overprize me, Sire," Anastasius said with what he hoped was becoming modesty. "It is the perfection of the sculpture, and not my inadequate words, which deserves your praise."

Gregory smiled. "Spoken with true *humilitas.*" He put his hand fondly on Anastasius's shoulder and said gravely, "It is God's work we do this day, Anastasius."

Anastasius studied the Pope's face. *He suspects nothing. Good.* Obviously, Gregory still believed that he could mediate a peace between the Emperor and his sons, still knew nothing of the secret arrangements that Anastasius had so carefully and quietly carried out, following his father's explicit instructions.

"Tomorrow's dawn will see a new peace in this troubled land," Gregory said.

That is true enough, thought Anastasius, *though the peace will not be of the kind you envision.*

If all went as planned, tomorrow at dawn the Emperor would awake to find that his troops had deserted in the night, leaving him defenseless before the armies of his sons. It was all agreed upon and paid for; nothing that Gregory said or did this day would make the slightest whit of difference.

But it was important that the papal mediation occur as planned. Negotiating with Gregory would allay the Emperor's suspicions and distract his attention at this crucial juncture.

It would be judicious to offer Gregory some encouragement. "It is a great thing you do today, Holiness," Anastasius said. "God will smile upon it, and upon you."

Gregory nodded. "I know it, Anastasius. More surely at this moment than ever before."

"Gregory the peacemaker, they will call you, Gregory the Great!"

"No, Anastasius," Gregory reproved. "If I succeed in this day's work, it will be God's doing, not mine. The future of the Empire, upon which Rome's security depends, hangs in the balance today. If we win through, it will be with His help alone."

Gregory's selfless faith fascinated Anastasius, who regarded it as a freak of nature akin to having six fingers on one hand. Gregory was a genuinely humble man, Anastasius decided—but then, considering his talents, he had every reason to *be* humble.

"Accompany me to the Emperor's tent," Gregory said. "I would like you to be there when I speak with him."

Everything is going smoothly, Anastasius thought. When this was over, he had only to return to Rome and wait. Once Lothar was crowned Emperor in his father's place, he would know how to reward Anastasius for the work he had done here.

Gregory went to the door of the tent. "Come then. Let us do what must be done."

They walked out onto the open field crowded with the tents and banners of the Emperor's army. It was hard to believe that by tomorrow morning the colorful riot of activity would all be gone. Anastasius tried to imagine the look on Louis's face when he stepped outside his tent and found the quiet fields stretching bare before him.

Passing the royal guard, they arrived at the imperial tent. Just outside, Gregory paused to murmur one last prayer. "*Verba mea auribus percipe, Domine . . .*"

Anastasius watched impatiently while Gregory's full, almost feminine lips soundlessly formed the words of the fifth psalm: ". . . *intende voci clamoris mei, rex meus et Deus meus . . .*"

Pious fool. At that moment Anastasius's contempt for the Pope was so strong that he had to make a conscious effort to keep his voice respectful.

"Shall we go in, Sire?"

Gregory raised his head. "Yes, Anastasius, I am ready."

14

Fulda

IN THE shadowy predawn moonlight, the brothers of Fulda descended the night stairs and walked serenely in single file through the inner courtyard to the church, their gray robes merging seamlessly with the darkness. The quiet slap of their plain leathern sandals was the only sound to break the profound silence; even the larks would not awaken for several hours. The brothers entered the choir and, with the sureness of long habit, moved to their assigned positions for the celebration of vigils.

Brother John Anglicus knelt with the others, shifting knees with practiced, unconscious movements to find the most comfortable place on the packed earth floor.

Domine labia mea aperies . . . They began with a versicle, then moved on to the third psalm, following the form laid down by St. Benedict in his blessed rule.

John Anglicus liked this first office of the day. The unchanging pattern of the ceremony left the mind free to roam while the lips mouthed the familiar words. Several brothers were already starting to nod, but John Anglicus felt marvelously awake, all senses quickened and alert to this little world lit by flickering candle flames, bounded by the comforting solidity of the walls.

The feeling of belonging, of community, was especially strong this time of night. Daylight's sharp edges, so quick to expose individual personalities, likes and dislikes, loyalties and grudges, were submerged in the muted shadows and the resonant unison of the brothers' voices, hushed and melodic in the still night air.

Te Deum laudamus . . . John Anglicus chanted the Alleluia with the others, their bowed, cowled heads as indistinguishable as seeds in a furrow.

But John Anglicus was not like the others. John Anglicus did not belong here among this renowned and distinguished brotherhood. It was not through any defect of mind or character that this was so. It was an accident of fate, or of a cruel, indifferent God, that set John Anglicus irrevocably apart. John Anglicus did not belong among the brothers of Fulda, because John Anglicus, born Joan of Ingelheim, was a woman.

FOUR years had passed since she had presented herself at the abbey foregate disguised as her brother John. "Anglicus" they named her, because of her English father, and even among this select brotherhood of scholars, poets, and intellects, she soon distinguished herself.

The very same qualities of mind that as a woman had earned her derision and contempt were here universally praised. Her brilliance, knowledge of Scripture, and quick-wittedness in scholarly debate became matters of community pride. She was free—no, *encouraged*—to work to the very limit of her abilities. Among the novices, she was quickly promoted to *seniorus;* this gave her greater freedom of access to the renowned Fulda library—an enormous collection of some three hundred and fifty codices, including an extraordinarily fine series of classical authors—Suetonius, Tacitus, Virgil, Pliny, Marcellinus, among others. She ranged among the neatly rolled stacks in a transport of delight. All the knowledge of the world was here, it seemed, and all was hers for the asking.

Coming upon her reading a treatise of St. Chrysostom one day, Prior Joseph was surprised to discover that she knew Greek, a skill no other brother possessed. He told Abbot Raban, who immediately set her to work translating the abbey's excellent collection of Greek treatises on medicine; these included five of Hippocrates' seven books of aphorisms, the complete Tetrabiblios of Aëtius, as well as fragments of works by Oribasius and Alexander of Tralles. Brother Benjamin, the community physician, was so impressed with Joan's work that he made her his apprentice. He taught her how to grow and harvest the plants in the medicinal herb garden, and how to make use of their various healing properties: fennel for constipation, mustard for coughs, chervil for hemorrhages, wormwood and willow-bark for fevers—there were curatives in Benjamin's garden for every human ailment imaginable. Joan helped him compound the various poultices, purges, infusions, and simples that were the mainstay of monastic medicine, and she accompanied him to the infirmary to tend the sick. It was fascinating work, exactly suited to her inquisitive, analytical mind. Between her studies and her work with Brother Benjamin, as well as the bells that rang regularly seven times a day, calling the brethren to canonical prayers, her days were busy and productive. There was a freedom and power in this man's existence that she had never experienced before, and Joan found that she liked it; she liked it very much.

"Perhaps I shouldn't be telling you this, for it will swell your head till it no longer fits the cowl," gossipy old Hatto, the porter, had said to her just the day before, smiling cheerfully to let her know he was only jesting. "But yesterday I heard Father Abbot tell Prior Joseph that you had the keenest mind of all the brethren and would one day bring great distinction to this house."

The words of the old fortune-teller from the St.-Denis fair echoed in Joan's ears: "Greatness will be yours, beyond your imaginings." Was this what she had meant? "Changeling," the old woman had called her and said, "You are what you will not be; what you will become is other than you are."

That much is certainly true, Joan thought ruefully, fingering the small hairless spot at the crown of her head, almost obscured by the thick ring of curly white-gold hair encircling it. Her hair—her mother's hair—had been Joan's only vanity. Nevertheless, she had welcomed being shaved. Her monk's tonsure, along with the thin scar on her cheek left by the Norseman's sword, enhanced her masculine disguise—a disguise upon which her life now depended.

When she had first come to Fulda, she faced each day full of apprehension, never knowing if some new and unanticipated aspect of the monastic routine would suddenly expose her identity. She worked hard to mimic a masculine carriage and demeanor but worried that she was giving herself away in dozens of unsuspected little ways, though no one seemed to take notice.

Fortunately, the Benedictine way of life was carefully designed to protect the modesty of every member of the community, from the abbot to the lowliest of the brothers. The physical body, sinful vessel, had to be concealed insofar as possible. The long, full robes of the Benedictine habit provided ample camouflage of her budding woman's shape; as an added precaution, however, she bound her breasts tightly with strong linen strips. The Rule of St. Benedict explicitly stated that the brothers must sleep in their robes and reveal no more than hands and feet even on the hottest nights of Heuvimanoth. Baths were prohibited, except for the sick. Even the *necessaria,* the community latrines, preserved brotherly modesty through the provision of sturdy concealing partitions between all of the cold stone seats.

Upon first adopting her disguise on the road from Dorstadt to Fulda, Joan had learned to contain her monthly bleeding with a thick wadding of absorbent leaves, which she could later bury. In the abbey, even this precaution proved unnecessary. She simply dropped the soiled leaves down the deep, dark holes of the necessaria, where they mixed indistinguishably with other excreta.

Everyone at Fulda accepted her unquestioningly as a boy. Once a person's gender was established, Joan came to realize, no one thought any more about it. This was fortunate, for discovery of her true identity would mean certain death.

It was that certainty that kept her, at first, from any attempt to contact Gerold. There was no one she could trust to bear a message, and no way for her to leave. As a novice she was closely watched at all hours of the day and night.

She had lain awake for hours on her narrow dormitory cot, tormented by doubt. Even if she could get word to Gerold, would he want her? When they had been together that last time at the riverbank, she had wanted him to make love to her—she blushed at the remembrance—but he had refused. Afterward, on the way home, he was distant and remote, almost as if angry. Then he had taken the first opportunity to go away.

"You shouldn't have taken him so seriously," Richild had said. "You are only the latest bead in Gerold's long necklace of conquests." Was Richild right? At the time it had seemed impossible to believe, but perhaps Richild had been telling the truth.

It would be absurd to risk everything, her very life, to contact a man who did not want her, who had perhaps never wanted her. And yet . . .

SHE had been at Fulda three months when she witnessed something that helped her decide what to do. She was passing through the grange court with a group of fellow novices on the way to their cloister when a lively commotion near the porter's gate drew their attention. She watched as an escort of mounted men rode through, followed by a lady, sumptuously arrayed in cloth of golden silk, as straight and elegant in the saddle as a marble pillar. She was beautiful, her delicate, rounded features and pale skin framed by a waterfall of lustrous, light brown hair, but her dark, intelligent eyes held a look of mysterious sadness.

"Who is she?" Joan asked, intrigued.

"Judith, wife of Viscount Waifar," replied Brother Rudolph, the master of novices. "A learned woman. They say she can read and write Latin like a man."

"*Deo, juva nos.*" Brother Gailo crossed himself fearfully. "Is she a witch?"

"She has a great reputation for piety. She has even written a commentary on the life of Esther."

"Abomination," said Brother Thomas, one of the other novices. A homely young man with a melon face, cleft chin, and heavy-lidded eyes, Thomas was convinced of his own superior virtue and seized every opportunity to display it. "A gross violation of nature. What can a woman, a creature of base passions, know of such things? God will surely punish her for her arrogance."

"He already has," Brother Rudolph replied, "for though the viscount needs an heir, his lady is barren. Just last month, she was delivered of another stillborn babe."

The noble procession pulled up before the abbatial church. Joan watched Judith dismount and approach the church door with solemn dignity, carrying a single taper.

"You should not stare, Brother John," Thomas remonstrated piously. He frequently curried favor with Brother Rudolph at the expense of his fellow novices. "A good monk should keep his eyes chastely lowered before a woman," he quoted sanctimoniously from the rule.

"You are right, Brother," Joan replied. "But I've never seen a lady like that, with one eye blue and the other brown."

"Do not compound your sin with falsehood, Brother John. Both the lady's eyes are brown."

"And how do you know that, Brother," Joan inquired slyly, "if *you* did not look at her?"

The other novices burst into laughter. Even Brother Rudolph could not suppress a smile.

Thomas glared at Joan. She had made him look a fool, and he was not one to forget such an injury.

Their attention was distracted by Brother Hildwin, the sacristan, who hurried to interpose himself between Judith and the church.

"Peace be with you, lady," he said, using the Frankish vernacular.

"*Et cum spiritu tuo,*" she replied smoothly in perfect Latin.

Pointedly, Brother Hildwin addressed her again in the vernacular. "If you require food and lodging, we stand ready to accommodate you and your entourage. Come, I will escort you to the house for distinguished visitors and inform our lord Abbot of your arrival. He will doubtless wish to greet you in person."

"You are most kind, Father, but I do not require *hospitalitas,*" she replied again in Latin. "I only wish to light a candle in the church for my dead babe. Then I will be on my way."

"Ah! Then it is my duty, as sacristan of this church, to inform you, Daughter, that you may not pass through these doors while you are still"—he sought a suitable word—"unclean."

Judith flushed but did not lose her composure. "I know the law, Father," she said calmly. "I have waited the requisite thirty-three days since the birthing."

"The babe of which you were delivered was a girl child, was it not?" Brother Hildwin said with an air of condescension.

"Yes."

"Then the time of . . . uncleanliness . . . is longer. You may not enter the sacred confines of this church for sixty-six days after the birth of the child."

"Where is this written? I have not read this law."

"Nor is it fitting that you should, being a woman."

Joan started indignantly at the brazenness of the affront. With the force of remembered experience, she felt the shame of Judith's humiliation. All the lady's learning, her intelligence, her breeding stood for naught. The vilest beggar, ignorant and mud streaked, could enter the church to pray, but Judith could not, for she was "unclean."

"Return home, Daughter," Brother Hildwin continued, "and pray in your own chapel for the soul of your unbaptized babe. God has a horror of what is against nature. Lay down the pen and pick up a womanly needle; repent of pridefulness, and He may lift the burden He has placed upon you."

The flush in Judith's cheeks spread its color across her face. "This insult shall not go unanswered. My husband shall know of it directly, and he will not be pleased." This was a piece of face-saving bravado, for Viscount Waifar's temporal authority carried no weight here, and she knew it. Holding her head high, she turned toward her waiting mount.

Joan came forward from the little group of novices.

"Give me the candle, lady," she said, holding out her hand. "I will light it for you."

Surprise and distrust registered in Judith's beautiful dark eyes. Was this a further attempt to humiliate her?

For a long moment the two women stood looking at each other, Judith the epitome of feminine beauty in her golden tunic, her long hair framing her face in a becoming cloud, Joan, the taller of the two, boyish and unadorned in her plain monk's garb.

Something in the compelling gray-green eyes that met hers with such intensity persuaded Judith. Wordlessly she placed the slim taper into Joan's outstretched hand. Then she remounted and rode through the gate.

Joan lighted the candle before the altar as she had promised. The sacristan was furious. "Intolerable cheek!" he declared. And that night, to Brother Thomas's evident delight, Joan was required to fast in penance for her crime.

AFTER this episode, Joan made a determined effort to put Gerold from her mind. She could never be happy living a woman's restricted existence. Besides, she reasoned, her relationship with Gerold was not what she had believed it to be. She had been a child, inexperienced and naive; her love had been a romantic delusion born of loneliness and need. Gerold had certainly not loved her, or he would never have left.

Aegra amans, she thought. Truly Virgil was right: love *was* a form of sickness. It altered people, made them behave in strange and irrational ways. She was glad she was done with it.

Never give yourself to a man. Her mother's words of warning came back to her. She had forgotten them in the fervor of her childish infatuation. Now she realized how lucky she had been to have escaped her mother's fate.

Over and over again Joan told herself these things, until at last she came to believe them.

⊱ 15 ⊰

THE brothers gathered in the chapter house, seated in order of seniority on the *gradines,* tiers of stone seats lining the walls of the house. The chapter meeting was the most important assembly of the day outside of the religious offices, for it was here that the temporal business of the community was conducted and matters regarding management, monies, appointments, and disputes were discussed. This was also where brothers who had committed transgressions of the rule were expected to confess their faults and be assigned their penances, or risk accusation by others.

Joan always came to chapter with a certain trepidation. Had she inadvertently given herself away with some incautious word or gesture? If her true identity were ever to be revealed, this was where she would learn of it.

The meeting always began with the reading of a chapter from the Rule of St. Benedict, the book of monastic regulations which guided the everyday spiritual and administrative life of the community. The rule was read straight through from beginning to end, a chapter a day, so that over the course of a year the brethren heard it in its entirety.

After the reading and benediction, Abbot Raban asked, "Brethren, have you any faults to confess?"

Before he finished uttering the words, Brother Thedo leapt to his feet. "Father, I do confess a fault."

"What is it, Brother?" Abbot Raban said with weary patience. Brother Thedo was always the first to accuse himself of wrongdoing.

"I have faltered in the performance of the *opus manuum.* Copying a life of St. Amandus, I fell asleep in the scriptorium."

"Again?" Abbot Raban lifted an eyebrow.

Thedo bowed his head meekly. "Father, I am sinful and unworthy. Please exact the harshest of penances upon me."

Abbot Raban sighed. "Very well. For two days you will stand a penitent before the church."

The brothers smiled wryly. Brother Thedo was so frequently to be found doing penance outside the church that he seemed part of the decoration, a living, breathing pillar of remorse.

Thedo was disappointed. "You are too charitable, Father. For so grievous a fault, I ask to be allowed to do penance for a week."

"God does not welcome pridefulness, Thedo, even in suffering. Remember that, while you are asking His forgiveness for your other faults."

The reprimand struck home. Thedo flushed and sat down.

"Are there any other faults to confess?" Raban asked.

Brother Hunric stood. "Twice I came late to night office."

Abbot Raban nodded; Hunric's tardiness had been noted, but because he admitted his fault freely and did not try to hide it, his penance would be light.

"From now until St.-Denis's day, you will keep night watch."

Brother Hunric bowed his head. The Feast of St.-Denis was two days away; for the next two nights, he must stay awake and watch the progress of the moon and the stars across the sky so he could determine as closely as possible the arrival of the eighth hour of the night, or two A.M., and then awaken the sleeping brothers for the celebration of vigils. Such watches were essential to the strict observance of the night office, for the sundial was the only other way of measuring the passage of time, and of course it was of no use in darkness.

"During your watch," Raban continued, "you will kneel in unceasing prayer on a pile of nettles, that you may be sharply reminded of your indolence and prevented from compounding your fault with sinful sleepfulness."

"Yes, Father Abbot." Brother Hunric accepted the penance without rancor. For so grave an offense, the punishment could have been far worse.

Several brothers stood in their turn and confessed to such minor faults as breaking dishes in refectory, errors in scribing, mistakes in the oratory, receiving their corresponding penances with humble acceptance. When they were finished, Abbot Raban paused to make certain no one else wished to confess. Then he said, "Have any other infractions of the rule been committed? Let those who will speak, for the good of their brothers' souls."

This was the part of the meeting Joan dreaded. Scanning the rows of brethren, her gaze fell on Brother Thomas. His heavy-lidded eyes were regarding her with unmistakable hostility. She shifted uneasily in her seat. *Does he mean to accuse me of something?*

But Thomas made no move to rise. From the row of seats just behind him, Brother Odilo stood.

"On Friday fastday, I saw Brother Hugh take an apple from the orchard and eat it."

Brother Hugh leapt nervously to his feet. "Father, it is true I picked the apple, for it was hard work pulling up the weeds, and I felt a great weakness in my limbs. But, Holy Father, I did not eat the apple; I merely took a small bite, to strengthen me so I could go on with the opus manuum."

"Weakness of the flesh is no excuse for violation of the rule," Abbot Raban responded sternly. "It is a test, sent by God to try the spirit of the faithful. Like Eve, the mother of sin, you have failed that test, Brother—a serious fault, especially as you did not seek to confess it yourself. In penance, you will fast for a week and forgo all pittances until Epiphany."

A week of starvation, and no pittances—the extra little treats that supplemented the spartan monastic diet of greens, pulse, and occasionally fish—until well after Christ Mass! This last part would be especially hard to bear, for it was during this holy season that gifts of food poured into the abbey from all over the countryside, as Christians looked guiltily to the welfare of their immortal souls. Honey cakes, pasties, sweet roast chickens, and other rare and wonderful indulgences would briefly grace the abbey tables. Brother Hugh looked evilly at Brother Odilo.

"Furthermore," Abbot Raban continued, "in grateful return to Brother Odilo for his attention to your spiritual well-being, you will prostrate yourself before him tonight and wash his feet with humility and thankfulness."

Brother Hugh bowed his head. He would perforce do as Abbot Raban had charged, but Joan doubted he would feel grateful. Penitent acts were easier to enjoin than penitent hearts.

"Are there any other faults that need to be disclosed?" Abbot Raban asked. When no one responded, he said gravely, "It grieves me to report that there is one among us who is guilty of the wickedest of sins, a crime detestable in the sight of God and Heaven—"

Joan's heart gave a leap of alarm.

"—the breaking of his holy vow made to God."

Brother Gottschalk jumped to his feet. "It was my father's vow, not mine!" he said chokingly.

Gottschalk was a young man, some three or four years older than Joan, with curly black hair and eyes set so deep in their sockets they looked like two dark bruises. Like Joan, he was an oblate, offered to the monastery by his father, a Saxon noble. Now that he was grown a man, he wanted to leave.

"It is lawful for a Christian man to dedicate his son to God," Abbot Raban said sternly. "Such offering cannot be withdrawn without great sin."

"Is it not an equal sin for a man to be bound against his nature and his will?"

"If a man will not turn, He will whet His sword," Abbot Raban said portentously. "He hath bent His bow and made it ready. He hath prepared for him the instruments of death."

"That is tyranny, not truth!" Gottschalk cried passionately.

"Shame!" "Sinner!" "For shame, Brother!" Scattered cries of outrage punctuated a chorus of hissing from the brethren.

"Your disobedience, my son, has placed your immortal soul in grievous danger," Abbot Raban said solemnly. "There is but one cure for such a disease—in the just and terrible words of the Apostle: *Tradere hujusmodi hominem in interitum carnis, ut spiritus salvus sit in diem Domini*—such a man must be handed over for the destruction of his flesh, that his spirit may be saved on the day of the Lord."

At Raban's signal, two of the *decani juniores,* brothers in charge of monastic discipline, took hold of Gottschalk and pushed him to the center of the room. He offered no resistance as they shoved him to his knees and roughly pulled up his robes, exposing his naked buttocks and back. From one corner of the room where it was kept for just this purpose, Brother Germar, the senior deacon, retrieved a sturdy willow stick, at the end of which were affixed thick strands of knotted, wiry rope. Positioning himself carefully, he raised the scourge high and brought it down hard on Gottschalk's back. The slap of the lash reverberated throughout the hushed assembly.

The scarred skin on Joan's back quivered. The flesh has its own memory, keener than the mind's.

Brother Germar raised the scourge again and brought it down even harder. Gottschalk's whole body shuddered, but he clamped his lips together, refusing to give Abbot Raban the satisfaction of hearing him cry out. Again the scourge rose and fell, rose and fell, and still Gottschalk did not break.

After the usual seven lashes, Brother Germar lowered the scourge. Abbot Raban angrily signaled him to continue. With a look of surprise, Brother Germar obeyed.

Three more lashes, four, five, and then there was an awful crack as the scourge struck bone. Gottschalk threw back his head and screamed—a great, terrible, tearing cry from the center of his being. The appalling sound hung in the air, then subsided into a long, shuddering sob.

Abbot Raban nodded, satisfied, and signaled Brother Germar to stop. As Gottschalk was lifted and half-led, half-dragged from the hall, Joan caught a flash of white in the middle of his crimsoned back. It was one of Gottschalk's ribs, and it had completely pierced his flesh.

THE infirmary was uncharactistically empty, for the day was warm and breezeless, and the old ones and the chronically ill had been taken outside for a touch of healing sun.

Brother Gottschalk lay prone on the infirmary bed, half conscious, his open wounds reddening the sheets. Brother Benjamin, the physician, bent over him, trying to staunch the bleeding with the aid of a few linen bandages, already completely saturated with blood. He looked up as Joan came in.

"Good. You are here. Hand me some bandages from the shelf."

Joan hurried to comply. Brother Benjamin peeled off the old bandages, threw them to the ground, and applied the new. Within moments, they were soaked through.

"Help me to shift him," Benjamin said. "The way he's lying, that bone is still making mischief. We must get that rib back into place, or we'll never stop the bleeding."

Joan moved to the opposite side of the bed, skillfully positioning her hands so that one quick forward motion would draw the bone back into place.

"Easy, now," Benjamin said. "Half sensible though he is, he'll feel it sharp. On my mark, Brother. One, two, *three!*"

Joan pulled while Brother Benjamin pushed. There was a fresh outpouring of blood; then the bone slid beneath the gaping flesh.

"*Deo, juva me!*" Gottschalk lifted his head in tortured petition, then fell back unconscious.

They sponged up the blood and cleansed Gottschalk's wounds.

"Well, Brother John, what needs doing next?" Brother Benjamin quizzed Joan when they had done.

She was quick with the answer. "Apply a salve . . . of mugwort, perhaps, mixed with some pennyroyal. Soak some bandages in vinegar, and apply them as a healing pad."

"Very good." Benjamin was pleased. "We shall put in some lovage as well, as a guard against infection."

They worked side by side, preparing the solution, the pungent smell of the new-crushed herbs rising headily around them. When the bandages were dipped and ready, Joan handed them to Brother Benjamin.

"You do it," he said, then stood back and watched approvingly as his young apprentice firmly pressed the ugly flaps of skin together and expertly positioned the bandages.

He came forward to inspect the patient. The bandaging was perfect—better, in fact, than he could have done himself. Nevertheless, he did not like the way Brother Gottschalk looked. His skin, cold and clammy to the touch, had gone white as new-sheared wool. His breathing came shallowly, and the pulse of his heart blood, faintly detected, was dangerously rapid.

He's going to die, Brother Benjamin realized with dismay, and the thought immediately followed: *Father Abbot will be furious.* Raban had exceeded himself in chapter and surely knew it; Gottschalk's death would serve as both reproach and embarrassment. And if news of it should reach King Ludwig . . . well, even abbots were not immune from censure and dismissal.

Brother Benjamin searched his mind for something more to do. His pharmacopoeia of medicines was useless, for he could not administer anything by mouth, not even water to replenish lost fluids, while his patient lay senseless.

John Anglicus's voice startled him from his reverie: "Should I start a fire in the brazier and set some stones to heating?"

Benjamin looked at his assistant with surprise. Packing a patient round with hot stones wrapped in flannel was standard medical procedure in winter, when the pervading chill was known to sap a sick man's strength, but now, in these last warm days of autumn . . . ?

"Hippocrates' treatise on wounds," Joan reminded him. She had given him her translation of the Greek physician's brilliant work only last month.

Brother Benjamin frowned. He enjoyed doctoring, and within the limited medical knowledge of the day, he was good at it. But he was no innovator; he felt more comfortable with safe, familiar remedies than with new ideas and theories.

"The shock of violent injury," Joan continued with a barely perceptible degree of impatience. "According to Hippocrates, it can kill a man with a penetrating chill that emanates from within."

"It is true that I have seen men die suddenly after injury, though their wounds did not appear to be mortal," Brother Benjamin said slowly. "*Deus vult,* I thought, God's will . . ."

The intelligent young face of John Anglicus was alight with expectancy, seeking permission to proceed.

"Very well," Brother Benjamin conceded, "fire up the brazier; it's unlikely to do Brother Gottschalk any harm, and it may do him good, as the pagan doctor says." He settled himself on a bench, grateful to rest his arthritic legs as his energetic young assistant bustled about the room, starting the fire and setting stones over it.

When the stones were hot, Joan wrapped them in thick layers of flannel cloth and carefully placed them all about Gottschalk. Two of the largest stones she positioned under his feet, so that they were slightly elevated, following Hippocrates' recommendation. She finished by laying a light woolen blanket over all, to hold in the warmth.

After a short while, Gottschalk's eyelids fluttered; he moaned and began to stir. Brother Benjamin went to the bed. A healthy pink tinge had returned to Gottschalk's skin, and he was breathing more normally. A quick check of his pulse revealed a strong, regular heartbeat.

"God be praised." Brother Benjamin breathed in relief. He smiled at John Anglicus across the bed. *He has the gift,* Brother Benjamin thought with an almost paternal pride, slightly tinged with envy. From the beginning the boy had shown brilliant promise—that was why Benjamin had asked for him as his assistant—but he had never expected him to come so far so fast. In just a few years, John Anglicus had mastered the skills it had taken Brother Benjamin a lifetime to acquire.

"You have the healing touch, Brother John," he said benevolently. "Today you have surpassed your old master; soon I will have nothing left to teach you."

"Do not say so," Joan responded with chagrin, for she was fond of Benjamin. "I still have much to learn, and I know it."

Gottschalk groaned again, his pinched lips drawing back to reveal his teeth.

"He begins to feel the pain," Brother Benjamin said. Working rapidly, he made a potion of red wine and sage, into which he infused a few drops of poppy juice. Such a preparation required the greatest care, for what could, in small doses, provide blessed relief from insupportable pain could also kill, the difference depending solely on the skill of the physician.

When he was done, Brother Benjamin handed the brimming cup to Joan, who carried it to the bed and offered it to Gottschalk. Proudly, he pushed it away, though the sudden movement caused him to cry out in pain.

"Drink it, Brother," Joan chided gently, and held the cup to Gottschalk's lips. "You must get well if you are ever to win your freedom," she added in a conspiratorial whisper.

Gottschalk flashed her a surprised look. He took a few sips, then drank rapidly, thirstily, like a man who comes upon a well after a hot day's march.

An authoritative voice sounded unexpectedly behind them. "Do not place your hopes in herbs and potions."

Turning, Joan saw Abbot Raban, followed by a score of the brethren. She put down the cup and rose.

"The Lord grants life to men and makes them sound. Prayer alone can restore this sinner to health." Abbot Raban signaled the brothers, who quietly surrounded the bed.

Abbot Raban led them in the prayer for the sick. Gottschalk did not join in. He lay unmoving, eyes closed as if asleep, though Joan could tell from his breathing he was not.

His body will heal, she thought, *but not his wounded soul.* Joan's heart went out to the young monk. She understood his stubborn refusal to submit to Raban's tyranny, remembering, too well, her own fierce struggle against her father.

"All praise and thanks to God." Abbot Raban's voice sounded clear above the rest of the brethren.

Joan joined in praising God, but in her mind she also gave thanks to the pagan Hippocrates, worshiper of idols, whose bones were dust many centuries before Christ was born, but whose wisdom had reached across the distant years to heal one of His sons.

"THE wound's mending nicely," Joan reassured Gottschalk after she unwrapped the bandages and laid his back bare for inspection. Two weeks had passed since the day of his scourging, and already the broken rib had knit and the jagged edges of the wound sealed neatly together—though, like her, Gottschalk would bear the marks of his punishment for life.

"Thanks for the trouble you've taken, Brother," Gottschalk replied, "but it will all be to do over, for it's only a matter of time till he has me scourged again."

"You only provoke him with open defiance. A milder approach would serve you better."

"I will defy him with the last breath in my body. He is evil," he cried passionately.

"Have you thought of telling him you'll forgo your claim to the land in return for your freedom?" Joan asked. An oblate was always offered to a monastery along with a substantial gift of land; if the oblate subsequently left, the land presumably would revert as well.

"Don't you think I've offered that already?" Gottschalk replied. "It's not the land he's after; it's me, or rather my submission, body and soul. And that he'll never have, though he kill me for it."

So it was a contest of wills between them—one that Gottschalk could not possibly win. Best to get him away from here before something terrible happened.

"I've been giving some thought to your problem," Joan said. "Next month there's a synod in Mainz. All the bishops of the Church will attend. If you submitted a petition for your release, they would have to consider it—and their ruling would supersede Abbot Raban's."

Gottschalk said bleakly, "The synod will never contravene the will of the great Raban Maur. His power is too great."

"The ruling of abbots, even of archbishops, has been overturned before," Joan argued. "And you've a strong argument in the fact you were offered as an oblate in infancy, before you had reached the age of reason. I searched the library and found some passages from Jerome that would support such an argument." She pulled a roll of parchment from under her robe. "Here, see for yourself—I've written it all down."

Gottschalk's dark eyes brightened as he read. He looked up excitedly. "It's brilliant! A dozen Rabans could not refute so well made an argument!" Then the dark clouds rolled in again. "But—there's no way for me to present this before the synod. *He* will never grant me permission to leave, even for a day, and certainly not to go to Mainz."

"Barthold, the cloth merchant, can take it for you. His business brings him here regularly. I know him well, for he comes to the infirmary to fetch medicine for his wife, who suffers from headache. He's a good man and can be trusted to bear the petition safely to Mainz."

Gottschalk asked with suspicion, "Why are you doing this?"

Joan shrugged. "A man should be free to live the life he chooses." To herself she added, *And so, for that matter, should a woman.*

EVERYTHING went off as planned. When Barthold came to the infirmary to pick up the medicine for his wife, Joan gave him the petition, which he bore away tucked safely in his saddlebag.

A few weeks later, the abbey received an unexpected visit from Otgar, Bishop of Trier. After the formal greeting in the forecourt, the bishop requested and received immediate audience with the abbot in his quarters.

The news the bishop brought was astonishing: Gottschalk was released from his vows. He was free to leave Fulda when he chose.

He chose to leave at once, not wishing to remain one moment longer than necessary under Raban's baleful eye. Packing was no problem; though he had lived all his life at the monastery, Gottschalk had nothing to bring away with him, for a monk could not own any personal property. Brother Anselm, the kitchener, put together a sack of food to see Gottschalk through the first few days on the road, and that was all.

"Where will you go?" Joan asked him.

"To Speyer," he answered. "I've a married sister there; I can stay with her for a while. Then . . . I don't know."

He had fought for liberty so long and with so little hope he had not stopped to consider what he would do if he actually achieved it. He had never known anything but the monastic life; its safe and predictable rhythms were as much a part of him as breathing. Though he was too proud to admit to it, Joan read the uncertainty and fear in his eyes.

The brethren did not gather for a formal leave-taking, for Raban had forbidden it. Only Joan and a few other brothers whose opus manuum brought them across the forecourt at that hour were there to see Gottschalk walk through the gate, a free man at last. Joan watched him make his way down the road, his tall, spare figure growing smaller and smaller until it disappeared on the horizon.

Would he be happy? Joan hoped so. But somehow he seemed a man fated always to yearn after that which he could not have, to choose for himself the rockiest, most difficult path. She would pray for him, as for all the other sad and troubled souls who must travel roads alone.

16

O N ALL Souls' Day, the brethren of Fulda gathered in the forecourt for the *separatio leprosorum,* the solemn liturgy segregating lepers from society. This year seven such unfortunates had been identified in the region surrounding Fulda, four men and three women. One was a youth of no more than fourteen, in whom the marks of the disease were as yet very indistinct; one an ancient woman of sixty or more, whose lidless eyes and absent lips and fingers attested to an advanced stage of the disease. All seven had been wrapped in black shrouds and herded into the forecourt, where they huddled in a wretched little band.

The brethren approached in solemn procession. First came Abbot Raban, drawn up tall in full abbatial dignity. To his right walked Prior Joseph, to his left, Bishop Otgar. Behind marched the remaining brethren in order of seniority. Two lay brothers brought up the rear of the procession, pushing a wheelbarrow heaped with earth taken from the graveyard.

"I hereby forbid you to enter any church, mill, bakery, market, or other place where people gather." Abbot Raban addressed the lepers with heavy solemnity. "I forbid you to use the common roads and paths. I forbid you to come near any living person without ringing your bell to give warning. I forbid you to touch children, or to give them anything."

One of the women began to wail. Two dark, wet patches stained the front of her worn woolen tunic. *A nursing mother,* Joan thought. *Where is her babe? Who will take care of it?*

"I forbid you to eat or drink in the company of anyone save lepers like yourselves," Abbot Raban continued. "I forbid you ever to wash your hands or face or any objects you may use at the riverbank, or at any spring or stream. I forbid you carnal knowledge of your spouse, or any other person. I forbid you to beget children, or to nurse them."

The woman's anguished wailing intensified, her tears coursing down her ulcerated face.

"What is your name?" With barely concealed irritation, Abbot Raban addressed the woman in the vernacular. Her unseemly display of emotion was marring the well-ordered symmetry of the ceremony, with which Raban had hoped to impress the bishop. For it was now apparent that Otgar had come to Fulda not merely to deliver the news of Gottschalk's release but also to observe and make report upon Raban's stewardship of the abbey.

"Madalgis," the woman snuffled in reply. "Please, lord, I must go home, for there are four fatherless little ones needing their dinner."

"Heaven will provide for the innocent. You have sinned, Madalgis, and God is afflicting you," Raban explained with elaborate patience, as if to a child. "You must not weep, but instead thank God, for you will suffer the less torment in the life to come."

Madalgis stood bewildered, as if she doubted she had heard aright. Then her face crumpled and her crying broke out anew, louder than before, her face crimsoning from the bottom of her neck to the roots of her hair.

That's odd, Joan thought.

Raban turned his back upon the woman. *"De profundis clamavi ad te, Domine . . ."* He began the prayer for the dead. The brethren joined in, their voices mingling in deep unison.

Joan mouthed the words mechanically, her eyes fixed on Madalgis with intent concentration.

Finishing with the prayer, Raban moved on to the final part of the ceremony, in which each of the lepers, in turn, would be formally separated from the world. He stood before the first, the relatively unmarked boy of fourteen. *"Sis mortuus mundo, vivens iterum Deo,"* Abbot Raban said. "Be dead unto the world, living in the eyes of God." He signaled to Brother Magenard, who plunged a spade into the wheelbarrow, lifted out a small pile of graveyard earth, and flung it at the boy, spattering his clothes and hair.

Five times the little ceremony was repeated, ending each time with the hurling of the earth. When it came Madalgis's turn, she tried to run, but the two lay brothers blocked her way. Raban frowned at her.

"Sis mortuus mundo, vivens iter—"

"Stop!" Joan shouted.

Abbot Raban broke off. Everyone turned to locate the source of this unprecedented interruption.

With all eyes upon her, Joan advanced toward Madalgis and

examined her with rapid skill. Then she turned to Abbot Raban. "Father, this woman is no leper."

"What?" Raban struggled to keep his anger reined, so the bishop would not observe it.

"These lesions are not leprotic. See how her skin colors, fed by the blood beneath? This affliction of the skin is not infectious; it can be cured."

"If she is not a leper, then what has caused these ulcers?" Raban demanded.

"There could be several causes. It is difficult to say without further examination. But whatever the reason, one thing is certain: it is not leprosy."

"God has marked this woman with the visible manifestation of sin. We must not defy His will!"

"She is marked, but not by leprosy," Joan responded sturdily. "God has provided us with the knowledge to discern between those whom He has chosen to bear this burden, and those whom He has not. Will He be pleased if we consign to a living death one whom He Himself has not elected?"

It was a clever argument. With dismay, Raban saw the others were moved by it. "How do we know whether you have correctly interpreted the signs of God's will?" he countered. "Is your pride so great you would sacrifice your brethren to it—for in order to minister to this woman you must put all in jeopardy."

This elicited a buzz of concern. Nothing, save the unimaginable torments of Hell, inspired more horror, revulsion, and fear than the disease of leprosy.

With a howl, Madalgis threw herself at Joan's feet. She had been following the discussion without understanding, for Joan and Raban had been speaking in Latin, but she had managed to discern that Joan had interceded on her behalf, and that the argument was not going well.

Joan patted her shoulder, as much to quiet as to comfort her. "None of the brethren needs be put at risk, saving myself. With your leave, Father, I will go with her to her home, bringing such medications as may be necessary."

"Alone? With a woman?" Raban's brows rose in pious horror. "John Anglicus, your purpose is perhaps innocent, but you are as yet a young man, subject to the baser passions of the flesh, from which it is my duty, as your spiritual father, to protect you."

Joan opened her mouth to respond, then closed it with frustration. No one could be safer from temptation by a woman than she, but there was no way she could explain that to Raban.

Brother Benjamin's rasping voice sounded behind her. "I will accompany Brother John. I am old, long past the time for such temptation. Father, you may trust in Brother John when he says the woman is no leper, for when he speaks with such certainty, he will not be wrong. His skill in such matters is very great."

Joan shot him a grateful glance. Madalgis clung to her, her wails tempered into muted whimpering by Joan's reassuring touch.

Abbot Raban hesitated. What he really wanted was to give John Anglicus a sound caning for his presumptuous disobedience. But Bishop Otgar was watching; Raban could not appear to be unbending or unmerciful. "Very well," he said grudgingly. "Brother John, after vespers you and Brother Benjamin may go from here with this sinner, and do what may be done in God's name to cure her of her affliction."

"Thank you, Father," Joan said.

Raban made the sign of the cross over them. "May God in His merciful goodness shield you from harm."

THE mule carrying bags of medical supplies plodded along placidly, indifferent to the westering sun. Madalgis's cottage lay some five miles on; at this languid pace, they would be hard-pressed to arrive before dark. Joan prodded the mule impatiently. To humor her, the beast took five or six quick steps in succession, then settled back comfortably into its original gait.

As they walked, Madalgis chattered on with the nervous energy that often follows a great fright. Joan and Benjamin learned her whole sad story. Despite her destitute appearance, she was no colona but a free-woman whose husband had held independent title to a manse encompassing some twelve hectares. After his death, she had tried to support her family by working the land herself, but this heroic endeavor was abruptly curtailed by her neighbor, Lord Rathold, who coveted the prosperous manse. Lord Rathold had brought Madalgis's labors to the attention of Abbot Raban, who forbade her, upon threat of excommunication, ever to take up tiller or hoe again. "It is ungodly for a woman to do the work of men," he told her.

Faced with starvation, Madalgis had been forced to sell the manse and its house to Lord Rathold for a fraction of its worth, receiving in return only a few solidi and a tiny hut in a nearby settlement with a small piece of pasturage for her cows.

She had taken up cheese making; in this way she had managed to eke out a minimal subsistence, bartering the fruits of her labor for other food and necessities.

As soon as she caught sight of her home, Madalgis gave a glad cry and ran ahead, quickly disappearing inside. Joan and Brother Benjamin followed a few minutes later and discovered her buried beneath a breathless tumble of children, all laughing, crying, and talking at the same time. Seeing the two monks enter, the children cried out in alarm and surrounded Madalgis protectively, fearing she would be taken from them again. Madalgis spoke to them and their smiles returned, though they studied the two strangers curiously.

A woman came in, holding a babe in each arm. She made a respectful bow to the two monks, then hurried past to hand one of the infants to Madalgis, who seized it joyfully and put it to her breast, where it began to suck hungrily. The other woman seemed a dame of fifty years or more, but then Joan saw that though her face was drawn and lined with care, she was not so old as that—no more perhaps than twenty-nine or thirty.

She has been nursing Madalgis's babe as well as her own, Joan realized. With sympathy she noted the woman's leaking breasts and sagging abdomen and the unhealthy pallor of her skin. Joan had seen the symptoms before: women often bore their first child by the age of thirteen or fourteen and thereafter existed in a state of virtually perpetual pregnancy, bringing forth one babe after another with dreary regularity. It was not uncommon for a woman to have twenty or more pregnancies during her lifetime—though inevitably some of these were cut short by miscarriage. By the time a woman reached her time of change—if indeed she lived that long, for childbirth carried with it a considerable hazard—her body was wasted, her spirit broken by exhaustion. Joan made a mental note to make up a tonic of powdered oak bark and sage to fortify the woman against the coming winter.

Madalgis spoke to her oldest child, a gangly boy of twelve or thirteen. He went out the door and returned a minute later with a loaf of bread and a chunk of blue-veined cheese, which he offered to Joan and Brother Benjamin. Brother Benjamin took the bread but refused the cheese, for it was obviously rotten with mold. Joan also found the cheese repellent, but to please the boy, she broke off a tiny piece and put it in her mouth. To her surprise, it tasted wonderful—pungent, rich, astonishingly flavorful—far superior to any cheese at Fulda's tables.

"Why, it's delicious."

The boy grinned.

"What's your name?" she asked him.

"Arn," he answered shyly.

As she ate, Joan took note of her surroundings. Madalgis's home was a small, windowless hut rudely constructed of crossed lathes daubed with mud and stuffed with straw and leaves. There were large gaps in the walls, through which the cool night air now swept, stirring the smoke from the hearth fire into a choking cloud. In one corner there was a pen for animals; in another month, Madalgis would bring in her cows for the winter—a common practice among the poor. Doing so not only protected the precious livestock but also brought a much-needed extra source of warmth into their homes. Unfortunately, in addition to their body heat, the animals brought pests: ticks, biting flies, fleas, and a host of other vermin, which burrowed into the floor rushes and the straw sleeping pallets. Most poor folk were covered with painful bites and rashes, a fact documented in the local churches, whose walls featured graphic representations of Job, his body covered with ulcers, scraping at his sores with a knife.

Some people—and Joan suspected Madalgis was one of these—developed unusually strong reactions to the insect bites over time. Their skin swelled into great sores, which, further irritated by clothes of coarse and unclean wool, finally erupted into festering lesions.

The test of Joan's diagnosis would have to wait, however, as it was now full dark. *Tomorrow,* Joan told herself as she prepared for sleep, *tomorrow we'll begin.*

THE next day they cleaned the little hut from top to bottom. The old rushes covering the ground were tossed out and the earth floor swept perfectly smooth and even. The sleeping pallets were burned, and new ones of fine fresh straw made up. Even the thatch roof, which had begun to sag and rot with age, was replaced.

The difficult part was persuading Madalgis to take a bath. Like everyone else, she washed her face, hands, and feet regularly, but the idea of total immersion was to her strange and even dangerous.

"I'll catch the flux and die!" she wailed.

"You'll die if you don't," Joan answered firmly. "A leper's existence is a living death."

The cool winds of Herbistmanoth had rendered the little creek that ran behind the settlement too cold for bathing. They had to haul the water up and heat it over the hearth fire, then pour it into a laundry tub. While the two monks stood with their backs to her, Madalgis lowered herself into the tub with a great deal of trepidation, then washed her body with soap and water.

After her bath, Madalgis donned a clean new tunic Joan had obtained from Brother Conrad, the cellarer, in anticipation of the need. Made of fine heavy linen, it was warm enough to see Madalgis through the winter yet was far smoother and less irritating than wool.

Bathed and cleaned, her house rid of vermin and gleaming from roof to floor, Madalgis immediately began to improve. Her lesions dried and began to show signs of healing.

Brother Benjamin was ecstatic. "You were right!" he said to Joan. "It isn't leprosy! We must return and show the others!"

"A few days more," Joan said cautiously. There must be no doubt whatsoever as to the cure when they returned.

"Show me another one," Arn pleaded.

Joan smiled at him. For the past few days she had been teaching the boy Bede's classical method of digital computation, and he had proved an apt and eager student.

"First you must show me that you remember what you've already learned. What do these represent?" She held up the last three fingers of her left hand.

"Units of one," the boy said unhesitatingly. "And these"—he indicated the left thumb and index finger—"are decimals."

"Good. And on the right hand?"

"These represent hundreds, and these, thousands." He lifted the appropriate fingers to illustrate.

"Very well, what numbers do you want to use?"

"Twelve, for that's my age. And"—he thought for a moment—"three hundred sixty-five, for that's the number of days in a year!" he said, proud to show off something else he had learned.

"Twelve times three hundred sixty-five. Let's see . . ." Joan's fingers moved swiftly, computing the total. "That's four thousand three hundred and eighty."

Arn clapped his hands with delight.

"You try it," Joan said, going through it again, more slowly, allowing time for him to mimic each motion. Then she had him do it on his own. "Excellent!" she said after he had executed it.

Arn grinned, delighted by the game and the praise. Then his round little face grew serious. "How high can you go?" he asked. "Can you do it with a hundred and a thousand? With . . . a thousand and another thousand?"

Joan nodded. "Just touch your chest like this . . . see? That gives you tens of thousands. And if you touch your thigh, like this, hundreds of thousands. So"—her fingers moved again—"one thousand one hundred times two thousand three hundred is . . . two million five hundred and thirty thousand!"

Arn's eyes flew wide with wonderment. The numbers were so enormous he could scarcely conceive them.

"Show me another!" he begged. Joan laughed. She enjoyed teaching the boy, for he drank in knowledge thirstily. He reminded her of herself as a child. *What a shame,* she thought, *that this bright spark of intelligence was destined to be extinguished in the darkness of ignorance.*

"If I can arrange it," she said, "would you like to study at the abbey school? You could go on learning there—not just numbers, but reading and writing as well."

"Reading and writing?" Arn repeated in wonder. Those extraordinary skills were reserved for priests and very great lords, not for such as he. He asked anxiously, "Would I have to become a monk?"

Joan was amused. Arn was of the age when boys begin to develop a strong interest in the opposite sex; the idea of a life of chastity was understandably abhorrent to him.

"No," she said. "You would study at the Outer School, the one for lay students. But it would mean leaving home and living at the abbey. And you'd have to study hard, for the teaching master is very strict."

Arn didn't hesitate for a moment. "Oh yes! Yes, please!"

"Very well. We're returning to Fulda tomorrow. I'll speak to the teaching master then."

☨

"AT LAST!" Brother Benjamin breathed with relief. Straight ahead, where the pebbled road met the horizon, the gray walls of Fulda rose starkly, backgrounded by the twin towers of the abbatial church.

The little group of travelers had endured a wearisome journey from Madalgis's cottage, and the chill damp had aggravated Benjamin's rheumatism, making every step a torment.

"We'll be there soon," Joan said. "You'll have your feet up before the brazier in the warming room within the hour."

In the distance, the beating of the boards was announcing their arrival—for no one approached the gates of Fulda unheralded. At the sound, Madalgis clutched her babe nervously. It had been all Joan and Brother Benjamin could do to convince her that she had to return to the abbey; she had agreed at last only on condition that her children accompany her.

The brethren were gathered in the forecourt to greet them, lined up ceremoniously in order of rank, with Abbot Raban himself, silver haired and majestically erect, in the front.

Madalgis shrank back fearfully, hiding behind Joan.

"Come forth," Raban said.

"It's all right, Madalgis," Joan reassured her. "Do as Father Abbot says."

Madalgis advanced and stood trembling in the midst of the alien company. An audible sigh of astonishment passed through the ranks of brethren at the sight of her. The open, ulcerous nodes and lesions had all disappeared; except for a few dry and healing marks, the sun-browned skin of her face and arms showed forth clear and firm, blooming with renewed health. There could be no further doubt: even the most inexperienced could tell that the woman who stood before them was no leper.

"O wondrous sign of grace!" Bishop Otgar exclaimed in awe. "Like Lazarus, she has been restored from death to life!"

The brethren crowded around, sweeping the little group of travelers triumphantly toward the church.

JOAN'S cure of Madalgis was regarded as nothing less than a miracle. All Fulda rang with John Anglicus's praise. When elderly Brother

Aldwin, one of the community's two priests, died in his sleep one night, there was little doubt among the brethren as to who should succeed him.

Abbot Raban, however, was of a different mind. John Anglicus had entirely too bold and presumptuous a nature for his liking. Raban preferred Brother Thomas, who, though admittedly less brilliant, was far more predictable—a quality Raban valued.

But there was Bishop Otgar to consider. The bishop knew of Gottschalk's near-death from whipping, an event that reflected badly on Raban's abbacy. If Raban passed over John Anglicus in favor of a less qualified brother, it might raise further questions about his stewardship of the abbey. And if the king should receive bad report of him, he might remove him as abbot—an unthinkable outcome. Best to be prudent in his choice of priest, Raban decided—at least for the moment.

At chapter he announced, "As your spiritual father, the right to appoint a priest from among you belongs to me. After much prayer and reflection, I have decided upon a brother well suited for the office by virtue of his great learning: Brother John Anglicus."

There was a murmur of approval from the brethren. Joan flushed with excitement. *I, a priest!* To be admitted to the sacred mysteries, to administer the holy sacraments! It had been her father's cherished ambition for Matthew and, after Matthew died, for John. How rich an irony if that ambition were finally realized through his daughter!

Seated across the room, Brother Thomas glowered at Joan. *This priesthood is mine,* he thought bitterly. *I was Raban's choice; didn't he say as much only a few weeks ago?*

John Anglicus's cure of the leper woman had changed everything. It was infuriating. Madalgis was a nobody, a slave, or little better. What difference did it make if she went to the leprosarium—or lived or died for that matter?

That the prize should go to John Anglicus was bitter gall. From the very first, Thomas had hated him—hated the quickness of his wit, of which he had often felt the barb, hated the ease with which he had mastered his lessons. Such things did not come easily to Thomas. He had had to slave to learn the forms of Latin and memorize the chapters of the rule. But what Thomas lacked in brilliance he made up for in persistence, and in the effort he put into the outward forms of faith. Whenever he finished with his meal, Thomas took care to lay his knife and spoon down perpendicularly, in tribute to the Blessed Cross. He never drank his wine straight down like the others but partook of it reverently, three sips at a time, in pious illustration of the miracle of the Trinity. John Anglicus didn't trouble himself with such acts of devotion.

Thomas glared at his rival, so angelic looking with his fine halo of white-gold hair. *May Hell dry him up with its flames, him and the God-cursed womb that engendered him!*

THE refectory, or monks' dining hall, was a masonry-walled structure forty feet wide and one hundred feet long, built large to accommodate all three hundred and fifty of the Fulda brethren at once. With seven tall windows on the south wall and six on the north, letting in direct sunlight year-round, it was one of the most cheerful of all the cloister buildings. The wide wooden beams and purlins supporting the rafters were colorfully painted with scenes from the life of Boniface, patron saint of Fulda; these added to the impression of brightness and light, so the room was as cheerful and pleasant now, in the cold, short days of Heilagmanoth, as it was in summertime.

It was noontime, and the brothers were assembled in the refectory for dinner, the first of the day's two meals. Abbot Raban sat at a long U-shaped table centered on the east wall, flanked by twelve brothers on his left and twelve on his right, representing Christ's apostles. The long planked tables bore simple plates of bread, pulse, and cheese. Mice scurried about on the earthen floor beneath, in furtive search of fallen crumbs.

In accordance with the Rule of St. Benedict, the brothers always took their meal without speaking. The strict silence was broken only by the clink of metal knives and cups and the voice of the lector for the week, who stood at the pulpit reading from the Psalms or the Lives of the Fathers. "As the mortal body partakes of earthly food," Abbot Raban liked to say, "so let the soul derive spiritual sustenance."

The *regula taciturnitis,* or rule of silence, was an ideal, commended by all but observed by few. The brothers had worked out an elaborate scheme of hand signs and facial gestures with which they communicated during meals. Entire conversations could be carried on in this manner, especially when, as now, the reader was poor. Brother Thomas read in a harsh, heavily accented voice that completely missed the lilting poetry of the Psalms; oblivious to his shortcomings, Thomas read loudly, his voice grating on the brethren's ears. Abbot Raban often asked Brother Thomas to read, preferring him to the monastery's more skilled readers, for, as he said, "too sweet a voice invites demons into the heart."

"Pssst." A muted hissing drew Joan's attention. She looked up from her plate to see Brother Adalgar signaling her across the table.

He held up four fingers. The number signified a chapter from the Rule of St. Benedict, a frequent vehicle for this kind of brotherly communication, which favored enigmatic references and circumlocutions.

Joan recalled the opening lines of chapter four: "*Omnes supervenientes hospites tamquam Christus suscipiantur,*" it read. "Let all who come be received like Christ."

Joan took Brother Adalgar's meaning at once. A visitor had come to Fulda—someone of note, or Brother Adalgar would not have troubled to mention it. Fulda received upward of a dozen visitors a day, rich and poor, fur-robed pilgrims and ragged paupers, weary travelers who came knowing that they would not be sent away, that here they would find a few days' rest, shelter, and food before continuing on their way.

Joan's curiosity was piqued. "Who?" she responded by a slight lift of her eyebrows.

At that moment Abbot Raban gave the sign, and the brothers rose from the table in unison, lining up in order of seniority. As they exited the refectory, Brother Adalgar turned to her.

"*Parens,*" he signed, and pointed at her emphatically. "Your parent."

WITH the calm, measured step and placid mien befitting a monk of Fulda, Joan followed the brethren out of the refectory. Nothing in her outward appearance betrayed her profound agitation.

Could Brother Adalgar be right? Had one of her parents come to Fulda? Her mother or her father? *Parens,* Adalgar had said, which could mean either. What if it was her father? He would not expect to see her but rather her brother, John. The idea filled Joan with alarm. If her father discovered her imposture, he would surely denounce her.

But perhaps it was her mother who had come. Gudrun would not betray her secret. She would understand that such a revelation would cost Joan her life.

Mama. It had been ten years since Joan had seen her, and they had parted badly. Suddenly, more than anything, Joan wanted to see Gudrun's familiar, beloved face, wanted to hold and be held by her, to hear her speak the lilting rhythms of the Old Tongue.

Brother Samuel, the hospitaler, intercepted her as she was leaving the refectory.

"You are excused from your duties this afternoon; someone has come to see you."

Torn between hope and fear, Joan said nothing.

"Don't look so serious, Brother; it isn't the Devil come for your immortal soul." Brother Samuel laughed heartily. He was a good-hearted, jovial man, fond of jests and laughter. For years Abbot Raban had chastised him for these unspiritual qualities, then finally given up and appointed him hospitaler, a job whose worldly duties of greeting and caring for visitors suited Brother Samuel perfectly.

"Your father is here," Samuel said cheerfully, glad to impart such good news, "waiting in the garden to greet you."

Fear splintered Joan's mask of self-control. She backed away, shaking her head. "I will not see him. I . . . I cannot."

The smile disappeared from Brother Samuel's lips. "Now, Brother, you don't mean that. Your father's traveled all the way from Ingelheim to speak with you."

She would have to offer some explanation. "There is bad blood between us. We . . . argued . . . when I left home."

Brother Samuel put his arm around her shoulders. "I understand," he said sympathetically. "But he *is* your father, and he has come a long way. It will be an act of charity to talk to him, if only for a little while."

Unable to disagree with this, Joan kept silent.

Brother Samuel took this for acquiescence. "Come. I will take you to him."

"No!" She shook off his encircling arm.

Brother Samuel was startled. This was no way to address the hospitaler, one of the seven obedientiary officers of the abbey.

"Your soul is troubled, Brother," he said sharply. "You need spiritual guidance. We will discuss this in chapter tomorrow."

What can I do? Joan thought in dismay. It would be difficult, if not impossible, to keep her true identity from her father. But a discussion in chapter could also be ruinous. There was no excuse for her behavior. If she was found to be disobedient, like Gottschalk . . .

"Forgive me, *Nonnus*"—she used the address of respect due a senior brother—"for my lack of temperance and humility. You took me by surprise, and in my confusion, I forgot my duty to you. I ask your pardon, most humbly."

It was a pretty apology. Brother Samuel's stern look dissolved into a smile; he was not a man to hold a grudge.

"You have it, Brother, most freely. Come. We will walk together to the garden."

As they made their way from the cloister past the livestock barns, the mill, and the drying kilns, Joan quickly calculated her chances. The last time her father had seen her, she had been a child of twelve. She had changed greatly in the ensuing ten years. Perhaps he would not recognize her. Perhaps . . .

They reached the garden with its neat rows of raised planting beds—thirteen in all, the number carefully selected to symbolize the holy congregation of Christ and the Twelve Apostles at the Last Supper. Each bed was exactly seven feet wide; this was also significant, for seven was the number of gifts of the Holy Ghost, signifying the wholeness of all created things.

In the rear of the garden, between beds of pepperwort and chervil, her father stood with his back to them. His short, squat body, thick neck, and resolute stance were immediately familiar. Joan pulled her head deep inside her voluminous cowl so the heavy material hung down in front, covering her hair and face.

Hearing their approach, the canon turned. His dark hair and beetling brows, which had once struck such terror in Joan, had gone completely gray.

"*Deus tecum.*" Brother Samuel gave Joan an encouraging pat. "God be with you." Then he left them.

Her father crossed the garden haltingly. He was smaller than she remembered; she saw with surprise that he used a stick to walk. As he drew near, Joan turned away and, without speaking, gestured him to follow. She led him out of the sharp glare of the midday sun into the windowless chapel adjoining the garden, where darkness would provide better concealment. Inside, she waited for him to take a seat on one of the benches. Then she seated herself at the far end, keeping her head low so the cowl hid her profile.

"*Pater Noster qui es in caelis, sanctficetur nomen tuum . . .*" Her father began the Lord's Prayer. His folded hands shook with palsy; he spoke in the quavering, brittle tones of an old man. Joan joined her voice to his, their mingled words echoing through the tiny, stone-walled chamber.

The prayer completed, they sat for a while in silence.

"My son," the canon said at last, "you have done well. Brother Hospitaler tells me you are to be a priest. You have brought honor to our family, as I once hoped your brother would."

Matthew. Joan fingered the medallion of St. Catherine that hung around her neck, the one Matthew had given her so long ago.

Her father caught the gesture. "My eyesight has grown thick. Is that your sister Joan's medallion?"

Joan let go of it, cursing her stupidity; she had not thought to hide it.

"I took it as a remembrance . . . afterwards." She could not bring herself to speak of the horror of the Norsemen's attack.

"Did your sister die without . . . dishonor?"

Joan had a sudden image of Gisla, screaming in pain and fear while the Norsemen took turns with her.

"She died inviolate."

"*Deo gratias.*" The canon crossed himself. "It was God's will, then. Headstrong and unnatural child, she could never have been at peace in this world; it is better so."

"She would not have said so."

If the canon caught the irony in her voice, he did not reveal it. "Her death was a very great grief to your mother."

"How fares my mother?"

For a long moment the canon did not respond. When at last he did, his voice was shakier than before.

"She is gone."

"Gone?"

"To Hell," the canon said, "to burn for all eternity."

"No." Understanding crowded the edges of Joan's consciousness. "No."

Not Mama with the beautiful face, the kind eyes, the gentle hands that brought kindness and comfort—Mama, who had loved her.

"She died one month ago," the canon said, "unshriven and unreconciled to Christ, calling upon her heathen gods. When the midwife told me she would not live, I did everything I could, but she would not accept the Blessed Sacrament. I put the Sacred Host in her mouth, and she spat it out at me."

"The midwife? You don't mean . . ." Her mother was over fifty, well past childbearing years; she had begotten no more children after Joan was born.

"They would not let me bury her in the Christian cemetery, not with the unbaptized babe still in her womb." He began to cry, great, choking sobs that shook his entire body.

Did he love her, then? He'd had an odd way of displaying it, with his brutal rages, his cruelty, and his lust, his selfish lust that had killed her in the end.

The canon's sobs slowly quieted, and he began the prayer for the dead. This time Joan did not join in. Quietly, under her breath, she began to recite the Oath, invoking the sacred name of Thor the Thunderer, just as Mama had taught her so long ago.

Her father cleared his throat uncomfortably. "There is one thing, John. The mission in Saxony . . . do you think . . . that is, could the brothers use my help, in their work with the heathens?"

Joan was perplexed. "What about your work in Ingelheim?"

"The fact is, my position in Ingelheim has become difficult. The recent . . . misfortune . . . with your mother . . ."

At once Joan understood. The strictures against married clergy, only feebly enforced during the reign of Emperor Karolus, had tightened under the reign of his son, whose religious zeal had earned him the title Louis the Pious. The recent synod in Paris had strongly reinforced both the theory and practice of clerical celibacy. Gudrun's pregnancy, visible evidence of the canon's lack of chastity, could not have come at a worse time.

"You have lost your position?"

Reluctantly, her father nodded. "But *Deo volente,* I have the strength and skill to do God's work yet. If you could intercede for me with Abbot Raban . . . ?"

Joan did not reply. She was overfull with grief, anger, and pain; there was no room left in her heart for compassion toward her father.

"You do not answer me. You have grown proud, my son." He stood, his voice taking on something of its old commanding tone. "Remember, it was I who brought you to this place, and to your current position in life. *Contritionem praecedit superbia, et ante ruinam exaltatio spiritus,*" he remonstrated sternly. "Pride goeth before destruction and a haughty spirit before a fall. Proverbs, chapter sixteen."

"*Bonum est homini mulierem non tangere,*" Joan retorted. "It is well for a man not to touch a woman, First Corinthians, chapter seven."

Her father raised his cane to strike her, but the movement caused him to lose his balance, and he fell. She put out her hand to help him, and he pulled her down to him, holding her fast.

"My son," his voice pleaded tearfully in her ear, "my son. Do not desert me. You are all I have."

Repelled, she pulled back so violently that her cowl slipped off her head. Hastily she pulled it on again, but it was too late.

Her father's face held an expression of horrified recognition. "No," he said, aghast. "No, it cannot be."

"Father—"

"Daughter of Eve, what have you done? Where is your brother, John?"

"He is dead."

"Dead?"

"Killed by Norsemen, in the church at Dorstadt. I tried to save him, but—"

"Witch! Mooncalf! Demon from Hell!" He traced the sign of the cross in the air before him.

"Father, please, let me explain—" Joan pleaded desperately. She had to calm him before his raised voice drew the others.

He retrieved his stick and struggled awkwardly to his feet, his whole body trembling. Joan moved to assist him, but he warded her off and said accusingly, "You killed your elder brother. Could you not have spared the younger?"

"I loved John, Father. I would never have harmed him. It was the Norsemen, they came without warning, with swords and axes." She tightened her throat against mounting sobs; she had to keep talking, make him understand. "John tried to fight, but they killed everyone, everyone. They—"

He turned toward the door. "I must put a stop to this, to you, before you do any further harm."

She grabbed hold of his arm. "Father, don't, please, they will kill me if—"

He rounded on her fiercely. "Changeling devil! You should have died in your heathen mother's womb before ever you were born!" He struggled to free himself, his face purpling alarmingly. "*Let me go!*"

Desperately she held on. If he walked through that door, her life was forfeit.

"Brother John?" A voice sounded from the doorway. It was Brother Samuel, his kindly face creased with concern. "Is anything wrong?"

Startled, Joan loosed her grip on her father's arm. He pulled free and went to Brother Samuel.

"Take me to Abbot Raban. I must . . . I mush—" He broke off suddenly with a look of puzzled surprise.

He looked strange. His skin had gone an even deeper purple; his face twisted grotesquely, the right eye drooping lower than the left, the mouth crooked peculiarly to one side.

"Father?" She approached hesitantly, holding out her hand.

He lunged for her, his right arm flapping wildly as if no longer under his control.

Terrified, Joan backed away.

He shouted something unrecognizable, then fell forward like a hewn tree.

Brother Samuel called for help. Immediately five brethren materialized in the doorway.

Joan knelt beside her father and supported him in her arms. His head lay heavy and unresisting against her shoulder, his thin gray hair twined between her fingers. Looking into his eyes, Joan was shocked by the malignant hatred she saw there.

His lips worked with a ghastly determination. "M . . . m . . . m . . . !"

"Don't try to speak," Joan said. "You are not well."

He blazed at her with savage fury. With one last, explosive effort, he spat out a single word: "M . . . m . . . m . . . Mulier!"

Woman!

His head turned convulsively to the side and froze there, his eyes set in their baleful glare.

Joan bent over him, seeking any sign of breath from the stretched lips, any pulse from the wasted neck. After a moment, she closed the staring eyes. "He is dead."

Brother Samuel and the others crossed themselves.

"I thought I heard him speak before he died," Brother Samuel said. "What did he say?"

"He . . . he called upon Mary, mother of Christ."

Brother Samuel nodded sagely. "A holy man." To the others he said, "Carry him to the church. We will prepare his body with all due ceremony."

✠

"*TERRA es, terram ibis*," Abbot Raban intoned. With the rest of the brethren, Joan stooped to scoop up a handful of earth, then tossed it into the grave, watching the dark, wet lumps smear unevenly across the smooth wood of her father's coffin.

He had always hated her. Even when she was little, before the lines of battle between them had been drawn, she had never elicited anything more from him than a sour, grudging tolerance. To him, she had always been only a stupid, worthless girl. Still, she was shocked to learn how willingly he would have exposed her, how unhesitatingly he would have consigned her to unspeakable death.

Nevertheless, as the last of the heavy earth was mounded on her father's grave, Joan felt an odd, unexpected melancholy. She could not remember a time when she had not resented her father, feared him, even hated him. Yet she felt a peculiar sense of loss. Matthew, John, Mama—all were gone. Her father had been her last link with home, with the girl she once had been. There was no Joan of Ingelheim anymore; there was only John Anglicus, priest and monk of the Benedictine house of Fulda.

⇥ 17 ⇤

Fontenoy | 841

THE meadow shimmered in the dim, gray light of early dawn, threaded through the middle with the sweetly curving lines of a silver creek. *An unlikely scene for a battle,* Gerold thought grimly.

Emperor Louis had been dead less than a year, but the smoldering rivalry among his three sons had already flared into full-fledged civil war. The eldest, Lothar, had inherited the title of Emperor, but the lands of the Empire were divided between Lothar and his two younger brothers, Charles and Ludwig—an unwise and dangerous arrangement that left all three sons dissatisfied. Even so, war might have been avoided had Lothar been more skilled in diplomacy. Peremptory and despotic by nature, Lothar treated his younger brothers with an arrogance that goaded them to league together in open rebellion against him. So the three royal brothers were finally come here to Fontenoy, determined to settle the differences between them with blood.

After considerable soul-searching, Gerold had cast his lot with Lothar. He knew Lothar's flaws of character well, but as the anointed Emperor, Lothar was the only hope for a united Frankland. The divisions that had racked the country over the past year had exacted a terrible toll: the Norsemen, taking advantage of the distraction the political upheaval afforded, had intensified their raids against the Frankish coast, wreaking great destruction. If Lothar could win a decisive victory here, his brothers would have no choice but to support him. A country ruled by a tyrant was better than no country at all.

The beating of the boards began, mustering the men. Lothar had arranged for an early mass to hearten his troops before the coming battle. Gerold left his solitary meditations and returned to the camp.

Robed in cloth of gold, the Bishop of Auxerre stood high upon a supply cart so all could see him. "*Libera me, Domine, de morte aeterna,*" he chanted in a ringing baritone as dozens of acolytes passed among the men, distributing the consecrated Host. Many of the soldiers were coloni and peasants with no previous experience at arms, men who would normally have been exempt from the imperial *bannum* requiring military service. But these were not normal times. Many had been torn from their homes without so much as an hour's leave to arrange their affairs or bid farewell to their loved ones. These last received the Host distractedly, being in no condition to prepare for death. Their minds were still firmly fixed upon the things of this world from which they had been so roughly severed: their fields, livelihoods, debts, their wives and children. Bewildered and frightened, they could not yet comprehend the enormity of their predicament, could not believe they were expected to fight and die on this unfamiliar ground for an Emperor whose name had, until a few days ago, been only a distant echo in their lives. *How many of these innocents,* Gerold wondered, *will live to see the sun set on this day?*

"O Lord of Hosts," the bishop prayed at the conclusion of the mass, "Champion against the enemy, Achiever of victories, grant us the shield of Thy aid, and the sword of Thy glory, for the destruction of our enemies. Amen."

"Amen." The air reverberated with the sound of thousands of voices. A moment later, the first narrow sliver of sun crested the horizon, spilling its light over the field, setting the tips of their spears and arrows gleaming like precious gems. A loud cheer went up from the men.

The bishop removed the pallium and handed it to an attending acolyte. Loosing his chasuble, he let it fall to the ground and stood revealed in a soldier's mail: *brunia,* the thick leather jacket soaked in heated wax and sewn with scales of iron, and *bauga,* metal leg guards.

He means to fight then, Gerold thought.

Strictly speaking, the bishop's holy office forbade him to spill another man's blood, but in practice this pious ideal was often ignored; bishops and priests fought alongside their kings like any other royal vassals.

One of the acolytes handed the bishop a sword engraved with the sign of the cross. The bishop swung the sword aloft so its golden cross glittered in the sun. "Praise Jesus Christ!" he shouted. "Forward, good Christians, to the kill!"

✠

GEROLD was in command of the left flank, positioned on the rise of a hill bordering the southern end of the field. On an opposite hill, Lothar's nephew Pippin commanded the right flank, a large, well-armed contingent of Aquitanians. The vanguard, commanded by Lothar himself, was drawn up just beyond the trees fronting the eastern end of the field, directly facing the enemy.

Gerold's bay stallion tossed its head and whinnied impatiently. Leaning over, Gerold ran a hand over its russet neck, gentling it. Best to reserve all that coiled energy for the charge, when it should come. "Soon enough, boy," he murmured steadyingly, "soon enough."

He checked the sky. It was rising six, the first hour of the morning. The sun, still low on the horizon, shone directly into the eyes of the enemy. *Good,* Gerold thought. *It's an advantage we can use.* He watched Lothar for the signal to advance. A quarter of an hour passed, and no signal came. The rival armies stood at opposite ends of the field, eyeing each other warily across the green expanse. Another quarter of an hour passed. Then another. And another.

Gerold broke rank and rode down the hill to the front line of the vanguard, where Lothar sat mounted under a flurry of banners.

"Majesty, why do we delay? The men are impatient to advance."

Lothar looked down his long nose irritably. "I am the Emperor; it is not meet that I should go to my enemies." He had no liking for Gerold, who had entirely too independent a mind for his taste—the result, no doubt, of the years he had spent among the pagans and barbarians in the northern march of the Empire.

"But, Sire, see the sun! Now the advantage is ours, but within the hour it will be gone!"

"Trust in God, Count Gerold," Lothar replied loftily. "I am Heaven's anointed king; He will not fail to grant us victory."

From the finality of Lothar's tone, Gerold understood that there was no point in further argument. He bowed stiffly, wheeled his horse, and rode back to his position.

Perhaps Lothar was right, and God did mean to award them victory. But might He not also expect a little help from men?

IT WAS rising ten; the sun was nearing midpoint. *Damn,* Gerold swore under his breath. *What on earth is Lothar thinking?* They had been waiting now almost four hours. The sun beat down on their iron mail, heating it until the men squirmed with discomfort. Those who had to relieve themselves were required to do so where they stood, for they could not break formation; the rank smell rose and hung about them in the breezeless air.

In these difficult circumstances, Gerold was glad to witness the arrival of a small corps of serving men, porting barrels of wine. The men were hot and thirsty; a strong cup of wine was just what was needed to revive their sagging spirits. A lusty cheer went up as the serving men began to circulate, ladling out cupfuls of thick red Frankish wine. Gerold took one himself and felt much the better for it. He did not, however, allow himself or his men more than this one drink. Where a little wine could bolster a man's courage, too much made him foolhardy and wild, a danger to himself and to his fellows.

Lothar showed no such concern. Benignly, he encouraged the drinking to continue. Shouting and chaffing, boasting of their skill at arms, the men of his vanguard jockeyed roughly for position, tripping over one another to win the honor of standing in the foremost rank, pushing and shoving like wayward boys—which indeed they were; except for a handful of experienced veterans, the greater part were no older than eighteen.

"They are coming! They are coming!"

The shout went up throughout the ranks. The opposing army was advancing, slowly as yet, so the unmounted men-at-arms and archers could keep in close proximity to the mounted cavalry which rode before them. The effect was solemn, majestic, more like a religious procession than the onset of a battle.

In Lothar's vanguard, there was a disorderly flurry as men scrambled to retrieve scattered helmets, lances, and shields. They had just managed to mount when the enemy cavalry spurred into a full forward charge, bearing down upon them with terrifying speed, causing the earth to reverberate with a deafening roar like that of a thousand thunderbolts.

The banners in the imperial vanguard dropped and rose, signaling the answering charge. The cavalry leapt forward, the horses' hooves tearing the smooth green turf as they drove ahead with straining necks.

Gerold's bay sprang in response; Gerold reined him in. "Not yet, boy." Gerold and his men must hold back; the left flank was to be last onto the field, after Lothar and Pippin.

Like two great waves, the opposing armies swept toward each

other forty thousand strong, the pride of the Frankish nobility riding knee to knee in solid lines a half mile wide and equally deep.

With a wild shout, a group from the imperial vanguard burst out of formation, spurring their horses into a disorderly run, racing against one another for the glory of being the first to engage the enemy before the eyes of their Emperor.

Gerold watched with chagrin. If they kept going as they were, they would reach the brook too soon and be caught laboring through the water while the enemy fought them from the solid ground of the far bank.

Reckless with wine and youth, they rode straight into the creek and collided with the enemy with an ear-splitting crack like two gigantic bones breaking. They fought with fierce courage at great disadvantage, for they had to strike from below at the enemy on the bank, their aim thrown off as their horses stumbled for footing on the slippery rocks. Those who were cut down fell into the water, where, mired in mud and struggling to rise against the weight of their mail, they were trampled by their own panicked, plunging horses.

The men in the rows behind saw what lay ahead but were coming on at such speed they could not check themselves without being violently overridden by those following. They, too, were forced to plunge down the muddied slope into the water, now churning alternately white and red with blood, driving the survivors of the first charge forward willy-nilly onto the spears of the enemy.

Only the rear of the cavalry, which now included Lothar, was able to check in time; they wheeled their horses and rode back across the field at a wild, undisciplined gallop that brought them crashing straight into the ranks of unmounted men-at-arms marching up behind. These were thrown into frenzied disarray as they cast aside their weapons and hurled themselves sideways to avoid the headlong rush.

It was a rout. The only hope now lay with the flanks, led by Pippin and Gerold. Positioned as they were, they could sweep down onto the field beyond the brook and strike directly at King Ludwig in the center. Looking to the opposite slope, Gerold saw that Pippin and his Aquitanians were turned, fighting with their backs to the field. King Charles must have circled round and come at them from behind.

No help to be had there.

Gerold looked back toward the field. The greater part of Ludwig's men had crossed the brook in pursuit of the retreating Lothar, and thus unwittingly thinned their ranks, leaving the king momentarily exposed. It was a chance in a thousand, but a desperate chance was better than none.

Gerold stood in his stirrups, raising his lance. "Forward!" he shouted, "in the Emperor's name!"

"The Emperor!" The cry went up like a great baying of hounds and was left shuddering in the air behind them as they streamed headlong down the slope, a great flying wedge aimed directly toward the spot where Ludwig's standard floated scarlet and blue in the summer sunlight.

The small band of men who had remained with the king scrambled to close ranks before him. Gerold and his men bore down upon them, shearing a path through their ranks.

Gerold took his first man with the lance, running him cleanly through the chest, the shaft of the lance splintering from the force of the blow. The man somersaulted out of the saddle, taking the shattered lance with him. Armed only with his sword, Gerold hurled himself forward with savage determination, striking left and right in great, powerful sweeps, hewing his way doggedly through the press toward the fluttering standard. His men drove in to the sides and behind, widening his path.

Yard by yard, inch by inch, Ludwig's guard gave way before the onslaught. Then, abruptly, the way ahead stood clear. Directly before Gerold rose the royal standard, a red griffin emblazoned on a field of blue. Before it, mounted on a white charger, was King Ludwig himself.

"Yield," Gerold shouted at full pitch to carry over the din. "Yield and you shall live!"

For answer, Ludwig brought his sword crashing down against Gerold's. Grimly, they fought man to man, an equal match of strength and skill, until a nearby horse pitched violently sidelong, felled by an arrow, causing Gerold's bay to rear and flinch away violently. Ludwig pressed this momentary advantage with a well-timed blow at Gerold's neck. Gerold ducked and thrust to the inside beneath the king's raised sword arm, driving his own blade in between the ribs.

Ludwig coughed, a froth of blood rising at his mouth; slowly his body twisted and slipped sideways from the saddle, thumping to the trampled ground.

"The king is dead!" Gerold's men shouted exultantly. "Ludwig is slain!" The cry was flung back echoing through the ranks.

Ludwig's body hung from the saddle, one foot caught in the trappings. His horse reared, pawing the air and dragging the king's body across the torn earth. The conical helmet with its protective nose plate loosened and dislodged, revealing a flat, broad-nosed, completely unfamiliar face.

Gerold swore. It was a coward's trick, unworthy of a king. This was not Ludwig but his counterfeit, decked out like the king to deceive them.

There was no time to lament, for they were immediately surrounded by Ludwig's troops. Guarding one another's flanks, Gerold and his men strove to extricate themselves from the enemy's noose, fighting with fierce determination toward the outer perimeter of the circle.

A brief flash of green and a breath of fresh, sweet-scented air sent Gerold's heart soaring. Another few yards and they would be free, with open field and a clear run before them.

A man flung himself in Gerold's path, planting himself as solidly as a tree. Quickly Gerold took his measure—a big man, fleshy, large stomached, powerful in the arms, wielding a mace, a weapon of strength, not skill. Gerold feinted with his sword to the left; when the man turned to answer it, Gerold drew back quickly to deliver a biting cut on the other arm. The man swore and quickly switched the mace to his left hand.

From behind came a humming sound like a beating of birds' wings. Gerold felt a sudden, numbing pain in his back as an arrow drove through his right shoulder. Helplessly he watched his sword slip from his suddenly nerveless fingers.

The big man raised the heavy mace and swung. Even as Gerold moved to evade it, he knew that he was too late.

Something seemed to explode inside his head as the crushing blow landed, spinning him into obliterating darkness.

THE stars shone down in imperturbable beauty upon the darkened field, strewn with the bodies of the fallen. Twenty thousand men who had wakened that morning lay dead or dying in that dark night—nobles, vassals, farmers, craftsmen, fathers, sons, brothers—the past greatness of an empire.

Gerold stirred and opened his eyes. For a moment he lay looking up at the stars, unable to remember where he was or what had happened. A strong odor rose to his nostrils, unpleasant and sickeningly familiar.

Blood.

Gerold sat up. The sudden movement caused an explosion of pain inside his head, and pain brought back memory. He touched his right shoulder; the arrow that had struck him was still lodged there, cut clean through the flesh just under his arm from back to front. It must come out, or the wound would fester. Clamping his arm against his side, he snapped off the iron tip, then reached back his left hand and, with one swift motion, drew out the feathered shaft.

He gasped and swore against the white-hot pain, fighting to remain conscious. After a while the pain began to ease and he was able to take account of his surroundings. All around him the ground was strewn with flung swords, broken shields, severed limbs, tattered standards, stiffening corpses—the ghastly debris of battle.

From the hill where Charles and Ludwig were encamped, the sounds of a victory celebration spilled down, bibulous jests and raucous laughter that floated eerily over the deep silence below. The light of the victors' torches shone down flickeringly, illuminating the field with a ghostly pallor. From the Emperor's camp on the opposite hill, not a single sound came, nor fire burned; the hill was silent, dark and still.

Lothar was defeated. His troops, what remained of them, had scattered into the surrounding woods, seeking what cover they could find from the pursuing enemy.

Gerold rose, fighting down a wave of nausea. A few feet away he found his bay stallion, horribly wounded, his hind legs twitching. He had been speared from beneath; his innards spilled from the gaping wound in his belly. As Gerold moved toward him, a shape, small and furtive, started up defensively: a mangy, starveling dog, come to feast on the night's rich banquet. Gerold waved his arms threateningly, and the dog skulked away, sidelong, resentful. Gerold knelt beside the bay, stroking his neck, murmuring to him; in response to the familiar touch, the anguished twitching slowed, but the eyes stared out in an agony of pain. Gerold took his knife from his belt. Pressing hard to be sure to sever the vein, he drew it across the bay's neck. Then he held him, speaking soothingly into his ear, until at last the great legs ceased flailing and the smoothly muscled flank relaxed beneath his hands.

A murmur of voices sounded behind Gerold.

"Look! Here's a helmet should fetch a solidus at least!"

"Leave it," said another voice, lower and more authoritative. "It's worthless, cleaved clean through at the back, can't you see? This way, lads, there's better pickings over here!"

Cutpurses. The aftermath of war drew such lawless types from the roads and byways that were their customary haunts, for the dead were easier prey than the quick. They moved furtively in the dark, stripping their victims of clothes, armor, weapons, and rings—whatever might be of value.

A voice sounded close by: "This one's alive!"

There was the sound of a blow, and a cry that broke off abruptly.

"If there are others," another voice said, "deal them the same. We want no witnesses to put a noose around our necks."

In a moment they would be upon him. Gerold stood, swaying. Then, keeping well to the shadows, he slipped into the darkness of the woods beyond.

⇥ 18 ⇤

THE brethren of Fulda remained largely unaffected by the feud among the royal Frankish brothers. Like a stone cast into a pond, the Battle of Fontenoy created great waves in the centers of power, but here, in the eastern march of the Empire, it caused scarcely a ripple. True, some of the larger landholders in the region had gone to serve in King Ludwig's army; according to law any freeman in possession of more than four manses had to answer the call to military service. But Ludwig's quick and decisive victory meant that all save two of these local men returned safe and sound to their homes.

The days passed as before, woven together indistinguishably in the unchanging fabric of monastic life. A string of successful harvests had resulted in a time of unprecedented plenty. The abbey granaries were full to bursting; even the lean, stringy Austrasian pigs grew fat from good feeding.

Then, abruptly, disaster struck. Weeks of unrelenting rain ruined the spring sowing. The earth was too wet to dig the small furrows necessary for planting, and the seeds moldered in the ground. Most disastrous of all, the pervasive damp penetrated the granaries, rotting the stored grain where it lay.

The famine of the following winter was the worst in living memory. To the horror of the Church, some even turned to cannibalism. The roads became more dangerous, as travelers were murdered not only for the goods they carried but for the sustenance their dead bodies could provide. After a public hanging in Lorsch, the starving crowd mobbed the platform and tore down the gallows, fighting over the still-warm flesh.

Weakened by starvation, people were easy prey for disease. Thousands died of the plague. The symptoms were always the same: headache, chills, and disorientation, followed by high fever and a violent cough. There was little anyone could do but strip the sufferers and pack them with cool cloths to keep their temperature down. If they survived the fever, they stood a chance of recovery. But very few survived the fever.

Nor did the sanctity of the monastic walls offer any protection against the plague. The first to be taken ill was Brother Samuel, the hospitaler, whose position brought him into frequent contact with the outside world. Within two days, he was dead. Abbot Raban ascribed this misfortune to Samuel's worldliness and immoderate fondness for jest; afflictions of the flesh, he affirmed, were only outward manifestations of moral and spiritual decay. Then Brother Aldoardus, acknowledged by all to be the embodiment of monkish piety and virtue, was struck down, followed in close order by Brother Hildwin, the sacristan, and several others.

To the surprise of the brethren, Abbot Raban announced that he was making a pilgrimage to the shrine of St. Martin to pray for the holy martyr's intervention against the plague.

"Prior Joseph will act for me in all things while I am gone," Raban said. "Give him due obedience, for his word is even as my own."

The abruptness of Raban's announcement, and his precipitate departure, occasioned a good deal of talk. Some of the brethren praised the abbot for undertaking so arduous a journey on behalf of all. Others muttered darkly that the abbot had absented himself in order to escape the local danger.

Joan had no time to debate such matters. She was kept busy from dawn till dusk saying Mass, hearing confession, and administering the increasingly frequent rites of *unctio extrema.*

One morning she noticed that Brother Benjamin was absent from his choir stall at vigils. Devout soul that he was, he never missed the daily offices. As soon as the service ended, Joan hurried to the infirmary. Entering the long, rectangular room, she breathed the pungent aroma of goose grease and mustard, known specifics for diseases of the lungs. The room was crowded to bursting; beds and pallets were placed side by side, and every one was occupied. Between the beds, the brothers whose opus manuum was in the infirmary circulated, straightening blankets, offering sips of water, praying quietly beside those too far gone to accept any other comfort.

Brother Benjamin was propped up in bed, explaining to Brother Deodatus, one of the junior brothers, the best way to apply a mustard plaster. Listening to him, Joan recalled the long-ago day when he had first taught her that same skill.

She smiled fondly at the memory. Surely, she thought, if Benjamin was still capable of directing things in the infirmary, he could not be critically ill.

A sudden fit of coughing interrupted Brother Benjamin's rapid flow of words. Joan hurried to his bed. Dipping a cloth in the bowl of rose-scented water that stood beside the bed, she held it gently to Benjamin's forehead. His skin felt incredibly hot. *Benedicite! How has he remained lucid with a fever so high?*

At last he stopped coughing and lay with eyes closed, breathing harshly. His graying hair ringed his head like a faded halo. His hands, those wide, squat plowman's hands possessed of such unexpected gentleness and skill, lay on the coverlet as open and helpless as a babe's. Joan's heart twisted at the sight.

Brother Benjamin opened his eyes, saw Joan, and smiled.

"You have come," he said raspingly. "Good. As you see, I am in need of your services."

"A bit of yarrow and some powdered willow-bark will have you right again soon enough," Joan said, more cheerfully than she felt.

Benjamin shook his head. "It's as priest, not as physician, that I need you now. You must help me into the next world, little brother, for I am done with this one."

Joan took his hand. "I'll not give you up without a fight."

"You've learned everything I had to teach you. Now you must learn acceptance."

"I won't accept losing you," she replied fiercely.

FOR the next two days, Joan battled determinedly for Benjamin's life. She used every skill he had ever taught her, tried every medicine she could think of. The fever continued to rage. Benjamin's large, well-fleshed body dwindled like the empty husk of a cocoon after the moth has flown. Beneath his feverish flush there appeared an ominous undertone of gray.

"Shrive me," he pleaded. "I wish to be in full possession of my senses when I receive the Sacrament."

She could deny him no longer.

"*Quid me advocasti?*" she began in the ceremonial cadences of the liturgy. "What do you ask of me?"

"*Ut mihi unctionem trados,*" he responded. "Give me unction."

Dipping her thumb in a mixture of ashes and water, Joan drew the sign of the cross on Brother Benjamin's chest, then laid a piece of sackcloth, symbol of penance, over the smudged design.

Benjamin was shaken with another violent fit of coughing. When it ended, Joan saw that he had brought up blood. Suddenly frightened, she hurried through the recitation of the seven penitential psalms and the ritual anointing of the eyes, ears, nose, mouth, hands, and feet. It seemed to take a very long time. Toward the end, Benjamin lay with his eyes closed, completely unmoving. Joan could not tell if he was still conscious.

At last the moment came to administer the viaticum. Joan held out the Sacred Host, but Benjamin did not respond. *It is too late,* Joan thought. *I have failed him.*

She touched the Host to Benjamin's lips; he opened his eyes and took it into his mouth. Joan made the sign of blessing over him. Her voice shook as she started the sacramental prayer: *"Corpus et Sanguis Domini nostri Jesu Christi in vitam aeternam te perducat . . ."*

HE DIED at dawn, as the sweet canticles of lauds filtered through the morning air. Joan was plunged into a profound grief. Since the moment twelve years ago when Benjamin had taken her under his wing, he had been her friend and mentor. Even when her duties as priest took her from the infirmary, he had continued to help her, encourage her, support her. He had been a true father to her.

Unable to find consolation in prayer, Joan threw herself into work. Daily mass was more crowded than ever, as the specter of death brought the faithful flocking to the church in unprecedented numbers.

One day while Joan was tipping the communal chalice for one of the communicants, an elderly man, she observed his oozing eyes and the dusky, feverish flush of his cheeks. She moved on to the next in line, a slim young mother with a small, sweet-faced girl still in arms. The woman held the child up to take the Sacrament; the tiny rosebud lips opened to drink from the same spot where the old man's mouth had just been.

Joan pulled the chalice away. Taking a piece of the bread, she wet it in the wine and gave it to the child instead. Startled, the girl looked toward her mother, who nodded encouragement; it was a departure from custom, but the abbey priest surely knew what he was doing. Joan continued down the line, wetting the bread in the wine, until the entire congregation had received the Sacrament.

Immediately after mass, Prior Joseph summoned her. Joan was glad it was Joseph and not Raban she would have to answer to. Joseph was not a man to cling undeviatingly to tradition, not if there was good and sufficient argument for change.

"You made an alteration in the Mass today," Joseph said.

"Yes, Father."

"Why?" The question was not challenging, merely curious.

Joan explained.

"The sick old man and the healthy infant," Joseph repeated thoughtfully. "A repulsive incongruity, I agree."

"More than an incongruity," Joan responded. "I believe it may be one way the disease is transmitted."

Joseph was confounded. "How can that be? Surely the noxious spirits are everywhere."

"Perhaps it's not noxious spirits that are causing the sickness—not alone, anyway. It may be passed along by physical contact with its victims, or with objects that they touch."

It was a new idea, but not a radical one. That some diseases were contagious was well known; this was, after all, why lepers were strictly segregated from society. It was also beyond dispute that sickness often passed through entire households, carrying off members of a family within days, even hours. But the cause for this phenomenon was unclear.

"Transmitted by physical contact? In what manner?"

"I don't know," Joan admitted. "But today, when I saw the sick man, and the open sores about his mouth, I felt—" She broke off, frustrated. "I cannot explain, Father, at least not yet. But until I know more, I would like to leave off passing the communal cup and dip the bread in the wine instead."

"You would undertake this change on the basis of a mere . . . intuition?" Joseph asked.

"If I am wrong, no harm will derive from my error, for the faithful will still have partaken of both the Body and the Blood," Joan argued. "But if my . . . intuition proves correct, then we will have saved lives."

Joseph considered a moment. An alteration in the Mass was not to be undertaken lightly. On the other hand, John Anglicus was a learned brother, renowned for his skill at healing. Joseph had not forgotten his cure of the leper woman. Then, as now, there had been little to go on other than John Anglicus's "intuition." Such intuitions, Joseph thought, were not to be scorned, for they were God-given.

"You may proceed for now," he said. "When Abbot Raban returns, he will of course render his own judgment upon the matter."

"Thank you, Father." Joan made her obeisance and left quickly, before Prior Joseph could change his mind.

INTINCTIO, they called the dipping of the Host, and apart from some of the elder brothers, who were set in their ways, the practice enjoyed widespread support among the brethren, for it was as satisfying to the aesthetics of the Mass as it was to the requirements of cleanliness and hygiene. A monk of Corbie, stopping by on his way home, was so impressed he carried the idea back to his own abbey, which adopted it as well.

Among the faithful, the frequency of new occurrences of the plague noticeably slowed, though it did not stop. Joan began to keep careful record of new cases of the disease, studying them in order to detect the cause of infection.

Her efforts were cut short by the return of Abbot Raban. Soon after his arrival, he summoned Joan to his quarters and confronted her with stern disapproval.

"The Canon of the Mass is sacred. How dare you tamper with it?"

"Father Abbot, the change is in form only, not in substance. And I believe it is saving lives."

Joan started to explain what she had observed, but Raban cut her off. "Such observations are useless, for they come not from faith but from the physical senses, which are not to be trusted. They are the Devil's tools, with which he lures men away from God and into the conceits of the intellect."

"If God did not wish us to observe the material world," Joan rejoined, "why then did He give us eyes to see, ears to hear, a nose to smell? Surely it is not sin to make use of the gifts He Himself has given us."

"Remember the words of St. Augustine: 'Faith is to believe what you do not see.'"

Joan responded without missing a beat, "Augustine also says that we could not believe at all if we did not have rational minds. He would not have us despise what sense and reason tell us must be so."

Raban scowled. His mind was of a rigidly conventional and

unimaginative cast, so he disliked the give-and-take of reasoned argument, preferring the safer ground of authority.

"Receive thy father's counsel and obey it," he quoted sententiously from the rule. "Return unto God by the difficult path of obedience, for thou hast forsaken Him by following thine own will."

"But, Father—"

"No more, I say!" Raban exploded angrily. His face was livid. "John Anglicus, as of this moment, you are relieved of your duties as priest. You will study humility by returning to the infirmary, where you will assist Brother Odilo, serving him with due and proper obedience."

Joan started to protest, then thought better of it. Raban had been pushed to his limit; any further argument could place her in gravest jeopardy.

With an effort of will, she bowed her head. "As you command, Father Abbot."

REFLECTING later upon what had happened, Joan saw that Raban was right; she had been prideful and disobedient. But of what use was obedience, if others must suffer by it? Intinction *was* saving lives; she was sure of that. But how could she convince the abbot? He would not tolerate further argument from her. But he might be persuaded by the weight of established authority. So now, in addition to the Opus Dei and her duties in the infirmary, Joan added hours of study in the library, searching the texts of Hippocrates, Oribasius, and Alexander of Tralles for anything that might support her theory. She worked constantly, sleeping only two or three hours a night, driving herself to exhaustion.

One day, poring over a section of Oribasius, she found what she needed. She was copying the crucial passage out in translation when she began having difficulty scribing; her head ached, and she could not hold the pen steady. She shrugged this off as the natural consequence of too little sleep and went on working. Then her quill inexplicably slipped from her grasp and rolled onto the page, scattering blobs of ink across the clean vellum, obscuring the words. *Curse the luck*, she thought. *I will have to scrape it clean and start over.* She tried to pick up the quill, but her fingers trembled so violently she could not get a grip on it.

She stood, holding on to the edge of the desk as dizziness swept

over her. Stumbling to the door, she thrust herself outside just as the
retching hit hard, doubling her up and thrusting her onto all fours,
where she heaved up the contents of her stomach.

Somehow she managed to stagger to the infirmary. Brother Odilo
made her lie down on an empty bed and put his hand to her forehead.
It was cold as ice.

Joan blinked with surprise. "Have you come from the washing
trough?"

Brother Odilo shook his head. "My hands are not cold, Brother
John. You're burning with fever. I fear the plague has you in its grip."

The plague! Joan thought woozily. *No, that can't be right. I'm
tired, that's all. If I can just rest for a while . . .*

Brother Odilo laid a cool strip of linen, steeped in rosewater, on
her forehead. "Now lie quiet, while I soak some fresh linen. I won't
be a minute."

His voice seemed to come from a long distance away. Joan closed
her eyes. The cloth felt cool against her skin. It felt good to lie still
with the sweet aroma around her, sinking peacefully into a welcome
darkness.

Suddenly her eyes flew wide. They were going to cover her in a
sheath of wet linen to bring the fever down. To do that they would
have to strip her bare.

She had to stop them. Then she realized that no matter how stren-
uously she resisted—and in her present condition she would not be
able to put up much of a fight—her protests would be dismissed as
mere feverish ravings.

She sat up, swinging her feet off the bed. Immediately the pain in
her head returned, pounding and insistent. She started for the door.
The room whirled sickeningly, but she forced herself to keep going
and made it outside. Then she headed quickly toward the foregate.
As she drew near the gate, she took a deep breath, willing herself
steady as she walked past Hatto, the porter. He looked at her curiously but made no move to stop her. Once outside, she headed
straight for the river.

Benedicite. The abbey's little boat was there, moored with a single
rope to an overhanging branch. She untied the rope and climbed in,
leaning against the grassy bank to push off. As the boat swung away
from the bank, she collapsed.

For a long moment the boat hung motionless in the water. Then the current took it, spinning it around before propelling it down the swiftly moving stream.

THE sky revolved slowly, twisting the high, white clouds into exotic patterns. A dark red sun touched the horizon, its rays burning hotter than fire, scorching Joan's face, searing her eyes. She watched fascinated as its outer edges shimmered and dissolved, forming human shape.

Her father's face floated before her, a ghastly, grinning death's-head stripped of flesh beneath the dark line of its brows. The lipless mouth parted. *"Mulier!"* it cried, but it was not her father's voice, it was her mother's. The mouth opened wider, and Joan saw that it was not a mouth at all but a hideous yawning gate opening into a great darkness. At the end of the darkness, fires burned, shooting up great blue-red pillars of flame. There were people in the flames, their bodies writhing in grotesque pantomimes of pain. One of them looked toward Joan. With a shock, Joan recognized the woman's clear blue eyes and white-gold Saxon hair. Her mother called to her, holding out her arms. Joan started toward her; suddenly the ground beneath dropped away and she was falling, falling toward the hideous mouth-gate. "Mamaaaaaaa!" she screamed as she fell into the flames . . .

She was in a snow-covered field. Villaris gleamed in the distance as the sun melted the snow on its roof, setting the water droplets sparkling like thousands of tiny gems. She heard the drumming of hooves and turned to see Gerold riding toward her on Pistis. She ran to him across the field; he drew up beside her, reached down, and hoisted her up before him. She leaned back, reveling in the tender strength of his encircling arms. She was safe. Nothing could harm her now, for Gerold would not permit it. Together they rode toward the gleaming towers of Villaris, the strides of the horse lengthening beneath them, rocking them gently, rocking, rocking . . .

THE motion had ceased. Joan opened her eyes. Above the level edge of the boat, the treetops were silhouetted black and unmoving against the twilit sky. The boat had come to a stop.

A murmur of voices came from somewhere above her, but Joan could not make out the words. Hands reached down, took hold of her, lifted her from the boat. Dimly she remembered: she must not let them take her, not while she was still sick, she must not let them carry her back to Fulda. She struck out ferociously with her arms and legs, striking flesh. Distantly she heard cursing. There was a short, sharp pain against her jaw, and then nothing else.

JOAN rose slowly out of a pool of blackness. Her head was pounding, her throat so dry it felt as if it had been scraped raw. She ran a dry tongue over parched lips, drawing tiny drops of blood from the cracked flesh. There was a dull ache in her jaw. She winced as her fingers explored a sensitive bump on her chin. *Where did I get that?* she wondered.

Then, more urgently, *Where am I?*

She was lying on a feather mattress in a room she did not recognize. Judging by the number and quality of the furnishings, the owner of the dwelling was prosperous: in addition to the enormous bed in which she was lying, there were benches upholstered with soft cloth, a high-backed chair covered with cushions, a long trencher table, a writing desk, and several trunks and chests, very finely carved. A hearth fire glowed nearby, and a pair of fresh loaves had been newly placed on the embers, their warm aromas just beginning to rise.

A few feet away, a plump young woman stood with her back toward Joan, kneading a mass of dough. She finished, wiping the flour from her tunic, and her eyes fell on Joan. She moved briskly to the door and called out, "Husband! Come quickly. Our guest has awakened!"

A ruddy-faced young man, long and gangly as a crane, came hurrying in. "How is she?" he asked.

She? Joan started as she caught the word. She looked down and saw that her monk's habit was gone; in its place she was clothed in a woman's tunic of soft blue linen.

They know.

She struggled to lift herself from the bed, but her limbs were heavy and weak as water.

"You mustn't exert yourself." The young man touched her shoulder gently, easing her back into the bed. He had a pleasant, honest face, his eyes round and blue as cornflowers.

Who is he? Joan wondered. *Will he tell Abbot Raban and the others about me—or has he already? Am I truly his "guest," or am I a prisoner?*

"Th . . . thirsty," she croaked.

The young man dipped a cup into a wooden bucket beside the bed and withdrew it brimming with water. He held it against Joan's lips and tipped it carefully, starting a slow stream of droplets into her mouth.

Joan grabbed the cup, angling it so the water poured faster. The cool liquid was sweeter than anything she had ever tasted.

The young man cautioned, "Best not take too much too soon. It's been over a week since we've been able to get anything into you beyond a few spoonfuls."

Over a week! Had she been here so long? She could not remember anything after climbing into the little fishing rig. "Wh . . . where am I?" she stammered hoarsely.

"You're in the demesne of Lord Riculf, fifty miles downstream from Fulda. We found your boat in a tangle of branches along the river's edge. You were half out of your mind with fever. Sick as you were, you fought hard to keep us from taking you."

Joan fingered the tender bump on her jaw.

The young man grinned. "Sorry. There was no reasoning with you in the condition we found you in. But take comfort, for you gave almost as good as you took." He pulled up his sleeve, revealing a large, ugly-looking bruise on his right shoulder.

"You saved my life," Joan said. "Thank you."

"You're welcome. It was only fair return for all you've done for me and mine."

"Do I . . . know you?" she asked, surprised.

The young man smiled. "I suppose I *have* changed a good deal since last we saw each other. I was only twelve then, rising thirteen. Let's see . . ." He began to figure on his hands, using Bede's classical method of computation. "That was some six years ago. Six years times three hundred sixty-five days . . . why, that's . . . two thousand one hundred and ninety days!"

Joan's eyes widened with recognition. "Arn!" she cried, and was immediately swept up into his enthusiastic embrace.

THEY did not speak further that day, for Joan was still very weak, and Arn would not allow her to weary herself. After she had taken a few spoonfuls of broth, she immediately fell asleep.

She awoke the next day feeling stronger, and, most encouraging of all, ravenously hungry. Breaking fast with Arn over a plate of bread and cheese, she listened intently as he told her all that had transpired since they last saw each other.

"As you foresaw, Father Abbot was so satisfied with our cheese that he accepted us as *prebendarii*, promising us fair living in exchange for a hundred pounds of cheese a year. But this much you must know."

Joan nodded. The extraordinary blue-veined cheese of repellent appearance and exquisite taste had become a staple at the refectory table. Guests of the abbey, both lay and monastic, were so taken with its quality that there was increasing demand for it throughout the region.

"How fares your mother?" Joan asked.

"Very well. She married again, a good man, a farmer with a herd of his own, whose milk they put toward making more cheese. Their trade grows daily, and they are happy and prosperous."

"No less than you." With a sweep of her arm, Joan indicated the large, well-kept home.

"My good fortune I owe to you," Arn said. "For at the abbey school I learned to read and to figure with numbers—skills that came in handy as our trade grew and it became necessary to keep accurate accounts. Learning of my abilities, Lord Riculf took me for his steward. I manage his estate here and guard against poachers of game or fish—that's how I came upon your boat."

Joan shook her head wonderingly, picturing Arn and his mother as they had been six years ago, living in their squalid hut as wretched as coloni—doomed, so it seemed, to a life of grinding poverty and semistarvation. Yet Madalgis was now remarried, a prosperous tradeswoman, and her son steward to a powerful lord! *Vitam regit fortuna,* Joan thought. *Truly, chance governs human life—my own as much as any.*

"Here," Arn said proudly, "is my wife, Bona, and our girl, Arnalda." Bona, a pretty young woman with laughing eyes and a quick smile, was even younger than her husband—seventeen winters at most. She was already a mother, and her swelling stomach revealed that she was once again with child. Arnalda was a cherub, all round blue eyes and curly blond hair, pink cheeked and adorable. She smiled dazzlingly at Joan, revealing a set of winning dimples.

"A fine family," Joan said.

Arn beamed and motioned to the woman and child. "Come and

greet . . ." He hesitated. "How shall I name you? 'Brother John' seems strange, knowing . . . what we know."

"Joan." The word was both alien and familiar to her ears. "Call me Joan, for that is my true name."

"Joan," Arn repeated, pleased to be trusted with this confidence. "Tell us, then, if you may, how it is that you came to live among the Benedictines of Fulda, for such a thing scarcely seems possible. How ever did you manage it? What brought you to do it? Did anyone share your secret? Did no one suspect?"

Joan laughed. "Time, I see, has not dulled your curiosity."

There was no point in deception. Joan told Arn everything, from her unorthodox education at the schola in Dorstadt to her years at Fulda and her accession to the priesthood.

"So the brothers still don't know about you," Arn said thoughtfully when she finished. "We thought perhaps you had been discovered and forced to flee. . . . Do you mean to return, then? You can, you know. I would die stretched upon the rack before anyone pried your secret out of me!"

Joan smiled. Despite Arn's manly appearance, there remained in him more than a bit of the little boy she had known.

She said, "Fortunately, there is no need for such a sacrifice. I got away in time; the brethren have no reason to suspect me. But . . . I am not sure that I *will* go back."

"What will you do, then?"

"A good question," Joan said. "A very good question indeed. As yet I don't know the answer."

ARN and Bona fussed over her like a pair of overanxious mother hens, refusing to let her rise from bed for several more days. "You are not yet strong enough," they insisted. Joan had little alternative but to resign herself to their solicitude. She passed the long hours by teaching little Arnalda her letters and numbers. Young as the child was, she had her father's aptitude for learning, and she responded eagerly, delighted by the attention of so diverting a companion.

When, at the end of the day, Arnalda was trundled off to sleep, Joan lay restlessly contemplating her future. Should she return to Fulda? She had been at the abbey almost twelve years, had grown up within its walls; it was difficult to imagine being anywhere else. But facts had to be faced: she was twenty-seven years old, already past the prime of life. The brethren of Fulda, worn down by the harsh climate, spartan diet, and unheated rooms of the monastery, seldom lived past forty; Brother Deodatus, the community elder, was fifty-four. How long could she hold out against the advances of age—how long before she would again be struck down by illness, forced anew to run the risk of disclosure and death?

Then, too, there was Abbot Raban to consider. His mind was firmly set against her, and he was not a man to turn from such a position. If she went back, what further hardships and punishments might she have to face?

Her spirit cried out for change. There was not a book in Fulda's library she had not read, not a crack in the ceiling of the dormitory she did not know by heart. It had been years since she had awakened in the morning with the happy expectation that something new and interesting might happen. She yearned to explore a wider world.

Where could she go? Back to Ingelheim? Now Mama was dead, there was nothing she cared about there. Dorstadt? What did she hope to find there—Gerold, still waiting, harboring his love for her after all these years? What folly. He was married again, more than likely, and would not be happy at Joan's sudden reappearance. Besides, she had long ago chosen a different life—a life in which the love of a man could play no part.

No, Gerold and Fulda both belonged to her past. She had to look determinedly toward the future—whatever that might be.

"BONA and I have decided," Arn said. "You must stay with us. It would be good to have another woman about the house to keep Bona company and help with the cooking and needlework—especially now, with the baby coming."

His condescension was irksome, but the offer was kindly meant, so Joan answered mildly, "That would prove a bad bargain, I fear. I was always a sorry seamstress, all thumbs with a needle and no use at all in the kitchen."

"Bona would be only too glad to teach y—"

"The truth is," she interrupted, "I have lived so long as a man I could not be a proper woman again—if, indeed, I ever was one! No, Arn"—she waved off his protest—"a man's life suits me. I like its benefits too well to be content without them."

Arn pondered this awhile. "Keep your disguise, then. It doesn't matter. You can help in the garden . . . or teach little Arnalda! You've charmed her already with your lessons and games, as once you did me."

It was a generous offer. She could not ask for greater ease or security than she would find in the bosom of this happy, prosperous family. But their world, snug and sheltered, was too small to contain her reawakened spirit of adventure. She would not trade one set of walls for another.

"Bless you, Arn, for a kind heart. But I've other plans."

"What are they?"

"I'm taking the pilgrim road."

"To Tours and the tomb of St. Martin?"

"No," Joan said, "to Rome."

"Rome!" Arn was stunned. "Are you mad?"

"Now the war is over, others will be making the same pilgrimage."

Arn shook his head. "My lord Riculf tells me that Lothar has not given up his crown, despite his defeat at Fontenoy. He has fled back to the imperial palace at Aachen and is looking for more men to fill the empty ranks of his army. My lord says he has even made overture to the Saxons, offering to let them return to worshiping their pagan gods if they will fight for him!"

How Mama would have laughed, Joan thought, *at such an unexpected turn of events: a Christian king offering to restore the Old Gods.* She could imagine what her mother would have said: the gentle martyr-God of the Christians might serve for ordinary purposes, but to win battles, one must call upon Thor and Odin, and the other fierce warrior-gods of her people.

"You cannot go, with things unsettled as they are," Arn said. "It's too dangerous."

He had a point. The conflict among the royal brothers had resulted in a complete collapse of civil order. The unguarded roads had become easy targets for roving bands of murderous brigands and outlaws.

"I'll be safe enough," Joan said. "Who'd want anything from a pilgrim priest, with nothing of value but the clothes upon his back?"

"Some of these devils would kill for the cloth, never mind the garment! I forbid you to go alone!" He spoke with an authority he would never have assumed had he still believed her to be a man.

She said sharply, "I am my own master, Arn. I go where I will."

Recognizing his mistake, Arn immediately retreated. "At least wait three months," he suggested. "The spice merchants come through then, peddling their goods. They travel well guarded, for they take no risks with their precious merchandise. They can provide you with safe escort all the way to Langres."

"Langres! Surely that is not the most direct route?"

"No," Arn agreed. "But it is the surest. In Langres there's a hostel for pilgrims headed south; you'll have no trouble finding a group of fellow travelers to keep you safe company."

Joan considered this. "You may be right."

"My lord Riculf made the same pilgrimage himself some years ago. He kept a map of the route he followed; I have it here." He opened a locked chest, took out a piece of parchment, and carefully unfolded it. It was darkened and frayed with age, but the ink had not faded; the bold lines stood out clearly, marking the route to Rome.

"Thank you, Arn," Joan said. "I'll do as you suggest. Three months' delay is not very long. It will give me more time with Arnalda; she's very smart, and coming along so well in her lessons!"

"Then it's settled." Arn began to roll up the parchment.

"I'd like to study the map a little longer, if I may."

"Take all the time you like. I'm off to the barns to oversee the shearing." Arn left smiling, pleased to have been able to persuade her so far.

Joan breathed deeply, filling her lungs with the sweet smells of early spring. Her spirit soared like a falcon loosed from its fetters, delivered suddenly to the miraculous freedom of wind and sky. At this hour, the brethren of Fulda would be gathered in the dark interior of the chapter house, crowded together on the hard stone gradines, listening to Brother Cellarer drone on about the abbey accounts. But she was here, free and unhindered, with the adventure of a lifetime before her.

With a surge of excitement, Joan studied the map. There was a good, wide road from here to Langres. There, the road turned south through Besançon and Orbe, descending along Lake St.-Maurice to LeValais. At the foot of the Alps, there was a monastic hostelry where pilgrims could rest and provision themselves for the hard trek across the mountains through the Great St. Bernard—the best and most frequently traveled of the Alpine passes. Once over the Alps, the wide, straight line of the Via Francigena led down through Aosta, Pavia, and Bologna into Tuscany, and beyond it to Rome.

Rome. The world's greatest minds gathered in that ancient city; its churches held untold treasures, its libraries the accumulated wisdom of centuries. Surely there, amidst the sacred tombs of the apostles, Joan would find what she was seeking. In Rome she would discover her destiny.

SHE was settling her saddlebag on the mule—Arn had insisted she take one for the journey—when little Arnalda came running out of the cottage, her blond hair still tousled from her night's sleep.

"Where are you going?" the cherubic little face demanded anxiously.

Joan knelt so her face was level with the child's. "To Rome," she replied, "the City of Marvels, where the Pope dwells."

"Do you like the Pope better than me?"

Joan laughed. "I've never met him. And there is no one I like better than you, little quail." She stroked the child's soft hair.

"Then don't go." Arnalda threw her arms around Joan. "I don't want you to go."

Joan hugged her. The small child-body cuddled warmly against her, filling her arms and her heart. *I could have had a little girl like this, if I had chosen a different path. A little girl to hold and to cuddle—and to teach.* She remembered the desolation she had felt when Aesculapius had gone away. He had left her a book, so she could continue to learn. But she, who had fled from the monastery with only the clothes on her back, had nothing to give the child.

Except . . .

Joan reached inside her tunic and pulled out the medallion she had worn ever since the day Matthew had first placed it about her neck. "This is St. Catherine. She was very smart and very strong, just like you." She related the story of St. Catherine.

Arnalda's eyes grew round with wonder. "She was a *girl,* and she did that?"

"Yes. And so may you, if you keep working at your letters." Joan took the medallion from her neck and hung it around Arnalda's. "She is yours now. Look after her for me."

Arnalda clutched the medallion, her little face contorted in a determined effort not to cry.

Joan said good-bye to Arn and Bona, who had come outside to see her off. Bona handed her a parcel of food and an oiled goatskin filled with ale. "There's bread and cheese, and some dried meat—

enough to see you through for a fortnight, by which time you will have reached the hostel."

"Thank you," Joan said. "I will never forget your kindness."

Arn said, "Remember, Joan. You are welcome here at any time. This is your home."

Joan embraced him. "Teach the girl," she said. "She is intelligent, and as hungry to learn as you were."

She mounted the mule. The little family stood around her, looking sad. It was her constant fate, it seemed, to leave behind those she loved. This was the price for the strange life she had chosen, but she had gone into it with eyes open, and there was no profit in regret.

Joan kicked the mule into a trot. With a last wave over her shoulder, she turned her face toward the southern road—and Rome.

≽┤ 19 ┝≼

Rome | 844

ANASTASIUS put down his quill, stretching his fingers to rid them of cramp. With pride, he studied the page he had just written—the latest entry in his masterpiece, the *Liber pontificalis,* or Book of the Popes, a detailed record of the papacies of his time.

Lovingly Anastasius ran his hand over the clean white vellum that lay ahead. On these blank pages the accomplishments, the triumphs, the glory of his own papacy would one day be recorded.

How proud his father, Arsenius, would be then! Though Anastasius's family had accumulated many titles and honors over the years, the ultimate prize of the papal throne had eluded them. Once it had seemed Arsenius might achieve it, but time and circumstance had conspired against him, and the opportunity had passed.

Now it was up to Anastasius. He must, he *would* vindicate his father's faith in him by becoming Lord Pope and Bishop of Rome.

Not immediately, of course. Anastasius's overarching ambition had not blinded him to the fact that his time had not yet come. He was only thirty-three, and his position as *primicerius,* though one of great power, was too secular a post from which to ascend to the Sacred Chair of St. Peter.

But his situation was soon to change. Pope Gregory lay on his deathbed. Once the formal period of mourning was over, there would be an election for a new Pope—an election whose outcome Arsenius had predetermined with a skillful blend of diplomacy, bribery, and threat. The next Pope would be Sergius, cardinal priest of the Church of St. Martin, weak and corruptible scion of a noble Roman family. Unlike Gregory, Sergius was a man who understood the way of the world; he would know how to express his gratitude to those who had helped him into office. Soon after Sergius's election, Anastasius would be appointed Bishop of Castellum, a perfect position from which to ascend the papal throne after Sergius, in his turn, was gone.

It was a pretty picture, but for one detail—Gregory still lived. Like an aging vine, roots driven deep to suck sustenance from arid soil, the old man stubbornly clung to life. Prudent and contemplative in his personal life as in his papacy, Gregory was proceeding with infuriating slowness even in this final act of dying.

He had reigned for seventeen years, longer than any Pope since Leo III of blessed memory. A good man, modest, well intentioned, pious, Gregory was well loved by the Roman people. He had been a solicitous patron of the city's teeming population of impoverished pilgrims, providing numerous shelters and houses of refuge, seeing that alms were distributed with a generous hand on all feast days and processions.

Anastasius regarded Gregory with a complicated mix of emotion, equal parts wonder and contempt: wonder at the genuineness of the man's piety and faith, contempt for his simplicity and slow-wittedness, which left him constantly open to deceit and manipulation. Anastasius himself had often taken advantage of the Pope's ingenuousness, never more successfully than on the Field of Lies, when he had arranged for the betrayal of Gregory's peace negotiations with the Frankish Emperor Louis under his very nose. That little stratagem had paid handsomely; the benefactor, Louis's son Lothar, had known how to render gratitude into coin, and Anastasius was now a wealthy man. Even more important, Anastasius had succeeded in winning Lothar's trust and support. For a time, it was true, Anastasius had feared that his carefully cultivated alliance with the Frankish heir might come to naught—for Lothar's defeat at Fontenoy had been admittedly disastrous. But Lothar had managed to come to terms with his rebellious brothers in the Treaty of Verdun, a remarkable piece of political legerdemain that permitted him to retain both his crown and his territories. Lothar was once again undisputed Emperor—a fact that should prove very valuable to Anastasius in the future.

The sound of bells jolted Anastasius from his reverie. The bells tolled once, twice, a third time. Anastasius slapped his thighs jubilantly. At last!

HE HAD already donned the robe of mourning when the expected knock came. A papal notary entered on silent feet. "The Apostolic One has been gathered to God," he announced. "Your presence, Primicerius, is requested in the papal bedchamber."

Side by side, without speaking, they threaded their way through the labyrinthine hallways of the Lateran Palace toward the papal quarters.

"He was a godly man." The notary broke the silence. "A peacemaker, a saint."

"A saint, indeed," Anastasius responded. To himself he thought, *What better place for him, then, than in Heaven?*

"When will come another?" The notary's voice cracked.

Anastasius saw the man was crying. He was intrigued by the display of genuine emotion. He himself was far too artful, too aware of the effect everything he said and did had on others, to engage in *lacrimae rerum.* Nevertheless, the notary's emotion reminded him that he should prepare his own show of grief. As they approached the papal bedchamber, he drew in his breath and held it, screwing up his face until he felt a sting behind his eyes. It was a trick he had, a way of bringing forth tears at will; he used it seldom, but always to good effect.

The bedchamber stood open to the gathering crowd of mourners. Inside Gregory lay on the great feather bed, eyes closed, arms, ritually crossed, clasped round a golden cross. The other *optimates,* or chief officers of the papal court, ringed the deathbed: Anastasius saw Arighis, the vicedominus; Compulus, the nomenclator; and Stephen, the vestiarius.

"The primicerius, Anastasius," the secretary announced as Anastasius entered. The others looked up to see him plunged into grief, his features etched with pain, his cheeks streaked with tears.

JOAN raised her head, letting the rays of warm Roman sun spill onto her face. She was still unaccustomed to such pleasant, mild weather in Wintarmanoth—or January, as it was called in this southern part of the Empire, where Roman, not Frankish, customs prevailed.

Rome was not what she had imagined. She had envisioned a shining city, paved with gold and marble, its hundreds of basilicas rising toward Heaven in gleaming testimony to the existence of a true *Civitas Dei,* a City of God on earth. The reality proved far different. Sprawling, filthy, teeming, Rome's narrow, broken streets seemed engendered in Hell rather than Heaven. Its ancient monuments—those that had not been converted to Christian churches—stood in ruin. Temples, amphitheaters, palaces, and baths had been stripped of their gold and silver and left open to the elements. Vines snaked across their fallen column shafts; jasmine and acanthus sprouted from the crevices of their walls; pigs and goats and great-horned oxen grazed in their decaying porticoes. Statues of emperors lay strewn upon the ground; the empty sarcophagi of heroes were reemployed as wash-tubs, cisterns, or troughs for swine.

It was a city of ancient and seemingly irreconcilable contradictions: the wonder of the world, and a filthy, decaying backwash; a place of Christian pilgrimage, whose greatest art celebrated pagan gods; a center of books and learning, whose people wallowed in ignorance and superstition.

Despite these contradictions, perhaps because of them, Joan loved Rome. The seething tumult of its streets stirred her. In these teeming corridors the far corners of the world converged: Roman, Lombard, German, Byzantine, and Muslim jostling one another in an exciting mix of customs and tongues. Past and present, pagan and Christian were intertwined in a rich and diverting tapestry. The best and worst of all the world were gathered within these ancient walls. In Rome, Joan found the world of opportunity and adventure which she had sought all her life.

She spent most of her time in the Borgo, where the various *scholae,* or societies, of foreigners were clustered. Arriving over a year ago, she had naturally gone first to the Schola Francorum but found no admittance there, as the place was overbursting with Frank-ish pilgrims and immigrants. So she had gone on to the Schola Anglo-rum, where her father's English ancestry, as well as her surname, Anglicus, had gained her a warm welcome.

The depth and breadth of her education soon earned her a reputa-tion as a brilliant scholar. Theologians came from all over Rome to engage her in learned discourse; they went away awed by the breadth of her knowledge and her quick-witted skill in disputation. How dis-mayed they would have been, Joan thought with an inward smile, had they known they had been bested by a woman!

Her regular duties included assisting at daily mass in the small church close beside the schola. After the midday meal, and a short nap (for it was the custom in the south to sleep away the sweltering afternoon hours), she went to the infirmary, where she passed the rest of the day tending the sick. Her knowledge of the medical arts stood her in good stead, for the practice of medicine here was nowhere near as advanced as in Frankland. The Romans knew little of the healing properties of herbs and plants, and nothing of the study of urine to diagnose and treat disease. Joan's successes as a healer put her services much in demand.

It was an active, busy life, one that suited Joan perfectly. It offered all the opportunities of monastic life with none of the disadvantages. She could exercise the full measure of her intelligence without check or censure. She had access to the schola library, a small but fine collection of more than fifty volumes, and no one stood over her shoulder to question her if she chose to read Cicero or Suetonius rather than Augustine. She was free to come and go as she pleased, to think as she liked, to express her thoughts without fear of flogging and exposure. The time passed quickly, measured out contentedly in the fulfillment of each day's work.

So things might have continued indefinitely had the newly elected Pope Sergius not fallen ill.

SINCE Septuagesima Sunday, the Pope had been beset by an assortment of vague but troubling symptoms: bad digestion, insomnia, heaviness and swelling of the limbs; shortly before Easter, he was stricken with a pain so intense as to be almost unendurable. Night after night, the entire palace was kept awake by his screaming.

The society of physicians sent a dozen of its best men to attend the stricken Pope. They tried a multitude of devices to effect a cure: they brought a fragment of the skull of St. Polycarp for Sergius to touch; they massaged his afflicted limbs with oil taken from a lamp that had burned all night on the tomb of St. Peter, a measure known to cure even the most desperate of afflictions; they bled him repeatedly and purged him with emetics so strong his whole body was racked with violent spasms. When even these powerful curatives failed, they tried to dispel the pain through counter-irritation, laying strips of burning flax across the veins of the legs.

Nothing availed. As the Pope's condition worsened, the Roman people were gripped with alarm: if Sergius should die so soon after his predecessor, leaving the Throne of St. Peter vacant again, the Frankish Emperor, Lothar, might seize the opportunity to descend on the city and assert his imperial authority over them.

Sergius's brother Benedict was also beset by worry—not out of any fraternal sentiment but because his brother's demise represented a threat to his own interests. Having persuaded Sergius to appoint him papal missus, Benedict had skillfully used that position to accrue the authority of the papal office for himself. The result was that, only five months into his papacy, Sergius ruled in name only; all real power in Rome was wielded by Benedict—to the considerable aggrandizement of his personal fortune.

Benedict would have preferred to have the title and honor of the papal office as well, but he had always known this to be beyond his reach. He had neither the education nor the polish for so great an office. He was a second son, and in Rome it was not the custom to divide property and title among heirs as in Frankland. As the firstborn, Sergius had been lavished with all the privileges the family could provide—the expensive clothes, the private tutors. It was terribly unfair, but there was nothing to be done about it, and after a while Benedict had left off sulking and sought consolation in worldlier pleasures, of which, he quickly discovered, Rome had no shortage. His mother had grumbled about his dissolute habits but made no serious attempt to curtail them; her interest and hopes had always been centered on Sergius.

Now, at last, the long years of being overlooked were at an end. It had not been difficult to get Sergius to appoint him papal missus; Sergius had always felt guilty about the preference he had been given over his younger brother. Benedict knew his brother was weak, but corrupting him had proved even easier than anticipated. After all the years of ceaseless study and monkish deprivation, Sergius was more than ready to enjoy life. Benedict did not try to lure his brother with women, for Sergius clung adamantly to the ideal of priestly chastity. Indeed, his feelings on this point approached obsession, so that Benedict was hard put to keep secret his own sexual adventuring.

But Sergius had another weakness—an insatiable appetite for the pleasures of the table. As he consolidated his own power, Benedict kept his brother distracted with an unending parade of gustatory delights. Sergius's capacity for food and wine was prodigious. He had been known to consume five trout, two roast hens, a dozen meat pasties, and a whole haunch of venison in a single sitting. After one such orgy, he had come to morning mass so gorged and bloated that he vomited up the Sacred Host onto the altar, to the horror of the congregation.

Following this shameful episode, Sergius resolved to reform, resuming the simple diet of bread and greens on which he had been raised. This spartan regimen restored him; he again began to take an

interest in affairs of state. This had interfered with Benedict's profitable schemes. But Benedict bided his time. Then, when he judged
Sergius had had enough of pious self-denial, he resumed tempting
him with extravagant gifts: rich and exotic sweetmeats, pasties and
pottages, roasted pigs, barrelfuls of thick Tuscan wine. Soon Sergius
was off on another feeding binge.

This time, however, the bingeing had gone too far. Sergius became
ill, dangerously ill. Benedict felt no compassion for his elder brother,
but he did not want him to die. Sergius's death would spell the end of
Benedict's own power.

Something had to be done. The physicians attending Sergius were
an incompetent lot who attributed the Pope's sickness to powerful
demons, against whose malignancy only prayer could avail. They surrounded Sergius with a multitude of priests and monks, who wept and
prayed beside his bed day and night, raising their voices stringently
toward Heaven, but it made no difference: Sergius continued to decline.

Benedict was not content to let his future hang upon the slender
thread of prayer. *I must do something. But what?*

"My lord."

Benedict was roused from his reverie by the small, hesitant voice
of Celestinus, one of the papal *cubicularii*, or chamberlains. Like
most of his fellows, Celestinus was the scion of a rich and aristocratic
Roman family that had paid handsomely for the honor of having
their young son serve as chamberlain to the Pope. Benedict regarded
the boy with dislike. What did this pampered child of privilege know
of life, of the hard scrabble to raise oneself up from obscurity?

"What is it?"

"My lord Anastasius requests an audience with you."

"Anastasius?" Benedict could not place the name.

"Bishop of Castellum," Celestinus offered helpfully.

"You dare instruct me?" Furious, Benedict brought his hand
down forcefully on Celestinus's cheek. "That will teach you respect
for your betters. Now be off, and bring the bishop to me here."

Celestinus hurried away, cradling his cheek tearfully. Benedict's
hand stung where it had contacted the boy; he flexed it, feeling better
than he had in days.

Moments later Anastasius swept regally through the doors. Tall
and courtly, the epitome of aristocratic elegance, he was well aware
of the impression he made on Benedict.

"*Pax vobiscus*," Benedict greeted him in mangled Latin.

Anastasius noted the barbarism but took care not to let his contempt show. "*Et cum spiritu tuo*," he responded smoothly. "How fares His Holiness the Pope?"

"Poorly. Very poorly."

"I grieve to hear it." This was more than politeness; Anastasius truly was concerned. The time was not yet right for Sergius to die. Anastasius would not be thirty-five, the minimum age required in a Pontiff, for more than a year. If Sergius died now, a younger man than he might be elected, and it could be twenty years or more before the Chair of St. Peter stood vacant again. Anastasius did not intend to wait that long to realize his life's ambition.

"Your brother is skillfully attended, I trust?"

"He is surrounded night and day by holy men offering prayers for his recovery."

"Ah!" There was a silence. Both men were skeptical of the efficacy of such measures, but neither could own his doubt openly.

"There is someone at the Schola Anglorum," Anastasius ventured, "a priest with a great reputation for healing."

"Oh?"

"John Anglicus, I believe he is called—a foreigner. Apparently he is a man of great learning. They say that he can perform veritable miracles of healing."

"Perhaps I should send for him," said Benedict.

"Perhaps," Anastasius agreed, then let the matter drop. Benedict, he sensed, was not a man to be pushed. Tactfully, Anastasius shifted the discussion to another matter. When he judged a reasonable amount of time to have passed, he stood to leave. "*Dominus tecum, Benedictus.*"

"*Deus vobiscus.*" Benedict mangled the form once again.

Ignorant oaf, Anastasius thought. That such a man could rise so far in power was an embarrassment, a stain upon the reputation of the Church. With a bow and an elegant sweep of his robes, Anastasius turned and left.

Benedict watched him go. *Not a bad sort, for an aristocrat. I will send for this healer-priest, this John Anglicus.* It would probably cause trouble, bringing in someone who was not a member of the society of physicians, but no matter. Benedict would find a way. There was always a way, when one knew what one wanted.

THREE dozen candles blazed at the foot of the great bed in which Sergius lay. Behind them knelt a clot of black-robed monks, droning litanies in deep-voiced unison.

Ennodius, chief physician of Rome, raised his iron lancet and drew it deftly across Sergius's left forearm, slicing into the chief vein. Blood welled from the wound and dripped into a silver bowl held by Ennodius's apprentice. Ennodius shook his head as he examined the blood in the bowl. It was thick and dark; the peccant humor that was causing the Pope's illness was compacted in the body and would not be drawn out. Ennodius left the wound open, letting the blood flow longer than usual; he would not be able to bleed Sergius again for some days, for the moon was passing into Gemini, an unpropitious sign for bloodletting.

"How does it look?" Florus, a fellow physician, asked.

"Bad. Very bad."

"Come outside," Florus whispered. "I must speak with you."

Ennodius staunched the wound, pressing the flaps of skin together and applying pressure with his hand. The task of binding the wound with grease-coated leaves of rue wrapped in cloth he left to his apprentice. Wiping the blood from his hands, he followed Florus out to the hall.

"They've sent for someone else," Florus said urgently as soon as they were alone. "A healer from the Schola Anglorum."

"No!" Ennodius was chagrined. The practice of medicine within the city was supposed to be strictly confined to members of the physicians' society—though in actuality a small and unrecognized army of medical dabblers plied their questionable skills among the populace. These were tolerated, as long as they operated anonymously among the poor. But a forthright acknowledgment of one of these, coming from the papal palace itself, represented an undeniable threat.

"John Anglicus, the man is called," Florus said. "Rumor has it he is possessed of extraordinary powers. They say he can diagnose an illness merely by examining a patient's urine."

Ennodius sniffed. "A charlatan."

"Obviously. But some of these medical pretenders are quite artful. If this John Anglicus can mount even an appearance of skill, it could be damaging."

Florus was right. In a profession such as theirs, where results were often disappointing and always unpredictable, reputation was everything. If this outsider should meet with success where they had been seen to fail . . .

Ennodius thought for a moment. "He makes a study of urine, you say? Well, then, we'll provide him with a sample."

"Surely the last thing we should do is help the foreigner!"

Ennodius smiled. "I said we'd provide him with a sample, Florus. I didn't say from whom."

SURROUNDED by an escort of papal guards, Joan walked quickly toward the Patriarchium, the enormous palace housing the papal residence as well as the multiplicity of administrative offices that constituted the seat of government in Rome. Bypassing the great Basilica of Constantine, with its magnificent line of round-arched windows, they entered the Patriarchium. Inside, they climbed a short flight of stairs which let upon the *triclinium major,* or great hall of the palace, whose construction had been commissioned by Pope Leo of blessed memory.

The hall was paved in marble and decorated with myriad mosaics, worked with a degree of artistry that left Joan awestruck. Never before had she seen colors so bright, nor figures so lifelike. No one in Frankland—bishop, abbot, count, not even the Emperor himself—could command such magnificence.

In the center of the triclinium, a group of men was gathered. One came forward to greet her. He was dark avised, with narrow, puffy eyes and a crafty expression.

"You are the priest John Anglicus?" he asked.

"I am."

"I am Benedict, papal missus and brother to Pope Sergius. I have had you brought here to cure His Holiness."

"I will do all I can," Joan said.

Benedict dropped his voice to a conspiratorial whisper. "There are those who have no wish to see you succeed."

Joan could well believe it. Many in the assemblage were members of the select and exclusive physicians' society. They would not welcome an outsider.

Another man joined them—tall, thin, with penetrating eyes and a beaked nose. Benedict introduced him as Ennodius, chief of the physicians' society.

Ennodius acknowledged Joan with the barest of nods. "You will discover for yourself, *if* you have the skill, that His Holiness is afflicted by demons, whose pernicious hold will not be dislodged by medicines or purgings."

Joan said nothing. She put little credence in such theories. Why look to the supernatural when there were so many physical and detectable causes of disease?

Ennodius held out a vial of yellow liquid. "This sample of urine was taken from His Holiness not an hour ago. We are curious to see what you can learn from it."

So I am to be tested, Joan thought. *Well, I suppose it's as good a way to start as any.*

She took the vial and held it up against the light. The group gathered round in a semicircle. Ennodius's beaked nose quivered as he watched her with vulpine expectancy.

She turned the vial this way and that until the contents showed clearly. Strange. She sniffed it, then sniffed again. She dipped a finger in, put it to her tongue, and tasted carefully. The tension in the room was now almost palpable.

Again she sniffed and tasted. No doubt about it.

A clever ruse, substituting a pregnant woman's urine for the Pope's. They had confronted her with a true dilemma. As a simple priest, and a foreigner, she could not accuse so august a company of deliberate deceit. On the other hand, if she did not detect the substitution, she would be denounced as a fraud.

The trap had been skillfully set. How to escape it?

She stood considering.

Then she turned and announced, straight-faced, "God is about to perform a miracle. Within thirty days, His Holiness is going to give birth."

BENEDICT shook with laughter as he led the way out of the triclinium. "The looks on those old men's faces! It was all I could do to keep from laughing out loud!" He was deriving an inordinate amount of pleasure from what had transpired. "You proved your skill and exposed their deceit without uttering a single word of accusation. Brilliant!"

As they approached the papal bedroom, they heard hoarse shouting from the other side of the door.

"Villains! Ghouls! I'm not dead yet!" There was a loud crash, as of something thrown.

Benedict opened the door. Sergius was sitting up in bed, crimson faced with fury. Halfway across the floor, a broken pottery bowl rocked wildly before a group of cringing priests. Sergius had snatched a golden cup from a bedside table and was about to hurl it at the hapless prelates when Benedict hurried over and pulled it from his grasp.

"Now, Brother. You know what the doctors said. You are ill; you must not exert yourself."

Sergius said accusingly, "I woke to find them anointing me with oil. They were trying to administer unctio extrema."

The prelates smoothed their robes with ruffled dignity. They appeared to be men of importance; one who wore the pallium of an archbishop said, "We thought it best, in view of His Holiness's worsening condition—"

"Leave at once!" Benedict interrupted.

Joan was astonished; Benedict must be powerful, indeed, to address an archbishop so uncivilly.

"Take thought, Benedict," the archbishop warned. "Would you endanger your brother's immortal soul?"

"Out!" Benedict swung his arms as if driving off a flock of blackbirds. "All of you!"

The prelates retreated hastily, exiting in shared indignation.

Sergius fell back weakly against his pillows. "The pain, Benedict," he whimpered. "I cannot bear the pain."

Benedict poured wine from a pitcher beside the bed into the golden cup and put it to Sergius's lips. "Drink," he said, "it will ease you."

Sergius drank thirstily. "More," he demanded as soon as he had drained it. Benedict poured him a second cup, and then a third. Wine spilled down the sides of Sergius's mouth. He was small boned but very fat. His countenance was a series of connecting circles: round face connecting to round chin, round eyes centered inside twin rings of flesh.

"Now," Benedict said, when Sergius's thirst was quenched, "see what I have done for you, Brother? I have brought someone who can help you. He is John Anglicus, a healer of great repute."

"Another physician?" Sergius said mistrustfully.

But he made no objection when Joan pulled back the covers to examine him. She was shocked at his condition. His legs were hugely swollen, the stretched flesh cracked and splitting from the strain. He was afflicted with a serious inflammation of the joints; Joan guessed the cause, but she had to make certain. She checked Sergius's ears. Sure enough, there they were: the telltale tophi, little chalky excrescences resembling crabs' eyes whose presence meant only one thing: Sergius was suffering an acute attack of gout. How was it possible that his doctors had not recognized it?

Joan ran her fingertips gently over the red, shiny flesh, feeling for the source of the inflammation.

"At least this one hasn't the hands of a plowman," Sergius conceded. It was astonishing he was still lucid, for he burned with fever. Joan felt his pulse, noting as she did the multiple wounds on his arm from repeated bleedings. His heartbeat was weak, and his coloring, now the fit of choler had passed, a sickly bluish white.

Benedicite, she thought. *No wonder he suffers from thirst. They have bled him within an inch of his life.*

She turned to a chamberlain. "Bring water. Quickly."

She had to reduce the swelling before it killed him. Thank heavens she had brought corm of colchicum. Joan reached into her scrip and withdrew a small square of waxed parchment, unfolding it carefully so as not to spill any of the precious powder. The chamberlain returned with a jug of water. Joan poured some into a goblet, then infused two drams of the powdered root, the recommended dosage. She added clarified honey to mask the bitter taste and a small dose of henbane to make Sergius sleep—for sleep was the best anodyne against pain, and rest the best hope for a cure.

She handed the goblet to Sergius, who gulped it thirstily. "Pah!" He spat it out. "This is water!"

"Drink it," Joan said firmly.

To her surprise, Sergius acquiesced. "Now what?" he asked after he had drained the cup. "Are you going to purge me?"

"I should have thought you'd had enough of such tortures."

"You mean to do no more than this?" Benedict challenged. "A simple draft and that is all?"

Joan sighed. She had encountered such reactions before. Common sense and moderation were not appreciated in the art of healing. People demanded more dramatic measures. The more serious the disease, the more violent the cure was expected to be.

"His Holiness is suffering from gout. I have given him colchicum, a known specific for the disease. In a few moments, he will sleep, and, *Deo volente*, the pain and swelling that have afflicted him will recede in a few days' time."

As if in demonstration of the truth of what she said, Sergius's ragged breathing began to ease; he relaxed against the pillows and closed his eyes peacefully.

The door swung open with a bang. In stalked a small, tensely coiled man with a face like that of a bantam cock spoiling for a fight. He brandished a roll of parchment beneath Benedict's nose. "Here are the papers. All that's needed is the signature." By his dress and manner of speech, he appeared to be a merchant.

"Not now, Aio," Benedict answered.

Aio shook his head fiercely. "No, Benedict, I will not be put off again. All Rome knows the Pope is dangerously ill. What if he dies in the night?"

Joan looked anxiously at Sergius, but he had not heard. He had slipped into a doze.

The man jingled a bag of coins before Benedict's eyes. "One thousand solidi, as agreed. Have the paper signed, now, and this"—he raised another, smaller bag—"is yours as well."

Benedict took the parchment to the bed and unrolled it on the sheet. "Sergius?"

"He is sleeping," Joan protested. "Do not rouse him."

Benedict ignored her. "Sergius!" He took his brother by the shoulder and shook him roughly.

Sergius's eyes blinked open. Benedict took a quill from the table beside the bed, dipped it in ink, and wrapped Sergius's hand around it. "Sign this," he commanded.

Dazedly, Sergius put the pen to the parchment. His hand shook, spilling the ink onto the parchment in an uneven scrawl. Benedict covered his brother's hand with his own and helped him trace the papal signature.

From where she stood, Joan saw the paper clearly. It was a *formata* appointing Aio Bishop of Alatri. The contract being made before Joan's very eyes was a bribe to buy a bishopric!

"Rest you now, brother," Benedict said, content now he had what he wanted. To Joan he said, "Stay with him."

Joan nodded. Benedict and Aio exited from the room.

Joan pulled the bedcovers over Sergius, smoothing them gently. Her chin was set in characteristic determination. Clearly, things in the papal palace were very much amiss. Nor were they likely to be righted as long as Sergius lay ill and his venal brother ruled in his stead. Her task was plain: restore the Pope to health, and that as quickly as possible.

FOR the next few days, Sergius's condition remained perilous. The constant chanting of the priests kept him from sound sleep, so at Joan's insistence their bedside vigil was terminated. Except for one brief excursion to the Schola Anglorum to retrieve more medicines, Joan did not leave Sergius's side. By day she carefully monitored his condition; by night she slept on a pile of cushions beside the bed.

On the third day, the swelling began to recede, and the skin covering it started to peel. In the evening, Joan woke from a restless sleep to find that Sergius had broken sweat. *Benedicite,* she thought. *The fever has passed.*

The next morning he awoke.

"How do you feel?" Joan asked.

"I . . . don't know," he said groggily. "Better, I think."

"You look a good deal better." The pinched look was gone, as was the unhealthy blue-gray cast of his skin.

"My legs . . . they're crawling!" He began to scratch at them violently.

"The itching is a good sign; it means the life is returning," Joan said. "But you must not irritate the skin, for there is still a danger of infection."

He withdrew his hand. But the itching sensation was too strong; a moment later he was clawing at his legs again. Joan administered a dose of henbane to calm him, and again he slept.

When he opened his eyes the next day, he was clearheaded, fully aware of his surroundings.

"The pain—it's gone!" He looked at his legs. "And the swelling!" The observation animated him; he pulled himself into a sitting position. Spying a chamberlain by the door, he said, "I'm hungry. Bring a raft of bacon and some wine."

"A plate of greens and a jug of water," Joan countermanded. The chamberlain hurried off before Sergius could protest.

Sergius's brows flew up with surprise. "Who are you?"

"My name is John Anglicus."

"You're not Roman."

"I was born in Frankland."

"The north country!" Sergius's eyes sharpened. "Is it as barbarous as they say?"

Joan smiled. "There are fewer churches, if that's what you mean."

"Why are you called 'Anglicus,'" Sergius asked, "if you were born in Frankland?" He was astonishingly alert in light of what he had been through.

"My father was English," Joan explained. "He came to preach the faith among the Saxons."

"The Saxons?" Sergius frowned. "A godless tribe."

Mama. Joan felt the old familiar surge of shame and love. She said, "Most are Christian now—as far as any can be who are brought to the Faith through fire and sword."

Sergius eyed her sharply. "You do not hold with the Church's mission to convert the heathen?"

"What value has any pledge exacted by force? Under torture, a person may confess to any number of lies, merely to put an end to pain."

"Yet our Lord bids us spread the word of God: 'Go, therefore, and teach all nations, baptizing them in the name of the Father and of the Son and of the Holy Spirit.'"

"True," Joan conceded. "But—" She broke off. She was doing it again—allowing herself to be drawn into imprudent and possibly dangerous debate—this time with the Pope himself!

"Go on," Sergius prodded.

"Forgive me, Holiness. You are not well."

"Nor yet too sick for reason," Sergius replied impatiently. "Go on."

"Well"—she chose her words carefully—"consider the order of Christ's commands: teach the nations first, then baptize them. We are not enjoined to bestow the sacrament of baptism before the mind embraces the Faith with rational understanding. First teach, Christ says, then dip."

Sergius contemplated her with interest. "You reason well. Where were you educated?"

"A Greek by the name of Aesculapius, a man of great learning, tutored me as a child. Later, I was sent to the cathedral school at Dorstadt, and later still to Fulda."

"Ah, Fulda! I have only recently received a volume from Raban Maur, beautifully illuminated, containing a poem of his own composition on the Holy Cross of Christ. When I write to thank him, I will tell him of your service to our person."

She thought she had put Abbot Raban behind her forever; would his tyrannous hatred follow her even here, blighting the new life she had made for herself? "You will not have good report of me from that quarter, I fear."

"Why is that?"

"The abbot holds obedience to be the greatest of the religious vows. Yet, to me, it has always come the hardest."

"And your other vows?" Sergius asked sternly. "What of them?"

"I was born into poverty and am accustomed to it. As for chastity"—she kept her voice free of any tinge of irony—"I have always resisted the temptations of women."

Sergius's expression softened. "I am glad to hear it. For in this matter, Abbot Raban and I do not agree; of all the religious vows, chastity is surely the greatest and most pleasing to God."

Joan was surprised that he should think so. The ideal of priestly chastity was far from universally practiced in Rome. It was not at all uncommon for a Roman priest to have a wife, as there was no prohibition against married men entering the priesthood, provided that they agreed to abjure all future conjugal relations—an agreement that predictably was observed more in the breach than in the practice. A wife rarely objected if her husband sought to become a priest, for she shared in the prestige of his position: "Priestess," the wife of a priest was respectfully titled, or "Deaconess," if the wife of a deacon. Pope Leo III had been married when he ascended the papal throne, and no one in Rome had thought worse of him for it.

The chamberlain returned with a silver dish of bread and greens that he placed before Sergius, who tore off a chunk of bread and bit into it hungrily. "Now," he said, "tell me all about you and Raban Maur."

⊱| 20 |⊰

IT WAS, Joan came to understand, as if Sergius were two different people—one dissolute, vulgar, and mean, the other cultivated, intelligent, and considerate. She had read of such cases in Celsus: *animae divisae*, he called them, divided spirits.

So it was with Sergius. But in his case, it was drink that triggered the metamorphosis. Gentle and kind when sober, he became a terror under the influence of wine. The palace servants, always ready to gossip, told Joan that Sergius had once condemned one of them to death merely for failing to deliver his supper in time. He had sobered up in time to stop the execution, but not before the unfortunate man had already been caned and pilloried.

His doctors had not been so far wrong after all, Joan decided: Sergius *was* possessed, though the demons that drove him were not of the Devil's making but his own.

Having gotten a glimpse of his better qualities, Joan made it her mission to restore him. She put him on a strict diet of greens and barley water. Sergius grumbled but submitted, fearing a return of pain. When she judged he was ready, Joan instituted a regimen of daily walks in the Lateran garden. In the beginning, he had to be carried there in his chair, three attendants groaning under his weight. The first day he barely managed to hobble a few steps before collapsing into his chair. With Joan's persistent encouragement, each day he went a little farther; at the end of a month he was able to make a full circuit of the garden. The residual swelling around his joints subsided, and the skin regained a healthy pink color. His eyes lost their puffiness, and as the contours of his face emerged more clearly, Joan could see that he was a much younger man than she had first thought—no more, perhaps, than forty-five or fifty.

"I feel a new man," Sergius said to Joan one day during their daily stroll. It was spring, and the lilacs were already in bloom, their heady scent perfuming the air.

"No dizziness, no weakness, no pain?" Joan asked.

"None. Truly, God has wrought a miracle."

"You might say that, Holiness," Joan said with a sideways smile. "But think what your condition was when God alone was serving as your physician!"

Sergius tweaked Joan's ear in playful recrimination. "God sent you here to me to effect His miracle!"

They smiled together, liking each other.

This is the moment, Joan thought. "If you truly feel quite well . . ." She let the words hang, tantalizingly.

"Yes?"

"I was just thinking . . . the papal court is in session today. Your brother Benedict is presiding in your place as usual. But if you're feeling strong enough . . ."

Sergius said irresolutely, "Benedict is accustomed to presiding. Surely there is no need . . ."

"The people did not choose Benedict for their lord. They need you, Holiness."

Sergius frowned. There was a long silence.

Joan thought: *I spoke too soon, and too boldly.*

Sergius said, "You speak truly, John Anglicus. I have been too long neglectful of such matters." The sadness in his eyes gave his face a look of grave wisdom.

Joan replied gently, "The remedy, my lord, lies in the doing."

Sergius contemplated this. Then he wheeled abruptly, heading for the garden gate. "Come on, then!" he called back to her. "What are you waiting for?"

Joan hurried after him.

Two guards leaned against the wall outside the council room, chatting idly. Seeing Sergius, they jumped to attention and pulled the doors open. "His Holiness Pope Sergius, Bishop and Metropolitan of Rome!" one announced in a ringing voice.

Sergius and Joan swept into the room. There was a moment's astonished silence, followed by a loud scraping of benches as everyone stood respectfully. Everyone, that is, but Benedict, who remained seated in the papal chair with his jaw agape.

"Close your mouth, Brother, unless you mean to catch flies," Sergius said.

"Holiness! Is this wise?" Benedict exclaimed. "Surely you should not risk your health by observing these proceedings!"

"Thank you, Brother, but I feel quite well," Sergius said. "And I have come not to observe but to preside."

Benedict stood up. "I rejoice to hear it, as does all Rome." He sounded anything but rejoiceful.

Sergius settled comfortably into the cushioned chair. "What is the case in hand?"

Quickly the notary outlined the details. Mamertus, a wealthy merchant, was suing for permission to renovate the Orphanotrophium, a shelter and school for orphans housed in a decaying structure close by the Lateran. Mamertus proposed to rebuild it entirely and turn it into a hostel for pilgrims.

"The Orphanotrophium," Sergius mused. "I know the place well; I stayed there some while myself, after my mother died."

"Holiness, the building is fallen into ruin," Mamertus said. "It is an eyesore, a blot upon our great city. What I propose will turn it into a palace!"

"What will become of the orphans?" Sergius asked.

Mamertus shrugged. "They can seek charity elsewhere. There are almshouses that will receive them."

Sergius looked doubtful. "It is a hard thing to be turned out from one's home."

"Holiness, this hostelry will be the pride of Rome! Dukes will not scorn to sleep there, nor kings neither!"

"Orphans are no less dear to God than kings. Has Christ not said, 'Blessed are the poor, for theirs is the Kingdom of God'?"

"Holiness, I beg you to consider. Think what the existence of such an establishment can do for Rome!"

Sergius shook his head. "I will not sanction the destruction of these children's home. The petition is denied."

"I protest!" Mamertus said heatedly. "Your brother and I are already agreed upon the arrangement; the compact has been struck, and the payment delivered."

"Payment?" Sergius arched a brow.

Benedict shook his head at Mamertus in urgent signal.

"I . . . I"—Mamertus raised his eyes, searching for words—"I made an offering, a most generous offering, at the altar of St. Servatius to speed the success of this enterprise."

"Then you are blessed," said Sergius. "Such charity carries its own reward, for you will suffer the less in the life everlasting."

"But—"

"You have our gratitude, Mamertus, for calling the poor state of repair of the Orphanotrophium to our attention. Restoring it shall become our immediate concern."

Mamertus's mouth opened and closed several times like that of a beached fish. With a last glare at Benedict, he stalked from the room.

Sergius winked at Joan, who smiled back.

Benedict caught the exchange. *So that's the weave of the wool,* he thought. He chided himself for not having noticed it sooner. It had been a busy season for the pontifical court, the most profitable time of year for Benedict; his time had been so heavily given over to these matters that he had not paid sufficient attention to the degree of sway the little foreign priest had acquired over his brother.

No matter, he told himself. *What's done can be undone. Every man has his weakness.* It was just a matter of discovering what that was.

JOAN hurried down the corridor on her way to the triclinium major. As Sergius's personal physician, she was expected to sup at his table—a privilege that allowed her to keep a close eye on everything the Pope ate and drank. His state of health was still far from robust; overindulgence could well bring on another attack of gout.

"John Anglicus!"

She turned to see Arighis, the vicedominus, or majordomo of the palace, coming toward her.

"A lady in the Trastevere is dangerously ill; you are called upon to attend her."

Joan sighed. Three times this week she had been called out on such an errand. The news of her cure of Pope Sergius had spread throughout the city. To the great dismay of the members of the physicians' society, Joan's services as a healer were suddenly very much in demand.

"Why not send a physician from the schola?" Joan suggested.

Arighis frowned. He was not accustomed to being challenged: as vicedominus, it was his right and his duty to exercise control over all matters relating to the papal household and its staff—a fact that this brash young foreigner did not seem to understand. "I have already committed your services."

Joan bristled at this assertion of authority; as Sergius's personal physician, she was not, strictly speaking, under Arighis's supervision. But the matter was scarcely worth battling over, and an urgent call for help must be answered, however inopportune the moment of its arrival.

"Very well," Joan agreed, "I'll get my bag of medicaments."

ARRIVING at the address, Joan found herself before a large residence, styled in the manner of an old Roman *domus*. A servant led her through a series of connecting courtyards and a garden to an interior chamber riotously decorated with brightly colored mosaics, stucco seashells, and fool-the-eye paintings designed to create the illusion of distant vistas and rooms. This fantastical room was suffused with a sweet smell, redolent of ripe apples. At the far side of the room stood a large feather bed, lit round with candles like an altar. In the middle of the bed, a woman was lying languorously.

She was the most beautiful woman Joan had ever seen, more beautiful than Richild, more beautiful even than her mother, Gudrun, whom Joan had believed until this moment to be the loveliest woman in creation.

"I am Marioza." The woman's voice was liquid honey.

"L-lady," Joan stammered, tongue-tied before such perfection. "I am John Anglicus, come in answer to your summons."

Marioza smiled, pleased with the effect she was having. "Come closer, John Anglicus," the honey-voice urged. "Or do you mean to examine me from there?"

The sweet-apple scent was stronger by the bed. Joan thought, *I know that scent.* But she could not, for the moment, place it.

Marioza held out a cup of wine. "Won't you drink my health?"

Politely, Joan drank, draining the cup according to custom. Up close, Marioza was even more beautiful, her skin a flawless ivory, her eyes huge, black-fringed orbs of deepest violet, darkened into ebony by the wide black pupils at the center.

Too wide, Joan suddenly realized. So great a dilation of the pupils was decidedly abnormal. The clinical observation broke the spell of Marioza's beauty. "Tell me, lady"—Joan set the cup down—"what ails you?"

"So handsome," she sighed, "and so businesslike?"

"I wish to help you, lady. What distress has called me to your side so urgently?"

"Since you insist"—Marioza pouted prettily—"it's my heart."

An unusual complaint for a woman of her age, Joan thought; Marioza could not be older than twenty-two. Well, such cases were known to occur, children born under an unlucky star with a worm in their hearts, every breath of their short existence a torment and a struggle. But those who suffered from such afflictions did not look like Marioza, whose whole being, apart from those mysteriously dilated pupils, radiated good health.

Joan took up Marioza's wrist and felt her pulse, finding it strong and regular. She examined Marioza's hands. The color was good, the tips of the fingers showing pink under the nails. The skin sprang back to the touch without mark or discoloration. Joan examined Marioza's legs and feet with equal care, again finding no sign of necrosis; everywhere Marioza's circulation appeared healthy and strong.

Marioza lay back against the pillows, watching through half-lidded eyes. "Looking for my heart?" she teased. "You'll not find it there, John Anglicus!" She pulled opened her silken bed robe, revealing a pair of flawless ivory breasts.

Benedicite! Joan thought. This must be the Marioza of legend, the most celebrated hetaera, or courtesan, in all of Rome! It was said that she numbered some of the most important men in the city among her clients. *She is trying to seduce me,* Joan realized. The absurdity of the idea caused her to smile.

Misinterpreting Joan's smile, Marioza was encouraged. This priest was not going to be so difficult to seduce as Benedict had indicated when he had purchased her services for that purpose. Priest or no, John Anglicus was nevertheless a man, and the man had not been born who could resist her.

With studied disinterest, Joan concentrated on her examination. She probed Marioza's sides, checking for bruised ribs; the pain from such an injury was often mistaken for a problem of the heart. Marioza did not wince or give any evidence of discomfort.

"What fine hands you have," she purred, arranging herself so the enticing curves of her body were displayed to advantage. "What fine, strong hands."

Joan bolted upright. "Satan's apple!"

How like a priest, Marioza thought, *to talk high-mindedly of sin at such a moment.* Well, she was no stranger to priests; she knew how to deal with these last-minute crises of conscience.

"Do not suppress your feelings, John, for they are natural and God-given. Is it not written in the Bible: 'The two shall become one flesh'?" Actually, Marioza was not sure the words came from the Bible, but she thought it likely; they had been told to her, under circumstances very similar to the present, by an archbishop. "Besides," she added, "no one will ever know what happens here between us, excepting ourselves."

Joan shook her head vehemently. "That's not what I meant. The scent in this room—it's mandragora—sometimes called Satan's apple." The yellow fruit was a narcotic; that explained Marioza's dilated pupils. "But where is the scent coming from?" Joan sniffed a candle near the bed. "What have you done, mixed the juice with candle wax?"

Marioza sighed. She had seen such reactions from virginal young prelates before. Embarrassed and unsure, they kept trying to turn the conversation to safer ground. "Come," she said, "leave off talk of potions. There are better ways for us to pass the time." She ran her hand across the front of John Anglicus's tunic, reaching for his privates.

Anticipating her, Joan jumped back. She snuffed the candle and took Marioza's hands firmly in her own. "Listen to me, Marioza. The mandragora—you use it for its aphrodisiac qualities, I know. But you must leave off, for its fumes are poison."

Marioza frowned. This was not going according to plan. Somehow she must get the man's mind off his doctoring.

There were footsteps in the hall below. No time left for persuasion. She grabbed the top of her robe with both hands and rent it with a strong downward pull. "Oh!" she gasped, "a pain comes now! Do but listen!" She clasped Joan's head and held it firmly to her breast.

Joan tried to pull away, but Marioza held her tight. "Oh, John," her voice was now pure liquid, "I cannot resist the force of your passion!"

The door burst open. A dozen papal guards stormed into the room and seized Joan, lifting her roughly off the bed.

"Well, Father, this is a strange kind of communion!" the leader of the guards said mockingly.

Joan protested. "This woman is ill; I was called here to physick her."

The man leered. "Indeed, many's the woman been cured of barrenness with such remedying."

There was a burst of raucous laughter. Joan said to Marioza, "Tell them the truth."

Marioza shrugged, her torn robe slipping from her shoulders. "They saw us. Why try to deny it?"

"Join the ranks, Priest!" jeered one of the guards. "The number of Marioza's lovers would fill the Colosseum to bursting!"

This was greeted with another explosion of laughter. Marioza joined in with the others.

"Come on, Father." The leader of the guards took Joan's arm, propelling her toward the door.

"Where are you taking me?" Joan demanded, though she knew the answer.

"To the Lateran. You'll answer to the Pope for this."

Joan wrenched herself from his grasp. To Marioza she said, "I don't know why you've done this, or for whom, but I warn you, Marioza: do not pin your fortunes on the favors of men, for they will prove as fleeting as your beauty."

Marioza's laughter died on her lips. "Barbarian!" she spat back contemptuously.

On a tide of laughter, Joan was carried from the room.

FLANKED by the guards, Joan walked in silence through the darkening streets. She could not bring herself to hate Marioza. Joan might have ended as such a one herself had fate not led her down a different path. The streets of Rome were filled with women offering themselves for no more than the price of a meal. Many had first come to the Holy City as pious pilgrims, even nuns; finding themselves without shelter or the means to buy return passage, they turned to the ready alternative. The clergy thundered against these "handmaids of the Devil" from the safety of their pulpits. Better to die chastely, they said, than live in sin. *But they,* thought Joan, *have never known hunger.*

No, Marioza was not to be blamed; she was only a tool. *But in whose hands? Who stands to gain by discrediting me?* Ennodius and the other members of the physicians' society were certainly capable of such chicanery. But surely they would aim their efforts at discrediting her medical skill.

If not them, then who? The answer came at once: *Benedict.* Ever since the business of the Orphanotrophium, he had resented her, jealous of her influence with his brother. The realization heartened her; at least she knew who the enemy was. Nor did she mean to let Benedict get away with this. True, he was Sergius's brother, but she was his friend; she would make him see the truth.

ARRIVING at the Lateran, Joan was dismayed when the guards marched her straight past the triclinium, where Sergius was dining with the optimates and other high officials of the papal court, down the hall to Benedict's quarters.

"Well, well. What have we here?" Benedict said mockingly as Joan and the guards entered. "John Anglicus, surrounded by guards like a common thief?" To the leader of the guard he said, "Speak, Tarasius, and tell me the nature of this priest's crime."

"My lord, we apprehended him in the rooms of the whore Marioza."

"Marioza!" Benedict affected a look of grave disapproval.

"We found him in the strumpet's bed, wrapped in her embrace," Tarasius added.

"It was a trick," Joan said. "I was called there on the false pretext that Marioza needed physicking. She knew the guards were coming and clasped me to her bosom just before they entered."

"You expect me to believe you were overpowered by a woman? For shame, false priest."

"The shame is yours, Benedict, not mine," Joan replied hotly. "You contrived the whole affair in order to discredit me. You arranged for Marioza to call me on the pretense of being ill, then sent the guards, knowing they would find us together."

"I own it readily."

The admission took Joan aback. "You confess your deceit?"

Benedict took a goblet of wine from a table and sipped from it, savoring the taste. "Knowing you to be unchaste, and not liking to see my brother's trust in you abused, I sought proof of your perfidy, that is all."

"I am not unchaste, nor have you any reason to think me so."

"Not unchaste?" Benedict sneered. "Tell me again how you found him, Tarasius."

"My lord, he lay with the wanton in her bed, and she was naked in his arms."

"Tsk, tsk. Think how distressed my brother will be to hear such damning testimony—the more so because of the great trust he has placed in you!"

For the first time Joan realized the seriousness of her situation. "Do not do this," she said. "Your brother needs me, for he is not yet out of danger. Without proper medical attention, he will suffer another attack—and the next one could kill him."

"Ennodius will attend my brother from now on," Benedict replied curtly. "Your sinner's hands have done harm enough."

"*I* do him harm?" Outrage obliterated the last of Joan's control. "You dare say that—you, who have sacrificed your brother to your own jealousy and greed?"

Wetness slapped her in the face; Benedict had hurled the contents of his cup at her. The strong wine burned her eyes, bringing forth tears; it coursed down her throat, causing her to choke and sputter.

"Take him to the dungeon," Benedict commanded.

"No!" With a sharp cry, Joan broke from the guards. She had to get to Sergius before Benedict could poison his mind against her. She ran swiftly down the hall toward the triclinium.

"Stop him!" Benedict shouted.

The guards' footsteps sounded behind her. Joan turned a corner and raced desperately toward the blazing lights of the triclinium.

She was a few yards away when she was tackled and sent sprawling. She struggled to rise, but the guards pinioned her arms and legs. Helpless, she was lifted and borne away.

She was carried down unfamiliar corridors and stairs that descended so steeply and for so long Joan began to wonder if they would ever end. At last the guards drew up before a heavy oak-planked door, barred with iron; they raised the bar and creaked the door open, then set Joan on her feet and thrust her roughly inside. She stumbled into murky darkness and landed with her feet in water. With terrifying solidity, the door slammed shut behind her, and the darkness became absolute.

THE footsteps of the guards retreated down the hall. Joan edged forward with arms held out, feeling at the darkness. She reached for her scrip—they had not thought to take it from her, a small blessing. She felt inside, fingering the various packets and vials, recognizing each by its shape and size. At last she found what she was looking for—the box containing her flint and kindling and the small stump of candle she used to warm her potions. She took up the flint and tapped it sharply against the side of the iron box, striking sparks into the dry tinder of straw. In a moment it quickened into flame. She held the candle to the tiny fire until the wick caught and steadied, casting its yellow light around her in a gentle arc.

The light shone precariously in the darkness, revealing flickering shapes and outlines. The dungeon was large, some thirty feet long by twenty feet wide. The walls were fashioned of heavy stone, smeared and darkened with age. From the slipperiness of the floor, Joan guessed it was also made of stone, though it was impossible to be sure, for it was covered with several inches of slimy, stagnant water.

She raised the candle higher, spreading its circle of light. In a far corner a pale shape shimmered into view—a human form, wan and insubstantial as a ghost's.

I am not alone. Relief flooded her, followed immediately by trepidation. This was, after all, a place of punishment. Was the apparition a madman or a murderer—or perhaps both?

"*Dominus tecum*," she said tentatively. The man did not respond. She repeated the greeting in the common tongue, adding, "I am John Anglicus, priest and healer. Is there aught I can do for you, Brother?" The man sat slumped against the wall, arms at his sides, legs spread wide. Joan moved closer. The light of the candle spilled onto the man's face—but it wasn't a face, it was a skull, a hideous death's-head covered with shreds of decaying flesh and hair.

With a cry, Joan turned and ran splashing toward the door. She pounded on the heavy oaken planks. "Let me out!" She knocked and pounded till her knuckles were rubbed raw.

No one replied. No one would come. They were going to leave her here to die alone in the dark.

She wrapped her arms around herself and held on tightly, trying to stop shaking. Gradually, the waves of terror and despair began to subside. Another feeling rose inside her—a stubborn determination to survive, to fight the injustice that had put her here. Her mind, temporarily numbed by fear, once again began to reason. *I must not give up hope,* she thought resolutely. *Sergius will not consign me to this dungeon forever. He'll be furious at first, when he hears Benedict's version of what happened with Marioza, but in a few days he'll calm down and send for me. All I have to do is endure until then.*

She began a careful circuit of the dungeon. She came across the remains of three other prisoners, but this time she was prepared, and they were not so frightful as the first, for their bones had long ago been picked clean of flesh. Her exploration also yielded an important discovery: one side of the dungeon was higher than the other; on the elevated side, the foul, slimy water stopped several feet short of the wall, leaving a long strip of dry floor. Against the wall, a discarded woolen cloak lay crumpled, tattered and honeycombed with holes, but still a useful protection against the penetrating chill of the underground chamber. In another corner of the room she made a further find: a straw pallet floating atop the water. The mattress was thick and well made, and so tightly woven that the top had remained dry. Joan dragged it over to the high side of the room and sat down on it, placing the candle beside her. She opened her scrip and took out some hellebore, scattering the poisonous black powder around her in a wide circle, a line of deterrent against rats and other vermin. Then she took out a package of powdered oak bark and another of dried sage; these she crumbled and infused into a small vial of wine mixed with honey. Tipping the vial of precious liquid carefully, she took a deep draft to fortify her against the foul and noxious humors of the place. Then she lay down on the pallet, snuffed the candle, and pulled the tattered cloak up over her.

She lay still in the dark. She had done all she could for the moment. Now she must rest and guard her strength until the time Sergius would send for her.

≽| 21 |≼

IT WAS the Feast of the Ascension, and the day's stational service was to be at the titular Church of St. Prassede. Though the sun had only just risen, spectators were already gathering, livening the street outside the Patriarchium with movement and color and chatter.

Soon the great bronze doors to the Patriarchium opened. The first to appear were the acolytes and others in minor clerical orders, walking humbly on foot. These were followed by a group of mounted guards, their sharp eyes raking the crowd for potential troublemakers. Behind them rode the seven regionary deacons and the seven regionary notaries, each preceded by a cleric bearing the banner with the *signa* of their ecclesiastical region. Then came the archpriest and the primicerius of the *defensores,* followed by their brethren. Finally Pope Sergius appeared, magnificently attired in a robe of gold and silver, astride a tall roan mare trapped in white silk. Immediately behind rode the optimates, the chief dignitaries of the papal administration, in order of importance: Arighis, the vicedominus, and then the vestiarius, the sacellarius, the arcarius, and the nomenclator.

The long procession crossed the open expanse of the Lateran courtyard and moved out with stately dignity, passing the great bronze statue of a she-wolf, *mater romanorum,* or mother of the Romans, believed by the ancients to have suckled Romulus and Remus. The statue had occasioned considerable controversy, for there were those who said it was blasphemy for a piece of pagan idolatry to stand before the walls of the papal palace, but others defended it with equal passion, praising its beauty and the excellence of its craftsmanship.

Just beyond the she-wolf, the procession turned north, passing beneath the great arch of the Claudian aqueduct, with its lofty, finely proportioned brickwork, onto the ancient Via Sacra, the sacred road that Popes had traversed for time beyond memory.

Sergius blinked back the piercing rays of the sun. His head ached, and the rhythmic swaying of his horse was making him dizzy; he gripped the reins to steady himself. *This,* he thought penitently, *is the price I pay for gluttony.* He had sinned again, gorging himself on rich food and wine. Despising his weakness, Sergius resolved, for the twentieth time that week, to reform.

With a pang of regret, he thought of John Anglicus. He had felt so much better when the foreign priest had been physicking him. But of course there could be no question of having him back, not after what he had done. John Anglicus was a detestable sinner, a priest who had broken the holiest of his vows.

"God bless the Lord Pope!" The cheering crowd brought Sergius's thoughts back to the present. He made the sign of the cross in blessing, fighting down nausea as the procession moved with stately dignity down the narrow line of the Via Sacra.

They had just passed the monastery of Honorius when the crowd scattered in sudden confusion as a mounted man rode in upon them. Horse and rider had been driven hard; the bay's mouth was lathered, its sides heaving. The rider's clothes were torn, his face blackened like a Saracen's with the mud of the road. He reined in and leapt to the ground in front of the procession.

"How dare you interrupt this sacred procession?" Eustathius, the archpriest, demanded indignantly. "Guards, strip this man and flog him. Fifty strokes will teach him a better respect!"

"He . . . is coming . . ." The man was so out of breath that the words were scarcely distinguishable.

"Hold." Sergius stayed the guards. "Who is coming?"

"Lothar," the man gasped.

"The Emperor?" Sergius said in astonishment.

The man nodded. "At the head of a large army of Franks. Holiness, he's sworn a blood revenge against you and this city for the grievance that's been done him."

A murmur of dismay came from the crowd.

"Grievance?" For a moment Sergius could not think what this could mean. Then it came to him. "The consecration!"

After Sergius's election, the city had gone ahead with the consecration ceremony without waiting for the Emperor's approval. This was a manifest breach of the charter of 824, which granted Lothar the right of imperial *jussio,* or ratification of an elected Pope prior to consecration. Nevertheless, the move had been widely applauded, for the people saw it as a proud reassertion of Roman independence from the distant Frankish crown. It was a clear and deliberate slight to Lothar, but as the jussio was more symbolic than substantive—for no Emperor had ever failed to confirm an elected Pope—no one believed Lothar would do much about it.

"Where is the Emperor?" Sergius's voice was a dry whisper.

"In Viterbo, Holiness."

Cries of alarm greeted this news. Viterbo was part of the Roman campagna, no more than ten days' march from Rome.

"My lord, he is a scourge upon the earth." The man's tongue was loosed now he had caught his breath. "His soldiers plunder all before them, ransacking the farms, carrying off the livestock, pulling up the vines by their roots. They take what they want, and what they do not want, they burn. Those who get in their way they kill without mercy— women, old men, babes in arms—none are spared. The horror"—his voice cracked—"the horror of it cannot be imagined."

Terrified and uncertain, the people looked to their Pope. But there was no comfort to be found there. Before the Romans' horrified eyes, Sergius's face went slack, his eyes rolled up into his head, and he toppled forward senseless onto his horse.

"O, he is dead!" The cry of lamentation found an echo on a dozen other tongues. Quickly the papal guards surrounded Sergius, plucking him from his horse and bearing him away into the Patriarchium. The rest of the procession followed close behind.

The frightened crowd thronged the courtyard, threatening to break into a dangerous panic. The guards rode in among them with whips and drawn swords, sending them scattering along the narrow, dark streets to the solitary terror of their homes.

ALARM and agitation grew as refugees thronged through the city gates from the surrounding campagna, from Farfa and Narni, Laurentum and Civitavecchia. They came in droves, their meager possessions bundled on their backs, their dead piled in carts. All had similar tales of Frankish depredation and savagery. These terrifying accounts spurred the city's efforts to strengthen its defenses: day and night the Romans toiled energetically to remove the layers of debris that had accumulated against the city walls over the centuries, making them easier for an enemy to surmount.

The priests of the city were kept busy from prime to vespers, saying Mass and hearing confession. The churches were filled to bursting, the ranks of the faithful swelled with a multitude of unfamiliar faces—

for fear had goaded many a fainthearted Christian into newfound faith. Piously they lighted candles and raised their voices in prayer for the safety of their homes and families—and for the recovery of the ailing Sergius, on whom all their hopes depended. *May the strength of God be with our Lord Pope,* they prayed, for surely he would have need of great fortitude to save Rome from the devil Lothar.

SERGIUS'S voice rose and fell in the fluid melodies of the Roman chant, truer and sweeter than that of any of the other boys in the *schola cantorum.* The singing master smiled approval at him. Encouraged, Sergius sang out more loudly, his young soprano rising higher and higher in joyous ecstasy, till it seemed as if it would lift him into Heaven itself.

The dream receded, and Sergius awoke. Fear, vague and undefined, crowded the edges of his consciousness, setting his heart racing before he understood why.

With a nauseating lurch, he remembered.

Lothar.

He sat up. His head throbbed, and there was a foul taste in his mouth. "Celestinus!" His voice cracked like a rusted hinge.

"Holiness!" Celestinus rose sleepily from the floor. With his soft pink cheeks, round child's eyes, and tousled blond hair, he resembled a heavenly cherub. At ten, he was the youngest of the cubicularii; Celestinus's father was a man of great influence in the city, so he had come to the Lateran earlier than most. *Well,* Sergius thought, *he is no younger than I was when I was taken from my parents' home.*

"Bring Benedict," he commanded. "I would speak with him." Celestinus nodded and hurried off, stifling a yawn.

One of the kitchen servants entered with a platter of bread and bacon. Sergius was not supposed to break fast until after his celebration of Mass—for the hands that touched the eucharistic gifts had to be free from any worldly stain. In private, though, such niceties of form were often disregarded—especially with a Pope of such prodigious appetite.

This morning, however, the smell of the bacon made Sergius's gorge rise. He waved the tray aside. "Take it away."

A notary entered and announced, "His Grace the Archpriest awaits you in the triclinium."

"Let him wait," Sergius responded curtly. "I will speak first with my brother."

Benedict's common sense in this crisis had proved invaluable. It had been his idea to take money from the papal treasury in order to buy off Lothar. Fifty thousand gold solidi should be enough to assuage even an Emperor's wounded pride.

Celestinus returned, not with Benedict but with Arighis, the vicedominus.

"Where is my brother?" Sergius asked.

"Gone, Holiness," Arighis replied.

"Gone?"

"Ivo the porter saw him ride out just before dawn with a dozen or so attendants. We thought you knew."

A rise of bile bathed Sergius's throat. "The money?"

"Benedict collected it last night. There were eleven coffers altogether. He had them with him when he left."

"No!" But even as Sergius's lips formed the denial, he knew the truth of it. Benedict had betrayed him.

He was helpless. Lothar would come, and there was nothing, nothing Sergius could do to stop him.

A wave of nausea overtook him. He leaned over the side of the bed, spilling the sour contents of his stomach onto the floor. He tried to rise but could not; pain stabbed at his legs, immobilizing him. Celestinus and Arighis ran to help him, lifting him back and down. Turning his head into the pillow, Sergius wept unrestrainedly, like a child.

Arighis turned to Celestinus. "Stay with him. I'm going to the dungeon."

JOAN stared at the bowl of food before her. There was a small crust of stale bread, and some gray, indistinguishable chunks of meat, threaded through with wriggling maggots; the rotten odor rose to her nostrils. It had been several days since she had eaten, for the guards, whether from carelessness or design, did not bring food every day. She stared at the meat, hunger doing battle with judgment. At last she put the bowl aside. Taking up the crust of bread, she bit off a small piece, chewing it slowly, to make it last longer.

How long had she been here—two weeks? Three? She had begun to lose count. The perpetual darkness was disorienting. She had used her piece of candle sparingly, lighting it only to eat or to prepare medications from her scrip. Nevertheless, the candle was reduced to a tiny stub of wax, good for no more than another hour or two of precious light.

Even more terrible than the darkness was the solitude. The utter and unremitting silence was unnerving. To stay alert, Joan set herself a series of mental tasks—reciting from memory the entire Rule of St. Benedict, all one hundred and fifty psalms, and the Book of Acts. But these feats of memory soon became too routine to keep her attention engaged.

She remembered how the great theologian Boethius, similarly imprisoned, had found strength and consolation in prayer. For hours she knelt on the cold stone floor of the dungeon, trying to pray. But at the core of her being, she felt nothing but emptiness. The seed of doubt, planted in her childhood by her mother, had taken deep root within her soul. She tried to weed it out, to rise up into the solacing light of grace, but she could not. Was God listening? Was He even there? As day after day passed with no word from Sergius, hope gradually slipped away.

The loud clank of metal jolted her as the bar on the door was lifted. A moment later the door swung wide, pouring dazzling light into the blackness. Shielding her eyes against the glare, Joan squinted toward the opening. A man stood silhouetted against the light. "John Anglicus?" he called uncertainly into the darkness.

The voice was instantly familiar. "Arighis!" Joan swayed lightheadedly as she rose and made her way through the stagnant water toward the papal vicedominus. "Have you come from Sergius?"

Arighis shook his head. "His Holiness does not wish to see you."

"Then why—?"

"He is gravely ill. Once before you gave him medicine that helped him; have you any with you now?"

"I have." Joan took a packet of powder of colchicum from her scrip. Arighis reached for it, but Joan quickly drew it back.

"What?" said Arighis. "Do you hate him so much? Beware, John Anglicus, for to wish harm upon Christ's chosen Vicar is to place your immortal soul in the gravest peril."

"I do not hate him," Joan said, and meant it. Sergius was not a bad man, she knew, only weak and overtrusting of his venal brother. "But I will not give this medicine into untrained hands. Its powers are very great, and the wrong dose could be lethal." This was not entirely true, for the powdered root was not as potent as she pretended; it would take a very large dose to do any real harm. But this was her chance at freedom; she would not let the door close upon it again.

"Besides," she added, "how do I know Sergius is suffering from the same ailment as before? To cure His Holiness, I first must see him."

Arighis hesitated. To free the prisoner would be an act of insubordination, a direct countermanding of the Lord Pope's order. But if Sergius died with the Frankish Emperor at the gates, the papacy, and Rome itself, might be forfeit.

"Come," he said, abruptly arriving at a decision. "I will take you to His Holiness."

SERGIUS lay against the soft silken pillows of the papal bed. The worst of the pain had passed, but it had left him drained and weak as a newborn kitten.

The door to the chamber opened, and Arighis entered, followed by John Anglicus.

Sergius started violently. "What is this sinner doing here?"

Arighis said, "He comes with a powerful medicine that will restore you to health."

Sergius shook his head. "All true physicking comes from God. His healing grace will not be transmitted through so impure a vessel."

"I am not impure," Joan protested. "Benedict lied to you, Holiness."

"You were in the harlot's bed," Sergius replied accusingly. "The guards saw you there."

"They saw what they expected to see, what they had been told to observe," Joan retorted. Quickly she explained how Benedict had contrived to trap her. "I did not want to go there," she said, "but Arighis insisted."

"That is true, Holiness," Arighis confirmed. "John Anglicus asked if I would not send one of the other physicians. But Benedict insisted that John Anglicus and no other should go."

For a long while, Sergius did not speak. Finally he said in a cracked voice, "If this is true, you have been grievously wronged." He burst out in despair, "Lothar's coming is God's just judgment against me for all my sins!"

"If God wanted to punish you, there are easier ways to do it," Joan pointed out. "Why sacrifice the lives of thousands of innocents when he could smite you with a single stroke?"

This took Sergius by surprise. With the customary self-absorption of the great, such a thought had not occurred to him.

"Lothar's coming is not a punishment," Joan persevered, "it is a test—a test of faith. You must lead the people with the strength of your example."

"I'm sick in body and in heart. Let me die."

"If you do, the will of the people dies with you. You must be strong, for their sake."

"What difference does it make?" Sergius said hopelessly. "We cannot prevail against Lothar's forces; it would take a miracle."

"Then," Joan said staunchly, "we will have to make one."

THE day after Pentecost Sunday, the date of Lothar's anticipated arrival, the piazza before the basilica of St. Peter began to fill with members of the various scholae of the city, dressed in their best finery. Lothar had not made a formal declaration of hostilities, so the plan was to accord him the reception due a personage of his exalted position. The unexpected show of welcome might disarm him long enough for the second part of Joan's plan to take effect.

By midmorning all was in readiness. Sergius gave the signal, and the first group, the *judices*, rode out, the yellow banners bearing their sign fluttering above them. Behind them rode the defensores and the deacons; then, on foot, the various societies of foreigners—Frisians, Franks, Saxons, Lombards, and Greeks. They called to one another bravely as they traveled down the Via Triumphalis, past the decaying skeletons of pagan temples lining the ancient road.

God grant they are not marching to their deaths, Joan thought. Then she turned her attention to Sergius. He had made good progress over the past few days but was still far from well. Would he be strong enough to endure the day's ordeal? Joan spoke to a chamberlain, who fetched a chair, into which Sergius sank gratefully. Joan gave him some lemon water mixed with honey to fortify him.

Fifty of the most powerful men in Rome were now gathered on the broad porch before the doors of the basilica: all the major officials of the Lateran administration, a select group of cardinal priests, the dukes and princes of the city, and their retinues. The archpriest Eustathius led them all in a short prayer, and then they stood in silence. There was nothing left to do but wait.

With taut faces they kept their eyes trained to where the road bent out of sight beyond the green hedges and meadows of the Neronian plain.

Time passed with unbearable slowness. The sun inched higher in a cloudless sky. The morning breeze diminished, then died, leaving the banners draped limply against their staffs. Swarms of flies circled lazily overhead, their irksome droning loud in the still, expectant air.

More than two hours had passed since the procession rode out. Surely they should have returned by now!

A barely perceptible noise came from the distance. They listened with pricked ears. The noise rose again, sustained and unmistakable—the sound of distant voices raised in song.

"*Deo gratias*," breathed Eustathius as the banners of the judices floated into view, topping the green horizon like yellow sails upon a sea. Moments later, the first riders appeared, followed by members of the various scholae, on foot. Behind them marched a dark multitude that stretched as far as the eye could see—Lothar's army. Joan drew in her breath; never before had she seen so great a host.

Sergius rose, leaning on his crosier for support. The vanguard of the procession drew up to the basilica and fanned out, creating a path through which the Emperor could pass.

Lothar rode through. Looking at him, Joan could well believe the tales of barbaric cruelty that had preceded him. He had a stocky body, crowned by a thick neck and massive head; his broad, flat face and shallow-set eyes registered a look of malevolent intelligence.

The two opposing groups faced each other, one dark and muddied from the rigors of the road, the other spotless and gleaming in their white clerical robes. Behind Sergius the roof of St. Peter's rose incandescently, its silver plates shimmering with the reflected light of the morning—the spiritual heart of the Church, the beacon of the world, the holiest shrine in all Christendom. Before such sacred grandeur, even Emperors had bowed.

Lothar dismounted, but he did not kneel to kiss the bottom step of the basilica in the customary show of reverence. Boldly he mounted the steps, followed by a group of armed men. The prelates gathered before the open doors of the basilica drew back in alarm; the papal guards surrounded Sergius protectively, their hands on their sword hilts.

All at once, the open doors of St. Peter's jolted and moved. Lothar jumped back. His men drew their swords, then stood bewildered, gazing wildly from one side to the other. But there was no one nearby. The doors swung slowly inward on their hinges as if supernaturally propelled. Then they closed with a final, definitive crack.

Now. Joan willed Sergius to act. As if he had heard her unspoken command, he drew himself up, extending his arms dramatically. Gone was the weak and sickly man of a few days ago; in his white *camelaucum* and golden robes, he looked imposing, magisterial.

He spoke in Frankish, to be sure Lothar's soldiers would understand. "Behold the hand of God," he intoned solemnly, "which has barred the holiest of His altars against you."

Lothar's men cried out fearfully. The Emperor stood his ground, wary and suspicious.

Now Sergius switched to Latin. "*Si pura mente et pro salute Reipublicae huc advenisti . . .* If you are come with a pure mind and goodwill toward the republic, enter, and welcome; if not, then no earthly power will open these doors to you."

Lothar hesitated, still mistrustful. Had Sergius conjured up a miracle? He doubted it, but he could not be certain: God's ways were mysterious. Besides, his own position was now considerably weakened, for his men were dropping in terror to their knees, their swords slipping from their hands.

With a forced smile, Lothar opened his arms to Sergius. The two men embraced, their lips meeting in the formal kiss of peace. "*Benedictus qui venit in nomine Domini,*" the choir chanted joyously. "Blessed is he who comes in the name of the Lord."

The doors jolted into motion again. As everyone watched, awestruck, the silver-plated panels swung outward until once again they stood full open. Arm in arm, with the joyous sounds of Hosanna ringing in their ears, Sergius and Lothar walked into the basilica to pray before the shrine of the Blessed Apostle.

THE difficulties with Lothar were not yet over—explanations still needed to be offered, apologies tendered, advantages negotiated, concessions made. But the immediate danger was past.

Joan thought of Gerold and how amused he would have been to see the use she had made of his hydraulic trick with the door. She pictured him, his indigo eyes alight with humor, his head thrown back in the generous laugh she remembered so well.

Strange, the workings of the heart. One could go on for years, habituated to loss, reconciled to it, and then, in a moment's unwary thought, the pain resurfaced, sharp and raw as a fresh wound.

>≽| **22** |≼

G EROLD breathed with relief as he and his men descended the final slope of Mt. Cenis. With the Alps behind them, the worst of the journey was over. The Via Francigena stretched ahead, blessedly flat and well kept, for it still retained its ancient paving of stone, laid down by the Romans in a time before memory.

Gerold spurred his horse into a canter. Perhaps now they could make up for time lost. An unseasonably late snowfall had made the narrow Alpine pass extremely treacherous; two men had died when their mounts lost their footing on the slippery ground, plunging horses and riders to their deaths. Gerold had been forced to call a halt until conditions improved; the delay put them even farther behind the vanguard of the imperial army, which must now be drawing close to Rome.

No matter; Lothar would scarcely miss them. This rear division numbered only two hundred men—lordlings and small landholders who had arrived late to the spring muster at the Marchfeld. It was an insulting command for a man of Gerold's stature.

In the three years since the Battle of Fontenoy, Gerold's relationship with Emperor Lothar had gone from bad to worse. Lothar had gradually become more and more tyrannical, surrounding himself with toadying followers who flattered him at every turn. He had absolutely no tolerance for fideles like Gerold, who continued to voice his opinions honestly—as, for example, when he had advised against this current campaign against Rome.

"Our troops are needed on the Frisian coast," Gerold argued, "to defend against the Norsemen. Their raids are becoming more and more frequent—and destructive."

It was true. Last year the Norsemen had attacked St.-Wandrille and Utrecht; the previous spring they had sailed brazenly down the Seine and burned Paris! This had sent a shock wave of fear over the countryside. If so great a city as Paris, in the very heart of the Empire, was not safe from the barbarians, then no place was.

Lothar's attention, however, was directed toward Rome, which had dared proceed with Pope Sergius's consecration without first asking for his sovereign approval—an omission which Lothar took as a personal affront.

"Send to Sergius and make your royal displeasure known," Gerold advised. "Punish the Romans by withholding payment of the *Romefeoh*. But let us keep our fighting men here, where they are needed."

Lothar had been enraged at this challenge to his authority. In retaliation, he had assigned Gerold command of the rear division.

They made good progress on the paved road, covering almost forty miles before dusk, but they did not pass a single town or village. Gerold had all but resigned himself to another restless night bedded down by the side of the road when he caught sight of a spiral of smoke circling lazily above the treetops.

Deo gratias! There was a village ahead, or at least a settlement of some kind. Now Gerold and his men were assured of a comfortable night's sleep. They had not yet crossed the border into papal lands; the Kingdom of Lombardy, through which they now rode, was imperial territory, and hospitality required that travelers be courteously welcomed—if not to beds in the house, then at least to soft berths of hay in a warm, dry stable.

They rounded a curve and saw that the smoke was not coming from a welcoming hearth fire but from the still-smoldering remains of houses burned to the ground. It must have been a thriving settlement; Gerold made out the blackened outlines of some fifteen buildings. The blaze had probably been started by a chance spark from a carelessly tended lamp or hearth fire; such calamities were not uncommon where houses were built of wood and thatch.

Riding past the blackened timbers, Gerold was reminded of Villaris. It had looked much the same on that long-ago day when he returned to find it burned by the Norsemen. He remembered digging through the rubble searching for Joan, seeking, yet afraid to find. Amazing—it had been fifteen years since he had last seen her, yet her image was imprinted on his mind as if it were yesterday: the crop of white-gold hair that curled beguilingly about her forehead, the full, throaty voice, the deep-set gray-green eyes so much wiser than their years.

He forced her image from his mind. Some things were too painful to dwell upon.

A mile beyond the ruined settlement, at the high cross marking the spot where two roads converged, a woman and five ragged children were begging alms. As Gerold and his men rode up, the little family drew back fearfully.

"Be at peace, good mother," Gerold reassured her. "We mean you no harm."

"Have you any food to spare, lord?" she asked. "For the children's sake?"

Four of the children ran to Gerold, holding their hands out in mute appeal, their small faces tight and anxious with hunger. The fifth, a pretty, black-haired girl some thirteen years of age, hung back and clung to her mother.

Gerold withdrew from his saddlebag the square of oiled sheepskin that held his ration of food for the next few days. There remained a good-sized loaf of bread, a block of cheese, and some dried salt venison. He started to break the loaf in half, then saw the children watching. *Ah, well,* he thought, handing over the whole parcel. *It's only a few more days to Rome; I can get by on the biscuits in the supply wagon.*

With a glad cry, the children fell upon the food like a swarm of starveling birds.

"Are you from the village?" Gerold asked the woman, pointing to the blackened ruin behind them.

The woman nodded. "My husband is the miller."

Gerold hid his surprise. The ragged figure before him appeared to be anything but a prosperous miller's wife. "What happened?"

"Three days ago, after the spring planting, soldiers came. The Emperor's men. They said we had to swear allegiance to Lothar or die immediately by their swords. So of course we swore."

Gerold nodded. Lothar's doubts about this part of Lombardy were not entirely unjustified, for it was a relatively new addition to the Empire, acquired by Lothar's grandfather, the great Emperor Karolus.

"If you took the oath of loyalty," he asked, "how did your village come to be destroyed?"

"They didn't believe us. Liars, they called us, and threw torches onto our roofs. When we tried to put the fires out, they held us back with their swords. Our stores of grain they torched as well, though we begged them not to, for the children's sake. They laughed and called them traitors' spawn, who deserved to starve."

"Villains!" Gerold exclaimed angrily. He had tried many times to convince Lothar that he could not win his subjects' loyalty with the use of force but only through just dealing and the rule of law. As usual, his words had fallen on deaf ears.

"They took all our men," the woman continued, "except the very young and the very old. The Emperor was marching to Rome, they said, and needed men to swell the foot ranks." She started to weep. "They took my husband and two of my sons—the younger is only eleven!"

Gerold scowled. Things had come to a sorry pass when Lothar needed children to fight his battles.

"My lord, what does it mean?" the woman asked anxiously. "Is the Emperor going to make war against the Holy City?"

"I don't know." Until this moment, Gerold had thought Lothar meant only to intimidate Pope Sergius and the Romans with a show of force. But the destruction of this village was an ominous sign; in so vengeful a mood, Lothar was capable of anything.

"Come, good mother," Gerold said. "We will take you with us to the next town. This is no safe place for you and the children."

She shook her head fiercely. "I'll not budge from this spot. How will my husband and sons find us when they return?"

If *they return*, Gerold thought grimly. To the black-haired girl he said, "Tell your mother to come with us, for the sake of the little ones."

The girl stared mutely at Gerold.

"She means no discourtesy, lord," her mother apologized. "She would answer if she could, but she cannot speak."

"Cannot speak?" Gerold said, surprised. The girl looked sound and showed no sign of being simple.

"Her tongue's cut out."

"Great God!" The loss of a tongue was a common punishment for thieves and other miscreants not quick enough to dodge the law's harsh justice. But surely this innocent young girl was guiltless of any crime. "Who did this? Surely it was not—"

The woman nodded grimly. "Lothar's men used her unlawfully, then cut out her tongue so she could not accuse them of the shameful deed."

Gerold was stunned. Such atrocities were to be expected of heathen Norsemen or Saracens—not of the Emperor's soldiers, defenders of Christian law and justice.

Brusquely Gerold gave orders. His men went to the wagons and took out a sack of biscuits and a small barrel of wine, which they placed on the ground before the little family.

"God bless you," the miller's wife said feelingly.

"And you, good mother," Gerold said.

They rode on, passing other plundered and deserted settlements along the way. Lothar had left ruin behind him wherever he passed.

Fidelis adjutor. As sworn fidelis to the imperial crown, Gerold was bound in honor to serve the Emperor faithfully. But what honor was there in serving a brute like Lothar? The disregard with which the Emperor cast aside the law and all other standards of human decency surely wiped clean the slate of obligation.

Gerold would lead this rearguard of the imperial army into Rome as he had promised. But afterward, he resolved firmly, he would quit the service of the tyrant Lothar forever.

BEYOND Nepi, the road deteriorated. The solid, hard-surfaced highway gave way to a narrow and decaying track, pitted with treacherous crevices and gulleys. The Roman paving was gone, the ancient stones removed and carted off for use in other construction—for such strong building materials were scarce in these dark times. Gerold read the marks of Lothar's passing in the dark earth, deeply rutted with the multiple tracks of wagons and horses. They had to take extra care with the horses, lest they lame themselves with an unlucky step.

During the night, a heavy rainfall turned the road into an impassable sea of mud. Rather than call another halt, Gerold decided to strike out through the open countryside and come round to the Via Palestrina, which would bring them into Rome through the eastern gate of St. John.

They rode swiftly through budding, sweet-scented meadows of gentian and woods sprouting with the gold-green leaves of spring. Emerging from a patch of dense scrub, they suddenly came upon a group of mounted men riding escort around a heavy wagon pulled by four strong cart horses.

"Greetings." Gerold addressed the man who appeared to be their leader, a dark-avised fellow with narrow, puffy eyes. "Can you tell us if we are headed toward the Via Palestrina?"

"You are," the man responded curtly. He turned to ride past.

"If you're bound for the Via Flaminia," Gerold said, "better think again. The road's washed out; your cart will be mired to its axles before you've gone ten yards."

The man said, "We're not headed there."

That was curious. Other than the road, there was nothing in the direction they were headed but deserted countryside. "Where are you going?" Gerold asked.

"I've told you all you need to know," the man snapped. "Ride on and leave an honest merchant to his business."

No ordinary merchant would address a lord so pridefully. Gerold's suspicions were aroused.

"What is your trade?" Gerold rode to the cart. "Perhaps you've something I'd be interested in buying."

"Leave that alone!" the man shouted.

Gerold wrenched the covers back, revealing the contents of the cart: a dozen bronze coffers secured with heavy iron locks, each marked unmistakably with the papal insignia.

The Pope's men, Gerold thought. *They must have been sent from the city to transport the papal treasure out of reach of Lothar's clutches.*

He toyed with the idea of commandeering the treasure and bringing it back to Lothar. Then he thought, *No. Let the Romans salvage what they may.* Pope Sergius would no doubt find a better purpose for the money than Lothar, who would only use it to finance more brutal and bloody military campaigns.

He was about to ride on when one of the Romans leapt from his horse and prostrated himself on the ground. "Mercy, lord!" he cried. "Spare us! We must not die unshriven with the weight of this great crime upon our souls!"

"Crime?" Gerold echoed.

"Hold your tongue, fool!" Their leader spurred his horse and would have trampled the other in the dirt, but Gerold intercepted him with drawn sword. Immediately Gerold's men drew their swords and surrounded the Romans, who, observing how greatly they were outnumbered, wisely kept their own blades scabbarded.

"Benedict's the one to blame!" the man on the ground sputtered in a burst of retaliatory anger. "It was his idea to steal the money, not ours!"

Steal the money?

The man called Benedict spoke placatingly. "I have no quarrel with you, lord, nor need our petty quarrels concern you. Let us pass in peace, and in token of our gratitude you may have one of these coffers." He smiled at Gerold conspiratorially. "There's gold enough inside to make you a wealthy man."

The offer and the manner of his making it resolved all doubt. "Bind him," Gerold commanded. "And the others. We'll take them and these coffers to Rome with us."

THE triclinium was ablaze with the light of a hundred torches. A phalanx of servants stood behind the high table at which Pope Sergius sat, flanked by the high dignitaries of the city: the priests of each of the seven regions of Rome to his left; their temporal counterparts, the seven defensores, to his right. Perpendicular to this table, and just as grand, was another, at which Lothar and his retinue were placed at seats of honor. The rest of the company, some two hundred men altogether, sat on hard wooden benches drawn up before long tables in the middle of the room. Plates, ewers, goblets, and platters crowded together on the tables, whose cloths already carried the marks of innumerable spills and stains.

As it was neither a Wednesday nor a Friday, nor any other fast day, the meal was not confined to bread and fish but included flesh meat and other rich viands. Even for a Pope's table, it was an extraordinary repast: there were platters of capons smothered with white sauce and ornamented with pomegranate and crimson sweetmeats; bowls of soup, filled with tender morsels of rabbit and woodcock swimming in a thick cream, giving off an aromatic steam; jellies of crayfish and loach; whole pigs larded with grease; and huge plates of roasted roe deer, kid, pigeon, and goose. In the center of Lothar's table, a whole cooked swan was displayed as if alive, its gilded beak and silvered body resting upon a mass of greens artfully arranged to appear like waves of the sea.

Seated at one of the tables in the center of the room, Joan cast a worried eye over the extravagant display. Such rich delights might well tempt Sergius into dangerous overindulgence.

"A toast!" The Count of Mâcon rose from his place beside Lothar and raised his cup. "To peace and friendship between our two Christian peoples!"

"Peace and friendship!" everyone chorused, and drained their cups. Servants hurried along the tables, pouring more wine.

There followed a multitude of toasts. When at last they ran out of subjects for liquid tribute, the feasting began.

Joan watched with alarm as Sergius ate and drank with reckless abandon. His eyes began to swell, his speech to slur, his skin to darken ominously. She would have to give him a strong dose of colchicum tonight to prevent a return attack of gout.

The doors to the triclinium opened, and a group of guards marched in. Sidestepping to avoid the innumerable serving boys who scurried nimbly about the room fetching and clearing dishes, the guards made their way briskly to the front of the room. A sudden quiet fell as the guests broke off talking, craning their necks to make out the cause of this extraordinary intrusion. This hush was followed by a murmur of surprise as they caught a glimpse of the man who walked in the midst of the guards with bound hands and lowered eyes: Benedict.

The cheerful circles of Sergius's face collapsed like punctured bladders. "You!" he cried.

Tarasius, the leader of the guards, said, "A troop of Franks found him in the campagna. He had the treasure with him."

Benedict had had a good deal of time on the trip back to Rome to consider his predicament. He could not deny taking the treasure, having been caught in the act. Nor could he think of a plausible excuse for what he had done, though he had racked his brain trying. He finally decided that the best course was to throw himself upon his brother's mercy. Sergius was tenderhearted to the core—a weakness Benedict despised, though now he hoped to use it to his gain.

He dropped to his knees, lifting his bound arms toward his brother. "Forgive me, Sergius. I have sinned, and I repent most humbly and sincerely."

But Benedict had not counted on the effects of the wine on his brother's temper. Sergius's face crimsoned as he swung unexpectedly into rage. "Traitor!" he shouted. "Villain! Thief!" He punctuated each word with a violent thump of his fist on the table, setting the plates clattering.

Benedict paled. "Brother, I beseech you—"

"Take him away!" Sergius ordered.

"Where should we take him, Holiness?" Tarasius asked.

Sergius's head was spinning; it was difficult to think. All he knew was that he had been betrayed, and he wanted to strike back, to wound as he himself had been wounded. "He's a thief!" he said bitterly. "Let him be punished as a thief!"

"No!" Benedict shouted as the guards took hold of him. "Sergius! *Brother!*" The last word was left echoing as he was dragged from the hall.

The color drained from Sergius's face, and he dropped into his chair. His head fell back, his eyes rolled, his arms and legs began to shake uncontrollably.

"It's the evil eye!" someone shouted. "Benedict's put a spell on him!" The guests cried out in consternation, crossing themselves against the workings of the Devil.

Joan raced through the crowded tables to Sergius's side. His face was turning blue. She took hold of his head and pried his clenched jaws open. His tongue was folded back upon itself, blocking the airway. Grabbing a knife from the table, Joan inserted the blunt end into Sergius's mouth, slipping it into the folded loop of tongue. Then she pulled. There was a sucking sound as the tongue flipped forward. Sergius gasped and began to breathe again. Joan pressed down gently with the knife, keeping the airway open. After a moment, the paroxysm subsided. With a muted groan, Sergius went limp.

"Take him to his bed," she ordered. Several serving boys lifted Sergius from his chair and carried him toward the door as the crowd pressed round curiously. "Make way! Make way!" Joan shouted as they bore the unconscious Pope out of the hall.

BY THE time they reached his bedroom, Sergius was conscious. Joan gave him black mustard mixed with gentian to make him vomit. Afterward he was dramatically improved. She gave him a strong dose of colchicum, just to be safe, mixing in some poppy juice to help him rest soundly.

"He'll sleep till morning," she told Arighis.

Arighis nodded. "You look exhausted."

"I *am* rather tired," Joan admitted. It had been a long day, and she had not yet recovered fully from her weeks of confinement in the dungeon.

"Ennodius and others from the physicians' society are waiting outside. They mean to interrogate you about His Holiness's relapse."

Joan sighed. She did not feel up to fending off a barrage of hostile questions, but apparently there was no help for it. Wearily she started for the door.

"Just a moment." Arighis beckoned her to follow him. At the far side of the room, he moved aside one of the tapestries and pushed on the wall beneath. The wall slid sideways, leaving an opening some two and a half feet wide.

"What on earth?" Joan was astonished.

"A secret passage," Arighis explained. "Built in the days of the pagan Emperors—in case they needed to make a quick escape from their enemies. Now it connects the papal bedroom to the private chapel, so the Apostolic One can enter and pray undisturbed any time of day or night. Come." He took a candle and entered the passage. "This way you can avoid that pack of jackals, at least for tonight."

Joan was touched that Arighis would share his knowledge of the secret passageway; it was a sign of the growing trust and respect between them. They descended a steep circular flight of stairs that leveled out before a wall into which was set a wooden lever. Arighis pulled it, and the wall moved aside, opening a passage. Joan slipped through, and the vicedominus pulled the lever again. The opening disappeared, leaving no trace of its existence.

She was behind one of the marble pillars in the rear of the Pope's private chapel, the Sanctum Sanctorum. Voices sounded near the altar. This was unexpected; no one should be here at this hour of night.

"It's been a long time, Anastasius," one voice said in gruff, heavily accented tones she recognized as Lothar's. He had called the other one Anastasius; that must be the Bishop of Castellum. The two men had obviously withdrawn to the chapel to speak privately. They would not look kindly upon an intruder.

What should I do? Joan wondered. If she tried to slip quietly through the door of the chapel, they might see her. Nor could she retrace her steps to the papal chamber; the lever that controlled the secret passage was on the other side of the wall. She would have to stay hidden until the meeting concluded and both men left. Then she could slip out of the chapel unnoticed.

"Most distressing, His Holiness's attack this evening," Lothar said.

Anastasius replied, "The Apostolic One is very ill. He may not live out the year."

"A great tragedy for the Church."

"Very great," Anastasius agreed smoothly.

"His successor must be a man of strength and vision," Lothar said, "a man who can better appreciate the historic . . . understanding between our two peoples."

"You must use all your influence, my liege, to ensure that the next Pontiff is such a man."

"Don't you mean—a man like you?"

"Have you reason to doubt me, Sire? Surely the service I did you at Colmar proved my loyalty beyond all question."

"Perhaps." Lothar was noncommittal. "But times change, and so do men. Now, my lord Bishop, your loyalty is to be put to the test again. Will you support the oath taking, or no?"

"The people will be reluctant to swear loyalty to you, my liege, after the damage your army has visited upon the countryside."

"Your family has the power to change that," Lothar responded. "If you and your father, Arsenius, take the oath, others will follow."

"What you ask is very great. It would require something great in return."

"I know that."

"An oath is only words. The people need a Pope who can lead them back to the old ways—to the Frankish Empire, and to you, my liege."

"I can think of no one better able to do that than you, Anastasius. I shall do everything in my power to see that you are the next Pope."

There was a pause. Then Anastasius said, "The people will take the oath, Sire. I will make certain of it."

Joan felt a surge of anger. Lothar and Anastasius had just bartered for the papacy like a pair of merchants at a bazaar. In return for the privileges of power, Anastasius had agreed to hand the Romans over to the Frankish Emperor's control.

There was a knock on the door, and Lothar's servant entered.

"The count has arrived, my liege."

"Show him in. The bishop and I have concluded our business."

A man entered, dressed in a soldier's brunia. He was tall and striking, with long, red hair and indigo eyes.

Gerold.

≽| 23 |≼

A STARTLED cry burst from Joan's lips.
"Who's there?" Lothar asked sharply.

Slowly Joan came out from behind the pillar. Lothar and Anastasius looked at her with astonishment.

"Who are you?" Lothar demanded.

"John Anglicus, my liege. Priest and physician to His Holiness Pope Sergius."

Lothar asked suspiciously, "How long have you been here?"

Joan thought quickly. "Some hours, Sire. I came to pray for His Holiness's recovery. I must have been more tired than I realized, for I fell asleep and only just awoke."

Lothar looked down his long nose disapprovingly. More likely the little priest had been trapped in the chapel when Anastasius and he had entered. There was no place to run and no place to hide. But it scarcely mattered. How much could he have overheard, and, more important, how much understood? Little enough. There could be no danger in the man; he was obviously no one of importance. The best course was to ignore him.

Anastasius had arrived at a different conclusion. Obviously John Anglicus had been eavesdropping, but why? Was he a spy? Not for Sergius, surely, for the Pope lacked the ingenuity to use spies. But if not, then for whom? And why? From now on, Anastasius decided, the little foreign priest would bear close watching.

Gerold was also studying Joan curiously. "You look familiar, Father," he said. "Have we met before?" He peered at her frowningly through the dim light. Suddenly his expression changed; he stared like a man who had just seen a ghost. "My God," he said chokingly. "It can't be . . ."

"You know each other?" Anastasius asked.

"We met in Dorstadt," Joan said quickly. "I studied some years at the cathedral school there; my *sister*"—she emphasized the word ever so slightly—"stayed with the count and his family during that time."

Her eyes flashed Gerold an urgent warning: *Say nothing.*

Gerold recovered his composure. "Of course," he said. "I remember your sister well."

Lothar broke in impatiently. "Enough of this. What have you come to tell me, Count?"

"My message is for your ears alone, my liege."

Lothar nodded. "Very well. The others may leave. We will speak again, Anastasius."

As Joan turned to go, Gerold touched her arm. "Wait for me. I would like to hear more . . . about your sister."

Outside the chapel, Anastasius went his way. Joan waited nervously under the baleful eye of Lothar's steward. The situation was extremely dangerous; one ill-considered word, and her true identity could be revealed. *I should leave now, before Gerold comes out,* she told herself. But she yearned to see him. She stood rooted there by a complex mix of fear and anticipation.

The chapel door opened, and Gerold emerged. "It *is* you, then?" he said wonderingly. "But how—?"

The servant was eyeing them curiously.

"Not here," Joan said. She led him to the little room where she kept her herbs and medicines. Inside, she lit the poppy oil lamps; they flared into life, enclosing the two in an intimate circle of light.

They stared at each other with the wonder of rediscovery. Gerold had changed in the fifteen years since Joan had last seen him; the thick, red hair was traced with gray, and there were new lines around the indigo eyes and wide, sensual mouth—but he was still the handsomest man she had ever seen. The sight of him set her heart hammering.

Gerold took a step toward her. All at once they were in each other's arms, holding on so tightly that Joan could feel the metal rings of Gerold's mail through her thick priest's robe.

"Joan," Gerold murmured. "My dearest, my pearl. I never thought to see you again."

"Gerold." The word blotted out all reasonable thought.

Gently his finger traced the faint scar on her left cheek. "The Norsemen?"

"Yes."

He bent and kissed it gently, his lips warm against her cheek. "They did take you, then—you and Gisla?"

Gisla. Gerold must never know, she must never tell him, the horror that had befallen his elder daughter.

"They took Gisla. I—I managed to escape."

He was astonished. "How? And to where? My men and I scoured the countryside looking for you but found no trace."

Briefly she told him what had happened—as much as she could tell in so hurried and constrained a circumstance: her escape to Fulda and acceptance as John Anglicus, the near-discovery of her identity and flight from the abbey, her pilgrimage to Rome and subsequent rise to the position of Pope's physician.

"And in all this time," Gerold said slowly when she had finished, "you never thought to send word to me?"

Joan heard the pain and bewilderment in his voice. "I—I did not think you wanted me. Richild said the idea of marrying me to the farrier's son was yours, that you had asked her to arrange it."

"And you believed her?" Abruptly he released her. "Great God, Joan, had we no better understanding between us?"

"I—I didn't know what to think. You had gone; I could not be certain why. And Richild knew—about us, about what happened at the riverbank. How could she have known, unless you told her?"

"I don't know. I only know that I loved you as I have never loved anyone before—or since." His voice tightened. "I drove Pistis almost beyond endurance on the road home, straining to catch sight of Villaris, for *you* were there, and I was wild with impatience to see you . . . to ask you to be my wife."

"Your wife?" Joan was dumbfounded. "But . . . Richild . . . ?"

"Something happened while I was gone—something that helped me see how empty my marriage was, how vital you were to my happiness. I was returning to tell you that I meant to divorce Richild, and marry you, if you would have me."

Joan shook her head. "So much misunderstanding," she said sorrowfully. "So much gone wrong."

"So much," he replied, "to make up for." He pulled her close and kissed her. The effect was like holding a candle to a wax tablet, dissolving what the years had written. Once again they were standing together in the river behind Villaris in the spring sunshine, young and giddy with new-discovered love.

After a long while he released her. "Listen, my heart," he said husk-ily. "I'm leaving Lothar's service. I told him so just now, in the chapel."

"And he agreed to let you go?" Lothar did not seem the kind of man to set aside willingly any man's obligation to him.

"At first he was difficult, but I got him to come round in the end. My freedom comes at a price; I've had to surrender Villaris with all its estates. I'm no longer a rich man, Joan. But I have the strength of my two arms, and friends who will stand by me. One of them is Siconulf, Prince of Benevento, whom I befriended when we served to-gether on the Emperor's campaign against the Obodrites. He needs good men around him now, for he's being hard-pressed by his rival Radelchis. Will you come with me, Joan? Will you be my wife?"

Brisk footsteps outside the door jolted them apart. A moment later the door opened and a head peeked in. It was Florintinus, one of the palace notaries.

"Ah!" he said. "There you are, John Anglicus! I've been looking all over for you." He looked sharply from Joan to Gerold and back again. "Am I . . . interrupting anything?"

"Not at all," Joan said quickly. "What can I do for you, Florintinus?"

"I've a terrible headache," he said. "I wondered if you could pre-pare one of your palliatives for me."

"I'd be happy to," Joan said courteously.

Florintinus lingered by the door, exchanging idle conversation with Gerold while Joan quickly prepared a mixture of violet leaves and willow-bark, decocting it in a cup of rosemary tea. She gave it to Florintinus, and he left at once.

"We can't talk here," she said to Gerold as soon as he was gone. "It's too dangerous."

"When can I see you again?" Gerold asked urgently.

Joan thought. "There's a Temple of Vesta on the Via Appia, just outside of town. I'll meet you there tomorrow after terce."

He took her in his arms and kissed her again, softly at first, then with an intensity that filled her with aching desire. "Till tomorrow," he whispered. Then he went through the door, leaving Joan's head spinning with a dizzying mix of emotions.

ARIGHIS peered sharply through the predawn light, checking the Lateran courtyard. All was in readiness. A lighted brazier had been placed alongside the great bronze statue of the she-wolf. A pair of

sturdy fire irons were set inside the flaming brazier, their tips beginning to glow red from the heat of the flames. Nearby stood a swordsman, sharpened blade at the ready.

The first rays of the sun crested the horizon. It was an unusual
hour for a public execution; such events normally took place after
mass. Despite the earliness of the hour, a crowd of spectators was already gathered—the eager ones always arrived well in advance to secure the best position for viewing. Many had brought their children,
who scampered about in excited anticipation of the gory spectacle.

Arighis had deliberately set the hour of Benedict's punishment for
dawn, before Sergius awakened and changed his mind. Others might
accuse him of proceeding with unseemly haste, but Arighis did not
care. He knew exactly what he was doing, and why.

Arighis had held the high office of vicedominus for over twenty
years; his entire life had been devoted to the service of the Patriarchium, to keeping the vast and complicated hive of pontifical offices
that composed the seat of government in Rome running smoothly
and efficiently. Over the years, Arighis had come to think of the papal
household as a living entity, a being whose continuing welfare was his
sole responsibility and concern.

That welfare was now threatened. In less than a year, Benedict had
turned the Patriarchium into a center of corrupt power brokering and
simony. Grasping and manipulative to the core, Benedict's very existence was a malignant canker upon the papacy. The only way to save
the patient was to amputate the diseased member. Benedict must die.

Sergius did not have the backbone for the deed, so it fell upon
Arighis to shoulder the burden. He did so unhesitatingly, knowing
that he acted for the good of Holy Mother Church.

Everything was in readiness. "Bring the prisoner," Arighis commanded the guards.

Benedict was marched in. Clothes rumpled, face drawn and ashen
from a sleepless night in the dungeon, he anxiously searched the courtyard. "Where is Sergius?" he demanded. "Where is my brother?"

"His Holiness cannot be disturbed," Arighis said.

Benedict whirled on him. "What do you think you are doing,
Arighis? You saw my brother last night. He was drunk; he didn't
know what he was saying. Let me talk to him, and you will see: he
will reverse the judgment against me."

"Proceed," Arighis commanded the guards.

The guards dragged Benedict to the center of the courtyard and forced him to his knees. They grabbed his arms and pulled them across the pedestal of the statue of the she-wolf so his hands rested levelly on the top.

Terror creased Benedict's face. "No! Stop!" he shouted. Raising his eyes toward the windows of the Patriarchium, he cried out, "Sergius! Sergius! Serg—!"

The sword sliced downward. Benedict screamed as his severed hands dropped to the ground, spurting blood.

The crowd cheered. The swordsman nailed Benedict's severed hands to the side of the she-wolf. According to ancient custom, they would remain there for one month as a warning to others tempted to the sin of thievery.

Ennodius the physician came forward. Pulling the hot irons from the brazier, he pressed them firmly against Benedict's bleeding stumps. The smell of burning flesh rose sickeningly in the air. Benedict screamed again and toppled into a faint. Ennodius bent to attend him.

Arighis leaned forward attentively. Most men died after such an injury—if not immediately from shock and pain then shortly afterward from infection or loss of blood. But some of the strongest managed to survive. One saw them on the streets of Rome, their grotesque mutilations revealing the nature of their crimes: severed lips, those who had lied under oath; severed feet, slaves who'd fled their masters; gouged-out eyes, those who had lusted after the wives or daughters of their betters.

The distressing possibility of survival was the reason Arighis had asked Ennodius and not John Anglicus to attend the condemned man, for the skill of the latter might be great enough to save Benedict.

Ennodius stood. "God's judgment has been rendered," he announced gravely. "Benedict is dead."

Christ be praised, Arighis thought. *The papacy is safe.*

JOAN stood on line in the *lavatorium,* waiting her turn for the ritual hand washing before mass. Her eyes were swollen and heavy from lack of sleep; all night she had tossed restlessly, her mind filled with thoughts of Gerold. Last night, feelings she believed long buried had resurfaced with an intensity that astonished and frightened her.

Gerold's return had reawakened the disturbing desires of her youth. *What would it be like to live as a woman again?* she wondered. She was accustomed to being responsible for herself, to having complete control of her destiny. But by law a wife surrendered her life to her husband. Could she trust any man so far—even Gerold?

Never give yourself to a man. Her mother's words echoed like warning bells in her mind.

She needed time to sort out the turmoil of emotions in her heart. But time was one thing she didn't have.

Arighis appeared beside her. "Come," he said urgently. He pulled her out of line. "His Holiness needs you."

"Is he ill?" Worriedly, she followed Arighis down the corridor to the papal bedroom. Last night's rich food and wine had been purged from Sergius's body, and the strong dose of colchicum Joan had administered should have staved off a return attack of gout.

"He will be if he keeps carrying on as he is."

"Why, what's wrong?"

"Benedict is dead."

"Dead!"

"The sentence was carried out this morning. He died immediately."

"Benedicite!" Joan quickened her steps. She could imagine the effect this news would have on Sergius.

Even so, when she saw him she was shocked. Sergius was scarcely recognizable. His hair was disheveled, his eyes red and swollen from weeping, his cheeks covered with scratches where his nails had scored them. He was on his knees beside the bed, rocking back and forth, whimpering like a lost child.

"Holiness!" Joan spoke sharply into his ear. "Sergius!"

He kept on rocking, blind and deaf in an extremity of grief. Clearly there was no way to reach him in his present condition. Taking some tincture of henbane from her scrip, Joan measured out a dose and held it to his lips. He drank distractedly.

After a few minutes, his rocking slowed, then stopped. He looked at Joan as if seeing her for the first time.

"Weep for me, John. My soul is damned for all eternity!"

"Nonsense," Joan said firmly. "You acted in just accordance with the law."

Sergius shook his head. " 'Be not like Cain, who was of the Evil One and murdered his brother,' " he quoted from the First Letter of John.

Joan countered with an answering passage. " 'And why did he mur-

der him? Because his own deeds were evil and his brother's righteous.'
Benedict was not righteous, Holiness; he betrayed you and Rome."

"And now he is dead, by my own word! O God!" He struck his
chest and howled in pain.

She had to divert him from his grief or he would work himself
into another fit. She took him firmly by the shoulders and said, "You
must make auricular confession."

This form of the sacrament of penance, in which one made private and regular confession *ad auriculam*, "to the ear" of a priest,
was widespread in Frankland. But Rome still held determinedly to
the old ways, in which confession and penance were made and given
publicly, only once in a lifetime.

Sergius seized on the idea. "Yes, yes, I will confess."

"I'll send for one of the cardinal priests," she said. "Is there someone you prefer?"

"I will make my confession to you."

"Me?" A simple priest and a foreigner, Joan was an unlikely candidate to serve as confessor to the Pope. "Are you sure, Holiness?"

"I want no other."

"Very well." She turned to Arighis. "Leave us."

Arighis shot her a grateful look as he left the room.

"Peccavi, impie egi, iniquitatem feci, miserere mei Domine . . ."
Sergius began in the ritual words of penitence.

Joan listened with quiet sympathy to his long outpouring of grief,
regret, and remorse. With a soul so burdened and tormented, it was
no wonder Sergius sought peace and forgetfulness in drink.

The confession worked as she had intended; gradually the wild
passion of despair subsided, leaving Sergius drained and exhausted
but no longer a danger to himself or others.

Now came the tricky part, the penance that had to precede forgiveness of sin. Sergius would expect his penance to be harsh—public
mortification, perhaps, on the steps of St. Peter's. But such an act
would only serve to weaken Sergius and the papacy in Lothar's eyes—
and that must be prevented at all costs. Yet the penance Joan imposed
must not be too light or Sergius would reject it.

She had an idea. "In token of repentance," she said, "you will ab-
stain from all wine and the meat of four-footed animals from this day
forward until the hour of your death."

Fasts were a common form of penance, but they usually lasted only a few months, perhaps a year. A lifetime of abstinence was stern punishment—especially for Sergius. And the penance would have the added benefit of helping protect the Pope from his own worst instincts.

Sergius bowed his head in acceptance. "Pray with me, John."

She knelt beside him. In many ways, he was like a child—weak, impulsive, needful, demanding. Yet she knew he was capable of good. And at this moment, he was all that stood between Anastasius and the Throne of St. Peter.

At the end of the prayer, she rose. Sergius clutched at her. "Don't leave," he pleaded. "I can't be alone."

Joan covered his hand with her own. "I won't leave you," she promised solemnly.

ENTERING through the crumbling portals of the ruined Temple of Vesta, Gerold saw with disappointment that Joan had not yet arrived. *No matter,* he told himself; *it's early yet.* He sat down to wait with his back against one of the slim granite pillars.

Like most pagan monuments in Rome, the temple had been stripped of its precious metals: the gilt rosettes that had once adorned the coffers of the dome were gone, as were the golden bas-reliefs ornamenting the pediment of the *pronaos*. The niches lining the walls were empty, their marble statues having been carted off to the lime kilns to be turned into building material for the walls of Christian churches. Remarkably, however, the figure of the goddess herself survived, ensconced in her shrine under the dome. One of her hands had broken off, and the lines of her garment were roughened, eroded by time and the elements, but the statue still had remarkable power and grace of form—testimony to the skill of its heathen sculptor.

Vesta, ancient goddess of home and hearth. She represented all that Joan meant to him: life, love, a renewed sense of hope. He breathed deeply, drinking in the damp sweetness of the morning, feeling better than he had in years. He had been low of late, weary of life's stale, unchanging round. He had resigned himself to it, telling himself it was the inevitable result of his years, for he was nearing forty-six, an old man's age.

Now he knew how wrong he had been. Far from being tired of life, he was hungry for it. He felt young, alive, vital, as if he had drunk from the fabled cup of Christ. The rest of his life stretched ahead bright with promise. He would marry Joan, and they would go to Benevento and live together in peace and love. They might even have children—it was not too late. The way he felt at this moment, anything was possible.

He started up as she came hurrying through the portal, her priest's robes billowing behind her. Her cheeks were rosy from the exertion of her walk; her cropped white-gold hair curled around her face, accentuating her deep-set gray-green eyes, eyes that drew him like pools of light in a darkened sanctuary. How ever had she succeeded in this man's disguise? he wondered. To his knowing eyes, she looked very womanly and wholly desirable.

"Joan." The word was part name, part supplication.

Joan kept a cautious distance between them. If once she let herself into Gerold's arms, she knew her resolve would melt.

"I've brought a mount for you," Gerold said. "If we leave now, we'll be at Benevento in three days' time."

She took a deep breath. "I'm not going with you."

"Not going?" Gerold echoed.

"I cannot leave Sergius."

For a moment he was too taken aback to say anything. Then he managed to ask, "Why not?"

"Sergius needs me. He is . . . weak."

"He's Pope of Rome, Joan, not a child in need of coddling."

"I don't coddle him; I doctor him. The physicians of the schola have no knowledge of the disease that afflicts him."

"He survived well enough before you came to Rome."

It was gentle mockery, but it stung. "If I leave now, Sergius will drink himself to death within a six-month."

"Then let him," Gerold answered harshly. "What has that to do with you and me?"

She was shocked. "How can you say such a thing?"

"Great God, haven't we sacrificed enough? The spring of our lives is already behind us. Let's not squander the time that is left!"

She turned away, so he would not see how much this affected her.

Gerold caught her by the wrist. "I love you, Joan. Come with me, now, while there's still time."

The touch of his hand warmed her flesh, sparking desire. She had a treacherous impulse to embrace him, to feel his lips on hers. Embarrassed by these weak and shameful feelings, she was suddenly, unreasonably angry with Gerold for having aroused them. "What did you expect?" she cried. "That I would run off with you the first moment you beckoned?" She let the wave of anger rise and crest within her, submerging her other, more dangerous emotions. "I've made a life here—a good life. I've independence and respect, and opportunities I never had as a woman. Why should I give it all up? What for? To spend the rest of my days confined to a narrow set of rooms, cooking and embroidering?"

Gerold said in a low voice, "If that's all I wanted in a wife, I'd have married long before now."

"Do so, then!" Joan retorted hotly. "I'll not stop you!"

A knot of bewilderment appeared between Gerold's brows. He asked gently, "Joan, what has happened? What's wrong?"

"Nothing is wrong. I've changed, that's all. I'm no longer the naive, lovesick girl you knew in Dorstadt. I'm my own master now. And I won't give that up—not for you, not for any man!"

"Have I asked you to?" Gerold responded reasonably.

But Joan did not want to hear reason. Gerold's nearness and her strong physical attraction to him were a torment. Savagely she tried to break its hold. "You cannot accept it, can you? The idea that I'm not willing to give up my life for you? That I'm one woman who's actually immune to your masculine charms?"

She had sought to wound, and she had succeeded.

Gerold stared at her as though he saw something new written upon her face. "I thought you loved me," he said stiffly. "I see I was mistaken. Forgive me; I'll not trouble you again." He went to the portal, hesitated, turned back. "This means we will never see each other again. Is that really what you want?"

No! Joan felt like crying. *It's not what I want! It's not what I want at all!* But another part of her cautioned her to hold back. "That's what I want," she said. Her voice sounded curiously distant in her own ears.

One more word of love and need from him, and she would have broken and run to his arms. Instead he wheeled abruptly and went through the portal. She heard him racing down the temple steps.

In another moment he would be gone forever.

Joan's heart rose like a cup filled to overbrimming. Then the cup tilted, spilling forth all her pent-up emotion.

She ran to the door. "Gerold!" she cried. "Wait!"

The loud clatter of hooves against stones drowned out her cry. Gerold rode swiftly down the road. A moment later he rounded a corner and was gone.

≯ 24 ≮

THE Roman summer arrived with a vengeance. The sun beat down relentlessly; by midday, the cobblestones were hot enough to blister a man's feet. The stench of rotting garbage and manure, intensified by the heat, rose into the still air and hung over the city like a suffocating pall. Pestilential fevers raged among the poor who lived in the damp and decaying tenements lining the low-lying banks of the Tiber.

Fearful of contagion, Lothar and his army quit the city. The Romans rejoiced at their departure, for the burden of maintaining so large a host had strained the city's resources to the limit.

Sergius was hailed as a hero. The adulation of the people helped soften his grief over Benedict's death. Buoyed by newfound health and energy—gained in large measure from the spartan diet Joan had imposed in penance—Sergius was a man transformed. True to his promise, he began rebuilding the Orphanotrophium. The crumbling walls were reinforced, a new roof added. Tiles of fine travertine marble were stripped from the pagan Temple of Minerva and used to line the floor of the great hall. A new chapel was constructed and dedicated to St. Stephen.

Where previously Sergius had frequently been too tired or ill to say Mass, he now celebrated the holy service every morning. In addition, he was often to be found praying in his private chapel. He threw himself into his faith with the same fervor with which he had once pursued the pleasures of the table—for he was not a man to do things by halves.

Two years of mild winters and plentiful harvests resulted in a time of general prosperity. Even the legions of poor who crowded the streets of the city seemed a little less wretched, as the pockets of their more prosperous brethren loosened and almsgiving increased. The Romans offered prayers of thanksgiving at the altars of their churches, well content with their city and their Lord Pope.

They did not suspect—how could they?—the catastrophe that was about to descend upon them.

✠

JOAN was with Sergius during one of his regular meetings with the princes of the city when a messenger burst in upon them.

"What's this?" Sergius inquired sternly.

"Holiness." The messenger knelt in obeisance. "I bring a message of utmost importance from Siena. A large fleet of Saracen ships has set sail from Africa. They are on a direct course toward Rome."

"Toward Rome?" one of the princes echoed thinly. "Surely the report is mistaken."

"There is no mistake," the messenger said. "The Saracens will be here within a fortnight."

There was a moment of silence while everyone took in this astonishing news.

Another of the princes spoke. "Perhaps it would be wise to remove the holy relics to a place of greater safety?" He was referring to the bones of the apostle Peter, the most sacred relics in all of Christendom, which lay housed in their namesake basilica outside the protection of the city walls.

Romuald, the greatest of the assembled princes, threw back his head and laughed. "You don't think the infidels would attack St. Peter's!"

"What's to prevent them?" Joan asked.

"They may be barbarians, but they're not fools," Romuald replied. "They know the hand of God would smite them flat the moment they set foot inside the sacred tomb!"

"They have their own worship," Joan pointed out. "They do not fear the hand of our Christian God."

Romuald's smile died. "What heathen blasphemy is this?"

Joan stood her ground. "The basilica is an obvious target for plunder, if only for the treasure that lies within. For safety's sake, we should bring these sacred objects and the saint's sarcophagus within the city walls."

Sergius was doubtful. "We've had other such warnings before, and nothing came of them."

"Indeed," Romuald said mockingly, "if we took fright at every sighting of a Saracen ship, the sacred bones would have been moving back and forth like a pair of shuttles on a loom!"

A burst of appreciative laughter was instantly cut off by the Pontiff's disapproving frown.

Sergius said, "God will defend His own. The Blessed Apostle will remain where he is."

"At least," Joan urged, "let us send to the outlying settlements, asking for men to help defend the city."

"It's pruning time," Sergius said. "The settlements need every able-bodied man to work in the vineyards. I see no need to risk the harvest, upon which all depend, when there is no immediate danger."

"But, Holiness—"

Sergius cut her off. "Trust in God, John Anglicus. There is no stronger armor than that of Christian faith and prayer."

Joan bowed her head in submission. But inside she thought rebelliously: *When the Saracens are at the gates, all the prayer in the world will not help half so much as a single division of good fighting men.*

GEROLD and his company were encamped just outside the town of Benevento. Within their tents the men were sleeping soundly after a long night of ribaldry—a boon Gerold had granted in reward for their resounding victory the day before.

For the past two years Gerold had commanded Prince Siconulf's armies, fighting to secure Siconulf's throne against the ambitious pretender Radelchis. A skilled commander who pushed his men hard while they were learning discipline and proficiency at arms, then trusted them to give good account of themselves on the field, Gerold had inflicted defeat after defeat on Radelchis's forces. Yesterday's victory was so resounding it had probably put an end to Radelchis's claim to the Beneventan throne forever.

Although armed sentries were posted all around the camp, Gerold and his men slept with swords and shields at their sides, where they were always ready at hand. Gerold took no chances, for an enemy could be dangerous even after defeat. The heat of revenge often drove men to rash and desperate action. Gerold knew of many encampments taken by surprise, their inhabitants slaughtered before they even had time to wake.

At the moment, however, such thoughts were far from Gerold's mind. He lay supine, arms behind his head, legs splayed carelessly. Beside him a woman covered in his cloak breathed soddenly, a rhythmic sound broken by occasional bursts of snoring.

In the light of dawn Gerold regretted the brief gust of passion that had brought her into his bed. There had been other such transient encounters over the years, each less satisfying and more forgettable than the one before. For Gerold still cherished in his heart the memory of a love that could never be forgotten.

He shook his head impatiently. It was idle to dwell upon the past. Joan had not shared his feelings, or she would not have sent him away.

The woman rolled onto her side. Gerold touched her shoulder and she woke, opening pretty brown eyes that stared back at him without depth or meaning.

"It's morning," Gerold said. He took a few coins from his scrip and handed them to her.

She jingled them and smiled happily. "Shall I come again tonight, my lord?"

"No, that won't be necessary."

She looked disappointed. "Didn't I please you?"

"Yes, yes, of course. But we're breaking camp tonight."

A short while later he watched her cross the field, her sandals slapping dully against the dry grass. Overhead the cloudy sky was lightening into a flat and pallid gray.

Soon it would again be day.

SICONULF and his chief fideles were already gathered in the great hall when Gerold entered. Dispensing with the usual courtesies, Siconulf announced abruptly, "I have just received word from Corsica. Seventy-three Saracen ships have set sail from the African coast. They are carrying some five thousand men and two hundred horse."

An astonished silence followed. So large a fleet was scarcely imaginable.

Eburis, one of Siconulf's fideles, gave a low whistle. "Whatever they intend, it's more than just another piratical raid upon our coast."

"They have set course for Rome," Siconulf said.

"Rome! Surely not!" said another of the fideles.

"Preposterous!" scoffed a third. "They'd never dare!"

Gerold scarcely heard them. His thoughts were racing ahead. "Pope Sergius will need our help," he said tautly.

But it was not Sergius he was thinking of. With a single stroke, the news of the approach of the Saracen fleet had erased all the bitter hurt and misunderstanding of the past two years. Only one thing mattered—to reach Joan and do everything within his power to protect her.

"What do you suggest, Gerold?" Siconulf asked.

"My prince, let me lead our troops to Rome's defense."

Siconulf frowned. "Surely the Holy City has defenders of her own."

"Only the *familia Sancti Petri*—a small and undisciplined group of papal militia. They will fall like summer wheat before the Saracens' blades."

"What about the Aurelian Wall? Surely the Saracens cannot breach it?"

"The wall seems strong enough," Gerold admitted. "But several of its gates are poorly reinforced. They won't withstand a sustained assault. And the tomb of St. Peter is entirely unprotected, for it lies outside the wall."

Siconulf considered this. He was reluctant to commit his troops to a cause other than his own. But he was a Christian prince, with a proper reverence for the Holy City and its sacred places. The idea of barbarian infidels defiling the Apostle's tomb was appalling. Besides, it occurred to him now that there might be some personal benefit in sending men to Rome's defense. Afterward, a grateful Pope Sergius might reward him with one of the rich papal patrimonies that bordered Siconulf's territory.

He said to Gerold, "You may have three divisions of troops. How long will you need to prepare to march?"

"The troops are battle hardened and ready. We can leave at once. If the weather holds, we'll be in Rome in ten days' time."

"Let us pray that will be sufficient. God go with you, Gerold."

IN ROME, an eerie sense of calm prevailed. Since the initial warning from Siena two weeks before, there had been no further word of the Saracen fleet. The Romans gradually began to relax their vigilance, convincing themselves that the reports of an enemy fleet had been false, after all.

The morning of August 23 dawned bright with promise. The stational mass was held at the Cathedral of Sancta Maria ad Martyres, known in pagan days as the Pantheon, one of the loveliest of Rome's churches. It was an especially beautiful service, with the sun filtering through the circular opening in the basilica's great domed roof, casting a golden glow over the entire congregation. Returning to the Patriarchium, the choir joyously chanted, *"Gloria in excelsis Deo."*

The song died on their lips as they entered the sun-dazzled piazza of the Lateran and saw a crowd of citizens milling anxiously round a weary and mud-stained messenger.

"The infidels have landed," the messenger announced grimly. "The town of Porto is taken, its people slaughtered and its churches defiled."

"Christ aid!" someone cried.

"What will become of us?" wailed another.

"They will kill us all!" a third shouted hysterically.

The crowd threatened to break into a dangerous disorder.

"Silence!" Sergius's voice rang above the uproar. "Cease this unworthy display!" The voice of authority cut commandingly through the din, compelling obedience.

"What," he said, "are we sheep, to cower so? Are we babes, to think ourselves defenseless!" He paused dramatically. "No! We are Romans! And this is Rome, protectorate of St. Peter, key bearer of the Kingdom of Heaven! 'Thou art Peter,' Christ has said, 'and upon this rock shall I build my church.' Why should you fear? Will God suffer His sacred altar to be defiled?"

The crowd stirred. Scattered voices cried out in response: "Yes! Listen to the Lord Pope! Sergius is right!"

"Have we not our guards and our militia?" With a sweep of his arm, Sergius indicated the papal guards, who obliged by raising their lances and shaking them fiercely. "The blood of our ancestors runs in their veins; they are armed with the strength of Omnipotent God! Who shall prevail against them?"

The crowd let out a ragged cheer. Rome's heroic past was still a source of pride, the military triumphs of Caesar and Pompey and Augustus the common knowledge of every citizen.

Joan watched Sergius in wonderment. Could this heroic figure be the same ailing, ill-tempered, disheartened old man she had encountered two years ago?

"Let the infidels come!" Sergius cried. "Let them hurl their weapons against this sacred fortress! They will crack their hearts against our God-protected walls!"

Joan felt the excitement, the swelling crest that rose thrillingly and broke upon the crowd in a roiling tumult of emotion. Her own feet were too firmly planted in reality to be so easily swept away. *The world is not as we would have it*, she thought, *no matter how skill-fully we may conjure it.*

The crowd were on their feet, heads lifted, faces aglow. All around Joan excited voices reverberated in unison: "Sergius! Sergius! Sergius! Sergius!"

AT SERGIUS'S command, the people spent the next two days fasting and praying. The altars of all the churches shone brightly, lit with a profusion of votive candles. Miracles were everywhere reported. The golden statue of the Madonna at the Oratory of St. Cosmas was said to have moved her eyes and sung a litany. The crucifix above the altar of St. Hadrian had shed tears of blood. These miracles were inter-preted as signs of divine blessing and favor. Day and night the sound of *Hosanna* rang out from churches and monasteries, as the clergy of the city rose to the Lord Pope's challenge and prepared to meet the enemy with the invincible strength of their Christian faith.

Shortly after dawn on August 26, the cry came down from the walls. "They're coming! They're coming!"

The terrified shrieks of the people penetrated even the thick stone walls of the Patriarchium.

"I must go to the parapets," Sergius announced. "When the peo-ple see me, they will know they have nothing to fear."

Arighis and the other optimates protested, arguing that it was far too dangerous, but Sergius was adamant. In the end they reluctantly led him to the wall, careful to choose a place where the stones rose somewhat higher, affording better protection.

There was a great cheer as Sergius ascended the steps. Then all eyes turned toward the west. A great cloud of dust rose shimmering in the air. The Saracens emerged from it at a rapid gallop, their loose garments flapping behind them like the wings of giant birds of prey. A terrible war cry rang out, a long, high ululation that rose and hung shuddering in the air, sending a chill of terror down the spines of all who stood listening.

"*Deo, juva nos*," one of the priests said tremblingly.

Sergius raised a small, gem-encrusted crucifix and cried, "Christ is our Savior and our Shield."

The city gates opened, and the papal militia marched out bravely to meet the enemy. "Death to the infidel!" they shouted, waving their swords and spears.

The opposing armies collided with a great noise of clashing steel, louder than the din of a thousand smiths. In minutes, it became evident the battle was hopelessly unequal; the Saracen cavalry rode straight over the front ranks of the Roman foot soldiers, cutting and slashing with their curved scimitars.

The militia in the rear could not see the slaughter up front. Still convinced of victory, they thronged forward, pushing against the backs of those before them. Line after line of men were driven relentlessly onto the Saracens' swords and fell, their bodies creating a treacherous stumbling ground for those who came after.

It was a massacre. Broken and terrified, the militia retreated in desperate disorder. "Run!" they screamed as they scattered across the field like seeds of grain before a wind. "Run for your lives!"

The Saracens did not trouble to pursue them, for their victory had gained them a much greater prize: the unprotected basilica of St. Peter. They surrounded it in a dark swarm. They did not dismount but rode their horses straight up the steps and through the doors in a great flying wedge.

Behind the walls, the Romans waited breathlessly. A minute passed. Then another. No thunderclap split the sky, no sea of flame poured from the heavens. Instead, the unmistakable noise of rending wood and metal issued from the basilica. The Saracens were pillaging the sacred altar.

"It cannot be," Sergius whispered. "Dear God, it cannot be."

A band of Saracens emerged from the basilica, waving the golden cross of Constantine. Men had died, it was said, simply for daring to touch it. Yet now the Saracens tossed it about mockingly, laughing as they pumped it up and down between their legs in obscene and beastly parody.

With a muted groan, Sergius dropped the crucifix and sank to his knees.

"Holiness!" Joan rushed to him.

He grimaced in pain, pressing one hand to his chest.

A seizure of the heart, Joan thought in alarm. "Take him up," she commanded. Arighis and several of the guards lifted the stricken Pope, cradling him in their arms, and carried him into a nearby house, where they laid him down on a thick straw mattress.

Sergius's breath was coming in labored gasps. Joan prepared an infusion of willow bark and hawthorn berries and gave it to him. It seemed to ease him, for his color improved and he began to breathe more easily.

"They're at the gates!" People were screaming outside. "Christ aid! They're at the gates!"

Sergius tried to raise himself from the bed, but Joan eased him back. "You must not move."

The effort had cost him; he pressed his lips together tightly. "Speak for me," he pleaded. "Turn their minds toward God. . . . Help them . . . Prepare them . . ." His mouth worked agitatedly, but no words came.

"Yes, Holiness, yes," Joan agreed. Clearly nothing else would pacify him. "I will do as you say. But now you must rest."

He nodded and lay back. His eyelids fluttered and closed as the medicine began to take effect. There was nothing to do now but let him sleep and hope the medicine would do its work.

Joan left him under the solicitous eye of Arighis and went out onto the street.

A rending noise, loud as a thunderclap, sounded close by. Joan started in fear.

"What's happening?" she called to a passing group of guards.

"The idolatrous swine are battering at the gate!" a guard called back as they marched past.

She returned to the piazza. Terror had driven the crowd into a frenzy. Men yanked the hairs violently from their beards; women shrieked and tore their cheeks with their nails till the blood ran. The monks of the Abbey of St. John knelt together in a solid clump, black cowls fallen from their heads, arms uplifted to Heaven. Several of their number tore off their robes and began to scourge themselves with split canes of wood in a frenzied attempt to propitiate the evident wrath of God. Frightened at this alarming display, children began to wail, their high-pitched voices threading reedily through the mad, discordant chorus.

Help them, Sergius had pleaded. *Prepare them.*

But how?

Joan climbed the steps to the wall. Picking up the crucifix Sergius had dropped, she thrust it aloft for all to see. The sun caught its gems, sparking a golden rainbow of light.

"Hosanna in excelsis," she began loudly. The high, clear notes of the holy canticle rang out over the crowd, strong and sweet and sure. The people nearest the wall raised tear-streaked faces toward the familiar sound. Priests and monks joined their voices in the song, kneeling on the cobbled stones beside masons and seamstresses. *"Christus qui venit nomine Domini . . ."*

There was another great crash, followed by the sound of splintering wood. The gates gave an inward heave. Light filtered through where a narrow crack had been opened.

Dear God, Joan thought. *What if they break through?* Until this moment such a possibility had seemed unthinkable.

Memory flooded her. She saw the Norsemen bursting through the doors of the cathedral at Dorstadt, swinging their axes. She heard the awful screams of the dying . . . saw John lying with his head crushed in . . . and Gisla . . . Gisla . . .

Her voice trembled into stillness. The people looked up in alarm. *Go on,* she told herself, *go on,* but her mind seemed frozen; she could not remember the words.

"Hosanna in excelsis." A deep baritone sounded beside her. It was Leo, Cardinal Priest of the Church of the Sancti Quattro Coronati. He had climbed up beside her on the wall. The sound of his voice jolted her from her fear, and together they went on with the canticle.

"God and St. Peter!" A loud cry resounded from the east.

The guards on the walls were jumping up and down, cheering, shouting, "God be praised! We are saved!"

She looked over the wall. A great army was galloping toward the city, its fluttering banners emblazoned with the emblems of St. Peter and the cross.

The Saracens dropped their battering rams and ran for their mounts.

Joan squinted into the sun. As the troops drew nearer, she gave a sudden, sharp cry.

At the head of the vanguard, his lance already poised for the throw, tall and fierce and heroic as one of her mother's ancient gods, rode Gerold.

THE ensuing battle was sharp and savage. The attack of the Beneventans had caught the Saracens off guard; they were driven back from the city walls and forced to retreat through the campagna all the way to the sea. At the coast, the infidels hauled their stolen treasure aboard their ships and set sail. In their haste to depart, they left great numbers of their brethren behind. For weeks Gerold and his men rode up and down the coast, hunting down scattered bands of the marauders.

Rome was saved. The Romans were torn between joy and despair—joy at their deliverance, despair at the destruction of St. Peter's. For the sacred basilica had been plundered beyond recognition. The ancient gold cross on the tomb of the Apostle was gone, as was the great silver table with the relief of Byzantium, given by Emperor Karolus the Great. The infidels had torn silver entablatures from the doors and gold plates from the floor. They had even—God darken their eyes!—carried away the high altar itself. Unable to remove the bronze coffin containing the body of the Prince of the Apostles, they had broken it open, scattering and defiling the sacred ashes.

All Christendom was plunged into grief. The footprints of the ages were preserved within this sanctum sanctorum of the Christian faith. Generations of pilgrims, including kings and emperors, had prostrated themselves before its sacred doors. Venerated popes rested within its walls. Yet this oldest and greatest of Christian churches, which neither Goths nor Vandals had dared to defile, had fallen before a band of African pirates.

Sergius blamed himself for the catastrophe. He withdrew to his rooms, refusing admittance to anyone save Joan and his closest advisers. And he took to drink again, downing cup after cup of Tuscan wine until at last he slipped into merciful oblivion.

The drinking had a predictable effect: his gout returned with a vengeance; to ease the pain, he drank even more. He slept badly. Night after night he woke screaming, tormented by nightmarish dreams in which he was visited by the vengeful specter of Benedict. Joan feared the strain this was putting on his already weakened heart.

"Remember the penance to which you agreed," she reminded him.

"It doesn't matter now," Sergius replied despondently. "I have no hope of Heaven. God has abandoned me."

"You must not blame yourself for what happened. Some things are beyond all mortal power to remedy or prevent."

Sergius shook his head. "The soul of my murdered brother cries out against me! I have sinned, and this is my punishment."

"If you will not think of yourself," Joan argued, "think of the people! Now, more than ever, they look to you for consolation and guidance."

She said it to hearten him, but the truth was otherwise. The people had turned against Sergius. There had been sufficient warning of the Saracens' approach, they said, plenty of time for the Lord Pope to have transported the holy sarcophagus inside the walls. Sergius's faith in God's deliverance, which at the time had been universally praised, was now universally condemned as the result of a sinful and disastrously mistaken pride.

"*Mea culpa*," Sergius responded, weeping. "*Mea maxima culpa.*"

Joan reasoned and scolded and cajoled, to no avail. Sergius's health deteriorated rapidly. Joan did everything she could for him, but it was no use. Sergius had set his mind on death.

Nevertheless, the dying took some time. Long after reason had departed and he had lapsed into unconsciousness, Sergius lingered, his body reluctant to relinquish the final spark of life. On a dark and sunless morning he finally died, his spirit slipping away so quietly that at first no one noticed the passing.

Joan genuinely mourned him. He had not been as good a man or a Pope as he might have been. But she had known, better than anyone else, what demons he had faced, had known how hard he had fought to free himself from them. That he had lost the fight in the end made the struggle no less honorable.

He was buried in the damaged basilica beside his predecessors, with a minimum of ceremony that bordered on the scandalous. The required days of mourning were barely observed, for the Romans had already turned their minds impatiently toward the future—and the election of a new Pope.

ANASTASIUS stepped out of the blustering January winds into the welcoming warmth of his family's ancestral palace. It was the grandest residence in all of Rome, save of course the Patriarchium, and Anastasius was justly proud of it. The vaulted ceiling of the reception hall rose over two stories and was constructed of pure white marble from Ravenna. Its walls were painted with brightly colored frescoes of scenes from the lives of the family ancestors. One depicted a consul making a speech before the Senate; another a general seated on a black charger, rallying the troops; still another a cardinal receiving the pallium from

Pope Hadrian. A panel of the front wall had been left blank in anticipation of the long-awaited day when the family would finally achieve
its greatest honor: the coronation of one of its sons as Pope.

Usually the hall was the scene of bustling activity. Today, but for
the presence of the family steward, it stood empty. Scorning to acknowledge the steward's effusive greeting—for Anastasius never
wasted time on underlings—he went directly to his father's room. Arsenius would normally have been in the great hall at this hour, engaged with the city's notables in the devious and gratifying politics of
power. But last month he had been stricken by a wasting fever that
had drained his formidable energies, confining him to his room.

"My son." Arsenius rose from his couch at Anastasius's entrance.
He looked gray and frail. Anastasius felt a curious, exhilarating surge
of strength, his own youth and energy somehow enhanced by contrast with his father's diminishing powers.

"Father." Anastasius went to him with arms stretched wide, and
they embraced warmly.

"What news?" Arsenius asked.

"The election is set for tomorrow."

"God be praised!" Arsenius exclaimed. It was just an expression.
Though he held the exalted title of Bishop of Orte, Arsenius had not
taken priest's orders and was not a religious man. His appointment to
the bishopric had been a politic acknowledgment of the enormous
power he wielded in the city. "The day cannot come too soon when a
son of mine will sit upon the Throne of St. Peter."

"That outcome may no longer be as certain as we once thought,
Father."

"What do you mean?" Arsenius asked sharply.

"Lothar's support of my candidacy may not be enough. His failure to defend Rome against the Saracens has turned many against
him. The people question why they should pay homage to an Emperor who does not protect us. There's a growing sentiment that
Rome should assert her independence from the Frankish throne."

Arsenius considered this carefully. Then he said, "You must denounce Lothar."

Anastasius was aghast. His father's mind, always so sharp and
discerning, was obviously slipping.

"If I did that," he responded, "I'd lose the support of the imperial
party, upon which our hopes depend."

"No. You will go to them and explain that you are acting strictly out of political necessity. Reassure them that no matter what you may be compelled to say, you are indeed the Emperor's man, and will prove it after your election with the award of valuable benefices and preferments."

"Lothar will be furious."

"By that time, it won't matter. We'll move directly to the ceremony of consecration after the election, without waiting for the imperial jussio. Under these circumstances no one will protest, for Rome obviously cannot remain leaderless one day longer than necessary under the continuing threat of the Saracens. By the time Lothar receives word of what has transpired, you'll be Lord Pope, Bishop of Rome—and there'll be nothing the Emperor can do to change it."

Anastasius shook his head admiringly. His father had taken measure of the situation at once. The old fox might be graying, but he had not lost any of his subtlety.

Arsenius held out a long iron key. "Go to the vaults and take what gold you need to win their minds to you. Damn!" he swore. "But for this God-cursed fever, I'd do it myself."

The key lay cool and hard in Anastasius's hand, imparting a gratifying sense of power. "Rest yourself, Father. I will take care of it."

Arsenius caught him by the sleeve. "Be careful, my son. It's a dangerous game you're playing. You have not forgotten what happened to your uncle Theodorus?"

Forgotten! The murder of his uncle in the Lateran Palace had been the defining moment of Anastasius's childhood. The look on Theodorus's face as the papal guards gouged out his eyes would haunt Anastasius till the day he died.

"I'll be careful, Father," Anastasius said. "Leave everything to me."

"Precisely," replied Arsenius, "what I intend."

AD TE, *Domine, levavi animam meam* . . . Joan prayed, kneeling on the cold stone of the Patriarchium chapel. But no matter how hard she prayed, she could not rise into the light of grace; the strong pull of a mortal attachment kept her rooted here below.

She loved Gerold. There was no longer any point in trying to evade or deny that simple truth. When she had seen him riding toward the city at the head of the Beneventan troops, her whole being had rushed toward him with a powerful conviction.

She was thirty-three years old. Yet she had no one to whom she was intimately connected. The practical realities of her disguise had not permitted anyone to get too close. She had been living a life of deceit, denying the truth of who she was.

Was this why God withheld His blessed grace? Did He want her to abandon her disguise and live the woman's life to which she had been born?

Sergius's death had freed her from any obligation to remain in Rome. The next Pope would be Anastasius, and there would be no place for Joan in his administration.

She had fought her feelings for Gerold for so long. What a blessed relief it would be just to let go, to follow the dictates of her heart and not her head.

What would happen when she and Gerold met again? She smiled inwardly, imagining the joy of that moment.

Anything was possible now. Anything might happen.

BY NOON on the appointed day of the election, a great crowd had gathered in the large open area to the southwest of the Lateran. According to ancient custom, formally affirmed in the constitution of 824, all Romans, lay and clergy, participated in the election of a new Pope.

Joan stood on tiptoe, straining to see over the tossing sea of heads and arms. Where was Gerold? Rumor had it that he had returned from his monthlong campaign against the Saracens. If so, he should be here. She was gripped with a sudden fear—had he gone back to Benevento without seeing her again?

The crowd parted respectfully as Eustathius, the archpriest, Desiderius, the archdeacon, and Paschal, the primicerius, came into the marketplace: the triumvirate of officials who by tradition ruled the city *sede vacante,* meaning in the interregnum between the death of one Pope and the election of another.

Eustathius led the people in a short prayer. "Heavenly Father, guide us in what we do here today, that we may act with prudence and honor, that hatred shall not destroy reason, and love shall not interfere with truth. In the Name of the holy and indivisible Trinity of the Father, Son, and Holy Spirit. Amen."

Paschal spoke next. "The Lord Pope Sergius having gone to God, it falls to us to elect his successor. Any Romans here assembled may speak and voice what sentiments God has inspired in them, that the general will may thereby be determined."

"My Lord Primicerius." Tassilo, the leader of the imperial faction and one of Lothar's agents, spoke up immediately. "One name commends itself above all others. I speak of Anastasius, Bishop of Castellum, son of the illustrious Arsenius. All the qualities of this man's nature commend him for the throne—his noble birth, his extraordinary scholarship, his indisputed piety. In Anastasius we will have a defender not only of our Christian faith but of our private interests as well."

"Of *your* interests, you mean!" a voice called mockingly from the crowd.

"Not at all," Tassilo retorted. "Anastasius's generosity and large-heartedness will make him a true father to you all."

"He's the Emperor's man!" the heckler cried again. "We want no tool of the Frankish throne for our Lord Pope!"

"That's right! That's right!" Several voices rose in vigorous agreement.

Anastasius ascended the platform. He raised his arms in a dramatic gesture, quieting the crowd. "My fellow Romans, you judge me wrongly. The pride of my noble Roman ancestors runs as strongly in my veins as in yours. I bend my knee before no Frankish overlord!"

"Hear, hear!" his supporters cheered enthusiastically.

"Where was Lothar when the infidel was at our gates?" Anastasius continued. "In failing to answer our need, he forfeited the right to call himself 'Protector of the Lands of St. Peter!' As Lothar's rank is exalted, I owe him honor; as he is a fellow Christian, I owe him courtesy, but my fealty is first and always to Mother Rome!"

He had spoken well. His supporters cheered again, and this time they were joined by others in the crowd. The tide of opinion was shifting toward Anastasius.

"It's a lie!" Joan cried. All around faces turned toward her in startled surprise.

"Who speaks?" Paschal peered into the crowd. "Let the accuser come forward."

Joan hesitated. She had spoken without thinking, sparked to anger by Anastasius's hypocrisy. But there was no backing out now. Boldly she mounted the platform.

"Why, it's John Anglicus!" someone said. A murmur of recognition swept the crowd; everyone knew or had heard of Joan's brave stand at the walls during the Saracen attack.

Anastasius blocked her way. "You have no right to address this assembly," he said. "You're not a Roman citizen."

"Let him speak!" a voice called out. Others took up the cry until at last Anastasius was forced to stand aside.

Paschal said, "Speak your accusation openly, John Anglicus."

Squaring her shoulders, Joan said, "Bishop Anastasius made compact with the Emperor. I overheard him promise to lead the Romans back to the Frankish throne."

"False priest!" "Liar!" The members of the imperial party began shouting in an attempt to drown her out.

Raising her voice over them, she described how she had overheard Lothar ask for Anastasius's help in getting the people to take the oath of loyalty, and how Anastasius had agreed in return for Lothar's support.

"This is a grave accusation," Paschal said. "What say you to it, Anastasius?"

"Before God the priest is lying," Anastasius said. "Surely my countrymen will not believe the word of a foreigner over that of a fellow Roman!"

"You *were* the first to support the oath taking!" someone called out.

"What of it?" countered another. "That proves nothing!"

A good deal of bickering followed. The debate grew heated, the mood of the crowd shifting first one way, then another as speaker after speaker rose to support or condemn Anastasius.

"My lord Primicerius!" Arighis, who until then had not spoken, came forward.

"Vicedominus." Paschal acknowledged Arighis respectfully, though with some surprise. Devoted and loyal servant to the papal throne that he was, Arighis had never meddled in politics. "Have you aught to add to this debate?"

"I do." Arighis turned to address the crowd. "Citizens of Rome, we are not free from danger. When spring comes, the Saracens may attempt another assault upon the city. Against this threat we must stand united. There can be no division among us. Whomever we choose for our Lord Pope, it must be one upon whom all can agree."

A murmur of assent swept through the crowd.

"Is there such a man?" Paschal asked.

"There is," Arighis replied. "A man of vision and strength, as well as learning and piety: Leo, Cardinal Priest of the Church of the Sancti Quattro Coronati!"

The suggestion was met with profound silence. So intent had they all been on debating the merits of Anastasius's candidacy, they had not stopped to consider anyone else.

"Leo's bloodlines are as noble as Anastasius's," Arighis went on. "His father is a respected member of the Senate. He has performed his duties as cardinal priest with distinction." Arighis saved his most telling point for last: "Can any of us forget how he stood bravely at the walls during the Saracen attack, rallying our spirits? He is a lion of God, another St. Lawrence, a man who can, who *will* protect us from the infidel!"

The exigency of the moment had spurred Arighis into uncharacteristic eloquence. Responding to the depth of his feeling, many in the crowd broke into a spontaneous cheer.

Sensing opportunity, the members of the papal faction took up the cry. "Leo! Leo!" they shouted. "We will have Leo for our lord!"

Anastasius's supporters mounted a countereffort on behalf of his candidacy. But the sentiment of the crowd had clearly changed. When it became apparent to the imperial faction that they could not carry the day, they swung their support to Leo. With one voice, Leo was proclaimed Lord and Pope.

Borne forward triumphantly on the shoulders of his countrymen, Leo ascended the platform. He was a short but well-formed man still in the prime of his years, his strong Roman features set off by a thick growth of curly brown hair and an expression that suggested intelligence and humor. With a sense of solemn occasion, Paschal prostrated himself before him and kissed his feet. Eustathius and Desiderius immediately followed suit.

All eyes turned expectantly toward Anastasius. For a fraction of a second he hesitated. Then he forced his knees to bend. Stretching himself full length upon the ground, he kissed the Pope-elect's feet.

"Rise, noble Anastasius." Leo offered him his hand, helping him to his feet. "From this day forth, you are Cardinal Priest of St. Marcellus." It was a generous gesture; St. Marcellus was among the greatest of Rome's churches. Leo had just presented Anastasius with one of the most prestigious sinecures in Rome.

The crowd cheered its approval.

Anastasius forced his lips into a smile as the bitter taste of defeat settled like dry ashes in his mouth.

"*MAGNUS Dominus et laudibilis nimis.*" The notes of the introit filtered through the window of the small room where Joan kept her medicaments. Because St. Peter's lay in ruins, the ceremony of consecration was being held in the Lateran Basilica.

Joan should have been in church with the rest of the clergy, witnessing the joyous coronation of a new Pope. But there was much to do here, hanging the new-picked herbs to dry, refilling jars and bottles with their appropriate medicines, setting things in order. When she was done, she scanned the shelves with their neatly stacked rows of potions, herbs, and simples—tangible testimony to all she had learned of the healing art. With a twinge of regret, she realized she would miss this little workshop.

"I thought I might find you here." Gerold's voice sounded behind her. Joan's heart gave a sudden leap of joy. She turned toward him, and their eyes met.

"*Tu,*" Gerold said softly.

"*Tu.*"

They beamed at each other with the warmth of reestablished intimacy.

"Strange," he said, "I almost forgot."

"Forgot?"

"Each time I see you I . . . discover you all over again."

She went to him, and they held each other tenderly, gently.

"The things I said the last time we were together . . . ," she murmured. "I didn't mean—"

Gerold put a finger to her lips. "Let me speak first. What happened was my fault. I was wrong to ask you to leave; I see that now. I didn't understand what you have accomplished here . . . what you have become. You were right, Joan—nothing I can offer you could possibly compare."

Except love, Joan thought. But she didn't say it. She said simply, "I don't want to lose you again."

"You won't," Gerold said. "I'm not returning to Benevento. Leo has asked me to remain in Rome—as superista."

Superista! It was an extraordinary honor, the highest military position in Rome: commander in chief of the papal militia.

"There's work to do here—important work. The treasure the Saracens plundered from St. Peter's will only encourage them to try again."

"You think they will come back?"

"Yes." To any other woman Gerold would have lied reassuringly. But Joan was not like any other woman. "Leo is going to need our help, Joan—yours and mine."

"Mine? I don't see what I can do."

Gerold said slowly, "You mean no one has told you?"

"Told me what?"

"That you are to be nomenclator."

"*What?*" She could not have heard aright. The nomenclator was one of the seven optimates, or highest officials, of Rome—the minister of charity, protector of wards, widows, and orphans.

"But . . . I'm a foreigner!"

"That doesn't matter to Leo. He's not a man to be bound by senseless tradition."

She was being offered the opportunity of a lifetime. But accepting it would also mean the end of any hope of a life with Gerold. Torn by opposing desires, Joan did not trust herself to speak.

Misinterpreting her silence, Gerold said, "Don't worry, Joan. I'll not trouble you again with proposals of marriage. I know now we can never be together in that way. But it will be good to work together again, as we once used to. We were always a good team, weren't we?"

Joan's mind was whirling; everything was coming out so differently from the way she had imagined. Her voice, when she answered, was a whisper. "Yes. We were."

"*Sanctus, Sanctus, Sanctus.*" The words of the sacred hymn reached their ears through the open window. The ceremony of consecration had concluded; the Canon of the Mass was about to begin.

"Come." Gerold held out his hand. "Let us go together to greet our new Lord Pope."

⨝ 25 ⨝

THE new Pontiff took up his duties with a youthful vigor that caught everyone by surprise. Overnight, it seemed, the Patriarchium was transformed from a dusty monastic palace into a bustling hive. Notaries and secretaries hurried down the halls, arms filled with rolls of parchment plans, statutes, cartularies, and benefices.

The first order of business was to fortify the city's defenses. At Leo's behest, Gerold undertook a thorough circuit of the walls, making careful note of every point of weakness. Following his suggestions, plans were drawn up and the work of repairing the walls and gates of the city began. Three of the gates and fifteen of the wall towers were completely rebuilt. Two new towers were constructed on opposite banks of the Tiber where the river entered the city at the gate of Portus. Chains of reinforced iron were strategically connected to each opposing tower; when the chains were stretched across the river, they formed an impassable barrier to ships. The Saracens would not be able to gain entry to the city by *that* means at least.

There still remained the difficult question of how to protect St. Peter's. To consider the problem, Leo convened a meeting of the high clergy and the optimates, including Gerold and Joan.

Several suggestions were put forth: posting a permanent garrison of militia around the basilica, enclosing its open portico, fortifying the doors and windows with bars of iron.

Leo listened without enthusiasm. "Such measures will only serve to delay a forced entry, not prevent it."

"With respect, Holiness," Anastasius said, "delay *is* our best defense. If we can hold the barbarians back until the Emperor's troops arrive—"

"*If* they arrive . . . ," Gerold interrupted dryly.

"You must trust in God, Superista," Anastasius rebuked him.

"Trust in Lothar, you mean," Gerold said. "And I do not."

"Pardon me, Superista," Anastasius said with exaggerated politeness, "for pointing out the obvious, but there is really nothing else we *can* do at the moment, since the basilica lies outside the city walls."

Joan said, "We can bring it inside."

Anastasius's dark brows arched sardonically. "What do you propose, John—moving the entire building stone by stone?"

"No," Joan replied. "I propose extending the city walls around St. Peter's."

"A new wall!" Leo's interest was sparked.

"Wholly impractical!" scoffed Anastasius. "So great a project has not been undertaken since the days of the ancients."

"Time, then," Leo said, "for another."

"We haven't the funds!" Gratius, the arcarius, or papal treasurer, protested. "We could bankrupt the entire treasury, and the work still wouldn't be half done!"

Leo considered this. "We will raise new taxes. After all, it is only fitting that the new wall, which will serve for the protection of all, should be completed with the help of all."

Gerold's mind was already racing ahead. "We could begin construction here"—he pointed to a map of the city—"by the Castel Sant'Angelo. Run the wall sideward up the Vatican Hill"—he traced an imaginary line with his finger—"circle it round St. Peter's, and bring it down in a straight line to the Tiber."

The horseshoe-shaped line Gerold had drawn enclosed not only St. Peter's and the monasteries and *diaconae* surrounding it but also the entire Borgo, in which were located the teeming settlements of the Saxons, Frisians, Franks, and Lombards.

"It's like a city of its own!" Leo exclaimed.

"Civitas Leonina," Joan said, "the Leonine City."

Anastasius and the others looked on with chagrin as Leo, Gerold, and Joan beamed in happy conspiracy.

AFTER weeks of consultation with the master builders of the city, the design for the wall was completed. It was an ambitious project. Formed of layers of tufa and tiles, the wall would stand a full forty feet high and twelve feet wide and be defended by no fewer than forty-four towers—a barrier that could withstand even the most determined siege.

In response to Leo's call, workers poured into the city from every town and colony of the papal campagna. They crowded into the hot and overcrowded tenements of the Borgo, straining the city's resources to the breaking point. Loyal and eager though they were, they were untrained, undisciplined workers, and their efforts proved difficult to organize. They showed up each day uncertain what to do, for there were not enough skilled builders to supervise their efforts. On the ides of May, an entire section of wall unexpectedly collapsed, killing several of the workers.

The clergy, led by the cardinal priests of the city, pleaded with Leo to abandon the project. The collapse of the wall was a clear indication of God's disfavor, they argued. The whole idea was folly; so tall a structure would never stand, and even if it did, it would never be completed in time to defend against the Saracens. Far better to direct the people's energies toward solemn prayer and fasting to turn aside the wrath of God.

"We will pray as if all depended on God, and work as if all depended on ourselves," Leo replied sturdily. Every day he rode out to check on the progress of the building and to urge the workers on. Nothing could deter him from his determination to see the wall completed.

Joan admired Leo's stubborn defiance of the skeptics. Utterly different from Sergius in character and temperament, Leo was a true spiritual leader, a man of drive and energy and enormous strength of will. But Joan's admiration for him was not shared by everyone. Sentiment in the city was divided between those who approved of the wall and those who opposed it. It soon became apparent that Leo's continued ability to govern was going to depend very much on the successful completion of the wall.

ANASTASIUS was well aware of the situation and the opportunity it presented. Leo's obsession with the wall left him dangerously vulnerable. If the project proved a failure, the resulting popular disapproval might provide Anastasius with just the opportunity he needed. His supporters in the imperial party could march to the Lateran, remove the discredited Pope from office, and install their candidate in his place.

Once he was Pope, Anastasius would protect the holy basilica of St. Peter by renewing and strengthening Rome's ties to the Frankish throne. Lothar's armies would prove a far better defense against the infidel than Leo's impractical wall.

But, Anastasius reminded himself, he must tread cautiously. Best not to take an open stand against Leo, not while people were still waiting to see the end result of the Pontiff's daring enterprise.

The wisest course was to support Leo publicly while doing all he could to bedevil the building project. To this end, Anastasius had already managed to arrange for the collapse of a section of wall. It had not been difficult; a few of his most trusted men had stolen out in the night and undermined the foundation with a bit of surreptitious digging. But the collapse had proved to be only a minor setback. Clearly something more was needed—a disaster of sufficient proportion to put an end to the whole ridiculous project once and for all.

Anastasius's mind twisted this way and that, seeking a way to strike. Again and again he came up without an idea. He fought a rising frustration. If only he could reach down with a giant hand, pluck the entire structure off the ground, and cast it into the flames of Hell with one great, irrefutable stroke.

The flames of Hell . . .

Anastasius sat bolt upright, energized by the sudden appearance of an idea.

JOAN woke to the new day slowly. For a moment she lay confused, staring at the unfamiliar configuration of wooden beams on the ceiling. Then she remembered: this was not the dormitory, but her own private quarters—one of the privileges of her exalted position as nomenclator. Gerold had also been awarded private quarters in the Patriarchium but had not slept there for several weeks, choosing instead to stay at the Schola Francorum in the Borgo, to be nearer the ongoing work on the wall.

Joan had seen him from a distance, riding around the construction site encouraging the workers or bending over a table discussing plans with one of the master builders. They had no opportunity to exchange anything more than a passing glimpse. Yet her heart rose excitedly each time she saw him. *Truly,* she thought, *this woman's body of mine is a traitor.*

With a deliberate effort, she fixed her attention on the day's work and the duties that awaited her.

The light of dawn was already coming through the window. With a start of surprise, she realized she must have overslept. If she didn't hurry, she would be late to her meeting with the head of St. Michael's hospice.

As she swung out of bed, she became aware that the light coming into her room was not the dawn. It could not be the dawn, for the window faced west.

She ran to the window. Behind the dark silhouette of the Palatine Hill, on the far side of the city, ribbons of red and orange light streamed into the moonless sky.

Flames. And they were coming from the Borgo.

Without pausing to slip into her shoes, Joan ran barefoot through the halls. "Fire!" she shouted. "Fire! Fire!"

Doors were thrown open as people spilled excitedly into the hall. Arighis came toward her, rubbing the sleep from his eyes.

"What's all this?" he demanded sternly.

"The Borgo is on fire!"

"Deo, juva nos!" Arighis made the sign of the cross. "I must wake His Holiness." He hurried off toward the papal bedroom.

Joan ran down the stairs and out the door. It was harder to see from here, for the numerous oratories, monasteries, and clergy houses surrounding the Patriarchium obscured the view, but she could tell the fire had spread, for the entire night sky was now illuminated with lurid brilliance.

Others were following Joan out to the portico. They fell to their knees, weeping and calling upon God and St. Peter. Then Leo appeared, bareheaded and in a simple tunic.

"Fetch the guard," he ordered a chamberlain. "Rouse the stableboys. Have them make ready every available horse and cart." The boy ran off to carry out his orders.

The horses were led up, restive and irritable at having been dragged from the comfort of their stables in the middle of the night. Leo mounted the foremost, a bay.

Arighis was aghast. "You do not mean to go yourself?"

"I do," Leo replied, taking up the reins.

"Holiness, I must object! It's far too dangerous! Surely it would be more fitting for you to remain here and lead a mass for deliverance!"

"I can pray just as well outside the walls of a church as within," Leo replied. "Stand aside, Arighis."

Reluctantly, Arighis complied. Leo spurred the bay and took off down the street. Joan and several dozen guards mounted and followed close behind.

Arighis frowned after them. He wasn't much of a rider, but his place was at the Pope's side. If Leo was bent upon this foolish course, then it was Arighis's duty to accompany him. He mounted awkwardly and set off after them.

They rode at a gallop, their torches reflecting wildly off the walls of the houses, their shadows chasing one another down the dark streets like demented ghosts. As they drew near the Borgo, the acrid smell of smoke rose to their nostrils, and they heard a great roar like the bellowing of a thousand wild beasts. Rounding a corner, they saw the fire straight ahead.

It was a scene out of Hell. The entire block was aflame, shrouded in a solid sheet of fire. Through a shimmering red haze, the wooden buildings writhed in the grip of the flames that consumed them. Silhouetted sharply against the fire, the figures of men capered about like the tortured souls of the damned.

The horses whinnied and backed away, tossing their heads. A priest came running toward them through the lowering smoke, his face smeared with sweat and soot.

"Holiness! Praise God you are come!" By his accent and manner of dress, Joan knew him for a Frank.

"Is it as bad as it looks?" Leo asked tersely.

"As bad, and worse," the priest replied. "The Hadrianium is destroyed, and the hospice of St. Peregrinus. The foreign settlements are gone as well—the Schola Saxonum is burned to the ground, along with its church. The houses of the Schola Francorum are in flames. I barely got out with my life."

"Did you see Gerold?" Joan asked urgently.

"The superista?" The priest shook his head. "He slept on one of the upper floors with the masons. I doubt if any of them got out; the smoke and fire spread too quickly."

"What about the survivors?" Leo asked. "Where are they?"

"Most have taken refuge in St. Peter's. But the fire is everywhere. If it isn't stopped, the basilica itself may be in jeopardy!"

Leo held out his hand. "Come with us; that's where we're headed now." The priest leapt up behind him on the bay, and they all rode off in the direction of St. Peter's.

Joan did not follow. She had a different thought in mind: to get to Gerold.

The line of fire rose solid and unbroken before her. No way to get through there. She circled around until she came to a line of blackened, ruined streets through which the fire had already passed, and turned down one that led in the direction of the Schola Francorum.

Scattered individual fires still burned on either side, and the smoke grew thicker. Fear tightened her throat, but she forced herself to go on. Her roan shied and fought, unwilling to advance; she shouted and kicked him, and he leapt forward skittishly. She passed through a landscape of horror—shriveled stumps of trees, hollowed skeletons of houses, charred and blackened bodies of those trapped in the act of fleeing. Joan's heart twisted within her; surely nothing living could have survived this holocaust.

Suddenly, improbably, the walls of a building rose before her. The Schola Francorum! The church and the buildings nearest it had been reduced to ashes, but wondrously, miraculously, the main residence still stood.

Her heart beat with renewed hope: perhaps Gerold *had* escaped! Or perhaps he was still inside, injured, needing help.

The roan stopped stiff, refusing to go farther. She kicked him again; this time he reared defiantly, tossing her to the ground. Then he took off at a wild gallop.

She lay stunned, the wind knocked out of her. Beside her lay a human corpse, shiny and black as melted obsidian, its back arched in the death agony. Gagging, she rose and ran toward the schola. She had to find Gerold; nothing else mattered.

Great burning pieces of ash were everywhere, on the ground, on her clothes, in her hair, suspended around her in a heavy, choking cloud. Hot embers scorched her bare feet; too late, she regretted not having put on her shoes.

The door to the schola came into view. Another few yards and she would be there. "Gerold!" she shouted. "Where are you?"

Wild and ungovernable as the wind that whipped it, the fire shifted direction, depositing a scatter of burning embers on the shingled roof, already dry as tinder from the fire's first passage. The embers glowed darkly and then caught; moments later, the whole building burst into flame.

Joan felt the hair on her scalp lift and fall in a violent rush of scorching air. The fire reached toward her with scalding tongues.

"Gerold!" she screamed again, driven back by the advancing flames.

✣

GEROLD had stayed up late into the night, poring over plans for the wall. When at last he snuffed out his candle, he was so exhausted he fell immediately into a deep and dreamless sleep.

He woke to the smell of smoke. *A lamp must be foundering,* he thought, and stood to put it out. The first breath he drew seared his lungs with a pain that drove him to his knees gasping for air. *Fire. But where is it coming from?* The thick smoke made it impossible to see more than a few feet in either direction.

The terrified cries of children sounded nearby. Gerold crawled in their direction. Frightened faces swam toward him in the darkness— two children, a boy and a girl, no more than four or five years old. They ran to him and clung, wailing piteously.

"It's all right." He pretended a confidence he did not feel. "We'll soon be out of here. Have you ever played horse-and-rider?"

The children nodded, wide-eyed.

"Good." He swung the girl onto his back, then the boy. "Hold on now. We're going to ride out."

He moved awkwardly with the added weight of the children on his back. The smoke had become even thicker; the children gasped and choked. Gerold fought a rising fear. Many victims of a fire died with no mark upon them, the breath stopped in their throats by smothering smoke.

Suddenly he was aware that he had lost his bearings. His eyes searched the darkness but could not make out the door in the ever-thickening smoke.

"Gerold!" A voice called through the choking gloom.

Bending low to get the best of the air, he lurched blindly toward the sound.

BEFORE the walls of St. Peter's, a pitched battle was being waged against the advancing fire. A crowd had gathered to defend the threatened basilica—black-robed monks from the neighboring monastery of St. John and their cowled counterparts from the Greek monastery of St. Cyril; deacons, priests, and altarboys; prostitutes and beggars; men, women, and children from all the foreign scholae of the

Borgo—Saxons, Lombards, Englishmen, Frisians, and Franks. Lacking any central coordination, the efforts of these disparate groups were largely ineffectual. They were making a chaotic attempt to locate vessels and jars and fetch back water from nearby wells and cisterns. A single well was surrounded with a great crowd of people while another stood entirely deserted. Shouting in a confusing variety of tongues, people pushed and shoved to get their vessels filled; jars collided and broke, spilling precious water on the ground. In the course of the struggle, the dipping beam of a well was broken; the only way to retrieve its water was to climb down the well shaft and pass the bucket up—a process so time consuming it was quickly abandoned.

"To the river! To the river!" people shouted, heading downhill to the Tiber. In the fear and confusion, some took off empty-handed, realizing only when they reached the riverbank that they had nothing to carry water in. Others brought enormous jars that, when filled with water, proved too heavy for their strength; halfway up the hill, they dropped them, weeping with grief and frustration.

In the midst of this chaos, Leo stood before the doors of St. Peter, as solid and immovable as the stones of the great basilica itself. People took heart from his presence. As long as their Lord Pope was here, all was not lost; there was still hope. So they kept battling the flames that moved forward inexorably as a tide, driving the line of sweating, straining firefighters relentlessly backwards.

To the right of the basilica, the library of the monastery of St. Martin was aflame; scraps of flaming parchment blew out the open windows and, borne by the wind, landed on the roof of St. Peter's.

Arighis tugged at Leo's sleeve. "You must leave now, Holiness, while there's still time."

Ignoring him, Leo continued praying.

I'll call the guards, Arighis thought desperately. *I'll have them carry him off by force.* As vicedominus he had the authority to do so. He hovered in tortured indecision. Could he bring himself to defy the Apostolic One, even to save him?

He spied the danger coming before anyone else. A great piece of silken altar cloth blew out through the burning walls of the monastery in a curling rope of fire. The wind caught it, straightening it into a blazing arrow headed straight for Leo.

Arighis hurled himself at Leo and pushed him out of the way. A moment later, the altar cloth slapped Arighis full in the face, searing his eyes, wrapping itself around his head and body in a white-hot caress. In an instant, his clothes and hair were on fire.

Blind and deafened by the flames, he ran leaping down the basilica steps until his legs gave way and he fell. In the last terrible moments while his body burned but his brain remained sharply aware, Arighis suddenly understood: this was his destiny, this the sacrificial moment toward which his entire life had been directed.

"Christ Jesus!" he screamed as the unspeakable pain pierced through to his heart.

THE cloud of smoke lifted a little, and Gerold saw the open door ahead. Beyond it, Joan's image shimmered in the heated air, her white-gold hair a shining halo in the firelight. With a final effort, Gerold heaved himself and the children upright and lurched through the door.

Joan saw him emerge from the smoky haze and ran toward him. She helped the sobbing children down and held them close to her own body, while her eyes remained fixed on Gerold, who stood swaying, unable to speak or move.

"Thank God," she said simply.

But the message in her eyes spoke so much more.

THEY left the children in the care of a group of nuns and hurried to the basilica, where Gerold saw at once that the firefighters were stationed in the wrong place; they were battling the blaze at close range.

Gerold took command. He ordered the men to fall back a safe distance and create a firebreak by uprooting bushes, twigs, and everything that would burn, then spading over the grass and watering the earth down.

Seeing the sparks showering down upon the basilica, Joan seized a bucket of water from a passing monk and climbed up onto the roof. Others followed her: two, then four, then ten. They formed a human chain, passing full buckets up from below and returning empty buckets to be filled. Pass, pour, pass, fill, pass, pour, pass, fill—they toiled side by side, arms aching with the effort, clothes and faces smeared with grime, open mouths gasping for breath in the smothering air.

On the ground below them, the fire crept closer, flames slicking across grass that blackened in an instant. Gerold and the men labored desperately to increase the area of the firebreak.

On the steps of the basilica, Leo made the sign of the cross, his face turned imploringly to the heavens. "O Lord God," he prayed. "Hear us now as we cry out unto Thee!"

The advancing fire reached the break line. The flames swelled, girding to leap forward over the denuded ground. Gerold and his men attacked with more buckets of water. The flames hesitated, drew back hissing angrily, then began to consume themselves.

The basilica was saved.

Joan felt the wet welcome of tears on her face.

THE first several days after the fire were spent burying the dead—those whose bodies could be found. The intense heat of the fire had reduced many of its victims to charred bones and ashes.

Arighis, as befitted his high position, was laid to rest with solemn ceremony. After a funeral mass in the Lateran, his body was interred in a crypt in a small chapel near the tombs of Popes Gregory and Sergius.

Joan mourned his loss. She and Arighis had not always gotten along, especially in the beginning, but they had come to respect each other. She would miss his quiet efficiency, his uncanny knowledge of every detail of the complicated inner workings of the Patriarchium, even the aloof pride with which he had carried out the duties of his office. It was fitting that he would now rest for all eternity near the Apostolic Ones, whom he had served with such devotion.

After the required days of mourning were observed, the grim accounting of the damage done by the fire began. The Leonine Wall, where the blaze had apparently started, had sustained only minor damage, but some three-quarters of the Borgo had been completely destroyed. The foreign settlements and their churches had been reduced to little more than blackened rubble.

That the Basilica of St. Peter had survived the holocaust was nothing short of a miracle—as it quickly came to be regarded. Pope Leo had stayed the fire, it was said, by making the sign of the cross against the advancing flames. This version of events was eagerly taken up by the Roman people, who were badly in need of reassurance that God had not turned against them.

They found an affirmation of their faith in Leo's miracle, fervently attested to by everyone who had been there. Indeed, the number of witnesses grew with every passing day, until it seemed that all of Rome must have been at St. Peter's that fateful morning.

All criticism of Leo was forgotten. He was a hero, a prophet, a saint, the living embodiment of the spirit of St. Peter. The people rejoiced in him, for surely a Pope who had worked such a miracle would be able to protect them from the Saracen infidels.

The rejoicing was not, however, universal. When word of Leo's miracle reached the Church of St. Marcellus, the doors were immediately closed and barred. All baptisms were postponed, all appointments abruptly canceled; those who inquired were told that no one could be admitted to the presence of Cardinal Priest Anastasius, for he was suddenly indisposed.

JOAN was working day and night, distributing clothing, medicine, and other supplies to the hospices and charitable homes in the city. The hospices were crowded with casualties of the fire, and there were too few physicians to tend them all, so she lent a hand wherever she could. Some burned and blackened bodies were past healing; there was little she could do for them but administer doses of poppy, mandragora, and henbane to ease their death agonies. Others had disfiguring burns that threatened to become corrupted; to these she applied poultices of honey and aloe, known specifics for burns. Still others, whose bodies were untouched by fire, suffered from having breathed in too much smoke. These lingered in torment, fighting for life with every shallow breath.

Shattered by the cumulative effect of so much horror and death, Joan was again afflicted by a crisis of faith. How could a good and benevolent God let such a thing happen? How could He so terribly afflict even children and babies, who were surely not guilty of any sin?

Her heart was troubled as the shadow of her ancient doubt fell upon her once again.

ONE morning she was meeting with Leo to arrange for the papal storehouses to be thrown open to the victims of the fire when Waldipert, the new vicedominus, entered unexpectedly. He was a tall, bony man whose pale skin and blond hair revealed his Lombard ancestry. Joan found it odd to see this stranger in Arighis's robes of office.

"Holiness," Waldipert said with an obeisance, "there are two citizens without who seek immediate audience."

"Have them wait," Leo replied. "I will hear their petition later."

"Pardon, Holiness," Waldipert persisted. "I believe you should hear what they have to say."

Leo raised an eyebrow. Had it been Arighis, Leo would have accepted his word without question, for Arighis's judgment had been known and trusted, but Waldipert was new and untried; unfamiliar as yet with the limitations of his position, he might be clumsily overreaching himself.

Leo hesitated, then decided to give Waldipert the benefit of the doubt. "Very well. Admit them."

Waldipert bowed and left, returning moments later with a priest and a boy. The priest was dark complexioned and squarely built. Joan recognized him as a stalwart of the faith, one of the many who toiled in honorable and impoverished obscurity in the lesser churches of Rome. The boy appeared by his dress to be in one of the minor orders—a lector, or perhaps an acolyte. He was a well-made youth, fifteen or sixteen years old, compact and comely with large, open eyes that must have normally radiated a cheerful good-naturedness, though at the moment they were clouded with grief.

The newcomers prostrated themselves before Leo.

"Rise," Leo said. "Tell us on what business you have come."

The priest spoke first. "I am Paul, Holiness, by God's grace and yours priest of the house of St. Lawrence in Damasco. This boy, Dominic, came to the chapel today requesting auricular confession, which service I was glad to render. What he told me was so shocking that I brought him here to tell it to you."

Leo frowned. "The privacy of such confessions may not be violated."

"Holiness, the boy comes here willingly, for he is in great distress of mind and spirit."

Leo turned to Dominic. "Is this true? Speak honestly, for there is no shame in refusing to repeat the secrets of the confessional."

"I want to tell you, Lord Father," the boy replied tremblingly. "I *must* tell you, for my soul's sake."

"Go on, then, my son."

Dominic's eyes blurred with tears. "I didn't know, Holy Father!" he burst out. "I swear on the relics of all the saints I didn't know what would happen, or I would never have done it!"

"Done what, my son?" Leo asked gently.

"Set the fire." The boy broke into a torrent of violent sobs.

There was a stunned silence, broken only by the sound of Dominic's crying.

"*You* set the fire?" Leo asked quietly.

"I did, and may God forgive me!"

"Why would you do such a thing?"

The boy swallowed his tears, struggling to master himself. "He told me the building of the wall was a great evil, for the money and time being squandered on it would be put to better use repairing churches and relieving the misery of the poor."

"He?" Leo said. "Did someone order you to set the fire?"

The boy nodded.

"*Who?*"

"My Lord Cardinal Anastasius. Lord Father, he must have had the Devil's tongue in him, for he spoke so convincingly that what he said seemed right and good."

There was another long silence. Then Leo said seriously, "Be careful of what you say, my son. You are certain it was Anastasius who commanded you?"

"Yes, Lord Father. It was to be only a small blaze," Dominic said in a strangled voice, "just enough to burn the scaffolding on the wall. God knows it was easy enough—I soaked a few rags in lamp oil and wedged them under a corner of the scaffolding, then set them alight. At first the fire stayed confined to the scaffolding, just as my lord cardinal had said it would. But then the wind came up and took it and—and—" He dropped weakly to his knees. "Oh, God!" he cried in sick despair. "The innocent blood! I'd not do it again, not if a thousand cardinals commanded me!"

The boy cast himself at Leo's feet. "Help me, Lord Father. Help me!" He raised his tormented face. "I cannot live with what I've done. Pronounce me my penance; I will bear any death, no matter how terrible, for my soul would be clean again!"

Joan stood stock-still, transfixed between horror and pity. To the list of Anastasius's crimes must surely be added the evil perversion of this boy's nature. His simple, honest-hearted soul had never been meant to commit such a crime, nor to bear its heavy weight on his conscience.

Leo laid a hand on the boy's head. "There has been death enough already, my son. What benefit to the world would there be in adding yours to the tally? No, Dominic, the penance I impose upon you is not death, but life—a life spent in atonement and penitence. From this day forward, you are banished from Rome. You will take the pilgrim road to Jerusalem, where you may pray before the Holy Sepulchre for divine forgiveness."

The boy raised bewildered eyes. "Is that all?"

"The road to atonement is never easy, my son. You will find the journey hard enough."

That, Joan thought, remembering her own pilgrimage from Frankland to Rome, was truer than young Dominic could possibly understand. He would have to live out his days far from his native land, separated from family and friends, from all that he had ever known. Along the way to Jerusalem he would have to brave a host of dangers—precipitous mountains and treacherous gorges, roads infested with thieves and brigands, starvation and thirst and a thousand other perils.

"Spend your life in unselfish service to your fellow men," Leo went on. "In all things conduct yourself in such a way that the scale of your good deeds will outweigh this one great evil."

Dominic flung himself to the ground and kissed the hem of Leo's robe. Then he rose, pale and resolute. "I am bound by you, Lord Father. I will do all exactly as you have commanded. I swear it by the sacred Body and Blood of Christ our Savior."

Leo made a sign of blessing over him. "Go in peace, my son."

Dominic and the priest left the room.

Leo said gravely, "Cardinal Anastasius comes from a powerful family; we must do everything in strict accordance with the law. I will draw up a writ specifying the charges against him. John, come with me; I may need your help. And, Waldipert—"

"Yes, Holiness?"

Leo nodded approval at him. "Well done."

"YOU'VE done well to bring me this news, Vicedominus," said Arsenius. He was in a private room of his palace with Waldipert, who had just finished reporting the details of the meeting between Pope Leo and the boy Dominic. "Allow me to express my gratitude for your help."

Arsenius unlocked a small bronze chest that stood upon his desk, took out twenty gold solidi, and handed them to Waldipert, who quickly pocketed the coins.

"I am glad to have been of service, my lord Bishop." With the briefest of bows, Waldipert turned and left.

Arsenius took no offense at Waldipert's hasty departure; it was imperative for the vicedominus to get back to the Patriarchium before his absence was noticed.

Arsenius congratulated himself on his foresight in having identified Waldipert as a young man with a future many years ago, when he was only a chamberlain in the papal household. It had been costly, buying the man's loyalty all these years. But now that Waldipert was vicedominus, the investment would pay off handsomely.

Arsenius rang for his servant. "Go to the Church of St. Marcellus and bid my son come at once."

HEARING the news, Anastasius sat down heavily in a chair opposite his father. Silently he cursed himself, humiliated that his father had learned how badly he had bungled things.

"Who would have guessed the boy would talk?" he said defensively. "To betray me, he had to condemn himself."

"It was a mistake to let him live," Arsenius said matter-of-factly. "You should have had his throat slit the moment the deed was done. Well, it's over now. We must look to the future."

"Future?" Anastasius echoed bleakly. "What future?"

"Despair is for the weak, my son, not for such as you and me."

"But what am I to do? Surely the situation is past all righting!"

"You must leave Rome. Now. Tonight."

"Oh, God!" Anastasius buried his face in his hands. His whole world was crumbling around him.

Arsenius said sternly, "Enough! Remember who and what you are."

Anastasius sat up, struggling to master himself.

"You will go to Aachen," Arsenius said, "to the Emperor's court."

Anastasius was bewildered. The sick fear gripping his heart was keeping him from thinking clearly. "But . . . Lothar knows I denounced him at the papal election."

"Yes, and knows as well why you were compelled to do so. He's a man who understands political necessity—how else do you think he managed to wrest the throne from his father and brothers? He's also a man in need of money." Arsenius took a leather pouch from his desk and handed it to Anastasius. "If the imperial feathers are still ruffled, this purse will help smooth them."

Anastasius stared dully at the heavy bag of coins. *Must I really leave Rome?* The idea of living out the remainder of his days among a tribe of barbarian Franks filled him with loathing. *Better, perhaps, to die now and have done with it.*

"Think of it as an opportunity," his father was saying. "A chance to win powerful friends at the imperial court. You'll need them, once you are Pope."

Once I am Pope. The words penetrated the heavy fog of Anastasius's despair. Then he was not being sent away forever.

"I'll look after your interests here, never fear," Arsenius said. "The tide of opinion cannot run in Leo's favor forever. Eventually it will crest, and then subside. When I judge the time to be ripe, I'll send for you."

The cold nausea that had gripped Anastasius began to recede. His father had not given up hope; therefore, neither must he.

"I've arranged for an escort," Arsenius said briskly. "Twelve of my best men. Come, I'll walk with you to the stables."

THE twelve guards were mounted and ready, armed with sword and pike and mace. Anastasius would not want for protection on the dangerous roads. His mount stood nearby, tossing its head impatiently—a strong and spirited beast; Anastasius recognized it as his father's favorite stallion.

"There's two or three hours of daylight yet—enough to give you a good start," Arsenius said. "They'll not come for you today, for they've no way of knowing you suspect anything, and Leo will surely take the precaution of drawing up an official writ for your arrest. It'll be morning before they start looking, and then they'll try St. Marcellus first. By the time they think of coming here, you'll be well away."

Struck with a sudden concern, Anastasius said, "What about you, Father?"

"They've no reason to suspect me. If they try to question me as to your whereabouts, they'll find they have a wolf by the tail."

Father and son embraced.

Can this actually be happening? Anastasius wondered. Things were moving so quickly it was bewildering.

"God go with you, my son," Arsenius said.

"And with you, Father." Anastasius mounted and turned his horse quickly so his father would not see the start of tears to his eyes. Just beyond the gate, he turned back for a last look. The sun was westering, spilling lengthening shadows over the sweet slopes of the

Roman hills, painting with red-gold hues the majestic skeletons of the Forum and the Colosseum.

Rome. Everything he had worked for, all he cared about, lay inside its sacred walls.

His last sight was of his father's face—pained but resolute, and steady and reassuring as the rock of St. Peter.

"*MEMBRUM putridum et insanibile, ferro excommunicationis a corpore Ecclesiae abscidamus . . .*"

In the cool dark of the Lateran Basilica, Joan listened to Leo pronounce the solemn and terrifying words that would sever Anastasius from Holy Mother Church forever. She noted that Leo had chosen the *excommunicatio minor,* the lesser form of excommunication, in which the condemned was enjoined from administering or receiving the sacraments (save for the last rites, from which no living soul could be excluded) but not from all intercourse with his fellow Christians. *Truly,* Joan thought, *Leo has a charitable heart.*

All the clergy of Rome and its patrimonies were gathered to witness the solemn ceremony; even Arsenius was here, for he would not jeopardize his own position as Bishop of Horta with a futile public opposition. Leo suspected, of course, that Arsenius had been complicit in his son's flight from justice. But there was no proof to substantiate such a charge and no other ground for complaint against him, since it was certainly no crime merely to be a man's father.

As the candle representing Anastasius's immortal soul was upended and extinguished in the dirt, Joan felt an unexpected twinge of sadness. *A tragic waste,* she thought. So brilliant a mind as Anastasius's could have been used to do much good, if his heart had not been twisted by obsessive ambition.

26

CONSTRUCTION on the Leonine Wall, as the structure was now universally called, proceeded apace. The fire intended to destroy it had done little actual harm; the wooden scaffolding used by the workers had burned to the ground, and one of the western ramparts had been badly blackened, but that was all. The problems that had plagued the project from the beginning now blessedly ceased. Work continued steadily throughout the winter and the following spring, for the weather remained blessedly mild, marked by long, cool, sunny days with no drop of rain. A constant supply of good-quality stone came in from the quarries, and the workers from the various domains of the papal campagna settled in to the work, laboring side by side in productive unison.

By Pentecost, the topmost row of stone reached a man's height. No one called the project folly now; no one complained of the time and money lavished on it. The Romans felt a growing pride in the work, whose immensity harked back to the ancient days of Empire, when such prodigies of construction were a commonplace, not a rarity. When finished, the wall would be magnificent, monumental, a towering barrier even the Saracens could never scale or breach.

But time ran out. On the calends of July, messengers arrived in the city with terrifying news: a Saracen fleet was gathering at Totarium, a small island off the east coast of Sardinia, in preparation for another attack on Rome.

Unlike Sergius, who had looked to the power of prayer to protect the city, Leo chose a more aggressive course of action. He sent immediately to the great maritime city of Naples, requesting a fleet of armed ships to engage the enemy at sea.

The idea was bold—and chancy. Naples still nominally owed allegiance to Constantinople, though in reality it had been independent for years. Would the Duke of Naples help Rome in her hour of need? Or would he use the opportunity to join forces with the Saracens and strike a blow against the Roman See on behalf of the Eastern Patriarchate? The plan was fraught with danger. But what alternative was there?

FOR ten days the city waited in tense expectation. When at last the Neapolitan fleet arrived at Porto, on the mouth of the Tiber, Leo set forth warily to meet them, accompanied by a large retinue of heavily armed militia under Gerold's command.

The Romans' anxieties were allayed when Caesarius, the commander of the fleet, prostrated himself before Leo and humbly kissed his feet. With a degree of relief he did not reveal, Leo blessed Caesarius, solemnly committing the sacred bodies of the apostles Peter and Paul to his protection.

They had survived the first roll of fortune's dice; on the next one all their futures would depend.

THE next morning the Saracen fleet appeared. The broad-stretched lateen sails spread across the horizon like opened talons. Bleakly Joan counted them—fifty, fifty-three, fifty-seven—still they kept coming—eighty, eighty-five, ninety—were there this many ships in the world?—one hundred, one hundred and ten, one hundred and twenty! *Deo, juva nos!* The Neapolitan vessels numbered only sixty-one; with the six Roman biremes still in serviceable condition, that made a total of sixty-seven. They were outnumbered almost two to one.

Leo stood on the steps of the nearby Church of St. Aurea and led the frightened citizens of Porto in prayer. "Lord, Thou who saved Peter from sinking when walking on the waves, Thou who rescued Paul from the depths of the sea, hear us. Grant power to the arms of Thy believing servants, who fight against the enemies of Thy church, that through their victory Thy holy name may be glorified among all nations."

In the open air, the voices of the people reverberated with a resounding "Amen."

Caesarius shouted orders from the deck of the foremost ship. The Neapolitans hurled themselves against the oars, muscles straining. For a moment the heavy biremes stood motionless in the water. Then, with an enormous groan of creaking timber, the ships began to move. The double banks of oars rose and dipped and rose and dipped, flashing like gems; the wind caught the sails, and the great biremes drove ahead, their ironclad prows cleaving the turquoise water into twin shafts of foam.

The Saracen ships turned to meet them. But before the two opposing fleets could engage, an earsplitting thunderclap signaled the advent of a storm. The sky darkened as black clouds rolled in rapidly from the sea. The heavy-drafted Neapolitan ships were able to make it back to safe harbor. But the Saracen vessels, crafted with low freeboards for speed and maneuverability in battle, were too flimsy to ride out the storm. They pitched and heaved on the rising waves, tossed about like pieces of bark, their iron rams striking their sister ships, breaking them apart.

Several of the ships headed into port, but as soon as they reached land, they were set upon. Fanned by the violent anger that follows terror, the Romans slaughtered the crews without mercy, dragging them from their ships and suspending them from gibbets hastily constructed along the shore. Witnessing their comrades' fate, the other Saracen ships struck out desperately for the open sea, where they were broken apart by giant, roiling waves.

In the moment of unexpected victory, Joan was watching Leo. He stood on the steps of the church, arms upraised, eyes lifted to Heaven in thanksgiving. He looked saintly, beatific, as if touched by a divine presence.

Perhaps he can *work miracles,* she thought. Her knees bent willingly as she bowed down before him.

"Victory! Victory at Ostia!" The news was cried jubilantly through the streets. The Romans spilled forth from their houses, the papal storehouses were thrown open, and wine flowed freely; for three days the city indulged in wild and drunken celebration.

Five hundred Saracens were marched into the city before jeering, hostile crowds. Many were stoned or hacked to death along the route. The survivors, some three hundred in number, were taken in chains to a camp in the Neronian Plain, where they were confined and required to labor on the Leonine Wall.

With the addition of these extra hands, the wall rose more quickly. In three years, it stood complete—a masterpiece of medieval engineering, the most extraordinary construction the city had seen in over four hundred years. The whole of the Vatican territory was enclosed within a structure twelve feet thick and forty feet tall, defended by forty-four massive towers. There were two separate galleries, one above the other; the lower gallery was supported by a series of graceful arcades opening within. Three gates gave entrance: the Posterula Sant'Angeli; the Posterula Saxonum, so named because it opened into the Saxon quarter; and the Posterula San Peregrinus, the principal gate through which future generations of kings and princes would pass to worship at the holy shrine of St. Peter.

Remarkable as the wall was, this was only the beginning of Leo's ambitious plans for the city. Dedicated to "restoring all the places of the saints," Leo embarked upon a great plan of rebuilding. The ring of anvils sounded day and night throughout the city as work went on in one after another of the city's churches. The burned basilica of the Saxons was restored, as well as the Frisian church of San Michele and the Church of the Sancti Quattro Coronati, of which Leo had once been cardinal.

Most important of all, Leo began the restoration of St. Peter's. The burned and blackened portico was completely rebuilt; the doors, stripped of their precious metal by the Saracens, were covered with new, light-diffusing silver plates on which myriad sacred histories were carved with astonishing skill. The great treasure that had been carried off by the Saracens was replaced: the high altar was covered with new plates of silver and gold and decorated with a massive gold crucifix set with pearls, emeralds, and diamonds; above it a silver ciborium weighing over a thousand pounds was mounted upon four great pillars of purest travertine marble, ornamented with gilt lilies. The altar was lit by lamps hung on silver chains, garnished with golden balls, their flickering light illuminating a veritable treasure trove of jeweled chalices, wrought silver lecterns, rich tapestries, and silken hangings. The great basilica gleamed with a splendor that outshone even its former magnificence.

OBSERVING the vast amounts of money pouring forth from the papal treasury, Joan felt troubled. Undeniably Leo had created a shrine of awe-inspiring beauty. But the majority of those who lived within sight of this glittering magnificence spent their days in brutish, degrading poverty. A single one of St. Peter's massive silver plates, melted into coin, would feed and clothe the population of the Campus Martius for a year. Did God's worship really require such sacrifice?

There was only one person in the world with whom Joan dared raise such a question. When she put it to him, Gerold considered soberly before replying. "I have heard it argued," he said finally, "that the beauty of a holy shrine provides the faithful with a different form of nourishment—food for the soul, not the body."

"It's difficult to hear the voice of God over the grumbling of an empty stomach."

Gerold shook his head affectionately. "You haven't changed. Remember the time you asked Odo how he could be certain the Resurrection had taken place, since there were no eyewitnesses?"

"I do." Joan flexed her hand ruefully. "I also remember how he answered me."

"When I saw the wound Odo gave you," Gerold said, "I wanted to strike him—and would have, if I hadn't known it would only make things more difficult for you."

Joan smiled. "You always were my protector."

"And you," he bantered, "always had the soul of a heretic."

They had always been able to talk like this, free from the world's restraints. It was part of the special intimacy that had bound them from the very first.

He looked at her now with a familiar warmth. Joan was keenly aware of him; she felt his nearness like a touch on her naked skin. But by now she was skilled at disguising her feelings.

She pointed to the pile of petitions on the table between them. "I must go hear these petitioners."

"Shouldn't Leo do that?" Gerold asked.

"He's asked me to see to it."

Lately Leo had been delegating more and more of his daily responsibilities to her so he could devote himself to the continuing plans for rebuilding. Joan had become Leo's ambassador to the people; she was so familiar a sight going about her charitable duties in the different regions of the city that she was hailed everywhere as "the little Pope" and greeted with some of the affection reserved for Leo himself.

As she reached for the pile of papers, Gerold's hand brushed hers. She drew her hand back violently, as if from a fire. "I . . . I'd better go," she said awkwardly.

She was immensely relieved, and a little disappointed, when he did not follow her.

BUOYED by the success of the Leonine Wall and the renovation of St. Peter's, Leo's popularity was soaring. *Restaurator Urbis,* he was called, Restorer of the City. He was another Hadrian, the people said, another Aurelius. Everywhere he went, crowds cheered him. Rome rang with his praises.

Everywhere, that is, but in the palace on the Palatine Hill, where Arsenius waited with gathering impatience for the day when he could call Anastasius home.

Things had not gone as expected. There was no way to depose Leo from the throne, as Arsenius had originally hoped, and even less hope that it would be left vacant through the happy accident of death: healthy and vigorous, Leo gave every evidence of living forever.

Now the family fortunes had suffered another blow. The week before, Arsenius's second son, Eleutheris, had died. He had been riding down the Via Recta when a pig darted between his horse's legs; the horse stumbled and Eleutheris fell, receiving a cut on the thigh. At first no one was concerned, for the wound was slight. But misfortune has a way of following upon misfortune. The wound became corrupted. Arsenius called in Ennodius, who bled Eleutheris profusely, but it availed nothing. Within two days his son lay dead. Arsenius immediately ordered a search for the owner of the pig; when he was discovered, Arsenius had his throat slit from ear to ear. But such revenge was cold comfort, for it could not bring back Eleutheris.

Not that there had been much love lost between father and son. Eleutheris was the exact opposite of his brother—soft, lazy, and undisciplined even as a child, he had scorned Arsenius's offer of a church education and chosen instead the more immediate gratifications of a lay existence—women, wine, gambling, and other forms of debauchery.

No, Arsenius mourned Eleutheris not for the man he had been or might have become, given time, but for what he had represented: another branch of the family tree, a branch that might yet have borne promising fruit.

For centuries, theirs had been the first family of Rome. Arsenius could trace his ancestry back in a direct line to Augustus Caesar himself. Yet this illustrious heritage was tarnished by failure, for none of its noble sons had ever achieved Rome's ultimate prize: the Throne of St. Peter. How many lesser men had sat upon that throne, Arsenius thought bitterly, and with what tragic result? Rome, once the wonder of the world, was sunk into ruinous and embarrassing decay. The Byzantines mocked it openly, pointing to the gleaming splendor of their own Constantinople. Who but one of Arsenius's family, Caesar's heirs, could lead the city back to her former greatness?

Now Eleutheris was gone, Anastasius was the last of the line, the only remaining chance the family would ever have to redeem its honor, and Rome's.

And Anastasius was banished to Frankland.

Arsenius felt dark despair close in on him. He shook it off brusquely, like an unwanted cloak. Greatness did not attend upon opportunity; it seized it. Those who would rule had to be willing to pay the price of power, however great.

DURING mass on the day of the Feast of St. John the Baptist, Joan first noticed something wrong with Leo. His hands trembled while receiving the offerings, and he faltered uncharacteristically over the *Nobis quoque peccatoribus.*

When Joan questioned him afterward, he dismissed his symptoms as nothing more than a touch of heat and indigestion.

The next day he was no better, nor the next, nor the next. His head ached constantly, and he complained of burning pains in his hands and feet. Each day he became a little weaker; each day it took more effort for him to rise from bed. Joan grew alarmed. She tried every remedy she knew for wasting diseases. Nothing helped. Leo continued to sink toward death.

THE voices of the choir rose loudly in the *Te Deum,* the final canticle of the Mass. Anastasius kept his face expressionless, trying not to grimace at the noise. He had never grown accustomed to the Frankish chant, whose unfamiliar tones grated upon his ears like the croaking of blackbirds. Remembering the pure, sweet harmonies of the Roman chant, Anastasius felt a sharp stab of homesickness.

Not that his time here in Aachen had been wasted. Following his father's instructions, Anastasius had set out to win the Emperor's support. He began by courting Lothar's friends and intimates, and making himself agreeable to Lothar's wife, Ermengard. He assiduously charmed and flattered the Frankish nobility, impressing them all with his knowledge of Scripture and especially of Greek—a rare accomplishment. Ermengard and her friends interceded with the Emperor, and Anastasius was readmitted to the royal presence. Whatever doubt or resentment Lothar might once have harbored against him was forgotten; once again Anastasius enjoyed the Emperor's trust and support.

I have done everything Father asked, and more. But when will come my reward? There were times, such as now, when Anastasius feared he might be left to languish forever in this cold, barbarian backwater.

Returning to his rooms after mass, he discovered a letter had arrived in his absence. Recognizing the hand as his father's, he took up a knife and eagerly cut the seal. He read the first few lines and cried out exultantly.

The time is now, his father had written. *Come claim your destiny.*

Leo lay on his side in bed, knees drawn up, suffering from sharp pains in his stomach. Joan prepared an emollient potion of egg whites beaten into sweetened milk, to which she added a little fennel as a carminative. She watched him drink it.

"That was good," he said.

She waited to see if he would keep it down. He did, then slept more restfully than he had in weeks. When he awoke hours later, he felt better.

Joan decided to put him on a diet of the potion, restricting all other food and drink.

Waldipert protested: "He's so weak; surely he needs something more substantial to keep his strength up."

Joan replied firmly, "The treatment is helping him. He must take no food other than the potion."

Seeing the determined look in her eyes, Waldipert backed down. "As you say, Nomenclator."

For a week, Leo continued to improve. His pain went away, his color returned, he even seemed to regain some of his old energy. When Joan brought him his evening dose of the healing potion, Leo eyed the milky mixture ruefully.

"How about a meat pasty instead?"

"You're getting your appetite back—a good sign. Best not to rush things, however. I'll look in on you in the morning; if you're still hungry, I'll let you try a bit of simple pottage."

"Tyrant," Leo responded.

She smiled. It was good to have him gibe with her again.

✣

EARLY the next morning, she arrived to find that Leo had suffered a relapse. He lay in bed moaning, too much in pain to reply when she spoke to him.

Quickly Joan prepared another dose of the emollient potion. As she did, her eyes fell upon an empty plate of crumbs on the table beside the bed.

"What's this?" she asked Renatus, Leo's personal chamberlain.

"Why, it's the meat pasty you sent him," the boy replied.

"I sent nothing," Joan said.

Renatus looked confused. "But . . . my lord Vicedominus said you ordered it specially."

Joan looked at Leo doubled over with pain. A horrible suspicion dawned.

"*Run!*" she told Renatus. "Call the superista and the guards. Don't let Waldipert leave the palace."

The boy hesitated only a moment, then ran from the chamber.

With shaking hands, Joan prepared a strong emetic of mustard and elder-root, spooning the mixture through Leo's tightened mouth. In a few moments, the cleansing spasm took him; his whole body heaved convulsively, but he brought up only a thin green bile.

Too late. The poison has left his stomach. Joan saw with distress that it had already begun its deadly work, tightening the muscles of Leo's jaw and throat, strangling him.

Desperately she tried to think of something else to do.

GEROLD ordered a search of every room of the palace. Waldipert was nowhere to be found. Immediately he was declared criminal and fugitive, and an intensive hunt was instituted throughout the city and into the surrounding countryside. But they searched in vain; Waldipert had completely disappeared.

Just as they were about to give up the pursuit, they found him. He was floating in the Tiber, his throat slit from ear to ear, his face fixed in a grimace of surprise.

✣

THE clergy and high officials of Rome were gathered in the papal bedchamber. They stood in a tight knot at the foot of the bed, as if to draw comfort from one another's nearness.

The poppy oil lamps burned low in their silver cressets. With the first of the dawn light, the senior chamberlain came to extinguish them. Joan watched as the old man loosened the cables and lowered the rings with exceeding care so none of the precious substance would be wasted. The simple domestic gesture seemed oddly out of place in the room's charged atmosphere.

Joan had not expected Leo to last the night. Long ago he had stopped responding to voice or touch. For hours his breathing had followed the same inexorable pattern, growing steadily noisier and more stertorous until it reached an alarming crescendo, then abruptly ceased. There was a pause during which no one in the room drew breath; then the terrifying cycle began again.

A flutter of cloth drew Joan's attention. Across the room Eustathius, the archpriest, was weeping, pressing his sleeve across his mouth to muffle the sound.

Leo let out a long, loud, rattling exhalation, then fell quiet. The silence dragged on and on. Joan crossed to the bed. The life was gone from Leo's face. She closed his eyes, then fell to her knees beside the bed.

Eustathius cried out in grief. The bishops and optimates knelt in prayer. Paschal, the primicerius, crossed himself, then left to carry the news to those waiting outside.

Leo, *Pontifex Maximus, Servus Servorum Dei,* Primate of the Bishops of the Church, and Lord Pope of the Apostolic See of Rome, was dead.

Outside the Patriarchium, the wailing began.

LEO was laid to rest in St. Peter's, before the altar of a new oratory dedicated to him. Burials were performed quickly this time of year, for no matter how saintly the soul that had inhabited it, a body did not withstand corruption long in the heat of a Roman July.

Shortly after the funeral, the ruling triumvirate proclaimed that in three days' time there would be a pontifical election. With Lothar to the north, the Saracens to the south, and Lombards and Byzantines between, Rome's situation was too precarious to allow the Throne of St. Peter to remain vacant any longer.

✦

TOO soon, Arsenius thought with chagrin as soon as he heard the news. *The election is too soon. Anastasius cannot arrive before then.* Waldipert, that bungling fool, had ruined things completely. He had been given explicit instructions on how to administer the poison gradually, in small doses; in that way, Leo would have lingered for a month or more—and his death would have aroused no suspicion.

But Waldipert had panicked and administered too large a dose, killing Leo at once. Then he'd had the gall to come cringing to Arsenius, asking for his protection. *Well, he's beyond reach of the law now, though not in the way he intended,* Arsenius thought.

He had ordered men killed before; it was part of the price of power, and only the weak balked at paying it. But he had never had to strike down anyone he knew as well as Waldipert. Distasteful as that had been, it was unavoidable. If Waldipert had been captured and questioned, he would have confessed under torture all he knew. Arsenius had merely done what he had to in order to protect himself and his family. He would destroy anyone who threatened the security of the family, break him as one breaks the flea that has bitten one with one's fingernails.

Nevertheless, Waldipert's death had left him feeling depressed and uneasy. Such violent acts, however necessary, took an inevitable toll.

With an effort of will, Arsenius turned his mind to more pressing matters. His son's absence complicated affairs; his election to the papacy would now be more difficult, but not impossible. The first thing to do was to get Eustathius, the archpriest, to overturn the sentence of excommunication against him. That would take some politic maneuvering.

Lifting a jeweled silver bell from his desk, Arsenius rang for his secretary. There was much to do, and very little time in which to do it.

IN HER workshop in the Patriarchium, Joan stood at her bench, crushing dried hyssop flowers to a fine powder in her mortar. Twist and grind and twist and grind; the familiar motions of hand and wrist were soothing balm to the grief battering her heart.

Leo was dead. It seemed impossible. He had been so vital, so forceful; he had loomed so much larger than life. Had he lived, he might have done much to lift Rome out of the quagmire of ignorance and poverty in which it had languished for centuries; he had the heart for it, and the will. But not the time.

The door opened, and Gerold entered. She met his eyes, feeling his presence as keenly as if he had touched her.

"I've just received word," he said brusquely. "Anastasius has left Aachen."

"You don't think he's coming here?"

"I do. Why else should he leave the Emperor's court so suddenly? He's coming to claim the throne that was denied him six years ago."

"But surely he can't be elected; he's excommunicate."

"Arsenius is trying to prevail upon the archpriest to reverse the sentence of excommunication."

"*Benedicite!*" This was very bad news. After his years of exile in the imperial court, Anastasius was surely more the Emperor's man than ever. If he was elected, Lothar's power would extend itself over Rome and all its territories.

Gerold said, "He will not have forgotten how you spoke against him at Leo's election. It will be dangerous for you to remain in Rome with him as Pope. He's not a man to forgive an injury."

Coming on top of her still-raw emotions over Leo's death, this realization was too much. Joan's eyes brimmed with tears.

"Don't cry, my heart." Gerold's arms were around her, strong and sure and comforting. His lips brushed her temples, her cheek, sparking currents of response. "Surely you've done enough, sacrificed enough. Come away with me, and we'll live as we were always meant to—together, as husband and wife."

She had a dizzying glimpse of his face close to hers, and then he was kissing her.

"Say yes," he said fiercely. "Say yes."

She felt as though she were being pulled below the surface of her conscious mind and carried off by a powerful current of desire. "Yes," she whispered, almost before she knew what she was saying. "Yes."

She had spoken without volition, responding impulsively to the force of his passion. But as soon as the words were out of her mouth, a great calm descended upon her. The decision had been made, and it seemed both right and inevitable.

He bent to kiss her again. Just then the bell rang, summoning everyone to the afternoon meal. A moment later, voices and hurrying footsteps sounded outside the door.

With murmured endearments, they parted quickly, promising to meet again after the papal election.

ON THE day of the election, Joan went to pray in the small English church that had been her own when she first came to Rome.

Burned to the ground during the great fire, the church had been reconstructed with materials stripped from Rome's ancient temples and monuments. As Joan knelt before the high altar, she saw that the marble pedestal supporting it bore the unmistakable symbol of the Magna Mater, ancient goddess of earth, worshiped by heathen tribes in a time beyond memory. Beneath the crude design was inscribed in Latin, "On this marble, incense was offered to the Goddess." Obviously when the great slab of marble had been brought here, no one understood the symbol or its inscription. This was not especially surprising, for many of the Roman clergy were barely literate, unable to decipher the ancient lettering, much less understand its meaning.

The incongruity of the sacred altar and its pagan base seemed to Joan a perfect symbol of herself: a Christian priest, she still dreamed of her mother's heathen gods; a man in the eyes of the world, she was tormented by her secret woman's heart; a seeker of faith, she was torn between her desire to know God and her fear that He might not exist. Mind and heart, faith and doubt, will and desire. Would the painful contradictions of her nature ever be reconciled?

She loved Gerold; about that there was no question. But could she be a wife to him? Never having lived as a woman, could she begin now, so late in life?

"Help me, Lord," Joan prayed, raising her eyes to the silver crucifix atop the altar. "Show me the way. Let me know what I must do. Dear God! Lift me into Thy bright light!"

Her words flew up, but her spirit remained below, weighted down by incertitude.

A door cracked open behind her. She turned from her place before the altar to see a head insert itself in the opening and as quickly withdraw.

"He's in here!" a voice shouted. "I've found him!"

Her heart pounded with sudden fear. Could Anastasius have moved against her so quickly? She rose to her feet.

The doors swung open, and the seven *proceres* entered, proceeded by acolytes carrying the banners of their office. They were followed by the cardinal clergy and then the seven optimates of the city. Not until Joan saw Gerold among them was she sure she was not going to be arrested.

In slow procession the delegation came down the aisle and halted before Joan.

"John Anglicus." Paschal, the primicerius, addressed her in formal tones. "By the will of God and of the Roman people, you have been elected Lord Pope of Rome, Bishop of the Roman See."

Then he prostrated himself before her and kissed her feet.

Joan stared at him disbelievingly. Was this some kind of ill-considered jest? Or a trap to lure her into expressing disloyalty to the new Pope?

She looked at Gerold. His face was taut and grimly serious as he dropped to his knees before her.

THE outcome of the election had taken everyone by surprise. The imperial faction, led by Arsenius, had stood staunchly for Anastasius. The papal faction countered by nominating Hadrian, priest of the Church of St. Mark. He was not the kind of leader who inspired confidence. Plump and short, with a face disfigured by smallpox, he stood with slumped shoulders, as if already burdened by the responsibility that had been placed upon him. He was a pious man, a good priest, but few would choose him to be the spiritual leader of the world.

Evidently Hadrian agreed with the general opinion, for he unexpectedly withdrew his name from nomination, informing those assembled that after much prayer and deep reflection he had decided to decline the great honor they would bestow on him.

This announcement caused a mild uproar among the members of the papal party, who had not been informed of Hadrian's decision in advance. There was a great deal of cheering from the imperialist side. Anastasius's victory now seemed certain.

Then a clamor arose from the rear of the assembly, where the lower ranks of the laity were gathered. "John Anglicus!" they shouted. "John Anglicus!" Paschal, the primicerius, sent guards to quiet them, but they would not be silenced. They knew their rights; the constitution of 824 gave all Romans, lay and clergy, high and low, the right to vote in a papal election.

Arsenius sought to head off this unexpected problem by making an open bid to buy the people's loyalty; his agents circulated swiftly through the crowd, offering bribes of wine, women, and money. But even these strong enticements did not prevail; the people were set against Anastasius, whom their beloved Pope Leo had seen fit to declare excommunicate. Vociferously they clamored for "the little Pope," Leo's friend and helpmate John Anglicus, and they would not be swayed.

Even so they might not have carried the day, for the ruling aristocracy would not have allowed its will to be overturned by a bunch of commoners, constitution or no. But the papal party, seeing in this popular insurgence an unlooked-for opportunity to block Anastasius from the throne, joined their voices to the people's. The deed was done, and Joan was elected.

ANASTASIUS and his party were camped outside Perugia, some ninety miles from Rome, when the courier arrived with the news. Anastasius barely finished reading the message before he let out a cry of pain. Without a word to his bewildered companions, he turned and reentered his tent, tying the flaps to prevent anyone from entering after him.

From inside the tent the men of his escort heard wild and unrestrained sobbing. After a time the sobbing became a kind of animal howling that went on through most of the night.

ROBED in scarlet silk woven with gold and seated on a white palfrey also clothed and bridled in gold, Joan rode in ceremony toward her coronation. From every door and window along the Via Sacra, streamers and banners fluttered in riotous color; the ground was strewn with sweet-smelling myrtle. Throngs of cheering people lined the street, pressing forward to catch a glimpse of the new Lord Pope.

Lost in her own reverie, Joan scarcely heard the noise of the crowd. She was thinking of Matthew, of her old master Aesculapius, of Brother Benjamin. They had all believed in her, encouraged her, but none could have dreamed of such a day as this. She could scarcely believe it herself.

When she had first disguised herself as a man, when she had been accepted into the Fulda brotherhood, God had not raised His hand against her. But would He truly allow a woman to ascend the sacred Throne of St. Peter? The question spun round in her mind.

The papal guards, led by Gerold, rode escort around Joan. Gerold kept his wary gaze fixed on the crowds lining the road. Now and again someone broke through the ranks of guards, and each time Gerold's hand strayed to the sword at his side, ready to defend Joan against attack. There was no occasion to draw his sword, however, for each time the interloper wanted only to kiss the hem of Joan's robe and receive her blessing.

In this slow and interrupted fashion, the long procession wound its way through the streets toward the Lateran. The sun was at midpoint in the sky when they drew up before the papal cathedral. As Joan dismounted, the cardinals, bishops, and deacons fell into place behind her. Slowly she climbed the steps and entered the shimmering interior of the great basilica.

REPLETE with ancient and elaborate ritual, the *ordo coronationis,* or coronation ceremony, took several hours. Two bishops led Joan to the sacristy, where she was solemnly vested in alb, dalmatic, and paenula before she approached the high altar for the singing of the Litany and the lengthy ritual of consecration, or anointing. During the recitation of the *vere dignum,* Desiderius the archdeacon and two of the regionary deacons held over her head an open book of the Gospels. Then came the mass itself; this lasted a good deal longer than usual because of the addition of numerous prayers and formularies befitting the importance of the occasion.

Throughout it all Joan stood solemn and erect, weighted down by the liturgical robes, as stiff with gold as those of any Byzantine prince. Despite the magnificence of her attire, she felt very small and inadequate to the enormous responsibility being laid upon her. She told herself that those who had stood here before her must also have trembled and doubted. And somehow they had carried on.

But they had all been men.

Eustathius, the archpriest, began the final benediction: "Almighty Lord, stretch forth the right hand of Thy blessing upon Thy servant John Anglicus, and pour over him the gift of Thy mercy . . ."

Will God bless me now? Joan wondered. *Or will His just wrath strike me down the moment the papal crown is placed upon my head?*

The Bishop of Ostia came forward bearing the crown on a cushion of white silk. Joan's breath caught in her throat as he raised the crown above her. Then the weight of the gold circlet settled upon her head.

Nothing happened.

"Life to our illustrious Lord John Anglicus, by God decreed our chief Bishop and Universal Pope!" Eustathius cried.

The choir chanted *Laudes* as Joan faced the assembly.

EMERGING onto the steps of the basilica, she was greeted by a thunderous roar of welcome. Thousands of people had been standing for hours in the blistering sun to greet their newly consecrated Pope. It was their will that she should wear the crown. Now they spoke that will in one great chorus of joyous acclamation: "Pope John! Pope John! Pope John!"

Joan raised her arms to them, feeling her spirit begin to soar. The epiphany, which only yesterday she had striven in vain to achieve, now came unlooked for and unbidden. God had allowed this to happen, so it could not be against His will. All doubt and anxiety were dispelled, replaced by a glorious, glowing certainty: *This is my destiny, and these my people.*

She was hallowed by the love she bore them. She would serve them in the Lord's name all the days of her life.

And perhaps in the end God would forgive her.

STANDING nearby, Gerold stared at Joan in wonderment. She was aglow, transformed by some unspeakable joy, her face a lovely shining lamp. He alone, who knew her so well, could guess at her inner hallowing of spirit, more important by far than the formal ceremony which had preceded it. As he watched her receive the acclamation of the crowd, his heart was torn by an unbearable truth: the woman he loved was lost to him forever, yet he had never loved her more.

≽ 27 ≼

JOAN'S first act as Pope was to undertake a walking tour of the city. Accompanied by an entourage of optimates and guards, she visited each of the seven ecclesiastical regions in turn, greeting the people and listening to their grievances and needs.

As she neared the end of her tour, Desiderius, the archdeacon, directed her up the Via Lata away from the river.

"What about the Campus Martius?" she said.

The others in the papal entourage looked at one another in consternation. The Campus Martius, the marshy, breezeless, low-lying region abutting the Tiber, was the poorest part of Rome. In the great days of the Roman Republic, it had been dedicated to the worship of the pagan god Mars. Now starving dogs, ragged beggars, and thieves wandered its once-proud streets.

"We daren't venture in there, Holiness," Desiderius protested. "The place is rife with typhus and cholera."

But Joan was already striding toward the river, flanked by Gerold and the guards. Desiderius and the others had no choice but to follow.

Rows of *insulae,* the narrow tenements of the poor, crowded together along the filthy streets edging the riverbank, their rotting timbers bending alarmingly. Some of the insulae had collapsed; the heaps of rotten timber lay where they had fallen, blocking the narrow streets. Overhead stretched the ruined arches of the Marcian aqueduct, once one of the engineering wonders of the world. Now its broken walls dripped filthy water that collected underneath in black, stagnant pools, breeding grounds for disease.

Groups of beggars huddled over pots of foul-smelling food simmering on little fires made from twigs and dried dung. The streets were covered with a layer of slime left behind by repeated floodings of the Tiber. Refuse and excrement plugged the gutters; the stench rose unbearably in the summer heat, attracting swarms of flies, rats, and other vermin.

"God's teeth," Gerold muttered darkly beside her. "The place is a pesthole."

Joan knew the face of poverty, but she had never seen anything to equal this appalling, brutish squalor.

Two small children crouched before a cooking fire. Their tunics were so threadbare Joan could see the whiteness of their skin beneath; their bare feet were wrapped with strips of filthy rags. One, a little boy, was obviously sick with fever; despite the summer heat, he was shivering uncontrollably. Joan removed her linen paenula and tucked it gently around him. The boy rubbed his cheek against the fine cloth, softer than anything he had felt in his life.

She felt a tug on the hem of her robe. The smaller child, a round-eyed cherub of a girl, was looking up at her questioningly. "Are you an angel?" the small voice chirruped.

Joan cupped the child's dirty chin. "You're the angel, little one."

Inside the pot, a small piece of stringy, unidentifiable meat was beginning to brown. A young woman with lank yellow hair came lumbering wearily up from the river hauling a bucket of water. The children's mother? Joan wondered. She was scarcely more than a child herself—surely no more than sixteen.

The young woman's eyes lit hopefully as she saw Joan and the other prelates. "Alms, good fathers?" She held out a grimy hand. "A bit of coin for the sake of my little ones?" Joan nodded at Victor, the sacellarius, who placed a silver denarius in the girl's outstretched palm. With a happy grin, the girl set down the water bucket to pocket the coin.

Raw sewage was floating in the water.

Benedicite! Joan thought. The filth in that water was doubtless what had made the boy sick. But with the aqueduct in ruins, what choice did his mother have? She must use the polluted water of the Tiber or die of thirst.

By now, others had begun to notice Joan and her entourage. People crowded around, eager to greet their new Lord Pope. Joan reached out to them, trying to touch and bless as many as she could. But as the crowd grew, the people packed round so closely she could scarcely move. Gerold gave commands; the guards shouldered the crowd back, opening a path, and the papal entourage retreated back up the Via Lata to the open sunshine and breezy, healthful air of the Capitoline Hill.

✠

"WE MUST rebuild the Marcian aqueduct," Joan said during a meeting with the optimates the next morning.

The brows of Paschal, the primicerius, lifted with surprise. "The restoration of a Christian edifice would be a more appropriate way to begin your papacy, Holiness."

"What need do the poor have of more churches?" she replied. "Rome abounds with them. But a working aqueduct could save untold lives."

"The project is chancy," Victor, the sacellarius, said. "It may well be that it can't be done."

She couldn't deny this. Rebuilding the aqueduct would be a monumental, perhaps an impossible, undertaking, given the sorry state of engineering of the day. The books which had preserved the accumulated wisdom of the ancients regarding these complicated pieces of construction had been lost or destroyed centuries ago. The parchment pages on which the precious plans were recorded had been scraped clean and written over with Christian homilies and stories of lives of saints and martyrs.

"We have to try," Joan said firmly. "We cannot allow people to go on living in such appalling conditions."

The others kept silent, not because they agreed but because it would be impolitic to offer further opposition when the Apostolic One's mind was so obviously set upon this course.

After a moment Paschal asked, "Who do you have in mind to oversee the building?"

"Gerold," Joan replied.

"The superista?" Paschal was surprised.

"Who else? He directed the construction of the Leonine Wall. Many believed that could not be done, either."

In the weeks since her coronation, she had sensed Gerold's growing unhappiness. It was difficult for them both, being near each other all the time. She, at least, had her work, a clear sense of mission and purpose. But Gerold was bored and restless. Joan knew this without his having to tell her; they had never needed speech between them to know what the other was feeling.

When Gerold came to her, she laid out her idea for the rebuilding of the Marcian aqueduct.

His brow furrowed thoughtfully. "Near Tivoli, the aqueduct runs underground, tunneling through a series of hills. If that section has fallen into decay, it will not be easy to repair."

Joan smiled as she saw his mind already beginning to engage with the idea, anticipating the problems involved.

"If anyone can do it, you can."

"Are you sure this is what you want?" Gerold's eyes met hers in a look of unmistakable longing.

She felt herself respond to him. But she dared not let her feelings show. To acknowledge their intimacy, even here in private, would be to court disaster. Matter-of-factly she replied, "I can think of nothing that would be of greater benefit to the people."

He looked away. "Very well, then. Mind you, I'm not promising anything. I'll look into it, see what's possible. I'll do all I can to see the aqueduct restored to working order."

"That's all I ask," she said.

SHE was coming to understand in an altogether new way what it meant to be Pope. Though nominally a position of great power, it was actually one of great obligation. Her time was completely taken up with the burdensome round of liturgical duties. On Palm Sunday, she blessed and distributed palm branches in front of St. Peter's. On Holy Thursday, she washed the feet of the poor and served a meal to them with her own hands. On the Feast of St. Anthony she stood before the Cathedral of Sancta Maria Maggiore and sprinkled holy water on the oxen, horses, and mules that had been brought by their owners to be blessed. On the third Sunday after Advent, she laid her hands upon each of the candidates brought forward to be ordained as priests, deacons, or bishops.

There was also the daily mass to lead. On certain days, this became a stational mass, preceded by a procession through the city to the titular church in which the service would be held, stopping along the route to hear petitioners; the procession and service took most of the day. There were over ninety stational masses, including the Marian feasts, the ember days, Christ Mass, Septuagesima and Sexagesima Sundays, and most of the Sundays and ferias in Lent.

There were feast days honoring Saints Peter, Paul, Lawrence,

Agnes, John, Thomas, Luke, Andrew, and Anthony, as well as the Nativity, the Annunciation, and the Assumption of the Virgin Mary. These were fixed or immovable feasts, meaning that they fell on the same day each year, like Christ Mass and Epiphany. Oblation, the Feast of St. Peter's Chair, the Circumcision of Christ, the Nativity of John the Baptist, Michaelmas, All Saints', and the Exaltation of the Cross were also fixed feasts. Easter, the holiest day of the Christian year, was a movable feast; its place in the calendar followed the time of the ecclesiastical full moon, as did its "satellite" holidays, Shrove Tuesday, Ash Wednesday, Ascension Day, and Pentecost.

Each of these Christian holidays was observed with at least four days of celebration: the vigil, or eve of the feast; the feast itself; the morrow, or day following; and the octave, or eighth day subsequent. All told, there were over one hundred and seventy-five Christian festival days, given over to elaborate and time-consuming ceremonial.

All of this gave Joan very little time to actually govern, or do the things she deeply cared about: bettering the lot of the poor and improving the education of the clergy.

IN AUGUST, the arduous liturgical routine was interrupted by a synod. Sixty-seven prelates attended, including all the *suburbicarii*, or provincial bishops, as well as four Frankish bishops sent by the Emperor Lothar.

Two of the issues addressed at this synod held particular interest for Joan. The first was intinction, the practice of bestowing Communion by dipping the eucharistic bread into the wine, rather than partaking of them separately. In the twenty years since Joan had introduced the idea at Fulda as a way of preventing the spread of disease, it had become so popular that in Frankland it was now almost universal custom. The Roman clergy, who were of course unaware of Joan's connection with intinction, regarded the novel practice with suspicion.

"It is a transgression of divine law," the Bishop of Castrum argued indignantly. "For the Holy Book clearly states that Christ gave His Body and Blood *separately* to His disciples."

There were nods of agreement all around.

"My lord Bishop speaks truly," Pothos, the Bishop of Trevi, said. "The practice has no precedent among the writings of the Fathers, and therefore must be condemned."

"Should we condemn an idea simply because it is new?" Joan asked.

"In all things we should be guided by the wisdom of the ancients," Pothos answered gravely. "The only truth of which we can be sure is that which has been vouchsafed in the past."

"Everything that is old was once new," Joan pointed out. "The new always precedes the old. Is it not foolish to scorn that which precedes and cherish that which follows?"

Pothos's brow furrowed as his mind wrestled with this complex dialectic. Like most of his colleagues, he had no training in classical argument and debate; he was comfortable only when quoting authority.

A lengthy discussion followed. Joan could, of course, have imposed her will by decree, but she preferred persuasion to tyranny. In the end the bishops were won over by her reasoning. The practice of intinction would continue in Frankland, at least for the present.

The next issue to be addressed was of deep personal interest to Joan because it involved her old friend Gottschalk, the oblate monk whose freedom she had once helped to win. According to the report of the Frankish bishops, he was again in serious trouble. Joan was saddened by this news but not especially surprised; Gottschalk was a man who courted unhappiness as ardently as a lover pursues his mistress.

Now he stood accused of the serious crime of heresy. Raban Maur, formerly Abbot of Fulda, since promoted to Archbishop of Mainz, had gotten wind of some radical theories Gottschalk had been preaching regarding predestination. Seizing the opportunity to wreak revenge upon his old nemesis, the archbishop had ordered Gottschalk imprisoned and savagely beaten.

Joan frowned. The cruelty with which supposedly pious men like Raban treated their fellow Christians never ceased to astound her. Pagan Norsemen aroused less fury in them than a Christian believer who stepped the slightest bit aside from the strict doctrines of the Church. *Why,* she wondered, *do we always reserve our worst hatred for our own?*

"What is the specific nature of this heresy?" she asked Wulfram, the leader of the Frankish bishops.

"First," Wulfram said, "the monk Gottschalk asserts that God has foreordained all men to either salvation or perdition. Second, that Christ did not die on the cross for all men, but only for the elect. And lastly, that fallen man can do no good apart from grace, nor exercise free will for anything but evil."

That sounds like Gottschalk, Joan thought. A confirmed pessimist, he would naturally gravitate to a theory that predestined man for doom. But there was nothing heretical, or even especially new, about his ideas. St. Augustine himself had said exactly as much in his two great works *De civitate Dei* and the *Enchiridion*.

No one in the room appeared to recognize this, however. Though all reverenced the name of Augustine, evidently none had taken the trouble to actually read his works.

Nirgotius, Bishop of Anagni, rose to speak. "This is wicked and sinful apostasy," he said. "For it is well known that God's will predestines the elect but not the condemned."

This reasoning was seriously flawed, as predestining the one group inevitably implied predestining the other. But Joan did not point this out, for she also was troubled by Gottschalk's preaching. There was a danger in leading people to believe they could not earn their own salvation by avoiding sin and trying to act justly. After all, why should anyone trouble to do good works if Heaven's roll was already made up?

She said, "I concur with Nirgotius. God's grace is not a predestining choice, but the overflowing power of His love, which suffuses all things that exist."

The bishops received this warmly, for it accorded well with their own thinking. Unanimously they voted to refute Gottschalk's theories. At Joan's instigation, however, they also included a condemnation of Archbishop Raban for his "harsh and unchristian" treatment of the erring monk.

Forty-two canons were passed by this synod, dealing mostly with the reform of ecclesiastical discipline and education. At the end of the week, the assembly was adjourned. All agreed that it had gone very well, and that Pope John had presided with unusual distinction. The Romans were especially proud to be represented by a spiritual leader of such superior intellect and learning.

THE goodwill Joan accrued from the synod did not, however, last very long. The following month, the entire ecclesiastical community was jarred to its foundations when she announced her intention to institute a school for women. Even those of the papal party who had supported Joan's candidacy were shocked: what manner of Pope had they elected?

Jordanes, the secundicerius, confronted Joan publicly on the matter during the weekly meeting of the optimates.

"Holiness," he said, "you do great injury in seeking to educate women."

"How so?" she asked.

"Surely you know, Holiness, that the size of a woman's brain and her uterus are inversely proportionate; therefore, the more a girl learns, the less likely she will ever bear children."

Better barren of body than of mind, Joan thought dryly, though she kept the thought to herself.

"Where have you read this?"

"It is common knowledge."

"So common, apparently, that no one has taken the trouble to write it down so all may learn from it."

"There is nothing to be learned from what is obvious to all. No one has written that wool comes from sheep, yet we all know it to be so."

There were smiles on all sides. Jordanes preened, pleased with the cleverness of his argument.

Joan thought for a moment. "If what you say is true, how do you account for the extraordinary fertility of learned women such as Laeta, who corresponded with St. Jerome, and who, according to his report, was safely delivered of fifteen healthy children?"

"An aberration! A rare exception to the rule."

"If I remember correctly, Jordanes, your own sister Juliana knows how to read and write."

Jordanes was taken aback. "Only a little, Holiness. Just enough to allow her to keep the household accounts."

"Yet according to your theory, even a little learning should have an adverse effect upon a woman's fertility. How many children has Juliana borne?"

Jordanes flushed. "Twelve."

"*Another* aberration?"

There was a long, embarrassed silence.

"Obviously, Holiness," Jordanes said stiffly, "your mind is quite made up on this matter. Therefore, I'll say no more."

And he didn't, at least not in that assembly.

"IT WAS not wise to insult Jordanes publicly," Gerold said afterward. "You may have driven him into the arms of Arsenius and the imperialists."

"But he's wrong, Gerold," Joan said. "Women are as capable of learning as men. Am I not proof of that?"

"Of course. But you must give people time. The world can't be remade in a day."

"The world won't ever be remade, if no one tries to remake it. Change must begin somewhere."

"True," Gerold allowed. "But not now, not here—not with you."

"Why not?"

Because I love you, he wanted to say, *and I'm afraid for you.*

Instead he said, "You can't afford to make enemies. Have you forgotten who and what you are? I can protect you from many things, Joan—but not from yourself."

"Oh, come—surely it's not as serious as all that. Will the world come to an end because a few women learn to read and write?"

"Your old tutor—Aesculapius, wasn't it?—what was it you told me he once said to you?"

"Some ideas are dangerous."

"Exactly."

There was a long silence.

"Very well," she conceded. "I'll speak to Jordanes and do what I can to smooth his ruffled feathers. And I promise to be more politic in the future. But the school for women is too important; I won't give up on it."

"I didn't think you would," Gerold replied, smiling.

In September, the school for women was formally dedicated. St. Catherine's School, Joan named it in loving memory of her brother Matthew, who had first acquainted her with the learned saint. Each time she passed the little building on the Via Merulana and heard the sound of female voices reciting, she thought her heart would split with joy.

She was as good as her word to Gerold. She was politic and courteous to Jordanes and the other optimates. She even managed to keep her tongue in check when she heard Cardinal Priest Citronatus preach that upon resurrection women's "imperfections" would be remedied, for all human beings would be reborn as men! Calling Citronatus to her, she offered in the guise of a helpful suggestion that eliminating that line from his sermons might help him achieve a better effect with his female parishioners. Couched in such diplomatic terms, the suggestion went over well; Citronatus was flattered by the papal attention and did not preach the idea again.

Patiently and uncomplainingly Joan endured the daily round of masses, audiences, baptisms, and ordinations. So the long, cool days of autumn passed with no further incident.

On the ides of November, the sky darkened and it began to rain. For ten days the rain came down in great driving sheets, drumming against the shingled roofs of the houses so the inhabitants had to plug their ears to shut out the maddening noise. The ancient sewers of the city were soon overwhelmed; on the streets water collected in growing pools that met and joined in quick-moving streams, turning the basalt stones into a treacherous slipping ground.

And still the rain came down. The waters of the Tiber rose dangerously, overrunning the embankments from the city to the sea, flooding the fields of the campagna, destroying the croplands, carrying off the cattle.

Within the city walls, the first region to be inundated was the low-lying Campus Martius, with its teeming population of poor. Some fled to higher ground as soon as the water began to rise, but many remained behind, unaware of the consequences of delay and reluctant to leave their homes and meager possessions.

Then it was too late. The waters rose above the height of a man, preventing any attempt at escape. Hundreds of people were trapped inside the rickety insulae; if the waters continued to rise, they would drown.

In such circumstances, the Pope usually retired to the Lateran cathedral and held a solemn litany, prostrating himself before the altar and praying for the city's deliverance. To the surprise and consternation of the clergy, Joan did no such thing. Instead, she summoned Gerold to discuss plans for a rescue.

"What can we do?" she asked. "There must be some way to save those people."

He replied, "The streets surrounding the Campius Martius are completely flooded. There's no way to get there except by boat."

"What about the boats moored at Ripa Grande?"

"They're only light fishing skiffs—flimsy vessels for such rough waters."

"It's worth an attempt," she argued urgently. "We can't just stand by idly while people drown!"

Gerold felt a rush of tenderness toward her. Not Sergius, not even Leo, would have showed such concern for the wretched population of the Campus Martius. Joan was different; seeing no distinction between rich and poor, she made none. In her eyes, all people were equally deserving of her care and attention.

"I'll call up the militia at once," he said.

They marched to the dock at Ripa Grande, where Joan used her authority to commandeer every dinghy in seaworthy condition. Gerold and his men got into the boats, and Joan spoke a few quick words of blessing over them, raising her voice to make herself heard over the pelting rain. Then she astonished everyone by clambering down into the boat with Gerold.

"What are you doing?" he asked in alarm.

"What does it look like?"

"You don't mean to come with us!"

"Why not?"

He gazed at her as if she were mad. "It's far too dangerous!"

"Where I am needed, I will go," she replied determinedly.

Eustathius, the archpriest, frowned down from the dock. "Holiness, think of the dignity of your position! You are Lord Pope, Bishop of Rome. Would you risk your life for a group of ragged beggars?"

"They are God's children, Eustathius, no less than you and I."

"But who will lead the litany?" he asked plaintively.

"You will, Eustathius. Do it well, for we have good need of your prayers." She turned impatiently to Gerold. "Now, Superista, will you row, or must I?"

Recognizing the look of stubborn determination in those gray-green eyes, Gerold took up the oars. There was no further time for debate, for the waters were rising quickly. He pulled on the oars, rowing strongly, and the boat drew away from the dock.

Eustathius shouted something after them, but his words were lost in the wind and driving rain.

The makeshift flotilla headed northwest toward the Campus Martius. The floodwaters had risen. The Tiber was coursing through this lower part of the city as if in its own channel. From the Porta Septimania to the foot of the Capitoline Hill, every church and house was flooded. The column of Marcus Aurelius was half submerged; waves lapped at the upper doorsills of the Pantheon.

Nearing the Campus Martius, they saw evidence of the terrible damage the flood had wreaked. Wooden debris, remains of the collapsed insulae, drifted swiftly by; bodies floated on the surface of the water, turning with every shift of the current. The terrified inhabitants of the remaining tenements had retreated to the upper stories. They leaned from the windows with outstretched arms, crying piteously for help.

The boats spread out, one or two to a building. The waves made it difficult to hold them steady. Some people panicked and jumped too soon, missing the bobbing, circling vessels. Others landed too far to the front or side of one of the boats, overturning it. There was a melee in the water as those who could not swim tried desperately to cling to those who could while the oarsmen cursed roundly and tried to right their flimsy craft.

Eventually all the boats were righted and they set off, following a route to the Capitoline Hill, where they let off their passengers. From this point, it was an easy climb to the safety of dry ground. Then the flotilla turned back to rescue more people.

They made trip after trip, drenched to the skin, clothes plastered to their bodies, aching from effort and fatigue. At last it seemed they had everyone. They were headed back toward the Capitoline Hill when Joan heard a child's voice crying for help. Turning, she saw a small boy silhouetted in one of the windows. Perhaps he had been asleep and only just awakened, or perhaps he had been too frightened to come to the window before.

Joan and Gerold looked at each other. Without a word, he turned the boat around and rowed back, pulling up beneath the window from which the boy now leaned and fanning the oars to hold the boat steady.

Joan stood, holding out her arms. "Jump!" she said. "Jump and I'll catch you!"

The boy stayed where he was, round eyes staring down in terror at the heaving boat below.

She fixed him with a compelling stare, willing him to move. "Jump now!" she commanded.

Timidly the boy slung one leg over the windowsill.

She reached for him.

At that moment there was a deafening roar. The ancient Posterula St. Agatha, northernmost gate of the Aurelian Wall, had given way under the pressure of the rising water. The Tiber came bursting into the city in a tidal wave of terrifying force.

Joan saw the boy's face framed in the window, his mouth forming a tiny O of terror as the entire building began to break apart. At the same moment, she felt the boat beneath her lift and shudder as it was sent spinning wildly on the onrushing flood.

She screamed, clinging desperately to the sides as the flimsy boat careered down the rapids, threatening at every moment to overturn. Water gushed over the sides; she raised her head, gulping for air, and caught an instant's glimpse of Gerold crouching near the bow.

There was a stunning jolt as the boat suddenly came to a halt, sending her crashing into the side.

For a while she lay dazed and uncomprehending. When at last she looked about her, she saw walls, a table, chairs.

She was indoors. The stupendous force of the flood had driven the little boat straight through an upper window of one of the insulae into the room within.

She saw Gerold lying in the front of the boat, facedown in several inches of water. She crawled over to him.

When she turned him over, he was limp and unresponsive, not breathing. She dragged him from the boat onto the floor of the room. Rolling him onto his stomach, she began pressing down on his back to force water out of his lungs. Press and release, press and release. *He can't die,* she thought. *He mustn't die.* Surely God could not be so cruel. Then she recalled the doomed young boy in the house and thought: *God is capable of anything.*

Press and release. Press and release.

Gerold's throat heaved, bringing up a great rush of water.

Benedicite! He was breathing again. Joan examined him carefully. No broken bones, no open wounds. But there was a large blue-black swelling just below his hairline, where he had received a nasty blow. This must have been what had knocked him senseless.

He should be coming round now, she thought. But Gerold remained sunk in his unnatural sleep, his skin pale and moist, his breathing shallow, his pulse faint and dangerously rapid. *What's wrong?* she wondered anxiously. *What else can I do?*

"The shock of violent injury can kill a man with a penetrating chill." The words of Hippocrates, words that had once saved Gottschalk's life, came back to her now.

She must get Gerold warm, and quickly.

Blasts of wind and rain were coming through the gaping hole left by the passage of the boat. She rose and began to explore the small tenement dwelling. Behind the front room there was a second, smaller one, windowless and therefore warmer and dryer. And—*Deo gratias!*—in the middle of the room there was a small iron brazier stacked with a few pieces of wood. On a nearby shelf she found a flint and some kindling. In a chest in the corner, there was a blanket of heavy wool, tattered but mercifully still dry.

Returning to the front room, she grasped Gerold under the shoulders and half-carried, half-dragged him into the back room, setting him down beside the brazier. Taking up the box of kindling, she struck the flint against the iron. Her hands were shaking so hard she had to try several times before she drew a spark. At last she got the little pile of straw to catch. She placed the flaming kindling in the brazier, and it flared upwards, licking at the logs above. The damp wood hissed and spat, reluctant to take. At last a tiny core of red glowed in one of the logs. She fanned the fragile fire, nursing it along with practiced skill. Just as it began to take hold, a breeze swept in from the other room and extinguished it.

She looked despairingly at the cold logs. There was no more kindling, no way for her to start the fire again. Gerold still lay unconscious, his skin an ominous bluish white, his eyes sunk in their sockets.

There was only one thing left to do now. Quickly she removed his wet clothes, baring his taut, slenderly muscular body, marked here and there with the fading scars of battle. Then she covered him with the blanket.

She stood and, shivering in the frigid air, began to take off her own soaked clothes: first the paenula and dalmatic, then the undergarments, the alb, amice, and cingulum. When she was stripped to the skin, she crawled under the blanket and lay full length against Gerold.

She held him close, warming his body with her own, willing her strength, her life into him.

Fight, Gerold, my dearest. Fight.

She closed her eyes and concentrated on making the link between them. All else was apart. The little room, the quenched fire, the boat, the storm outside—none of it was real. There was only the two of them. They would live joined, or perish.

Gerold's eyelids fluttered, then opened. His indigo eyes regarded her without surprise; he knew she had been with him.

"My pearl," he murmured.

For a long while they lay silent, joined in wordless communication. Then he raised his arm to draw her closer, and his fingers brushed against the raised scars on her back.

"The marks of a lash?" he asked quietly.

She flushed. "Yes."

"Who did this to you?"

Slowly, haltingly, she told him of the beating she had received from her father when she refused to destroy Aesculapius's book.

Gerold said nothing, but the muscles in his jaw tightened. He bent over her and began to kiss each jagged scar.

Over the years, Joan had trained herself to rein her emotions in, to hold tight against pain, not to cry. Now the tears slid down her cheeks unchecked.

He held her tenderly, murmuring endearments, until her tears stopped. Then his lips were on hers, moving softly with a skill and tenderness that filled her with surging warmth. She slid her arms around him and closed her eyes, letting the sweet, dark wine of her senses rush over her, mind's will yielding at long last to body's desire.

Dear God! she thought. *I didn't know, I didn't know!* Was this what her mother had warned her against, what she had run from all these years? This wasn't surrender; it was a wondrous, glorious expansion of self—a prayer not of words but of eyes and hands and lips and skin.

"I love you!" she cried at the moment of ecstasy, and the words were not profanation but sacrament.

IN THE Great Hall of the Patriarchium, Arsenius waited with the optimates and members of the high clergy of Rome for news. When he had first received word of what Pope John had done, Arsenius could scarcely believe it. But then what else could one expect from a foreigner—and a commoner at that?

Radoin, second in command of the papal militia, entered the hall.

"What news?" Paschal, the primicerius, asked impatiently.

"We managed to rescue several score of the inhabitants," Radoin reported. "But I fear His Holiness has been lost."

"Lost?" Paschal repeated thinly. "What do you mean?"

"He was in a skiff with the superista. We thought they were following us, but they must have turned back to rescue another survivor.

That was just before the gate of St. Agatha collapsed and sent a wall of water crashing into that area."

This news was followed by scattered cries of alarm and dismay. Several of the prelates crossed themselves.

"Is there any chance they survived?" Arsenius asked.

"None," Radoin replied. "The force of the flood swept away everything in its path."

"God have mercy upon them," Arsenius said gravely, using all his control to conceal his elation.

"Shall I give the order to sound the bells of mourning?" Eustathius, the archpriest, asked.

"No," Paschal replied. "We must not be precipitate. Pope John is God's chosen Vicar; it is yet possible that God has worked a miracle to save him."

"Why not return and search for them?" Arsenius suggested. He had no interest in a rescue, but he did need to assure himself that the Throne of St. Peter was again vacant.

Radoin replied, "The collapse of the northern gate has rendered the entire area impassable. We can do nothing more until the floodwaters subside."

"Then let us pray," said Paschal. "*Deus misereatur nostri et benedicat nobis . . .*"

The others joined in, bowing their heads.

Arsenius recited the words by rote, while his mind ranged to other matters. If, as it now appeared certain, Pope John had died in the flood, then Anastasius had a second chance at the throne. *This time,* Arsenius thought determinedly, *nothing must go wrong with the election.* This time he would use all his power to make certain his son's candidacy did not fail.

"*. . . et metuant eum omnes fines terrae. Amen.*"

"Amen," Arsenius echoed. He could hardly wait for the news the next day would bring.

WAKING toward morning, Joan smiled to see Gerold sleeping beside her. She let her eyes linger on his long, spare, proud face—as startling now in its manly beauty as when she had first glimpsed it across a banquet table twenty-eight years ago.

Did I know even then, she wondered, *in the very first moment? Did I know that I loved him? I think I did.*

At last she had come to accept what she had fought so long to deny—Gerold was part of her, *was* her in some unfathomable way she could neither explain nor deny. They were twin souls, linked inextricably and forever, two halves of one perfect whole that would never again be complete without both.

She did not let herself dwell upon the full implications of this wondrous discovery. It was enough to live in the present moment, in the supreme happiness of being here, now, with him. The future did not exist.

He lay on his side, his head close to hers, lips slightly parted, long, red hair tousled about his face. In his sleep, he looked vulnerable and young, almost boyish. Moved by an inexpressible tenderness, Joan reached out and gently smoothed a stray tendril off his cheek.

Gerold's eyes opened, gazing at her with so intense an expression of love and need that it left her breathless. Wordlessly he reached for her, and she went to him.

THEY were dozing again, entwined in each other's arms, when Joan started alert, aware of a strange sound. She lay still, listening with pricked ears. All was quiet. Then she realized that it wasn't noise that had awakened her but silence—the absence of the loud, steady drumming on the roof overhead.

The rain had stopped.

She rose and went to the window. The sky was overcast and gray, but for the first time in over ten days patches of blue showed on the horizon, with shafts of sunlight spilling through the clouds.

Praise God, she thought. *Now the flooding will end.*

Gerold came up behind her and put his arms around her. She leaned back against him, loving the feel of him.

"Will they come for us soon, do you think?" she asked.

"Very soon, now the rain's stopped."

"Oh, Gerold!" She buried her head in his shoulder. "I've never been so happy, nor so unhappy."

"I know, my heart."

"We can never be together again, not like this."

He stroked her bright hair. "We needn't go back, you know."

She looked at him with surprise. "What do you mean?"

"No one knows we're here. If we don't signal the rescue boats when they come, they'll go away. In a day or so, when the floodwaters recede, we'll slip away from the city by night. No one will come after us, for they'll think we both died in the flood. We'll be free and clear—and we'll be together."

She made no answer but turned to look out the window again.

He awaited her decision, his life, his happiness hanging in the balance.

After a while she turned back to him. Looking into the depths of those gray-green eyes, haunted with grief, Gerold knew that he had lost.

She said slowly, "I cannot walk away from the great responsibility with which I've been entrusted. The people believe in me; I can't abandon them. If I did, it would turn me into someone else, someone different from the person you love."

He knew he would never have more power over her than he had at this moment. If he used that power, if he took her in his arms and kissed her, she might yet agree to come away with him. But that would be unfair. Even if she yielded, it would be a surrender that might not last. He would not try to persuade her to do anything she might afterward regret. She must come to him of her own free will or not at all.

"I understand," he said. "And I'll not press you further. But there's something I want you to know. I'll say it only once, and never again. You are my true wife on this earth, and I your true husband. No matter what happens, no matter what time and fate may do to us, nothing can ever change that."

They dressed, to be ready when rescue should come. Then they sat together, holding each other close, Joan's head resting lightly on Gerold's shoulder. They were sitting like that, rapt in each other, when the rescue boats arrived.

As they were rowed back toward the Patriarchium, Joan kept her head bowed as if in prayer. Aware of the watchful eyes of the guards, she did not dare look at Gerold, for she was not sufficiently in control of her feelings.

Arriving at the dock, they were immediately surrounded by a jubilant, cheering crowd. There was time for only one last backward glance before they were triumphantly borne off to their separate quarters.

≽∤ 28 ∤≼

PAPA POPULI, they called her, the people's Pope. Over and over the story was told of how the Lord Pope had gone forth from his palace on the day of the flood, risking his life to save those of his people. Wherever Joan went in the city, she was given a riotous welcome. Her path was strewn with sweet-smelling petals of acanthus, and from every window people called down blessings upon her. She drew strength and solace from their love, dedicating herself to them with renewed fervor.

The optimates and high clergy, on the other hand, were scandalized by Joan's behavior on the day of the flood. For the Vicar of St. Peter to rush off to the rescue in a dinghy—why, it was absurd, an embarrassment to the Church and the dignity of the papal office! They regarded her with growing disaffection, amplified by the very real differences they had with her: she was a foreigner, and they were native-born Romans; she believed in the power of reason and observation, and they believed in the power of sacred relics and miracles; she was forward looking and progressive, and they were conservative, bound by habit and tradition.

Most had entered the ranks of the clerical bureaucracy in childhood. By the time they reached maturity, they were thoroughly steeped in Lateran tradition and quite inimical to change. In their minds there was a right way and a wrong way to do things—and the right way was what had always been done.

Understandably, they were disconcerted by Joan's style of governance. Wherever she saw a problem—a need for a hospice, the injustice of a corrupt official, a shortage in the food supply—she sought to move quickly to correct it. Frequently she found herself thwarted by the papal bureaucracy, the vast and cumbersome system of government that over the course of centuries had evolved into a labyrinthine complexity. There were literally hundreds of departments, each with its own hierarchy and its own jealously guarded responsibilities.

Impatient to get things done, Joan looked for ways to circumvent the ponderous inefficiency of the system. When Gerold ran short of funds for the ongoing work on the aqueduct, she simply withdrew the money from the treasury, bypassing the usual course of putting a request through the office of the sacellarius, or papal paymaster.

Arsenius, alert as ever to opportunity, did what he could to exploit the situation. Seeking out Victor, the sacellarius, he broached the subject with politic art.

"I fear His Holiness lacks a sufficient appreciation of our Roman ways."

"So he would, not being born to them," Victor responded noncommittally. A cautious man, he would not reveal his hand until Arsenius played his.

"I was shocked to hear that he withdrew funds from the treasury without going through your office."

"It was rather . . . inappropriate." Victor conceded.

"Inappropriate!" Arsenius exclaimed. "My dear Victor, in your place I would not be so charitable."

"No?"

"If I were you," Arsenius said, "I'd look to my back."

Victor dropped his air of studied indifference. "Have you heard anything?" he asked anxiously. "Does His Holiness mean to replace me?"

"Who can tell?" Arsenius replied. "Perhaps he means to dispense with the position of sacellarius altogether. Then he can take whatever funds he likes from the treasury without having to explain to anyone."

"He'd never dare!"

"Wouldn't he?"

Victor didn't answer. Like a skilled fencer, Arsenius gauged his timing and thrust home.

"I begin to fear," he said, "that John's election was a mistake. A serious mistake."

"The thought has occurred to me," Victor admitted. "Some of His Holiness's ideas—the school for women, for example . . ." Victor shook his head. "God's ways are certainly mysterious."

"God didn't put John on the throne, Victor; we did. And we can remove him."

This was too much. "John is Christ's Vicar," Victor said, deeply shocked. "I admit he's . . . odd. But to move forcibly against him? No . . . no . . . surely it has not come to that."

"Well, well, you may be right." Artfully Arsenius let the matter drop. There was no need to pursue it further; he had planted the seed and knew it could be trusted to grow.

SINCE their parting on the day of the flood, Gerold had not seen Joan. The remaining work on the aqueduct was not within the city but at Tivoli, some twenty miles distant. Gerold was closely involved with every aspect of the construction, from overseeing the design of the repair to supervising the work crews. Frequently he bent his own back to the work, helping lift the heavy stones and cover them with new mortar. The men were surprised to see the lord superista stoop to such menial work, but Gerold welcomed it, for only in hard physical labor did he find momentary respite from the aching sadness inside.

Better, he thought, *far better if we had never lain together like man and wife.* Perhaps then he could have gone on as before. But now . . .

It was as if he had lived all the years before in blindness. All the roads he had traveled, all the risks he had taken, all he had ever done or been had led to one person: *Joan.*

When the aqueduct was finished, she would expect him to resume his position as leader of the papal guard. To be near her again every day, to see her and know that she was hopelessly out of reach . . . it would be unendurable.

I'll leave Rome, he thought, *as soon as the work on the aqueduct is complete. I'll return to Benevento and resume command of Siconulf's army.* There was an appealing simplicity to a soldier's life, with its definable enemies and clear objectives.

He drove himself and his men relentlessly. Within three months' time, the work was completed.

THE restored aqueduct was formally dedicated on the Feast of the Annunciation. Led by Joan, the entire clergy—acolytes, porters, lectors, exorcists, priests, deacons, and bishops—circled the massive peperino arches in solemn procession, sprinkling the stones with holy water while chanting litanies, psalms, and hymns. The procession halted, and Joan spoke a few words of solemn blessing. She looked up to where Gerold stood waiting atop the foremost of the arches, lean, long legged, taller by a head than the others around him.

She nodded to him, and he pulled a lever, opening the sluice gates. The cheers of the people rang out as the cold, pure, healthful waters of the springs of Subiaco, which lay some forty-five miles outside the city walls, flowed within the Campus Martius for the first time in over three hundred years.

CRAFTED in the imperial style, the papal throne was a massive, high-backed piece of richly carved oak studded with rubies, pearls, sapphires, and other precious gems, as comfortless as it was impressive. Joan had been ensconced in it for over five hours, granting audience to a stream of petitioners. Now she shifted restlessly, trying to ease the growing discomfort in her back.

Juvianus, the head steward, announced the next petitioner. "Magister Militum Daniel."

Joan frowned. Daniel was a difficult man, thorny and irascible—and he was a close associate of Bishop Arsenius. His presence here could only mean trouble.

Daniel entered briskly, nodding greeting at several of the notaries and other papal officials.

"Holiness." He saluted Joan with the most minimal of bows, then began with rude abruptness. "Is it true that at the March ordinations, you intend to install Nicephorus as Bishop of Trevi?"

"It is."

"The man's a Greek!" Daniel protested.

"Why should that matter?"

"So important a position must go to a Roman."

Joan sighed inwardly. It was true that her predecessors had used the episcopacy as a political tool, distributing bishoprics among the noble Roman families like so many choice plums. Joan disagreed with this practice, for it had resulted in a great number of *episcopi agraphici*—illiterate bishops, who had spawned all kinds of ignorance and superstition. How, after all, could a bishop correctly interpret the word of God to his flock if he could not even read it?

"So important a position," she replied equably, "should go to the person best qualified. Nicephorus is a man of learning and piety. He will make a fine bishop."

"You would think so, being yourself a foreigner." Daniel deliberately used the insulting term *barbarus* rather than the more neutral *peregrinus*.

There was an audible intake of breath from the others in the room.

Joan looked Daniel straight in the eye. "This has nothing to do with Nicephorus," she said. "You are guided by selfish motives, Daniel, for you want your own son Peter to be bishop."

"Well, why not?" Daniel said defensively. "Peter is well suited for the position by virtue of family and birth."

"But not by ability," Joan said bluntly.

Daniel's mouth gaped in astonishment. "You dare . . . you dare . . . my son—"

"Your son," Joan interrupted, "reads equally well from a lectionary placed right side up or upside down, for he knows no Latin. He has committed to memory the few scriptural passages he knows. The people deserve better. And in Nicephorus they shall have it!"

Daniel drew himself up, stiffly offended. "Mark my words, Holiness: you have not heard the end of this!"

And with that he turned and left.

Joan thought, *He will go straight to Arsenius, who will no doubt find some way to make further trouble.* About one thing Daniel was certainly right; she had not heard the end of this.

Suddenly she was inexpressibly weary. The air in the windowless room seemed to close in upon her; she felt queasy and faint. She tugged on her pallium, pulling it away from her neck.

"The lord superista," Juvianus announced.

Gerold! Joan's spirits rose. They had not spoken since the day of their rescue. She had hoped he would come today, though at the same time she feared their meeting. Aware of the watchful eyes of the others, Joan kept her face impassive.

Then Gerold entered, and her treacherous heart leapt at the sight of him. The flickering lamplight played across his features, illuminating the handsomely chiseled angles of his brow and cheekbone. He returned her gaze; their eyes locked in silent communication, and for a brief moment they were quite alone in the midst of that great company.

He came forward and knelt before the throne.

"Rise, Superista," she said. Did she imagine it, or was her voice somewhat unsteady? "This day your head is crowned with honor. All Rome is indebted to you."

"I thank you, Holiness."

"Tonight we will celebrate your great accomplishment with a feast. You shall sit at my table in the place of honor."

"Alas, I regret that I will not be able to attend. I leave Rome today."

"Leave Rome?" She was taken aback. "What do you mean?"

"Now that the great work with which you charged me is complete, I am resigning as superista. Prince Siconulf has asked me to return to Benevento to resume command of his armies—and I have accepted the post."

Joan kept her rigid posture on the throne, but her hands gripped the arms. "You can't do that," she answered brusquely. "I won't permit it."

The assembled prelates raised their eyebrows. True, it was unusual to resign so prestigious a post, but Gerold was a free Frank, at liberty to commit his services wherever he chose.

"In helping Siconulf," Gerold answered reasonably, "I will be continuing to serve Rome's interests as well, for Siconulf's territories provide a strong Christian bulwark against the Longobards and Saracens."

Joan set her mouth firmly. Turning to the others, she commanded, "Leave us."

Juvianus and the rest exchanged surprised glances, then exited the room with a flurry of respectful obeisances.

"Was that wise?" Gerold asked after they had gone. "Now their suspicions may be aroused."

"I had to talk to you alone," she replied urgently. "Leave Rome? What on earth can you be thinking of? No matter, I won't allow it. Let Siconulf find someone else to lead his armies. I need you here, with me."

"Oh, my pearl." His voice was a caress. "Look at us—we cannot so much as look at each other without betraying how we feel. A single unwary glance, a careless word, and your life could be forfeit! I *must* go, can't you see?"

Joan knew what he was saying, even knew he was right in a way. But it didn't matter. The prospect of his leaving filled her with dismay. Gerold was the one person who truly knew her, the only one upon whom she could absolutely depend.

She said, "Without you, I'd be utterly alone. I don't think I could bear it."

"You are stronger than you know."

"No," she said. She rose from the throne to go to him and swayed as a strong wave of dizziness swept her.

Instantly Gerold was at her side. He took her arm, supporting her. "You're ill!"

"No, no. Just . . . overtired."

"You've been working too hard. You need rest. Come, I'll help you to your quarters."

She gripped him fiercely. "Promise me you won't go until we've had a chance to talk again."

"Of course I won't leave." His eyes were filled with concern. "Not until you're feeling quite well again."

JOAN lay on her bed in the quiet of her room. *Am I truly ill?* she wondered. *If so, I must discover the cause and treat it quickly before Ennodius and the other physicians of the schola get wind of it.*

She applied her mind to the problem, putting questions to herself as if she were her own patient.

When did the first symptoms begin?

Now she thought about it, she had not felt well for several weeks.

What are the symptoms?

Fatigue. Lack of appetite. A feeling of bloatedness. Queasiness, especially upon first arising . . .

Sudden terror struck her.

Desperately she thought back, trying to recall the time of her last monthly bleeding. Two months ago, perhaps three. She had been so busy, she had paid no attention.

All the symptoms fit, but there was one way to be certain. She leaned over and picked up the bedpan that rested on the floor beside her bed.

A short while later, she set it down again with shaking hands.

The evidence was unmistakable. She was with child.

ANASTASIUS pulled off his velvet buskins and leaned back comfortably on the divan. *A good day,* he thought, pleased with himself. *Yes, it's been a very good day.* This morning he had shone at the imperial court, impressing Lothar and his entire retinue with his wisdom and learning.

The Emperor had asked his opinion of *De corpore et sanguine Domini,* the treatise that was causing such a stir among the country's theologians. Written by Paschasius Radbertus, Abbot of Corbie, the treatise advanced the daring theory that the Eucharist contained the true Body and true Blood of Christ the Savior—not His symbolic but his actual, historic flesh: "that which was born of Mary, suffered on the cross, and rose from the tomb."

"What do you think, Cardinal Anastasius?" Lothar inquired of him. "Is the sacred Host Christ's Body in mystery, or in truth?"

Anastasius was ready with an answer. "In mystery, my liege. For it can be shown that Christ has two distinct bodies: the first born of Mary, the second represented symbolically in the Eucharist. *'Hoc est corpus meum,'* Jesus said of the bread and wine at the Last Supper. 'This is my body.' *But he was still present bodily with his disciples when he said it.* So clearly He must have meant the words in a figurative sense."

So clever was this argument that when he'd finished speaking, all had applauded him. The Emperor had lauded him as "another Alcuin." Plucking several hairs from his beard, he had presented them to Anastasius—a gesture of highest honor among these strange, barbarian people.

Anastasius smiled, reliving the pleasure of the moment. He poured wine from the pitcher on the table beside him into a silver cup, then picked up the parchment scroll containing the latest letter from his father. He broke the wax seal and unrolled the fine white vellum. His eyes scanned the scroll, reading with eager interest. He stopped at the report of the theft of the corpses of Ss. Marcellinus and Peter from their cemetery.

Not that the taking of saints' bodies from their tombs was unusual; Christian sanctuaries all over the world constantly clamored for these holy relics in order to attract throngs of the faithful with the promise of miracles. For centuries the practical-minded Romans had made capital out of this foreign obsession with relics by conducting a regular trade in them. The countless pilgrims who swarmed to the Holy City were willing to dole out substantial sums for a finger of St. Damian, a collarbone of St. Anthony, or an eyelash of St. Sabina.

But the bodies of Ss. Marcellinus and Peter had not been sold; they had been stolen, dragged ignominiously from their graves at night and smuggled out of the city. *Furta sacra*—the theft of sacred things—such crimes were called. They had to be stopped, for they robbed the city of its greatest treasures.

"After this disgraceful theft," his father wrote, "we asked Pope John to double the number of guards posted in the churchyards and cemeteries. But he refuses. He says men are better employed in the service of the living than the dead."

Anastasius knew that John had put great numbers of the papal militia to work building schools, hospices, and houses of refuge. He had devoted his time and attention—and the greater part of the papal finances—to such secular projects, while the city's churches were left to languish. His own father's church had not received so much as a single golden lamp or silver candelabrum since John had taken office. Yet Rome's innumerable cathedrals, oratories, baptisteries, and chapels were her claim to glory. If they were not constantly embellished and improved, Rome could not hope to compete with the splendor of her eastern rival, Constantinople, which now brazenly called itself New Rome.

If—no, Anastasius corrected himself—*when* he was Pope, things would be different. He would lead Rome back to the days of her greatness. Under his solicitous patronage, her churches would once again gleam with fabulous riches, more resplendent than even the finest palaces of Byzantium. This, he knew, was the great work that God had put him on this earth to do.

He returned to reading his father's letter, but with diminishing interest, for the last part was taken up with items of minor importance: the list of names of those to be ordained at the coming Easter ceremonies had finally been published; his cousin Cosmas had married again, this time to a widowed deaconess; a certain Daniel, magister militum, was greatly aggrieved because his son had been passed over for a bishopric in favor of a Greek.

Anastasius sat up. A Greek to be bishop! His father seemed to regard the move as just another example of Pope John's regrettable lack of *romanità*. Was it possible that he had completely overlooked the possibilities of the situation?

This, Anastasius thought with mounting excitement, *is the chance for which I've been waiting*. At long last, fortune had delivered opportunity into his hands.

He rose quickly and went to his desk. Taking up a quill, he began to write. "Dear Father. Waste no time upon receiving this letter, but send the magister militum Daniel here to me at once."

JOAN paced the floor of the papal bedroom. *How*, she asked herself, *could I have been so blind?* It had simply not occurred to her that she could be pregnant. After all, she was over forty-one, well past the normal time for childbearing.

But Mama was older still when she quickened with child for the last time.

And died in the birthing.

Never give yourself to a man.

Fear, cold and unreasoning, gripped Joan's heart. She struggled to calm herself. After all, what had happened to Mama might not happen to her. She was strong and healthy; she had a good chance of surviving childbirth. But even if she did, what then? In the watchful beehive that was the Patriarchium, there was no way to keep her labor and delivery secret, no way to hide the child when it came. Her womanhood would surely be discovered.

What kind of death would be considered sufficient punishment for such a crime? It was certain to be terrible. They might put her eyes out with red-hot irons and flay her to the bone. Or she might be slowly dismembered, then burned while still alive. Some such hideous end was inevitable when this child came.

If it came . . .

She put both hands on her abdomen; there was no hint of movement from the babe growing within. The thread of life was as yet wound very thin; it would not take much to break it.

She went to the locked chest where she kept her medicaments. She had transferred them from her herbarium soon after her consecration; they were easier to hand here and safer against theft. Her hands ranged among the various vials and bottles until she found what she was looking for. With swift skill, she infused a measure of ergot into a cup of strong wine. In small doses, it was a beneficial medicine; in larger doses, it could induce abortion—though it didn't always work and was not without serious risk to the woman taking it.

What other choice did she have? If she did not end this pregnancy, she would face a death far more horrible.

She lifted the cup to her lips.

The words of Hippocrates came unbidden to her mind: *The medical art is a sacred trust. A physician should use his skill to help the sick according to his ability and judgment, but absolutely never to do harm.*

Resolutely Joan pushed the thought aside. All her life this woman's body of hers had been a source of grief and pain, an impediment to everything she wanted to do and to be. She would not now let it rob her of her life.

She tipped the cup and drank.

Never to do harm. Never to do harm. Never to do harm.

The words burned into her, searing her heart. With a sob, she threw the empty cup to the ground. It rolled away, the last drops streaking an erratic scarlet pattern across the floor.

SHE lay in her bed and waited for the ergot to take effect. Time passed, but she felt nothing. *It's not working,* she thought. She was frightened and at the same time greatly relieved. As she sat up, she was taken by a great fit of trembling. Her whole body shook with uncontrollable spasms. Her heart pounded; when she felt at her wrist, her pulse was wildly erratic.

Pain gripped her. She was stunned by its intensity, like a hot knife plunged into her innards. She rolled her head from side to side, biting her lip to keep from crying out. She dared not risk drawing the attention of the papal household.

The next few hours passed in a kind of haze as Joan moved in and out of consciousness. At one point she must have hallucinated; it seemed to her that her mother sat with her, called her "little quail," and sang to her in the Old Tongue as she used to, placing cool hands on her fevered brow.

Before dawn she awoke, weak and shaky. For a long while, she lay quite still. Then she slowly began to examine herself. Her pulse was regular, her heartbeat strong, her skin color good. There was no effusion of blood, no sign of any lasting harm.

She had survived the ordeal.

But so had the child within her.

THERE was only one person she could turn to now. When she told Gerold of her condition, he reacted at first with shocked disbelief.

"Great God! . . . is it possible?"

"Evidently," Joan said dryly.

He stood for a moment, his gaze fixed and reflective. "Is that why you've been ill?"

"Yes." She did not mention the abortifacient; even Gerold could not be expected to understand that.

He took her in his arms and held her close, cradling her head against his shoulder. For a long moment they remained quite still, silently sharing what was in their hearts.

He said quietly, "Do you remember what I said to you on the day of the flood?"

"We said many things to each other that day," she replied, but she felt her pulse quicken, for she knew what he meant.

"I said you were my true wife on this earth, and I your true husband." He put his hand under her chin, raising her eyes to his. "I understand you better than you think, Joan. I know how your heart's been torn. But now fate has decided things for us. We'll go away from here and be together as we were meant to."

She knew he was right. There was nothing else to do. All the roads that had lain before her were narrowed now to a single path. She felt sad and anxious, and at the same time strangely excited.

"We can leave tomorrow," Gerold said. "Dismiss your chamberlains for the night. Once everyone's asleep, it shouldn't be difficult for you to slip out the side door. I'll be waiting there with women's garments for you to change into once we're outside the city walls."

"Tomorrow!" She had accepted the idea of leaving but had not realized it would be so soon. "But . . . they'll come looking for us."

"By the time they do, we'll be well away. And they'll be looking for two men, not a simple pilgrim husband and his wife."

It was a daring plan, but it could work. Nevertheless, she resisted it. "I can't leave now. There's still so much I want to accomplish here, so much that needs doing."

"I know, my heart," he said tenderly. "But there's no other choice; surely you must see that."

"Wait until after Easter," she offered. "Then I'll go with you."

"Easter! Why, that's almost a month away! What if someone guesses your condition before then?"

"I'm only four months along. Under these great robes of mine, I can keep the pregnancy hidden for another month."

Gerold shook his head emphatically. "I can't let you risk it. You must get away from here now, while there's still time."

"No," she answered with equal conviction. "I won't leave my people without their Pope on the holiest day of the year."

She's frightened and upset, Gerold thought, *and therefore not thinking clearly.* He would go along with her for the present, having small choice, but quietly he would make things ready for a quick departure. If at any time danger threatened, he would whisk her away to safety—by force if necessary.

O N *nox magna*, the Great Night of the Easter celebration, thousands of people crowded in and around the Lateran cathedral to join in the celebration of the paschal vigil, baptism, and mass. The long service began on Saturday evening and would continue into the early hours of Easter morning.

Outside the holy cathedral, Joan lit the paschal candle, then handed it to Desiderius, the archdeacon, who carried it ceremoniously into the darkened church. Joan and the rest of the clergy followed after, chanting the *lumen Christi*, hymn to the light of Christ. Three times the procession paused on its way down the aisle while Desiderius lit the candles of the faithful from the paschal candle. By the time Joan reached the altar, the great nave was ablaze with a thousand tiny flames, their flickering light reflecting dazzlingly off the polished marble of the walls and columns in dramatic representation of the Light brought into the world by Christ.

"*Exultet jam angelica turba caelorum. Exultent divina mysteria!*"

Joyously, Desiderius began the *Exultet*. The time-honored chant, with its beautiful and striking ancient melody, rang in Joan's ears with special poignancy.

I will never stand before this altar and hear these sweet sounds again, she reflected. The thought brought a strong sense of loss. Here, amid this inspiring celebration of redemption and hope, she came closest to experiencing a true faith in God. "*O vere beata nox, quae expoliavit Aegyptios, ditavit Hebraeos! Nox, in qua terrenis caelestia junguntur . . .*"

EXITING the cathedral at the conclusion of the mass, Joan saw a man with torn and mud-stained clothes waiting on the steps. Taking him for a beggar, she signaled Victor, the sacellarius, to give him alms.

The man waved off the proffered coins. "I am no alms seeker, Holiness, but a messenger, come with urgent news."

"Let's have it then."

"Emperor Lothar and his army are marching through Paterno. At the rate they are traveling, they will be in Rome in two days' time."

A murmur of alarm rose from the prelates standing nearby.

"Cardinal Priest Anastasius rides with him," the messenger added.

Anastasius! His presence among the imperial entourage was a very bad sign.

"Why do you call him Cardinal Priest?" Joan asked reproachfully. "Anastasius no longer has claim to that title, being excommunicate."

"Beg pardon, Holiness, but so I heard the Emperor address him."

This was the worst news of all. The Emperor's disregard of Leo's sentence of excommunication was a direct, unmistakable defiance of papal authority. In such a frame of mind, Lothar was capable of anything.

That night, discussing this turn of events, Gerold pressed her again to keep her promise. "I have waited until after Easter, as you wished. You must leave now, before Lothar arrives."

Joan shook her head. "If the papal throne is vacant when Lothar arrives, he will use his power to have Anastasius elected Pope."

Gerold had no better liking for the idea of Anastasius as Pope than she did, but her safety was his first concern. He said, "There will always be some reason or other to keep us from leaving, Joan. We cannot delay forever."

"I will not abuse the people's trust by leaving them in *his* hands," she replied stubbornly.

Gerold had an almost irresistible impulse to simply pick her up and carry her off, away from the web of danger that was tightening around her. As if sensing his thoughts, Joan quickly spoke again.

"It's only a matter of a few days," she said in a conciliatory tone. "Whatever Lothar's purpose is in coming, he's unlikely to stay any longer than he needs to accomplish it. As soon as he's gone, I'll leave with you."

He weighed this for a moment. "And you'll offer no further argument against leaving?"

"No further argument," Joan promised.

THE next day, Joan waited on the steps of St. Peter's while Gerold rode out to greet Lothar. Sentries were posted all along the Leonine Wall to keep watch.

A short time later the cry went up from the wall, "The Emperor has arrived!" Joan ordered the gate of San Peregrinus opened.

Lothar rode in first. Anastasius was at his side, brazenly wearing the cardinal's pallium. His high-browed patrician face registered a look of haughty pride.

Joan acted as though she were oblivious to his presence. She waited on the steps for the Emperor to dismount and come to her.

"Be welcome, Majesty, to this Holy City of Rome." She extended her right hand, the one that bore the papal ring.

Lothar did not kneel but bent stiffly from the waist to kiss the symbol of her spiritual authority.

So far, so good, she thought.

The first rank of Lothar's men parted, and she saw Gerold. His face was taut with anger, and around his wrists was a tight cord of rope.

"What is the meaning of this?" Joan demanded. "Why is the superista bound?"

Lothar replied, "He has been arrested on a charge of treason."

"Treason? The superista is my loyal helpmate. There is no one I trust more."

Anastasius spoke for the first time. "The treason is not against your throne, Holiness, but the imperial one. Gerold is accused of conspiring to return Rome to Greek control."

"Nonsense! Who makes such an unfounded charge!"

Daniel rode out from behind Anastasius and fixed Joan with a look of malignant triumph. "I do," he said.

LATER, in the privacy of her room, Joan bent her mind to the problem, trying to think of a way to respond. It was, she realized, a diabolically clever plot. As Pontiff, she herself could not be put on trial. But Gerold could—and if he was found guilty, she would be implicated as well. The plan had the mark of Anastasius all over it.

Well, he won't get away with it. She set her chin defiantly. Let Anastasius do what he could. He would not prevail. She was still Pope, with power and resources of her own.

29

THE Great Triclinium was a relatively new addition to the Patriarchium, but it was already rich in historical significance. The paint on these walls had only just dried when Lothar's grandfather Karolus Magnus and Pope Leo III met here with their followers to forge the epic agreement that would raise Karolus from King of France to Emperor of the Holy Roman Empire and change the face of the world forever.

The fifty-five years that had passed since then had done nothing to dim the splendor of the hall. Its three large apses were paved with slates of flawless white marble and adorned with finely hewn columns of porphyry carved with decorations of marvelous complexity. Above the marble revetment, the walls were covered with colorful murals depicting the life of the apostle Peter, each drawn with wondrous artistry. But even these marvels were outshone by the great mosaic that rested over the arch of the central apse. In it St. Peter was depicted magnificently enthroned, surrounded by a round saint's nimbus. To his right knelt Pope Leo and to his left Emperor Karolus, each one's head surrounded by a square nimbus, the sign of the living—for they had been alive at the time the triclinium was built.

In the front of the hall, Joan and Lothar were ensconced upon two great, jewel-encrusted thrones. They appeared *sedentes pariter,* meaning that they were seated with equal ceremony; the two thrones were carefully placed side by side, level with each other so as not to give an appearance of greater importance to either one. The archbishops, cardinal priests, and abbots of Rome were seated facing them on high-backed chairs of Byzantine design, softly cushioned in green velvet. The other *sacerdotes,* the optimates, and the rest of the leading men of the Franks and Romans stood behind, filling the great hall to capacity.

When everyone was in place, Gerold was led in by Lothar's men, hands still bound before him. Joan's lips tightened as she saw dark bruises on his face and neck; obviously he had been beaten.

Lothar addressed Daniel. "Come forward, Magister Militum, and speak your accusation so all may hear."

Daniel said, "I overheard the superista tell Pope John that Rome should form an alliance with the Greeks in order to rid the city of Frankish domination."

"Liar!" Gerold growled, and was immediately rewarded with a hard cuff from one of his guards.

"Stand off!" Joan spoke sharply to the guard. To Gerold she said, "You deny these charges, Superista?"

"I do. They are false and wicked lies."

Joan took a deep breath. She must take the plunge now, or not at all. Speaking loudly so all could hear, she said, "I confirm the superista's testimony."

There was a shocked murmur from the assembled prelates. By responding in this way, Pope John had turned himself from judge to accused, in effect putting himself on trial along with Gerold.

Paschal, the primicerius, interjected soberly, "Holiness, the accusation is not for you to support or deny. Remember the words of the great Karolus: *Judicare non audemos.* You are not on trial here, nor can you be judged by any earthly court."

"I know that, Paschal. But I am prepared to answer these charges of my own free will, in order to free men's minds from any unjust suspicion." She nodded to Florentinus, the vestiarius. Following their prearranged signal, he immediately came forward bearing a large volume, magnificently bound—the gospel-book, containing the holy word of the apostles John, Luke, Mark, and Matthew. Joan clasped the book reverently. In a ringing voice she declared, "Upon these sacred gospels, wherein the Word of God is revealed, I swear before God and St. Peter that such a conversation never took place. If I am not speaking truth, may God strike me where I stand."

The dramatic gesture appeared to have worked. During the awed silence that followed, no one moved or spoke.

Then Anastasius stepped forward, taking up a position beside Daniel. "I offer myself as *sacramentale* for this man," he declared boldly.

Joan's heart sank. Anastasius had responded with a perfect counterthrust. He had invoked the law of *conjuratio*, according to which guilt or innocence was proved by whichever side in a dispute was able to amass the greatest number of *sacramentales,* or oath helpers, to support his sworn word.

Quick to take measure of the situation, Arsenius rose from his seat and joined his son. One by one, others slowly came forward to stand with them. Jordanes, the secundicerius, who had opposed Joan in the matter of the school for women, was among them. So was Victor, the sacellarius.

Ruefully Joan recalled Gerold's repeated words of caution to her to take things slowly and be more politic with her opponents. In her eagerness to get things done, she had not paid sufficient heed to his advice.

Now the reckoning was come.

"I will serve as sacramentale for the superista." A voice sounded clearly from the rear of the assembly.

Joan and the others turned to see Radoin, second in command of the papal guard, shouldering his way through the crowd. Staunchly he stood beside Gerold. His action emboldened others; in short order Juvianus, the head steward, came forward, followed by the cardinal priests Joseph and Theodore and six of the *suburbican* bishops, as well as several dozen of the lesser clergy who, being closer to the people, could better appreciate what Joan had done for them. The rest of the assembly held back, unwilling to commit themselves.

When all who wished to had come forward, the count was made: fifty-three men on Gerold's side and seventy-four on Daniel's.

Lothar cleared his throat. "God's judgment is here made manifest. Stand forth, Superista, to receive your sentence."

The guards started toward Gerold, but he shook them off. "The charge is false, no matter how many choose to perjure themselves by supporting it. I claim the right of ordeal."

Joan drew her breath in sharply. Here, in the southern part of the Empire, the ordeal was by fire, not water. An accused man had to walk barefoot over a twenty-foot row of white-hot plowshares. If he made it over, he was judged innocent. But very few people survived the ordeal.

Across the room, Gerold's eyes blazed an urgent message at Joan: *Do not try to stop me.*

He intended to sacrifice himself for her. If he made it over the coals, his innocence—and hers—would be proven. But he would probably die in the proving.

Just like Hrotrud, Joan thought. The memory of the village mid-wife's grisly death brought a sudden flash of inspiration.

She said, "Before proceeding further, there are some questions I would like to put to the magister militum."

"Questions?" Lothar frowned.

Anastasius protested. "This is highly irregular. If the superista wishes to undergo the ordeal, that is his right. Or does His Holiness doubt the workings of divine justice?"

Joan responded evenly, "Not at all. Neither do I scorn the workings of God-given reason. What harm can there be in asking a few questions?"

Unable to think of a reasonable reply, Anastasius shrugged and fell silent. But his face registered his vexation.

Joan's brow furrowed as she concentrated on recalling Cicero's six evidentiary questions.

Quis.

"Who," she asked Daniel, "apart from you, was witness to this alleged conversation?"

"No one," he replied. "But the testimony of these sacramentales is surety for my word."

Joan went on to the next question.

Quomodo.

"How did you come to overhear so private a conversation?"

Daniel hesitated only a moment before replying. "I was passing by the triclinium on my way to the dormitory. Seeing the door standing open, I went to close it. That's when I heard the superista talking."

Ubi.

"Where was the superista standing at the time?"

"Before the throne."

"About where he is now?"

"Yes."

Quando.

"When did this happen?"

Daniel pulled nervously on the neck of his tunic. The questions were coming so fast he had no time to think. "Aah . . . on the Feast of St. Agatha."

Quid.

"What exactly did you overhear?"

"I have already told the court that."

"Were those the superista's actual words, or an approximate rendering of the conversation?"

Daniel smirked. Did Pope John think he was stupid enough to fall into so obvious a trap? He said firmly, "I reported the superista's words exactly as he spoke them."

Joan sat forward on the papal throne. "Let me see if I have understood you correctly, Daniel. According to your testimony, on the Feast of St. Agatha you stood outside the door of the triclinium and heard every word of a conversation in which the superista told me that Rome should form an alliance with the Greeks."

"Correct," Daniel said.

Joan turned to Gerold. "Where were you on the Feast of St. Agatha, Superista?" she asked.

Gerold answered, "I was in Tivoli, finishing the work on the Marcian aqueduct."

"Are there any who can bear witness to that?"

"Dozens of men labored beside me all day long. They can all testify to my whereabouts that day."

"How do you explain this, Magister Militum?" Joan asked Daniel. "Surely a man cannot be in two places at once?"

Daniel was now looking decidedly pale. "Ah . . . ah. . . ," he stammered, desperately seeking a reply.

"Might you be mistaken about the date, Magister Militum?" Anastasius prompted. "After all these months, so small a detail might well be difficult to recall."

Daniel seized the proffered chance. "Yes, yes. Now I think back, it happened earlier than that—on the Feast of St. Ambrose, not St. Agatha. A thoughtless mistake."

"Where there is one mistake, there may be others," Joan responded. "Let us return to your testimony. You say you heard every word that was spoken while you were standing outside the door?"

"Yes," Daniel answered slowly, mistrustful now.

"You have sharp ears, Magister Militum. Please demonstrate this extraordinary acuity for us by repeating this feat."

"What?" Daniel was completely at a loss.

"Go stand outside the door, as you were before. The superista will speak a few words. When you come back, tell us what he said."

"What kind of trumpery is this?" Anastasius objected hotly.

Lothar looked at Joan disapprovingly. "Surely, Holiness, the use of jongleur's tricks undermines the gravity of these proceedings."

"Majesty," Joan replied, "what I have in mind is no trick, but a test. If Daniel is telling the truth, he should be able to hear the superista as well now as he did then."

"My liege, I protest!" Anastasius said. "Such a thing is contrary to all the customary proofs of law"

Lothar considered the matter. Anastasius was right; the use of evidence to prove or disprove an accusation was a strange and novel idea. On the other hand, Lothar had no reason to believe Daniel was lying. No doubt he would pass Pope John's unusual "test"—and that would lend greater credence to his testimony. Too much rested on the outcome of this trial for there to be any question afterward as to its fairness.

Lothar waved his hand imperiously. "Let the test proceed."

Reluctantly Daniel crossed the length of the great hall and stood on the other side of the door.

Joan put a finger to her lips, signaling Gerold to keep silent. "*Ratio in lege summa justitia est,*" she said in a high, clear voice. "Reason is the highest justice in law." She nodded to the guard at the door. "Bring Daniel back.

"Well," she asked when he stood before her again. "What did you hear?"

Daniel groped for a likely answer. "The superista repeated his protestation of innocence."

Those who had come forward to stand witness for him cried out in shocked dismay. Anastasius turned away in disappointment. Lothar's perpetual dark frown deepened even more.

Joan said, "Those are not the words that were spoken. And it was not the superista but I who spoke them."

Cornered, Daniel burst out angrily, "What difference does it make if I actually overheard the conversation or not? Your actions have demonstrated your true sympathies! Did you not ordain the Greek Nicephorus as bishop?"

"Ah!" Joan said. "That brings us to the last of the questions: *Cur.* Why? Why did you make false report of such a conversation to the Emperor? You were not motivated by truth, Daniel, but by envy—because your own son was passed over for the position Nicephorus received!"

"Shame!" a voice shouted from the crowd, and was quickly echoed by others. "Traitor!" "Liar!" "Rogue!" Even Daniel's own sacramentales joined in the torrent of abuse, eager to dissociate themselves from him now.

Joan raised a hand, silencing the assembly. Expectantly they waited for her to pronounce sentence against Daniel. For so serious a crime, the punishment would surely be very great: first the tongue that had uttered the treasonous lie would be cut out, then Daniel would probably be drawn and quartered.

Joan had no inclination to exact so terrible a price. She had accomplished what she wanted, which was to vindicate Gerold. There was no need to take Daniel's life; he was an unpleasant little man, spiteful and covetous, but no worse or more wicked than others she had known. And, Joan was certain, in this instance he had been little more than a tool in Anastasius's hands.

"Magister Militum Daniel," she said gravely. "From this moment forward, you are stripped of your title with all its lands and privileges. You will leave Rome today and remain forever banished from the Holy City and its sacred shrines."

The crowd was hushed by this astonishing display of *caritas*. Eustathius, the archpriest, seized the moment. "Praise be to God and St. Peter, Prince of the Apostles, through whom the truth has been made manifest! And long life to our Lord and Supreme Pontiff, Pope John!"

"Long life!" the others shouted. The sound echoed off the walls of the room, shaking the lamps in their silver cressets.

"WHAT did you expect?" Arsenius paced the floor of his room agitatedly in front of his son, who was seated at ease on one of the divans. "Pope John may be guileless, but he's no fool. You underestimated him."

"True," Anastasius conceded. "But it doesn't matter. I'm back in Rome—with the full support of the Emperor and his troops."

Arsenius stopped pacing. "What do you mean by that?" he asked sharply.

"I mean, Father, that I am now in a position to take what we could not win by election."

Arsenius stared. "Take the throne by force of arms? *Now?*"

"Why not?"

"You've been away too long, my son. You don't know how things stand here. It's true Pope John has made enemies, but there are many who support him."

"What do you suggest, then?"

"Be patient. Return to Frankland, trim your sails, and wait."

"For what?"

"For the winds of fortune to change."

"When will that happen? I have waited long enough to claim what is mine by right!"

"There is danger in moving too precipitously. Remember what happened to John the Deacon."

John the Deacon had been the opposing candidate in the election that had raised Sergius to the papal throne. After the election, the disappointed John had marched to the Patriarchium with a large group of armed retainers and forcibly occupied the throne. But the princes of the city rallied against him; within hours the Patriarchium was retaken and John deposed. The next day, Sergius was ceremoniously ordained as Pope—and John's severed head rested atop a pike in the Lateran courtyard.

"That won't happen to me, Father," Anastasius said confidently. "I've thought about this very carefully. God knows I've had time for thinking, stranded all these years in that alien backwater."

Arsenius felt the sting of his son's unspoken rebuke. "What exactly do you propose?"

"Wednesday is the Feast of Rogation. The stational mass is at St. Peter's. Pope John will lead the procession to the basilica. We'll wait until he is well away, then take the Patriarchium by storm. It will all be over before John even suspects what is happening."

"Lothar will not order his troops to attack the Patriarchium. He knows such an act would unite all Rome against him, even those of his own party."

"We don't need Lothar's soldiers to take the Patriarchium; our own guards can handle that. Once I'm clearly in possession of the throne, Lothar will come to my support—of that I'm certain."

"Perhaps," Arsenius said. "But taking the papal palace will not be easy. The superista is a formidable fighter, and he commands the loyalty of the papal guard."

"The superista's chief concern is for the Pope's personal safety. With Lothar and his army in the city, Gerold will be riding guard on the procession, along with the better part of his men."

"And afterward? Surely you realize Gerold will come against you with all the power at his disposal?"

Anastasius smiled. "Don't worry about Gerold, Father. I have a plan that will take care of him."

Arsenius shook his head. "It's too risky. If you should fail, it will mean the ruin of our family, the end of all we have worked toward these many years."

He's afraid, Anastasius thought. The realization brought a quiet satisfaction. All his life, he had relied upon his father's help and counsel and at the same time had resented the fact that it was so. For once, he was proving the stronger. *Perhaps,* Anastasius thought, regarding the old man with a mix of love and pity, *perhaps it was this very fear, this failure of the will at the crucial moment of testing, that kept him from greatness.*

His father was looking at him strangely. In the depths of those familiar and well-loved eyes, faded now with the years, Anastasius read concern and worry, but something more, something Anastasius had never seen there before—respect.

He put a hand on his father's shoulder. "Trust me, Father. I will make you proud, I promise."

THE Holy Day of Rogation was a fixed feast, invariably celebrated on April 25. Like so many other of the fixed feasts—the Feast of Oblation, the Feast of St. Peter's Chair, the ember weeks, Christ Mass—the roots of its celebration could be traced all the way back to pagan times. In ancient Rome, April 25 was the date of the Robigalia, the heathen festival honoring Robigo, God of Frost, who just at this season could visit great damage on the budding fruits of the earth if not placated with gifts and offerings. Robigalia was a joyous festival, involving a lively procession through the city into the cornfields, where animals were reverently sacrificed, followed by races and games and other forms of merriment in the open fields of the campagna. Rather than try to suppress this time-honored tradition, which would only alienate those they sought to win to the True Faith, the early Popes wisely chose to keep the festival but give it a more Christian character. The procession on the Holy Day of Rogation still went to the cornfields, but it stopped first at St. Peter's Basilica, where a solemn mass was celebrated to honor God and implore, through the intercession of the saints, His blessing on the harvest.

The weather had cooperated with the occasion. The sky above was blue as new-dyed cloth and clear of any trace of cloud; the sun sparkled a golden light on the trees and houses, its heat relieved by a welcome touch of coolness from a northerly breeze.

Joan rode in the middle of the procession behind the acolytes and defensores, who went on foot, and the seven regionary deacons, who were mounted. Behind her rode the optimates and other dignitaries of the Apostolic Palace. As the long line with its colorful signs and banners moved through the Lateran courtyard, past the bronze statue of the mater romanorum, she shifted uncomfortably on her white palfrey; the saddle must have been badly fitted, for already her back hurt with a dull but painful ache that came and went at intervals.

Gerold was ranging back and forth along the side of the procession with the other guards. Now he drew up beside her, tall and breathtakingly handsome in his guard's uniform.

"Are you well?" he asked anxiously. "You look pale."

She smiled at him, drawing strength from his nearness. "I'm fine."

The long procession turned onto the Via Sacra, and Joan was immediately greeted with a roar of acclamation. Aware of the threat that the presence of Lothar and his army represented, the people had turned out in record numbers to demonstrate their love and support of their Lord Pope. They thronged the road to a depth of twenty feet and more on either side, cheering and calling out blessings, so the guards were forced to keep pushing them back in order for the procession to move through. If Lothar required any proof of Joan's popularity with the people, he had it there.

Chanting and waving incense, the acolytes made their way down the ancient street, traveled by the Popes since time beyond memory. The pace was even slower than usual, for there were a great many petitioners stationed along the route, and, as was the custom, the procession stopped frequently so Joan could hear them. At one of the stops, an old woman with gray hair and a scarred face flung herself on the ground before Joan.

"Forgive me, Holy Father," the woman pleaded, "forgive the wrong I've done you!"

"Rise, good mother, and be comforted," Joan replied. "You've done me no injury I know of."

"Am I so changed you do not even know me?"

Something in the ravaged face raised imploringly to hers struck a sudden chord of recognition.

"*Marioza?*" Joan exclaimed. The famous courtesan had aged thirty years since Joan last saw her. "Great God, what has happened to you?"

Ruefully Marioza raised a hand to her scarred face. "The marks of a knife. A parting gift from a jealous lover."

"*Deus misereatur!*"

Marioza said bitterly, "Do not pin your fortunes on the favors of men, you once told me. Well, you were right. The love of men has proved my ruin. It's my punishment—God's punishment for the evil trick I played upon you. Forgive me, Lord Father, or else I am damned forever!"

Joan made the sign of blessing over her. "I forgive you willingly, with my whole heart."

Marioza clutched Joan's hand and kissed it. The people nearby cheered their approval.

The procession moved on. As they were passing the Church of St. Clement, Joan heard a sudden commotion off to the left. A group of ruffians at the rear of the crowd were jeering and throwing stones at the procession. One struck her horse on the neck, and it reared wildly, slamming Joan against the saddle. A jolt of pain shot through her. Stunned and breathless, she clung to the golden trappings as the deacons hurried to her side.

GEROLD spied the group of troublemakers before anyone else. He turned his horse and was riding in after them before the first volley of rocks even left their hands.

Seeing him come, the ruffians ran off. Gerold spurred after them. Before the steps of the Church of St. Clement, the men abruptly wheeled, pulled weapons from the hidden folds of their garments, and came at Gerold.

Gerold drew his sword, signaling urgently to the guards following him. But there was no answering call, no sound of hooves drumming up behind. He was alone when the men surrounded him in a jabbing, thrusting swarm. Gerold wielded his sword with economical skill, making each blow count; he injured four of his assailants, taking only a single knife wound in his thigh before they dragged him from his horse. He let himself go limp, feigning insensibility, but kept a tight hand on his sword hilt.

No sooner had he hit the ground than he sprang back to his feet, sword in hand. With a cry of surprise, the nearest attacker came at him with drawn sword; Gerold moved sideways, wrong-stepping him, and when the man faltered, Gerold brought his sword down on his arm. The man dropped, his half-severed arm spurting blood. Several others came at him, but now Gerold heard the shouts of his guard approaching from behind. Another moment and help would be at hand. Keeping his sword before him, Gerold backed away, keeping a wary eye on his ambushers.

The dagger took him from behind, slipping between his ribs with noiseless stealth, like a thief into a sanctuary. Before he was aware of what had happened, his knees buckled and he folded softly to the ground, marveling even as he did that he felt no pain, only the warm blood streaming down his back.

Above him he heard fresh sounds of shouting and clashing steel. The guards had arrived and were fighting off the attackers. *I must join them,* Gerold thought and went to reach for his sword on the ground beside him, but he could not stir a hand.

CATCHING her breath, Joan looked up and saw Gerold turn aside in pursuit of the rock throwers. She saw the other guards start to follow him, only to be checked by a group of men standing among the crowd on that side of the road; the group closed together, blocking the way as if acting on some unseen signal.

It's a trap! Joan realized. Frantically she cried warning, but her words were drowned in the noise and confusion of the crowd. She spurred her horse to go to Gerold, but the deacons kept tight hold of the bridle.

"Let go! Let go!" she shouted, but they held on, not trusting the horse. Helplessly Joan watched the ruffians surround Gerold, saw their hands reach up to grab him, clutching at his belt, his tunic, his arms, dragging him from his horse. She saw a last bright glint of red hair as he disappeared beneath the swirling crowd.

She slid off the horse and ran, shoving her way through the group of milling, frightened acolytes. By the time she reached the side of the road, the crowd was already parting, making way for the guards, who came toward her bearing Gerold's limp body.

They set him on the ground, and she knelt beside him. Blood was trickling in a thin froth from one corner of his mouth. Quickly she removed the long rectangle of the pallium from around her neck, wadded it, and pressed hard against the wound in his back, trying to staunch the flow of blood. No use; within minutes the thick fabric was soaked through.

Their eyes met in a look that was deeply intimate, a look of love and painful understanding. Fear gripped Joan, fear like she had never known before. "No!" she cried, and clasped him in her arms, as if by sheer physical closeness she could stave off the inevitable. "Don't die, Gerold. Don't leave me here all alone."

His hand groped the air. She took it in hers, and his lips moved in a smile. "My pearl," he said. His voice was very faint, as if speaking from a long distance away.

"Hold on, Gerold, hold on," she said tautly. "We'll take you back to the Patriarchium; we'll—"

She sensed his going even before she heard the death rattle and felt his body grow heavy in her arms. She crouched over him, stroking his hair, his face. He lay still and peaceful, lips parted, eyes fixed blindly on the sky.

It was impossible that he was gone. Even now his spirit might be nearby. She raised her head and looked around her. If he were somewhere near, there would be a sign. If he were anywhere, he would let her know.

She saw nothing, sensed nothing. In her arms lay a corpse with his face.

"He is gone to God," Desiderius, the archdeacon, said.

She did not move. As long as she kept hold of him, he was not entirely gone, a part of him was still with her.

Desiderius took her arm. "Let us carry him to the church."

Numbly she heard and understood. He must not lie here in the street, open to the gaze of curious strangers. She must see him honored with all the proper rites and dignities; it was all that was left her to do for him now.

She laid him down gently, to keep from hurting him, then closed his staring eyes and crossed his arms on his chest so the guards could bear him away with dignity.

As she went to stand, she was taken with a pain so violent it doubled her over, and she fell to the ground gasping. Her body heaved with great spasms over which she had no control. She felt an enormous pressure, as if a weight had been dropped on her; the pressure moved lower until she felt it would surely split her apart.

The child. It's coming.

"Gerold!" The word shuddered into a terrible groan of pain. Gerold could not help her now. She was alone.

"Deus Misereatur!" Desiderius exclaimed. "The Lord Pope is possessed of the Devil!"

People screamed and wept, cast into an extremity of terror.

Aurianos, the chief exorcist, hurried forward. Sprinkling Joan with holy water, he intoned solemnly, *"Exorcizo te, immundissime spiritus, omnis incursio adversarii, omne phantasma ..."*

All eyes were fixed on Joan, watching for the evil spirit to issue forth from her mouth or ear.

She screamed as with one last, agonizing pain the pressure inside suddenly gave way, spilling forth from her in a great red effusion.

The voice of Aurianos cut off abruptly, followed by a long, appalled silence.

Beneath the hem of Joan's voluminous white robes, dyed now with her blood, there appeared the tiny blue body of a premature infant.

Desiderius was the first to react. "A miracle!" he shouted, dropping to his knees.

"Witchcraft," cried another. Everyone crossed themselves.

The people pressed forward to see what had happened, pushing and shoving and climbing over one another's backs to get a better view.

"Stay back!" the deacons shouted, wielding their crucifixes like clubs to keep the unruly crowd at bay. Fighting broke out up and down the long line of the procession. The guards rushed in, shouting rough commands.

Joan heard it all as if from a distance. Lying on the street in a pool of her own blood, she was suddenly suffused with a transcendent sense of peace. The street, the people, the colorful banners of the procession glowed in her mind with a strange brightness, like threads in an enormous tapestry whose pattern she only now discerned.

Her spirit swelled within her, filling the emptiness inside. She was bathed in a great and illuminating light. Faith and doubt, will and desire, heart and head—at long last she saw and understood that all were one, and that One was God.

The light grew stronger. Smilingly she went toward it as the sounds and colors of the world dimmed into invisibility, like the moon with the coming of dawn.

⊱ Epilogue ⊰

Forty-two Years Later

ANASTASIUS sat at his desk in the Lateran scriptorium, writing a letter. His hands, stiff and arthritic with age, ached with every stroke of the quill. Despite the pain, he went on writing. The letter was extremely urgent and had to be dispatched at once.

"To His Imperial Majesty the most worshipful Emperor Arnulf," he scrawled.

Lothar was long dead, having died only a few months after leaving Rome. His throne had gone first to his son Louis II, and then, after his death, to Lothar's nephew Charles the Fat, both weak and undistinguished rulers. With the death of Charles the Fat in 888, the Carolingian line begun by the great Karolus—or Charlemagne, as he was now widely known—had come to an end. Arnulf, Duke of Carinthia, had managed to wrest the imperial throne from a host of challengers. On the whole, Anastasius thought the change in succession a good one. Arnulf was smarter than Lothar, and stronger. Anastasius was counting on that. For something had to be done about Pope Stephen.

Just last month, to the horror and scandal of all Rome, Stephen had ordered the body of his predecessor Pope Formosus dragged from its grave and brought to the Patriarchium. Propping the corpse up in a chair, Stephen had presided over a mock "trial," heaped calumnies upon it and finished by cutting off three fingers of its right hand, the ones used to bestow the papal blessing, in punishment for Formosus's "confessed" crimes.

"I appeal to Your Majesty," Anastasius wrote, "to come to Rome and put an end to the Pope's excesses, which are the scandal of all Christendom."

A sudden cramp in Anastasius's hand shook the quill, scattering droplets of ink over the clean parchment. Cursing, Anastasius blotted up the spilled ink, then put down the quill and stretched his fingers, rubbing them to ease the pain.

Odd, he reflected with grim irony, *that a man such as Stephen should succeed to the papacy when I, so perfectly suited to the office by every qualification of birth and learning, was denied it.*

He had come close, so close to gaining the coveted prize. After the shocking revelation and death of the female Pope, Anastasius had occupied the Patriarchium, claiming the throne for himself with Emperor Lothar's blessing.

What might he not have accomplished had he remained on the throne! But it was not to be. A small but influential group of clerics had adamantly opposed him. For several months, the issue of the papal succession had been hotly debated, with first one side, then the other appearing to prevail. In the end, persuaded that a substantial group of Romans would never be reconciled to Anastasius as Pope, Lothar chose the expedient course and withdrew his support. Anastasius was deposed and sent in ignominy to the monastery of Trastevere.

They all thought I was finished then, Anastasius thought. *But they underestimated me.*

With patience, skill, and diplomacy, he had fought his way back, eventually winning the confidence of Pope Nicholas. Nicholas had raised him to the office of papal librarian, a position of power and privilege he had held for over thirty years.

Having reached the extraordinary age of eighty-seven, Anastasius was now revered and respected, universally praised for his great learning. Scholars and churchmen from all over the world came to Rome to meet him and to admire his masterwork, the *Liber pontificalis,* the official chronicle of the Popes. Just last month a Frankish archbishop by the name of Arnaldo had asked permission to make a copy of the manuscript for his cathedral, and Anastasius had graciously agreed.

The *Liber pontificalis* was Anastasius's bid for immortality, his legacy to the world. It was also his final revenge upon his detested rival, the person whose election on that black day in 853 had denied him the glory for which he had been destined. Anastasius obliterated Pope Joan from the official record of the Popes; the *Liber pontificalis* did not even mention her name.

It was not what he had most deeply desired, but it was something.

The fame of Anastasius the Librarian and his great work would ring down through the ages, but Pope Joan would be lost and forgotten, consigned forever to oblivion.

The cramp in his hand was gone. Picking up the quill, Anastasius once again began to write.

IN THE scriptorium of the Episcopal Palace at Paris, Archbishop Arnaldo labored over the last page of his copy of the *Liber pontificalis*. Sunlight streamed through the narrow window, illuminating a shaft of floating dust. Arnaldo put the finishing flourish on the page, looked it over once, then wearily set down the quill.

It had been a long and difficult labor, copying out the entire manuscript of *The Book of the Popes*. The palace scribes had been quite surprised when the archbishop had taken on the task himself rather than assign it to one of them, but Arnaldo had his reasons for doing so. He had not merely duplicated the famous manuscript; he had corrected it. Between the chronicles of the lives of Pope Leo and Pope Benedict, there was now an entry on Pope Joan, restoring her pontificate to its rightful place in history.

He had done this as much out of a feeling of personal loyalty as from a desire to see the truth told. Like Joan, the archbishop was not what he seemed. For Arnaldo, née Arnalda, was actually the daughter of the Frankish steward Arn and his wife, Bona, with whom Joan had resided after her flight from Fulda. Arnalda had been only a small girl then, but she had never forgotten Joan—the kind and intelligent eyes that had regarded her so attentively; the excitement of their daily lessons together; the shared joy of accomplishment as Arnalda had begun to read and write.

She owed Joan a great debt, for it was Joan who had rescued Arnalda's family from poverty and despair, pointed the way from the dark abyss of ignorance to the light of knowledge, and made possible the high station which Arnalda now enjoyed. Inspired by Joan's example, Arnalda had also chosen, on approaching adulthood, to disguise herself as a man in order to pursue her ambitions.

How many others like us are there? Arnalda wondered, not for the first time. How many other women had made the daring leap, abandoning their female identities, giving up lives that might have been filled with children and family, in order to achieve that from which they would otherwise have been barred? Who could know? It might be that Arnalda had unknowingly passed by another such changeling in cathedral or cloister, toiling along in secret and undisclosed sisterhood.

She smiled at the thought. Reaching inside her archbishop's robes, she clasped the wooden medallion of St. Catherine that hung around her neck. She had worn it constantly ever since the day Joan had given it to her over fifty years ago.

Tomorrow she would have the manuscript bound in fine leather embossed with gold and placed in the archives of the cathedral library. Somewhere, at least, there would remain a record of Joan the Pope, who, though a woman, was nevertheless a good and faithful Vicar of Christ. Someday her story would be found and told again.

The debt is repaid, Arnalda thought. *Requiesce in pace, Johanna Papissa.*

≽| Author's Note |≼

Was There a Pope Joan?

"Partout où vous voyez une légende, vous pouvez être sûr, en allant au fond des choses, que vous trouverez une histoire."

"Whenever you see a legend, you can be sure, if you go to the very bottom of things, that you will find history."

— VALLET DE VIRIVILLE

POPE Joan is one of the most fascinating, extraordinary characters in Western history—and one of the least well known. Most people have never heard of Joan the Pope, and those who have regard her story as legend.

Yet for hundreds of years—up to the middle of the seventeenth century—Joan's papacy was universally known and accepted as truth. In the seventeenth century, the Catholic Church, under increasing attack from rising Protestantism, began a concerted effort to destroy the embarrassing historical records on Joan. Hundreds of manuscripts and books were seized by the Vatican. Joan's virtual disappearance from modern consciousness attests to the effectiveness of these measures.

Today the Catholic Church offers two principal arguments against Joan's papacy: the absence of any reference to her in contemporary documents, and the lack of a sufficient period of time for her papacy to have taken place between the end of the reign of her predecessor, Leo IV, and the beginning of the reign of her successor, Benedict III.

These arguments are not, however, conclusive. It is scarcely surprising that Joan does not appear in contemporary records, given the time and energy the Church has, by its own admission, devoted to expunging her from them. The fact that she lived in the ninth century, the darkest of the dark ages, would have made the job of obliterating her papacy easy. The ninth century was a time of widespread illiteracy, marked by an extraordinary dearth of record keeping. Today, scholarly research into the period relies on scattered, incomplete, contradictory, and unreliable documents. There are no court records, land surveys, farming accounts, or diaries of daily life. Except for one questionable history, the *Liber pontificalis* (which scholars have called a "propagandist document"), there is no continuous record of the ninth-century Popes—who they were, when they reigned, what they did. Apart from the *Liber pontificalis,* scarcely a mention can be found of Joan's successor, Pope Benedict III—and *he* was not the target of an extermination campaign.

One ancient copy of the *Liber pontificalis* with a record of Joan's papacy still exists. The entry on Joan is obviously a later interpolation, clumsily pieced into the main body of the text. However, this does not necessarily render the account untrue; a subsequent annalist, convinced by the testimony of less politically suspect chroniclers, may have felt morally obliged to correct the official record. Blondel, the Protestant historian who examined the text in 1647, concluded that the entry on Joan was written in the fourteenth century. He based his opinion on variations in style and handwriting—subjective judgments at best. Important questions about this document remain. When was the passage in question written? And by whom? A reexamination of this text using modern methods of dating—which has never been attempted—might yield some interesting answers.

Joan's absence from contemporary church records is only to be expected. The Roman clergymen of the day, appalled by the great deception visited upon them, would have gone to great lengths to bury all written report of the embarrassing episode. Indeed, they would have felt it their duty to do so. Hincmar, Joan's contemporary, frequently suppressed information damaging to the Church in his letters and chronicles. Even the great theologian Alcuin was not above tampering with the truth; in one of his letters he admits destroying a report on Pope Leo III's adultery and simony.

As witnesses for the denial, then, Joan's contemporaries are deeply suspect. This is especially true of the Roman prelates, who had strong personal motives for suppressing the truth. On the rare occasions when a papacy was declared invalid—as Joan's would have been when her female identity was discovered—all of the deposed Pope's appointments immediately became null and void. All the cardinals, bishops, deacons, and priests ordained by that Pope were stripped of their titles and positions. No great surprise, then, that records kept or copied by these very men make no mention of Joan.

In modern history, the eighteen-minute gap in the Nixon tapes is a telling demonstration of the way embarrassing or incriminating evidence can be made to disappear. The sealing of JFK assassination records, which will not be revealed in their entirety until 2017, is another example. These attempts to control the historical record were accomplished in a time of widespread literacy and audio-visual media. How much easier this would have been in the ninth century, a time before printed books, when 95 percent of the population could not read or write, and all that was required was to "lose" or to alter a few handwritten manuscripts!

It is only after the distancing effect of time that the truth, kept alive by unquenchable popular report, gradually begins to emerge. And, indeed, there is no shortage of documentation for Joan's papacy in later centuries. Frederick Spanheim, the learned German historian who conducted an extensive study of the matter, cites no fewer than *five hundred* ancient manuscripts containing accounts of Joan's papacy, including those of such acclaimed authors as Petrarch and Boccaccio.

Today, the church position on Joan is that she was an invention of Protestant reformers eager to expose papist corruption. Yet Joan's story first appeared hundreds of years before Martin Luther was born. Most of her chroniclers were Catholics, often highly placed in the church hierarchy. Joan's story was accepted even in official histories dedicated to Popes. Her statue stood undisputed alongside those of the other Popes in the Cathedral of Siena until 1601, when, by command of Pope Clement VIII, it suddenly "metamorphosed" into a bust of Pope Zacharias. In 1276, after ordering a thorough search of the papal records, Pope John XX changed his title to John XXI in official recognition of Joan's reign as Pope John VIII. Joan's story was included in the official church guidebook to Rome used by pilgrims for over three hundred years.

Another striking piece of historical evidence is found in the well-documented 1413 trial of Jan Hus for heresy. Hus was condemned for preaching the heretical doctrine that the Pope is fallible. In his defense Hus cited, during the trial, many examples of Popes who had sinned and committed crimes against the Church. To each of these charges his judges, all churchmen, replied in minute detail, denying Hus's accusations and labeling them blasphemy. Only one of Hus's statements went unchallenged: "Many times have the Popes fallen into sin and error, for instance when Joan was elected Pope, who was a woman." Not one of the twenty-eight cardinals, four patriarchs, thirty metropolitans, two hundred and six bishops, and four hundred and forty theologians present charged Hus with lying or blaspheming in this statement.

As for the Church's second argument against Joan, that there was not sufficient time between the papacies of Leo IV and Benedict III for her to have reigned—this too is questionable. The *Liber pontificalis* is notoriously inaccurate with regard to the times of papal accessions and deaths; many of the dates cited are known to be wholly invented. Given the strong motivation of a contemporary chronicler to conceal Joan's papacy, it would be no great surprise if the date of Leo's death was moved forward from 853 to 855—through the time of Joan's reported two-year reign—in order to make it appear that Pope Leo was immediately succeeded by Pope Benedict III.*

History provides many other examples of such deliberate falsification of records. The Bourbonists dated the reign of Louis XVIII from the day of his brother's death and simply omitted the reign of Napoleon. They could not, however, eradicate Napoleon from the historical records because his reign was so well recorded in innumerable chronicles, diaries, letters, and other documents. In the ninth century, by contrast, the job of obliterating Joan from the historical record would have been far easier.

There is also circumstantial evidence difficult to explain if there was never a female Pope. One example is the so-called chair exam, part of the medieval papal consecration ceremony for almost six hundred years. Each newly elected Pope after Joan sat on the *sella stercoraria* (literally, "dung seat"), pierced in the middle like a toilet, where his genitals were examined to give proof of his manhood. Afterward

---

*Two of the strongest material proofs against Joan's papacy are predicated on the assumption that Leo IV died in 855. (1) A coin bearing the name of Pope Benedict on one side and Emperor Lothar on the other. Since Lothar died on September 28, 855, and the coin shows Benedict and Lothar alive together, Benedict could obviously not have assumed the throne later than 855. (2) A decretal written on October 7, 855, by Pope Benedict confirming the privileges of the monastery of Corbie, again indicating that he was at that time in possession of the throne. But these "proofs" are rendered meaningless if Leo died in 853 (or even 854), for then there was time for Joan's reign before Benedict assumed the throne in 855.

the examiner (usually a deacon) solemnly informed the gathered people, *"Mas nobis dominus est"*—"Our Lord Pope is a man." Only then was the Pope handed the keys of St. Peter. This ceremony continued until the sixteenth century. Even Alexander Borgia was compelled to submit to the ordeal, though at the time of his election his wife had borne him four sons, whom he acknowledged with pride!

The Catholic Church does not deny the existence of the pierced seat, for it survives in Rome to this day. Nor does anyone deny the fact that it was used for centuries in the ceremony of papal consecration. But many argue that the chair was used merely because of its handsome and impressive appearance; the fact that it had a hole in it is, they say, quite irrelevant.

Figure 1. The *sella stercoraria*.

This argument seems doubtful. The chair had obviously once served as a toilet, or possibly an obstetric chair. (See figure 1.) Is it likely that an object with such crude associations would be used as a papal throne without some very good reason? And if the chair exam is a fiction, how does one explain the innumerable jests and songs referring to it that were rife among the Roman populace for centuries? Granted, these were ignorant and superstitious times, but medieval Rome was a close-knit community: the people lived within yards of the papal palace; many of their fathers, brothers, sons, and cousins were prelates who attended papal consecrations and who would have known the truth about the *sella stercoraria*. There even exists an eyewitness account of the chair exam. In 1404, the Welshman Adam of Usk journeyed to Rome and remained there for two years, keeping close record of his observations in his chronicle. His detailed description of Pope Innocent VII's coronation includes the chair exam.

Another interesting piece of circumstantial evidence is the "shunned street." The Patriarchium, the Pope's residence and episcopal cathedral (now St. John Lateran) is located on the opposite side of Rome from St. Peter's Basilica; papal processions therefore frequently traveled between them. A quick perusal of any map of Rome will show that the Via Sacra (now the Via S. Giovanni) is by far the shortest and most direct route between these two locations—and so in fact it was used for centuries (hence the name Via Sacra, or "sacred road.") This is the street on which Joan reportedly gave birth to her stillborn child. Soon afterward, papal processions deliberately began to turn aside from the Via Sacra, "in abhorrence of that event."

The Church argues that the detour was made simply because the street was too narrow for processions to pass along until the sixteenth century, when it was widened by Pope Sixtus V. But this explanation is patently not true. In 1486, John Burcardt, Bishop of Horta and papal master of ceremonies under five Popes—a position which gave him intimate knowledge of the papal court—described in his journal what transpired when a papal procession broke from custom and traversed the Via Sacra:

> On going as in returning, [the Pope] came by way of the Coliseum and that straight road where . . . John Anglicus gave birth to a child. . . . For that reason . . . the Popes, in their cavalcades, never pass through that street; the Pope was therefore

blamed by the Archbishop of Florence, the Bishop of Mas-
sano, and Hugo de Bencii the Apostolic Subdeacon ...

A hundred years *before* the street was widened, this papal procession passed down the Via Sacra with no difficulty. Burcardt's account also makes it plain that Joan's papacy was accepted at the time by the highest officials of the papal court.

Given the obscurity and confusion of the times, it is impossible to determine with certainty whether Joan existed or not. Historians are divided on the subject of Joan's historicity. After the publication of my novel, several scholarly studies were released, either for the first time, or in newly available English translations.

1. Peter Stanford, former editor of the *Catholic Herald* (official journal of Catholic dioceses), came out with a book entitled *The She-Pope*. After an extensive review of historical manuscripts, folklore records, and Roman artifacts/statuary, Stanford concludes, "Weighing all the evidence, I am convinced that Pope Joan was an historical figure."

2. Alain Boureau, whose entry on the subject, *La Papesse Jeanne*, was written in French and published in 1988, saw an English translation of his work in 2001. (Too late for me! When doing my research, I had to plod through the somewhat ponderous tome in French.) Boureau makes a strong argument against Joan's historical existence, some of which is compelling—though note he did not directly examine ancient and original handwritten manuscripts, like Joan Morris (cited below).

3. Emmanuel Rhoides, a Greek scholar of the nineteenth century, devoted much of his life to the defense of Pope Joan—for which he was excommunicated. His novel, written in Greek and translated into English by Lawrence Durrell, has long been available on bookshelves (though it credits Durrell as writer, not translator). Rhoides's novel is not useful in determining Joan's historicity. But his scholarly work, titled *Pope Joan: An Historical Romance* is. When researching my novel, I could only access this work through special library collections. But it has been newly released in an edition by Charles Collette Hastings, now widely available.

4. Joan Morris, who received her graduate degree in liturgical re-search at the University of Notre Dame, is the only person since the seventeenth century to conduct an extensive, direct examination of original, handwritten, ninth-century pontificals. Her scholarly study titled *Pope John VIII: Alias Pope Joan* was published in 1985—and her argument in favor of Joan's existence is well-documented and persuasive. Unfortunately, this work is available only through rare book sources, university libraries, and other special collections.

THE truth of what happened in A.D. 855 may never be fully known. This is why I have chosen to write a novel and not a historical study. Though based on the facts of Joan's life as they have been reported, the book is nevertheless a work of fiction. Little is known about Joan's early life, except that she was born in Ingelheim of an English father and that she was once a monk at the monastery of Fulda. I have neces-sarily had to fill in some missing pieces of her story.

However, the major events of Joan's adult life as described in *Pope Joan* are all accurate. The Battle of Fontenoy took place as described on June 25, 841. The Saracens did sack St. Peter's in the year 847 and were later defeated at sea in 849; there was a fire in the Borgo in 848 and a flood of the Tiber in 854. Intinction gained popularity as a reg-ular method of communion in Frankland during the ninth century. Blue cheese is believed to have been discovered in this part of Europe in the ninth century, by accident, very much in the way described.

Anastasius was in fact excommunicated by Pope Leo IV; later, after his restitution as papal librarian for Pope Nicholas, he is widely credited as the author of the contemporary lives in *Liber pontificalis*. The murders of Theodorus and Leo in the papal palace actually hap-pened, as did the trial pitting the magister militum Daniel against the papal superista. Pope Sergius's gluttony and gout are matters of his-torical record as is his rebuilding of the Orphanotrophium. Anasta-sius, Arsenius, Gottschalk, Raban Maur, Lothar, Benedict, and Popes Gregory, Sergius, and Leo are all real historic figures. The details of the ninth-century setting have been meticulously researched.

In this new edition, information on ninth-century clothing, food, and medical treatment is even more accurate, thanks in part to read-ers who wrote to suggest helpful corrections.

Among the most useful reader-generated suggestions:

1. Substitution of honey for sugar as a ninth-century sweetener. Sugar was not readily available in ninth-century Western Europe. But it was not unknown, sugar cane having been cultivated for centuries in Persia (where it was called "the reed that gives honey without bees"). From there Arab traders carried it to Africa, Sicily, and the Mediterranean.

Trade in these dark times had slowed to a trickle, but it did exist. Contemporary chronicles describe two gifts from Caliph Harun-al-Rashid of Baghdad to Charlemagne: a marvelous mechanical water clock and . . . an elephant! If an elephant could make it to the Frankish empire, then sugar certainly did.

But history-buff readers are correct in pointing out that sugar was a rarity, reserved—and used only seldomly—for the tables of the great. Honey was the common sweetener of the ninth century, a fact reflected in this new edition.

2. Removal of horns from ninth-century Viking helmets. Many readers wrote to say that Viking helmets did not have horns. So I reviewed the literature on this subject. References to horned helmets go back as far as Plutarch, who wrote that Viking ancestors wore helmets "made to resemble the heads of horned beasts." Archeological digs have unearthed horned helmets, mostly from Denmark. There is even one ninth-century depiction of a Viking wearing a horned helmet on the Oseberg Tapestry from Norway.

Nevertheless, readers who argued this point are probably right. Most experts believe that horned helmets were used for ceremonial, not martial, purposes. The most persuasive argument I read was that of one scholar who pointed out that a horned helmet would be a serious disadvantage in battle, for it provided a foe with a convenient handhold to steady you as he slit your throat!

I admit I had trouble letting go of this one, for horned Viking helmets are ingrained in popular imagination. Hagar the Horrible will never be the same for me! But I decided to come down on the side of historical realism, so in this edition the Viking attackers of Dorstadt do not wear horned helmets.

3. Change in Gerold's age. Some astute readers did the math and realized that Gerold must have fathered Gisla when he was only

twelve years old—and naturally they found this puzzling. Boys of that age today are considered children.

Certainly twelve was very young for fathering, even in the ninth century. But back then twelve-year-old boys were considered young adults. They could marry, have children, ride to war, and die in battle alongside their elders. And many did.

However, in consideration of reader sensibilities, Gerold is three years older in this new edition. This was an easy change to effect, for Gerold is an entirely fictional character, born of the need to account for Joan's death in childbirth, attested to in hundreds of chronicle records.

4. Excision of *boiled corn* in the meal Joan's family serves to Aesculapius. Many readers have been troubled by the use of corn in a novel about ninth-century Europe, believing that it is a New World food. But I took the description of this particular meal right off the pages of a ninth-century manuscript. Here's where the problem arises: *Corn* is an ancient word, used generically to mean *grain* or *seed*. What we call *corn* is actually *maize*—a New World crop. Over time, the two words have become confused.

Though not a historical error, the use of the word *corn* was a poor writer's choice. Why create doubt in the minds of readers? So in this edition, the family sits down to a meal of boiled barley-corn.

I did make some adjustments in the interest of telling a good story. I needed a Viking raid on Dorstadt in the year 828, although it didn't actually take place until 834. Similarly, I had Emperor Lothar descend twice upon Rome to chastise the Pope, though in fact he actually dispatched his son Louis, King of Italy, to do the job for him the first time. The bodies of Ss. Marcellinus and Peter were stolen from their graves in 827, not 855; John the Antipope, Sergius's predecessor, was not killed after his deposition but merely imprisoned and then banished. Anastasius died in 878, not 897. These deliberate errata are, I trust, exceptions; on the whole I tried to be historically accurate.

Some things described in *Pope Joan* may seem shocking from our perspective, but they did not seem so to the people of the day. The collapse of the Roman Empire and the resulting breakdown of law and order led to an era of almost unprecedented barbarism and violence. As one contemporary chronicler lamented, it was "a sword age, a wind age, a wolf age." The population of Europe had been almost halved by a disastrous series of famines, plagues, civil wars, and "barbarian" invasions. The average life expectancy was very short: less than a quarter of the population ever reached their fifties. There were no longer any real cities; the largest towns had no more than two to three thousand inhabitants. The Roman roads had fallen into decay, the bridges on which they depended disappeared.

The social and economic order which we now call feudalism had not yet begun. Europe was as yet one country: Germany did not exist as a separate nation, nor did France, or Spain, or Italy. The Romance languages had not yet evolved from their parent Latin; there were no French or Spanish or Italian languages, only a variety of forms of degenerating Latin and a host of local patois. The ninth century marked, in short, a society in transition from one form of civilization, long dead, to another not yet born—with all the ferment and unrest that this implies.

Life in these troubled times was especially difficult for women. It was a misogynistic age, informed by the antifemale diatribes of church fathers such as St. Paul and Tertullian:

> *And do you not know that you are Eve? . . . You are the gate of the devil, the traitor of the tree, the first deserter of Divine Law; you are she who enticed the one whom the devil dare not approach . . . on account of the death you deserved even the Son of God had to die.*

Menstrual blood was believed to turn wine sour, make crops barren, take the edge off steel, make iron rust, and infect dog bites with an incurable poison. With few exceptions, women were treated as perpetual minors, with no legal or property rights. By law, they could be beaten by their husbands. Rape was treated as a form of minor theft. The education of women was discouraged, for a learned woman was considered not only unnatural but dangerous.

Small wonder, then, if a woman chose to disguise herself as a man in order to escape such an existence. Apart from Joan, there are other women who successfully managed the imposture. In the third century, Eugenia, daughter of the Prefect of Alexandria, entered a monastery disguised as a man and eventually rose to the office of abbot.

Her disguise went undetected until she was forced to reveal her sex as a last resort to refute the accusation of having deflowered a virgin. In the twelfth century, St. Hildegund, using the name Joseph, became a brother of Schönau Abbey and lived undiscovered among the brethen until her death many years later.*

The light of hope kindled by such women shone only flickeringly in a great darkness, but it was never entirely to go out. Opportunities were available for women strong enough to dream. *Pope Joan* is the story of one of those dreamers.

---

*There are other, more modern examples of women who have successfully passed themselves off as men, including Mary Reade, who lived as a pirate in the early eighteenth century; Hannah Snell, a soldier and sailor in the British navy; a nineteenth-century woman whose real name is unknown to us but who, under the name of James Barry, rose to the rank of full inspector-general of British hospitals; and Loreta Janeta Velaquez, who fought for the Confederate side at the Battle of Bull Run under the name Harry Buford. Teresinha Gomes of Lisbon spent eighteen years pretending to be a man; a highly decorated soldier, she rose to the rank of general in the Portuguese army and was discovered only in 1994, when she was arrested on charges of financial fraud and forced by the police to undergo a physical exam. In 2006, Norah Vincent published her book *Self-Made Man*, in which she describes the year she spent in male disguise, during which time she spent three months in a monastery with her true identity completely undetected.

A Reader's Guide

FOR many years, I've been joining the conversation with reading groups by speakerphone.* Some questions come up very frequently. To these FAQs, I provide answers below. Afterward, I include a list of questions to which even *I* don't know the answer, but which lead to lively and productive book group discussion—the "best of the best" based on my years of experience chatting with reading groups.

Q: Why did you write this novel?

A: Having written four nonfiction books, I wanted to switch to historical fiction—my favorite form of leisure reading. When I stumbled across Joan's story in a piece of chance reading, I knew I had found my subject. What an extraordinary lost mystery-legend of history, documented even better than King Arthur's! How was it possible that I had never even *heard* of her?

    The more I learned about Joan, the more I liked her. To me, she's an inspiring example of female empowerment through learning—an issue deeply relevant in today's world, where women in many countries are still discouraged, or even prevented, from going to school. I had my own daughter very much in mind as I wrote this novel. I hope that Joan's story inspires young women to pursue their education so they can have full exercise of mind, heart, and spirit.

Q: Are you Catholic?

A: No. Oddly, this turned out to have an unexpected advantage. Were I Catholic, raised in the traditions, rituals, and theology of today's Church, I would have approached ninth-century Christian faith with a lot of very wrong preconceptions. In my novel I

---

*Reading groups interested in setting up a "Chat with the Author" should go to popejoan.com for information or to make a request.

have tried to show the many ways in which the worship of a thousand years ago differed from our own. If there's one thing that the study of history teaches us, it is that yesterday's heresies are often today's truths—and vice versa.

Q: What response has the book had from the Vatican?

A: None. And that's only to be expected. In today's world, controversy sells things. If the Vatican denounced my novel, the very next day it would probably be on the *New York Times* bestseller list.

The best way to bury any story is to ignore it—as Joan's millennium-old story proves.

Q: Why did you choose that ending for Pope Joan?

A: I didn't. The historical records on Joan are nearly unanimous in saying that she died in childbirth while in papal procession on the Via Sacra. This ending is also supported by the centuries-old tradition of the "shunned street" (described in the author's note).

If Joan had died behind the walls of the papal palace, no one would ever have known that she was a female. For that to become known, her death had to be public.

Q: Why is there such brutality in the novel—for example, the rape of Gisla during the Viking attack on Dorstadt?

A: The question implies that I intensified the savagery of life in the ninth century in the interest of sensational storytelling. The truth is that I took it easy on readers; life in the ninth century was far more brutal and unjust than anything depicted in my novel.

Recent and continuing world events reveal that crimes against humanity are not relegated only to history. Upsetting as reading about such things can be, my feeling is this: if people, past and present, can endure such terrible things, then the least we can do is bear witness. I see no advantage whatsoever to "cleaning up" history. As George Santayana said, "Those who do not study history are condemned to repeat it."

"Best of the Best" Reading Group Questions

1. How important is it to this story to believe in its historicity? Are there lessons to be learned from Joan's story whether it's legend or fact? What are they?

2. Francis Bacon, the seventeenth-century philosopher, said, "People believe what they prefer to be true." How does this relate to Joan's story compared to, say, that of King Arthur? What is it about Joan's story that people might not "prefer to be true"?

3. Are reason and faith incompatible? What do you make of Aesculapius's argument that *lack* of faith leads people to fear reason? What about Joan? Does her study of reason in the work of classical authors such as Lucretius diminish her faith?

4. Joan sacrificed much because she loved Gerold. Do you know women who have sacrificed opportunities to exercise mind, heart, and spirit for love of a man? For love of a child? Are such sacrifices justified?

5. What implications does Joan's story have with regard to the role of women in the Catholic Church? Should nuns play a greater— or different—role? If so, what should that role be? Should women be priests? What effect would women priests have on the Church and its liturgy? What effect have they had on the Episcopal Church?

6. One reviewer wrote: "Pope Joan . . . is a reminder that some things never change, only the stage and the players do." Are there any similarities between the way women live in some places of the world today and the way they lived back then?

7. What causes any society to oppress womankind? What are the root causes of misogyny? Are they based in religion or in society? Both? Neither?

8. Why might medieval society have believed so strongly that education hampered a woman's ability to bear children? What purpose might such a belief serve?

9. What similarities or differences do you see between Pope Joan and Saint Joan of Arc? Why was one Joan expunged from history books and the other made a saint?

10. If Joan had agreed to leave with Gerold when he first came to Rome, what would her life have been like? Did she make the right choice or not?

11. What causes Joan's inner conflict between faith and doubt? How do these conflicts affect the decisions she makes? Does she ever resolve these conflicts?

About the Author

A New York City native, DONNA WOOLFOLK CROSS graduated cum laude, Phi Beta Kappa, from the University of Pennsylvania in 1969 with a B.A. in English. She moved to London, England, after graduation and worked in a small publishing house on Fleet Street, W. H. Allen and Company. Upon her return to the United States, Cross worked at Young and Rubicam, a Madison Avenue advertising firm, before going on to graduate school at UCLA where she earned a master's degree in literature and writing in 1972.

In 1973, Cross moved to Upstate New York and began teaching writing at an upstate New York college. She is the author of two books on language, *Word Abuse* and *Mediaspeak,* and coauthor of the college textbook *Speaking of Words.* The product of seven years of research and writing, *Pope Joan* is her first novel. Cross is at work on a new novel set in seventeenth-century France.